THE SEVEN

THE LOST TALE OF DELLERIN

ROBERT J POWER

DEPAOR PRESS

THE SEVEN

First published in Ireland by DePaor Press in 2019.
ISBM 978-1-9999994-5-2

Available in eBook, Audiobook, Paperback and Large Print Paperback

www.RobertJPower.com

For Rights and Permissions contact:
Hello@DePaorPress.com

CONTENTS

For Jan.

*Without you I could never have written a line and without you
I never would have wanted to.*

You are my muse, you always have been.

PROLOGUE

The dreadful roar of explosions filled the night, each one fiercer than the last. Beneath the cacophony of terrible thunder, two vanquished fighters stumbled down through the deserted side streets unnoticed. There was no pride in retreat, and both carried their heads low in desolation. She carried both his pack and her own. She wanted to help the old warrior more, but he was too prideful to show weakness from his injury, particularly with what they had faced only hours before.

Anguis, The Dark One.

Erin thought it a feeble and unimaginative title for such a beast. Whatever suitable title fitted him didn't matter now though, for another revolution had collapsed at the final hurdle. Beside her, Rhendell tripped and collapsed against one of the alley walls, leaving a warm smear of blood upon the surface. The Dark One's monstrous hounds could track such a stain, she thought bitterly.

She slid down on the other side of the wall and took a few deep breaths to ease the burn of her exhausted lungs. How long had they been running? It felt like an eternity, for all time stopped when running for your life. She had discovered this peculiar knowledge early as a child, but this race was worse than before. All around them, the glow of fire and misery was giving way to the light of dawn. With the birth of a new day would be certain capture.

"I won't make it out of the city. I am lost," Rhendell gasped as he tentatively tightened the tourniquet around his leg. It was a futile gesture if he continued at this pace.

"No, sir. We are both lost," Erin said, watching for movement in the diminishing night. "It would take the entire Dellerin army an age to find us among the ruins this miserable day. We are two bleeding wretches in a militia of scattered insurgents, and there are countless others still fighting, I expect," she lied.

She held her voice, lest the horror of what she had seen steal what nerve she still had. A lesser soldier might have fallen to their knees in despair knowing the size of their task, but she was wily enough to know with their allies decimated and fleeing the ruins of the city, the acolytes would still have a task on their hands hunting down and killing every single one. There was just as much pride in hiding through the unforgiving day in one of the ruined structures surrounding them as there was in retreating.

Erin pulled her comrade to his unsteady feet. "Come on, you old fool."

Despite his subdued protest, she helped him across the street to a three-storied house sitting among dozens of similar buildings. Something drew her to the place, and if Erin trusted anything in the world, it was her instincts. She used to trust her platoon, but they were dead—apart from the unlucky few who survived the first wave of that dreadful black fire. She knew The Dark One's ways. She knew they would suffer a terrible fate at his vengeful hands. Those he had captured would know it too.

Like every other building in this quarter of the city, the house was abandoned and likely untouched for many years. The owner had left the door locked, but most of the broken windows were low enough to scale through. It was the finest deed of her night, helping her comrade climb into its engulfing darkness, alerting no battalion of patrolling acolytes. They crept through the ruined house like thieving rats. Their most precarious moments were climbing some creaking, rickety stairs. At the top floor, they found sanctuary in an old abandoned room full of ash, mould, and ruined books.

"Yes, this will suit us. This is polished," Rhendell declared as most captains did when successful plans not of their creation became their creation once it assured success.

Erin smiled and dared not argue. As he made himself comfortable, leaning up against one of the ruined bookshelves, there appeared a little of the colour back in his grizzled features.

"Though, I'll still likely catch an infection in this grotty den," he muttered and rummaged through his pack for a needle and thread—and maybe a little bottle of sine while he was at it. He found the bottle and administered a shot to his lips for the pain.

"That Venistrian cur was waiting," he muttered and shook his head.

"That fire," she whispered, and he nodded.

"Those demons." For a moment, he was lost in recent memories of horrible things. She knew this because she couldn't stop thinking of those horrible things either.

Erin slipped over to the one window in the little room and dared to ease the torn curtain halfway across its rail. It was not enough to notice from this far up but enough to let a little light in. If this were to be her last day, she would rather see the blue sky above one last time although, as it was, the clouds were thick and unpleasant. They matched the smoke from the many fires burning throughout the city of Dellerin, and she sighed weakly. What a waste.

They thought they were ready, but no matter how far they marched, The Dark One was everlasting, and his wrath was eternal. Her head spun suddenly, and she stumbled away from the window and dropped to a knee in front of one bookcase. Her hand reached out to steady herself and fell upon a thick book, lined and fitted with its brethren. As swiftly as it appeared, the dizziness left her. Instinctively, Erin took the book in her hand.

"There's little point in setting a fire up here. Whatever books aren't ruined with dampness will just fall to dust," Rhendell said from across the room. He gazed upon a few books in equal disrepair. "And even if there are still a few we can burn, acolytes might spot whatever smoke we make."

Erin ignored him and held the book as though it was some cherished volume of *Mipsey the Meddling Munket* from a lost childhood. It had no title, nor decoration. Age and dampness within this abandoned room had taken its toll, yet beneath the cover, the pages felt crisp and dry. Many other books in the bookcase had rotted to ruin, yet this one was in a fair condition. It could burn well for quite a time if one were so inclined to announce themselves to a searching army.

Erin opened its pages. As before, she felt as compelled to the book as she had the building it lay in. Beneath the first page, she read in delicate cursive scroll two words, and her mind reeled.

"The Seven," she whispered.

4

"Oh, here we go again—you and your tales of The Seven," Rhendell mocked.

Erin bit back a retort, knowing its pointlessness.

There were some who believed the tales of The Seven. Most of those tales prophesied that The Seven might tear The Dark One from his perch eventually. They were only tales for children, but even now, she'd always felt a kinship to such a mysterious group. Whether they still lived or, in fact, ever existed at all, was something else entirely.

The Dark One had forbidden all stories of The Seven spoken aloud. She'd heard tell on more than one occasion of bards entertaining crowds in taverns as far out as the Dellerin coast with humorous tales of heroism, bravado, and a fine bit of lewd humour involving Heygar and his Hounds. However, come the dawn, those same bards might mysteriously disappear.

Erin had never heard the bards' tales for herself. Perhaps this was a charmless fable from the bitter mouth of their ruler, eliciting further control of a miserable land rife with starvation, pestilence, and other ungodly things. There were numerous things considered forbidden under his laws. Who knew what wonderments he had denied her knowledge of? Erin, hardly an old maiden at twenty-three years, had no memory of a world before him. Still, she had faith—even in the darkest times, when armies marched and faded—that light would still win out. Not all things could remain secret. Not even mysterious, childish tales when they fought wars for the good of the people, nor when the words "heroic" and "nobility" were words held precious. Childish tales.

"Well, go on. Can you make any of it out?" Rhendell asked, and Erin realised he hadn't taken his eyes off the book either. His wound was open and fighting the alcohol he had dripped across the deep opening. In his hands were a needle and thread. He trusted no one to sew stitches, and he did not trust her now.

Erin ran her fingers across the delicate text, and it seemed to hum in her mind as she read silently. The book itself wasn't printed. Instead, its contents were meticulously scribed with a steady hand in dark black ink. It had a foreword.

"They say The Seven would tear the great darkness from this shattered world, and they would do it at the right price. The darkness is eternal. So, too, must be The Seven," she whispered and left the blank page to turn to the next. After a few moments, she tilted her head and sighed again.

"It starts strangely," she said.

"Oh, just start it, Corporal. I need the distraction," Rhendell said and stuck the needle into his skin.

THE BOUNTY

"You will kill him," whispered the king, toying with the piece of fruit in his quivering hands. It sounded like an order. Most royals did not insist; they merely requested with the veiled threat of a kingdom echoing at their backs. Any in their earshot were advised to listen.

The king had the pompous voice and imposing look, but Heygar, who was born without a noble drop of blood in his veins, was never a man to be intimidated. It should have been the other way around.

"Will I now?" asked Heygar, taking an apple from the large bowl atop the cedar table separating the two men. He leaned back in the wooden stool and ignored the loud creak under his weight. Too many ales without a grand undertaking, he mused. And what a fine undertaking this king had presented him this evening. His Hounds would be happy.

"I understand a man with your talents charges quite a price for this deed," the king said as though bartering with such a man was below his stature. In truth, it was below him, but in these times, keeping up appearances meant any competent royal would do what was needed. And Heygar was exactly what was needed.

It was good to be the king, but it was better to be a legend, and recruiting a legend was something the royal did not trust his advisers with. There was a revolution in the air—there had been for many months. All it took was a spark and, in this quiet little room, the king was attempting to blow the fires of change away from his table.

If Heygar accepted the task, the king would no doubt appear strong and merciless. However, were the legendary mercenary to refuse the bounty, word would swiftly spread throughout the kingdom of Dellerin. Perhaps as far as Venistra. Words like this would only add kindling to the fires of discontent.

Heygar enjoyed these moments. It reminded him exactly how far he'd come. How much respect he commanded. How much he would miss this life when it was over.

"I think my services are a fair price." Heygar shrugged as though bartering with royalty was equally beneath him. He heard more creaking again and decided it was his heavy steel armour that tested the stool's stability. In hindsight, he could have favoured a heavy cloak for a secretive liaison, but when one was a living legend, one had to maintain a certain appearance. Besides, if it all went wrong, it was unlikely a cloak would protect him from a thousand royal guards and their pointy little spears.

He caught sight of himself in the reflection of a silver chalice brimming with cherry red wine, and he thought himself rather fetching in this light. Terrifying, barbaric, and magnificent. Heavyweight or not, he decided he had made the right decision. He also chose not to drink with royalty this evening.

"Fifty gold for Mallum's head," King Lemier said. A

decent opening gambit. A man could find an entire year of rapture in the pleasure nests of Castra with that wealth, though he would have to live off little more than corn and grape ale for sustenance. Heygar was no great fan of grape ale, and what would Cherrie think of such endeavours anyway?

"My Hounds would baulk at that price," Heygar said, eyeing his secretive surroundings. He swallowed his discontent. It was little more than a forgotten nook in the middle of a grand palace. A dozen feet each way were wooden shelves bearing glass jars of preserved foods, grain sacks, and hanging salted meats. They had invited him into a storage room.

Once King Lemier had his pledge secured, however, everyone in the court would know of Heygar's loyalty. As young as the king was, he was already adept in the art of maintaining public opinion—at least with the lords of the court.

"Perhaps you shouldn't feed your precious Hounds such grand meats," the king hissed and chewed a piece of the red fruit. After a few moments of uncomfortable silence, he spat the mulched contents into the small fire behind them with just the right amount of contempt.

"Thurken waste of my time," muttered Heygar. It was a fine reply when defending his merry little group of mercenaries. "There are seven in my pack, and we don't play well together when reaping scraps."

They were far more than simple mercenaries. They were renowned throughout the land. "Heygar's Hounds" was the current title given by the masses, but to Heygar, they would always be The Seven.

"One hundred gold," the mercenary mumbled.

The king slammed his fist down upon the table. "How

dare you!" he snarled, letting the echo resonate around the grim meeting place. The fire danced in answer to the outburst. A spitting ember leapt from its infernal nest behind them, hissed, and then died in the grate. Heygar took a breath before replying. He was again grateful he had chosen the armour.

"One hundred gold apiece is a fair price for such an undertaking," he said as though he argued the price of a wedding ring in Dellerin's market with a stubborn vendor who should really know better. King Lemier didn't know better either.

Rage had drawn his face flush, or perhaps he sat too near the fire. Perhaps the rich, silken gowns were too suffocating in a snug little room like this. "You dare to charge one hundred gold apiece? It is one insignificant man in an insignificant part of the world. I could get a hundred mercenaries for that price."

Heygar felt fine and cool in his new armour. He doubted the king would even have the strength to don such a suit. And if he could march in it, he wouldn't have the nerve to march to "insignificant" Venistra. Few mercenaries from Dellerin would dare to. Not with the troubling reports he'd heard, anyway.

Had there not been the whisperings of a famine? Of civil revolt? Monsters rising? Typical whispered embellishments. Regardless, a hundred other mercenaries would make the journey, but most of them would find imaginative ways to seek their deaths along the way. The Seven, however, could make the trip with no bother at all.

Heygar loved the art of bartering. He always knew when to add fuel to a furnace as well. "One hundred and twenty gold apiece so." He took an apple and wiped away a blemish before holding it out for further inspection. It was a fine apple, rich and green, like the lands this king ruled over.

Venistra, however, was a nasty pit of an island a few hundred miles off the coast, through a tempestuous ocean, gloomy and grey with an economy of wretchedness. It was a stain on the rest of the many islands off the four coasts of Dellerin. Whenever new taxes were introduced, it was always Venistra who felt most aggrieved. Though he was no scholar in any of the lands beyond the one in which he lived most of his life, Heygar knew Venistra was a country in itself and presided over by a royal house who answered to the king sitting in front of him.

However, these last few months, Venistra had argued louder than usual, and he had even heard the hushed name of the weaver calling himself Mallum, who was growing in popularity. A fine surname from a regal house, he imagined. They were all the same, inevitably. Like most of Heygar's targets, Mallum, too, would die under the unforgiving blade.

There should have been a guild of assassins to remove the man quietly from this plain, but secret killings would not serve King Lemier at all. Venistra offered a resounding "no", so the king needed to make an example, lest voices closer to home whispered these same rebellious words. Royalty were dethroned and hung for less. An invasion from the king's royal guard on such a small island, however, would easily be construed as a considerable overreaction to a paltry crime.

A little bit of assassination by a famous band of mercenaries, however, would deliver the right message to the rest of Dellerin's empire. Fall in line or Heygar's Hounds will get you.

"One hundred and twenty gold apiece is a mugging!" roared the king. This, too, was a fine reply. He slammed his fist down on the table. The table appeared unperturbed by such an assault, as was the mercenary.

"One hundred and thirty gold apiece."

"You dare to barter with me in such a way?" Lemier cried, looking every day his twenty years. Heygar was double this span and thrice as experienced. He had seen and led wars, and Lemier had done little more than taste a lover's gift and enter a biased tournament or two.

"You should know who you dare challenge. One hundred and fifty," whispered Heygar. This was going splendidly. He slid a thin, iridescent dagger from his wrist gauntlet smoothly. Eralorien, his weaver, had spent hours casting a fragile illusion on it, and it took a moment for Heygar's eyes to acclimatise to its deadliness. It took the king even less.

The mercenary shook the enchantment from the blade as though covered in droplets from the rain, and he watched the weapon reveal itself in all its glory. King Lemier's face grew pale. He eyed the doorway from which he'd entered, a few feet away. He might make the precarious journey before Heygar charged him down, but he made no move to do so.

Heygar could read the man's thoughts easily enough. What type of foolish king allowed himself to sit and negotiate with an armed mercenary? A king that would require new guards with a keener eye for weakly concealed weapons. They had taken his longsword and shield and assumed a man of his integrity would leave himself defenceless. They did not know his legend at all, did they? They never would.

The city gallows would know ample business come dawn, he imagined. Heygar should have felt guilt for knowingly damning the three men who had secretly escorted him into these chambers, but money was money. There was nothing like a little fear to loosen the pockets of a parsimonious royal.

"It would take but a cry from my mouth for the guards to

stream through the doorway," the king whispered, feigning confidence.

Heygar laughed.

"And when the first fell, I would have two weapons in my hands. You could send an entire legion into this room, and they would fall under my blade, but you would never see the eventual outcome regardless. So, cry out, my liege."

The royal said nothing.

"Don't worry, Your Majesty. It is possible you might escape with most of your limbs intact, and I would eventually fall, probably out in the gardens somewhere among the waterlilies, and that would be the end of the infamous Heygar. But remember this: I still have my six remaining Hounds, and I am uncertain what retaliation they would take on the kingdom. I have led them for a time. I am their king in everything but entitled blood." He slid the blade through his apple, carving a thin slice and popping it into his mouth. Delicious. "One hundred and sixty."

"Can you do this deed loudly?" the king asked after a few cautious breaths.

"The Seven can do anything asked as long as there is payment." Heygar had never known true defeat, even in war. He had been a fine enough general, he supposed, but as a leader of a wild group of mercenaries, he had found something close to divinity. Had the king not heard the tales? Had he not hummed the songs? He probably had, hence the lack of outcry to a pack of doomed guardians standing guard outside the door.

"And what if Mallum offers thrice for you to return the favour?"

Heygar couldn't decide if he were trying to insult him. The young man's hands were still shaking, so he forgave him the insinuation.

"You may accuse me of lashing a hard bargain, but if I give my word, it is a gift worth more than gold. Think of it as this, Your Highness. If I accepted payment from every man or woman who pleaded for their predestined lives with oaths of quadrupled payments, I'd have retired many a year ago or else never received a second bout of employment due to earning myself a bad name. If you pay me, Mallum will die," Heygar said with a coldness shared only by a man who treated death with the respect it deserved.

The king took a few moments to consider this. Heygar could have truthfully added that he did, in fact, favour this king's seat. He was no great political mind, and he had brought no great prosperity to the people, but crime was at an unprecedented low, and hunger was scarce enough across the land. Under a different ruler, everything could easily change. Heygar was no saint, but a few bags of gold were no excuse to hurt those who idolised him and his Hounds. He intended to do the king's biddings. He could have said this, but that would have set his opponent's worries at ease. Business was business, and he still wanted payment.

"For your word, I will pay two hundred apiece. One quarter now, and the rest upon your return," Lemier whispered and placed his hands upon the table.

Heygar dared a smile. He thought it a fine counter-offer. The king was speaking his language and winning his favour outright.

"Deal struck, my liege." Heygar spat into his hand and held it out. It was a crude gesture used by commoners, and to his surprise, the king mimicked the act and shook his hand firmly.

For only the briefest moment, Heygar imagined the king may have been willing to part ways with a little more, but it didn't really matter. He had more than enough to pay off the last payment on the ring he intended for Cherrie. And after that? Well, retirement was but a breath or two away.

There was the matter of a little bit of killing in the world's most unforgiving place. Once word spread that The Seven were marching, Mallum would know well his fate, and he would be waiting. Heygar thought it doubtful that the dead man would step into the source without a terrible fight.

CAST A LURE

As Heygar suspected, the king had him escorted from the palace, but not before they paraded him through the court. Every visit to this room always impressed him, with its obsidian floor, marble walls, and decorative sheets of glistening hanging silk. A lesser man might lose the run of himself, imagining himself becoming a king and sitting upon the lavish throne of silver and crystal, but Heygar had little aspirations for such a title.

His footsteps echoed loudly as the crowd of privileged dukes and regents fell silent to his peasant's march. He could read it on their powder-painted faces, and they were correct. The weaver known as Mallum was about to learn the full reach of his king.

Heygar concealed his disdain for the insincere bows offered. Replying with a slight tilt of his head to all other males in attendance, he did almost enough to show deference. The ladies of the court, regardless of age or status, thrust out their chests that little more, for he was the dominant male in this room—the real king, should he try. To them, he offered a polite smile of acknowledgement, and to those with fancier allurements, he allowed his eyes to drop further to enjoy their gifts a little more. Let them take it as a compliment. Besides, he was a full-blooded man, was he not?

Waiting guards opened the court's doors of golden adornment. Freedom from such wealthy decadence was all but a step away. Then a large, booming voice called out to him.

"Good hunting, Heygar of The Seven. May no demons be upon your back," King Lemier declared, displaying none of the anger or uncertainty he had shown moments before as he seated himself upon his throne. If there had been any doubt why the mercenary was visiting the king at court, there was little now.

Heygar knew well to play his part. He spun around gracefully despite his heavy burden and bowed magnificently. They had paid him a fine fortune. May as well offer all the accoutrements. He placed his hand across his chest, suggesting allegiance.

"For the good of the kingdom, and for the good of my king, I will serve my liege." That sounded just right.

The king knew well the depth of his loyalty, but such a pledge would keep the howling wolves from the noble gates that little while longer. They whispered words as Heygar left the room. The wheels of rumour had already begun their turning.

Heygar allowed himself a wry smile as the doomed guards escorted him out through the gardens to the city. By the time they locked the gates behind him, he had convinced himself that when retirement came, he might survive the political cutthroats and the privileged vermin of the royal court. Cherrie would need a little time to adapt to becoming a divine lady of court though.

He laughed to himself at such a thought as he made his

way down through the cobbled streets of Dellerin City to meet with his little pack of maniacs. However, not before he made one more secretive liaison with an old friend.

Bereziel's house was like many others in the centre of the richest part of the city, but it was a mansion without an owner's love. Heygar never believed Bereziel had truly loved much in his life, apart from fighting with the Hounds, studying the source, or perhaps bedding down with Cherrie. He looked up at the three-story monstrosity and shook his head in dismay. His oldest friend had let the place fall to ruin. It hadn't tasted a lick of paint since its construction, the impressive gates were rusted right through, and the garden hadn't received a cutting of any kind in many a season.

Heygar knocked upon the oak doorway. When there was no reply, he turned the handle and stepped into the domain of the finest weaver of the source he had ever known.

"Are you dead?"

The artificial smell of lemongrass permeating throughout the claustrophobic home disguised the smell of damp, age, and rancidness. The door closed behind him, leaving him in near darkness but for a dim light a few floors up.

"General," croaked a voice from above.

"Not dead, so."

Heygar began the precarious climb up the wooden stairs. Stacks of archaic tomes and forgotten scrolls, likely scribed with invaluable incantations and weavings, were disregarded upon each step like a toy after its child had grown weary of play. While each creased and tied scroll or stained book were appreciated well enough by Bereziel, to the rest of the ignorant world, they would have been invaluable. The weaver had the finest collection of words gathered upon the source and its weavings, but Bereziel never liked to share. Ever.

Heygar followed the light until he reached the small study

on the top floor. It was overflowing with rune stones, bottled ingredients, and mysterious weaving assortments. With even more ancient books filling large bookcases on either side of the room, it was no surprise his friend had let his home fall into disrepair. All the weaver could ever need or desire was in this room.

Bereziel sat perfectly still behind his messy desk as if he were a porcelain figurine—fragile and priceless. With mounds of notes and script on either side of him, he could easily have remained concealed with his head dipped, hiding beneath his long white hair. It was even whiter than Heygar remembered, and it had only been a few months since they had last spoken.

Oh, Bereziel, what have you done to yourself?

"When have you last looked up from one of these books?" Heygar mocked, running his fingers along the nearest volume from his resting place in the doorway. It was *The Medicinal History of the Snakewood Shrub, Volume Two*.

Fascinating.

Bereziel looked up from his book to this jest, and Heygar cursed in surprise. The improper use of manipulating energies had aged the man. It did with all weavers, but Bereziel had aged as though a century had passed since they last spoke. They were born in the same year, yet Bereziel resembled less a brother and more a grandfather. His skin was tight and yellow, as if wild cancer ran freely through his blood, and his eyes sat in deep, emaciated sockets. The wrinkles that had formed through the unnatural use of the arcane had transformed the man from an intimidating warrior into a decrepit wretch.

"You've been weaving something terrible, haven't you, my old friend?" Heygar said. He felt the weight of the coins in his waist pouch, heavier than before.

"An old man in my position has additional costs. One must accept employment where one can," the weaver said softly.

Heygar recognised the lie for what it was. Bereziel needed no money. He desired to know more of the world beyond this one, to step where no weaver had in the few hundred years since the first of their kind emerged from their nonexistence. Heygar knew more about weavers than most, but even he was denied any truth or history. He was not their kind.

He wondered if the mystery of their origins was known even to themselves. Perhaps every child who displayed the trait intrinsically knew of their own lineage or learned it from their master. Any time a mere legend as Heygar asked questions of the source and weavings, every weaver he had ever met would leave the question unanswered. A smart man wouldn't continue pushing at an adawan nest, lest the inhabitants bite. They were as human as the next with unusual abilities, clueless how best to control them.

Bereziel knew how to control his abilities, but soon enough he would spend too much of his soul into weavings and die. Heygar sighed, eyed his friend, and lamented how things had turned out.

With shaking fingers, Bereziel wiped the ash clear of an incense burner and dropped a few stalks of dried lemongrass inside. With a pestle, he ground the plant down and set it alight with a candle. Before the flames could overcome the plant, he blew it out and the embers released a fresh fragrance into the air. Watching how strenuous such a menial task had become for him depressed Heygar greatly. Another great man lost to unnatural things.

"You still spend your fortunes on female company. I thought a few years living in Venistra would shake such urges from you?" Heygar mocked, though the humour was lost in the tragedy he saw in front of him. This was the cost of losing a soul.

He eyed the room's ramshackle appearance and felt a little guiltier. How many incantations had this man performed for him throughout their life? First, as a general upon the battlefield, and then even more after the last war was won. A great weaver should have focused his efforts on greater things, like love, family, or the unhealthy pursuit of unlimited power. Instead, Bereziel had offered his soul up for the benefit of Heygar's rising star. However, he *had* been one of The Seven, so that was something at least.

"Not all of them would charge the rates that Cherrie would," the weaver said.

Heygar saw the glimmer in the eyes of his old friend. Bereziel had taken her to bed first. He would never allow him to forget that.

Heygar eventually stepped into the room. "Perhaps I'll tell her you've returned from your exile in that cursed place and suggest she drop in and earn herself a little of the gold I'm about to pay you."

Bereziel's face darkened. "You gave your word you wouldn't tell anyone I had returned. Nothing good can come from any soul knowing I am here."

Heygar laughed. "You've always suggested dark things are stirring, yet still, I see no sign."

"Yeah, well, one of these decades I'll be right, and when I am, I'd rather no one knows where to find Bereziel of The Seven."

"I'll know."

"True, but I can take you in a fight, Heygar." Bereziel smiled and accepted the embrace from his friend. He felt like ragged bones in Heygar's grip. Whatever wanderings he had taken in Venistra had left him at death's door.

The old weaver shuffled back to his desk and collapsed in his seat. "The king has plans for you, has he not?" As he spoke, he swiped a large tower of ancient scrolls from his eye line. They toppled from his desk and scattered among the countless others along the floor. Bereziel didn't seem to notice, and Heygar wondered how desperate Iaculous, his youngest Hound and apprentice weaver, would be to spend time in this room, studying any of the mysterious enchantments so casually discarded. It was unlikely the young man would ever be welcome, however. Many of their kind might think it a shame that Bereziel would soon die without passing on his knowledge first.

"Venistra."

"You ask me to cast a lure on your pack," Bereziel whispered. He eyed the doorway as though eager ears were about—as though casting a lure was against the law, and its punishment was death. It was, but it would take a brave battalion to hunt either of the men down.

Heygar removed the pouch from his waist and dropped it on the desk. With the loss of the money, he felt even guiltier. He took a seat and waited for the usual argument. How many times would Bereziel challenge his honour on such matters before acquiescing to his demands? This evening would be no different from any other as long as Bereziel still had any incantations left in his broken form.

"The dark world has gifted me many things, but it has left me a shell, at least for now."

"You are still fierce," Heygar insisted. He thought again of the pledge ring paid off in full and the possibility of retirement in a house bigger than this. Cherrie was still young enough for one pup. A wife and child settled in a vineyard would be a grand thing. Sacrificing his friend's soul was just another price to pay.

"Every time I weave darkness like this, more of my soul disappears into oblivion," the weaver whispered and reached for his bag of gems. Heygar wasn't even sure Bereziel knew what his fingers were up to. He moved as though something in the dark parts of his mind controlled him. "I'm not sure how much of me is even left." Bereziel placed seven gemstones into a little stone case. He rubbed his fingers across the surface and sighed as the realisation struck him. "I don't want to cast this. Of all the enchantments, this one is the most treacherous."

Here we go.

"My masters always believed enchantments to be godly things, but any enchantment requiring a prayer to a demon will never end well."

Yes, yes, Bereziel, I know this already.

Heygar exhaled. "The gods are dead; so are all the demons. Lures, enchantments, and stirring evils, they're all the same thing really."

"The gods are most certainly dead." Bereziel drifted off, his eyes focusing on faraway things, and Heygar sighed loudly to pull him from his dramatics.

Nothing changes.

"It was perfectly fine casting a lure in the wars when it suited, so why argue now?" Heygar didn't mind being under the influence of a lure, especially those he had cast upon himself. A lure made everything easier.

"I'm not talking about a thousand unsuspecting soldiers being lured into believing what they fought for was righteous. I'm talking about your brethren. I'm talking about the family you surround yourself with. I'm talking about the woman you intend to marry," Bereziel wheezed. The effort appeared to exhaust him.

"What makes you think I intend to marry Cherrie?" Some things a weaver just knew. *Like dark things stirring?* That close to the world beyond, there might be glimmers of precognition. It didn't really matter. Heygar was planning to pledge himself to her before the night's end. "Will you just do it?" He gestured to the gold.

"Even I don't know how a lure will fully behave once cast? But, I do know your comrades will follow you regardless. You need not prey upon their greed, my friend. Venistra is a terrible place. Give them free will to face it. Each of them is destined for great things. That much I know."

He took Heygar's hand. There was a renewed desperation to the fading man's pleas. *What has he discovered in Venistra to cause such fear?* He hadn't begged like this in almost two decades—since Heygar had first asked for a lure. Back then, there was only a hint of silver showing up in the weaver's black hair, and they would race each other to the brothel to earn Cherrie's company for the night. Bereziel had been the finer sprinter; Heygar had won the marathon.

"In Venistra, where the light is hazy, the wet air is bitter, and hopelessness is a potent fever, a lure is what will keep our spirits raised. A lure is what will keep us going when everything is lost. A lure is what might save us all," Heygar muttered. *Time to seal the deal.* "You value your privacy here. Do you want me to tell Cherrie you are back in Dellerin City? How well will your concealing enchantment work if she knows of its existence? Do you want her to see you like this?" Heygar said coldly, and then he felt the full weight of guilt. *Too far.* He could see the pain on his friend's prideful face, and he knew he had crossed the line. He tapped the pouch of gold.

Bereziel nodded and placed both his fingers upon the case. He took a sharp blade and slit the tips of three of his fingers in a swift motion. He cupped his hand and swiftly turned it over, allowing a few delicate streams of crimson to flow into the box of gemstones. His eyes were shut tightly in concentration, and what colour he had had swiftly left his face. Was this another step too far? Heygar almost thought about stopping his friend but instead, he remained still.

"Siiiiiilllllleeeennnnciiiiiiooooo." A shudder ran down Heygar's back as his oldest friend chanted deeply. Bereziel drew his hand away and recovered the first stone. It was black and dull.

"The rat. Maybe I should have lured him with a little cheese." Bereziel's voice had changed completely as the source energy took hold. It was strong, cruel, and familiar. He appeared weaker, but forbidden practices infused him somewhat. It would not last, however. He was the vessel for a brief time, and what was stolen from the soul and weaved into the enchantment left a dreadful hollowness in its wake.

"Do not refer to Silvious as that," warned Heygar of his fateful little companion. Freakish-looking as he was, he was a kind little beast.

The weaver shrugged indifferently and removed a dark-green stone, regal and smooth.

"Denan," whispered Bereziel and nodded approvingly. "He still hasn't escaped your clutches? A fine man like that will always be hard to entice, even if he is enticed by the wrong things. Perhaps returning home will help him find his way." Bereziel held his fingers over both stones. For a moment, Heygar felt unsteady, as though the floor shook gently.

"He is more than ready to form his own group, but for now, he only wishes a place as my right hand." Heygar wondered why he needed to explain his or his current best friend's actions. Denan loved their group. He could earn a fortune with his name alone, but in Heygar's Hounds, they could be legends.

"I merely made a comment," Bereziel sniffed.

"Well … don't."

The next was Cherrie's stone. Wild red and clear. It shimmered in the candlelight. Bereziel touched it gently. Heygar never liked that part and was happy when her former customer moved on to the next rock.

"You know this is your one," Bereziel said in a strange, forceful voice as he held a raw sapphire out in front of him. "This is the pinnacle. Are you sure you wish to do this?" he warned in one last attempt.

Heygar knew well that a lure was one of the finer enchantments when weaving, and it was invaluable to the right leader. It was the desire to accomplish a task. It preyed upon one's reservations. The more fears and doubts pressed on the nerves, the greater the enticement. Heygar knew his comrades well. They would obsess on the reward, and the lure would drive them. Greed was a powerful ally, but with mercenaries, it was almost sacrosanct.

Yes, there was always a little danger with any enchantment, but no lure had steered him wrong. For some unknown reason, the weavers' guild had outlawed the practice many years ago, and it was likely Bereziel was the only weaver capable of such weaving nowadays. When he died, so, too, might this art. It was a trivial matter. He needed this enchantment this evening, and he was receiving it. Why worry of the things to come?

"You know what I desire. Enchant me."

"I warn you I will not lure them to follow you mindlessly. I will lure them to complete their task in Venistra. Should one of you fall, the lure's effect shall add itself to those remaining, at least, until the task is completed. Only then will the weaving dissipate," Bereziel whispered.

Heygar nodded. "I'd best make sure we don't die."

After a moment, Bereziel held his hands over all three and closed his eyes, and he reached for another stone. There was a glimmer of recognition, and Bereziel smiled warmly. He lifted a second from the chest and eyed them carefully.

"Iaculous, the child, and Arielle, the beauty. When I saw them last, there was only a spark, but now it has taken fire," Bereziel said of the white rock and crystal stone. He took a deep breath and placed both rocks in his hands for a breath of time. Both rocks glowed for a few moments before dimming. "I've never seen that before," he said with delicate awe. "The lure sees something in them that I cannot."

"He is no child anymore. He has been a capable healer the last three years, and Arielle is no beauty compared to her sister."

"To him, she is, and she is deserving of someone who sees her for what she truly is," Bereziel said. He caressed the stone gently as if holding her soul itself.

"Maybe I could send her to you, instead of Cherrie." Heygar laughed.

He felt a little crude, thinking of Arielle offering her body for coin. If truth be told, she wasn't built for the harshness of the mercenary life. She could fight like the rest of them, but it had not escaped him that she spent many a lonely hour in the darkness, crying for any blood spilled. He had been killing from a far younger age, but she never took to it like her sister. If he'd had his way, she would never march with them, but Cherrie was loath to leave her alone for very long, lest she fall into a much darker world. Lest she flee the one she was already in.

Bereziel stared at him irritably before placing both stones side by side. They glowed again, and he laughed giddily. "They could be soulmates, like nothing I've ever seen before," he whispered.

"Are you saying that me and Cherrie aren't?"

"Take no offence, friend. Souls are lonely, solitary things, but sometimes two can intertwine. I'm sure you and your love can perfectly become intertwined—if not with the spirit, then at least with the flesh." Bereziel laughed, but his eyes stayed upon the stones.

"He still hasn't hupped upon her," Heygar muttered under his breath. Bereziel ignored this. "Hasn't even tried to kiss her either."

"He will," the weaver said. "Their child could rule the entire world," he blurted in that same strange voice. Ancient, knowing, and lost.

"I'd best keep them in the group, so," quipped Heygar. He wondered if he was mocking his friend, the source, or even himself.

"I would very much like to meet with them both. I would find it interesting to know the effect a lure might have upon their souls," Bereziel said, and then he reached for the last stone before Heygar could reply.

"Ah, yes. Eralorien, your fabled weaver. The old man with the wandering thoughts and wandering hands too," Bereziel spat and dropped the plain glass shard on the table. After a moment, he flicked it with a withered, irritated finger.

Heygar smiled. "Oh come now, Bereziel, jealousy does not suit you. One of the finest weavers I've ever hired."

"He's a thurken fraud," snapped Bereziel. "His hair is barely greying, and he's twice my age. What type of weaver looks that healthy?" he added as if he had something to prove. As if Heygar didn't believe Eralorien was a weak

28

replacement. He was fine enough a weaver for casting a few wards of healing but little else, and his apprentice displayed just as little aptitude for the arcane. "I don't know how Iaculous hasn't stagnated under his instruction too," Bereziel noted.

"I disagree. I suspect Eralorien has learned to reverse the ageing upon the body while weaving," mocked Heygar.

Bereziel recoiled ever so. Not enough to give a great deal away in a game of chance, but enough that Heygar might surmise his activities this next year.

"Oh, Bereziel," he lamented, and his friend shrugged as though it were trivial that he'd sacrificed what remained of his life trying to undo the terrible ageing process that weaving had inflicted upon the body. A body withered far quicker with little soul to call upon. Even Heygar knew there was no returning of the soul. Any weaver who said differently was a liar or worse, disillusioned.

"If you thought so highly of his skill, it would be him weaving from his soul," the weaver muttered and held his hand over the stone. The room appeared to shake once more and fell still just as soon as it occurred. "It is done," Bereziel whispered, and he held his head in his hands. He shook uncontrollably, and all strength left his voice. The vibrant man of the source had diminished back to the ancient shell once more.

"I feel no different."

"How many years have you been stating that? You will know when it happens," Bereziel said.

Heygar smiled. "Until we meet again, my friend."

"I know I will meet you all again in some shape or form. Be wary in Venistra. There is darkness there that is not of this world. Something waiting in the darkness. Mallum is not what the king will have you believe him to be. I am glad I am no part of this task," Bereziel said, and then he leaned back in his chair suddenly, closed his eyes, and fell asleep immediately like a strangler's puppet left to rest at the end of a performance.

Heygar nodded and bowed. "We will meet again, if not in this life, then perhaps in the world beyond," he whispered to the wind. Then he left the fading man to his silence.

CUSTOMS BEFORE THE MARCH

The air was cool on Heygar's face as he strode from Bereziel's house, down through the winding streets of Dellerin. He passed the abandoned market square, long closed since the call of the night, and headed along the delicate flow of the canal until he came to the finest establishment in the entire kingdom: The Drunken Assassin.

Heygar and his comrades had always stayed in this six-story behemoth before setting out in search of their next task and never once tasted failure. The ale was warm, and the food was tepid. Why break from tradition? Mercenaries were a superstitious bunch, and Heygar was no different.

He met Silvious, the rodenerack, in the doorway. Heygar always thought him a fascinating rogue with an uncanny ability to squirm out of precarious trouble. He was mostly human, unlike many of his brethren from the Addakkas inlets, but not for a moment did that grant him any grace among most humans. The Hounds were fond of him but never showed him the respect he deserved.

Silvious was almost four and a half feet in height but could out-leap any man twice over and slice any cur's throat with his clawed fingers quicker than any serrated dagger. "Mostly human with a little rat thrown in," he was inclined to point out to any fiend who took umbrage at his presence. He hid his unnatural ears beneath a thin hood and, with his propensity for shaving, he allowed himself to blend in among humankind—at least, at first glance.

But if one were to look a little closer, it was plain to see that his jaw was a little too sharp, his nose a little too pronounced, and his bucked teeth razored. And if one looked even closer, they might even see the strength and fire in his dark, beady eyes.

"It's a little chilly out here, Silvious," Heygar said, nodding to the inviting light of the tavern within.

"I didn't want it to be like last time. I wanted to wait until everyone was here. 'Sides, I don't mind the cold," Silvious whispered and twitched his nose unnaturally—unnatural for a human; perfectly natural for a rat.

The low murmur of conversation, jests, downing pints, and popular songs filled the night, and Heygar felt for his companion. He was too human for acceptance by his rodenerack kind, and man never needed an excuse to strike out at anything that was extraordinary. No one knew why the rodenerack were as they were. Some said it was the work of demons from a millennium ago. Others said it was simple cunning on the rodents' part to integrate themselves into civilisation. As if rats weren't despicable enough without mimicking their human counterparts. Maybe they were just the next step in evolution. Or a step behind.

It didn't really matter to Heygar. Silvious was a master thief, and he trusted the beast with his life. There were worse companions to have when travelling into unforgiving lands. He wondered if Venistrians were as nasty to their kind as he had heard.

"I imagine I'm the last to arrive," Heygar said, marching through the door. The rodenerack followed swiftly behind.

It was the music blaring from a talented troupe in the corner which caught his attention first. Only the best musicians were likely to make a living in any tavern in the city, and this troupe were no different. They enraptured the crowd with simple melodies and drove the room towards merriment and drunkenness. Heygar listened for a few bars as he surveyed the room for obvious threats.

It had only been two hours since the king had openly proclaimed the Hounds were saviours of the kingdom, and despicable plans might already be in motion. Just because he was a legend didn't mean assassination was not around the corner or sitting at the bar. Any mercenary company that took out any of The Seven was likely to make a fine name for themselves. And though such an exact ill fate had befallen this group before, the company responsible usually and mysteriously disappeared without a trace before the season was out.

Heygar's eyes focused on a young man in the corner. His eyes were still, and his face was pale with worry while all around him sang and drank heavily. Now, why was a young lad in a fine establishment like this daring not to enjoy himself? After a few breaths of time, a young girl sat down beside him. His face lit up. Immediately, they engaged in conversation as if their young lives depended on it. Heygar smiled at his miscalculation. A fresh courting was a wonderful thing to behold. If he could, he might keep that in mind when the fighting began.

Content that most patrons were present for respectable reasons, he walked the room once before leaving a handful of silver coins at the counter for their half-night stay. He didn't bother trying to catch the eye of his comrades, who were spread out, engaging in good times. They had been since he had left them a few hours earlier.

Heygar grabbed a stool and seated himself at an occupied table in the middle of the room. "Leave," he said, and the owners of the table leapt from their seats, lest the legend tear them apart.

Silvious sniggered and took an empty seat. Within a few pulses of blood, the rest of his Hounds flocked around him. Arielle and Iaculous dropped their playing cards mid-bet and took the empty seats beside each other. Always beside each other. Never too far apart either, Denan and Cherrie emerged from a secluded corner and sat down on either side of him, his closest allies and confidants. They'd been with him since the beginning. With Bereziel, they were first known as "The Luistra Four," but time was ever-moving, and now there were more potential legends to call upon and a hundred stories between them. Eralorien was last to sit with them. Vibrant and intimidating, he carried his illusions and delusions softer than most.

"What is the good word, General?" Denan, his second in command, asked. He was a few years younger than Heygar. With a strong, sharp jaw, black hair, and a matching goatee, it was no surprise that most women fell under his charms easily enough. He was gentle and quiet when at peace, but in the raging movements of war, he was fierce and brutal. It was the Venistrian blood in him.

Already, the eyes in the inn focused on the impressive collection at the table. Conversation dropped, and ears became more eager. The troupe were constant, as most talented troupes were. They played loud enough to cover the conversation. Despite the melodies, every patron knew exactly why this meeting was taking place and guessed every word spoken. Mallum had terrible things coming to him for rebelling against the king, did he not? If the Hounds knelt at Lemier's crown, well, he really wasn't that bad, now was he?

"The word is gold, and it shines. Our beloved king will offer one hundred apiece." Heygar produced his bag of coin. He dropped it on the table, and Silvious swiped it up swiftly. "Twenty apiece to start, and the rest to whoever survives," laughed Heygar as the rodenerack dealt the coin out to his comrades.

His twitching fingers assured honesty, and no one argued. They merely accepted the coin and placed them in their own pouches, but not before blowing thrice upon the chinking pieces and kissing the fabric for luck.

Let this not be the final payment.

"Was it as we suspected?" Cherrie asked.

She was flush, and Heygar thought her beautiful even though she was almost forty years in age. Old for a goddess without a ring upon her finger. She was taller than most, but she met Heygar at just the right height. When a rare smile left her perfect lips, it was enough to quell a storm. When she laughed, Heygar swore it was the actions of a deity within the source, and when she stripped naked, he felt he was never adequate enough to writhe with her. But she loved him. They were fine true lovers for five whole years. It was time to step into betrothal, regardless of their fears for it.

"This Mallum has to have fine tricks to have attained power in a place like Venistra," Eralorien said, running his fingers through his greying yet unmistakably healthy-looking hair. His other hand fell upon his temple, which he massaged gently. His eyes watching Cherrie as she played with her dark amber hair.

As the only real weaver of the source among them, it was no surprise he was more cautious than the rest. Some said Mallum could weave pure flame of death. It was hard to face something like that with a few enchantments of healing or concealment. Well, at least Denan had his sword, which would cut through anything the source could muster.

"Any man'll fall to an arrow," Silvious hissed. If he had a tail, Heygar imagined it would twitch wildly. One drunken night, the little beastie had confessed that he had cut it off as a little fledgling. Heygar had laughed and assumed him jesting. They hadn't spoken of it since.

"Well, if the rat's not scared, what do we have to fear?" Iaculous muttered, and Arielle slapped him across the back of the head. He grinned devilishly and feigned terrible hurt.

Iaculous was a delicate little whelp of a pup with an unremarkable face. Perhaps as he grew beyond his nineteen years, he might earn a little charm or develop a deep stare to set himself apart from his averageness. As it was, he was an apprentice weaver of the source, and Eralorien suggested him unremarkable. He was brave and followed orders to the letter though, so he was worthy of his place among them.

"Don't call him that," Arielle mocked, and then she reached across to the offended thief and stroked his face lovingly.

The rodenerack laughed and accepted the jest as camaraderie. All he wanted was acceptance and a family. In Heygar's Hounds, he had nearly both. Nearly, but not quite.

Arielle drank from the nearest abandoned goblet without shame. She was no beauty like her older sister, but her blonde hair was elegant enough, and with rosy cheeks and youthful laugh lines already appearing on her face, she was a pleasure to be around. She could silence a room with her smile like Cherrie, but her constant laughter was infectious and could rouse any man from dreariness. Iaculous was probably a fine enough fit. Perhaps in a year or two, they could both escape the mundanity of the close friendship both hung their banners upon.

"I've never liked Venistra," said Cherrie. She played with her hair a little more, eyeing Denan for a sign of offence. She was harder than the rest, earning her steel through a life of struggle before she earned her place as a master tracker, master of the bow, master of the blade, and master of killing when he thought of it. He thought her the finest mercenary of them all, but he would never let her know such a thing. Caution followed almost every move she ever took. A lifetime protecting her sister would do that to anyone, he supposed. Her age dictated that she was closer to being Arielle's mother and often behaved as so. Their actual mother was dead long ago. He had never met her.

"A hundred gold would earn us quite an adventure in the pleasure nests of Castra," Denan said. "Just you and me, eh, Heygar?" He eyed Cherrie for the reaction of her own. She slapped him across the back of the head.

"We could bring little Iaculous and make a man out of him," agreed Heygar, wondering if the lure was taking place. Deep down, he felt a warmth in his stomach.

Someone placed a full tray of chinking ales down in front of the group, and enthusiastic hands reached out and retrieved the mugs without offering payment. The innkeeper bowed and left a little poorer. Still, The Seven as locals was worth its weight in gold. It was a small matter. Soon enough, they would pay him in full.

"Ooh, can I come and watch Iaculous lose his innocence?" Arielle asked excitedly.

"The more, the merrier. We might even reserve a few boys for you," suggested Denan.

"Oh, no. My first with a boy needs to be with roses, candles, and silken sheets. Keep that in mind, Iaculous,"

Arielle said. The apprentice's face reddened, and he hid himself in his ale. "I'll take a few girls though. They would know where everything goes."

"That is very much something I would like to see," said Silvious.

"I'd only charge you half-price, my little pet. The rest would need to cough up all the coin in advance," Arielle pledged, and the table laughed.

"Will you join us blowing our wealth in paradise?" Heygar asked of Eralorien, who shrugged noncommittally and stared at his drink.

"I'm adequate enough to attain female companionship without the need to pay for it," the old weaver sniffed. He drained his drink as though it were an antidote to a dreadful disease. He slipped his bag of coin into one of the many hidden pockets underneath his cloak and wiped the hairs in his long beard around his mouth.

Unlike the rest of The Seven, he carried no armour or blade, instead relying on his luck and wards to keep him safe. Of all The Seven, he brought little to the table, but to walk into battle without a weaver of any skill was folly. Weavers were a rare thing in Dellerin, and perhaps because Eralorien had replaced Bereziel, he had never fully warmed to the man.

"Eralorien and myself shall have a fine time ourselves while the rest of you furrow until poor," Cherrie jested coldly. Talk of prostitution was always a touchy subject with the girl.

"Are you charging again?" Arielle asked, and the table exploded into laughter.

"Well, if you are charging…" Eralorien said. More laughter.

"We'll talk about it when they're off in Castra," Cherrie muttered through clenched teeth.

Heygar saw her feelings were almost hurt, but she was as

tough as deyrawn leather. Though they laughed, there was uneasiness at the table. It was the same feeling when cracking wit at learning of a rival mercenary's untimely demise. Before a task, there was always the fear. So, they ordered another round.

Soon, that apprehension seemed to dissipate, and Heygar wondered if it was the beverage. Reassuring thoughts flooded his mind and drowned suggestions of Venistra's hazards mercilessly. They were The Seven. They would know victory. Why did he even need to have a lure cast, anyway? They were fierce, and they would follow him regardless. This Mallum was no great threat at all. They only needed to be as clever and composed as usual.

He looked across the table and found the group had fallen silent. Each one of them was brave and exquisite. Each one of them stared blankly into nothingness as a collective realisation came upon them.

"We have to kill Mallum extravagantly," Heygar declared and felt just fine about it.

"We'll take his thurken head," Denan suggested and sighed contentedly.

"We'll lance it on a stake for the rest of Venistra to see," Cherrie said, daring a smirk.

"Then we'll return it to King Lemier on a silver platter," Eralorien said, nodding in approval.

"Wherein he can shower us with all the gold in the land," Iaculous declared and licked his lips greedily.

"So, we can buy all the shiny," said Arielle giddily.

"And then we go out and do it all over again," whispered Silvious, counting his riches for the third time.

They drank with good cheer for a few hours more until, at midnight, Heygar declared their tab needed repayment. They stripped their armour and sent Silvious to cover the debt.

The creature downed his ale and stumbled through the crowd, eager to find the sturdiest bunch of troublemakers. He quickly found his quarry in a corner by the door. Heygar watched his thief trip and crash wonderfully into a dozen other mercenaries at their table. Feigning apology and awe, he swiped a couple of money pouches from unsuspecting belts before brazenly marching to the bar to clear the debt.

Denan cracked his fingers loudly. "Here we go."

Silvious returned the pouches to the mercenaries by dropping the empty pieces of cloth on the table. "Thanks, lads," was all he managed before the aggrieved brutes fell on him as one enraged unit.

Within a pulse, Arielle was beside him. A pulse after that, five other comrades were at war. Two fiends grabbed Silvious and flung him through a window. "Get out of here, rat!" one of them screamed as glass and mostly human waste was removed into the cold street outside.

"Don't call him that!" Iaculous roared and swung a chair on both assailants. Arielle leapt at both men and took one through another window while Iaculous finished the other. Denan surged into the main body of aggrieved men and destroyed all in his path. With a grinning face, he struck without prejudice while at his flank, the tall legs of Cherrie kicked and pinned any fools unlucky to strike a girl. With her green dress flowing out behind her, she was a tempest, and the melee soon grew beyond both parties.

There was a simple rule to a bar fight. It didn't matter who you struck as long as you struck ferociously with the foot or fist.

As mayhem erupted all around them, only Eralorien avoided the brutality. With a faint blue glow emanating from his fingers, he weaved healing where appropriate. Not enough to drain himself, but enough to stem Cherrie's bleeding nose or lessen the swelling around Denan's eye. He would take care of any deep cuts at the end, and only those of his comrades.

"Woo!" cried Heygar, ducking away from a larger opponent. He countered the weak left with a swift knee to the groin and delivered a quick combination to the falling man. All was fair in a decent brawl. Though Heygar's Hounds were a group to be respected, few mercenaries would pass up the opportunity to say they manhandled a legend without paying too severe a price.

Heygar spun among the skirmish and turned into a swinging strike from the young man he had gazed upon before. It caught him under the chin, but it did little more than irritate. It was a fine technique though, and the youth had seen a fight or two. In the blink of an eye, Heygar spotted his assailant's potential mate looking on. She was fearful as her man took on the most famous warrior in the world, but beneath the fear, he spotted primal pride. Heygar swayed and stumbled backwards and crashed into a table, sending drinks, splinters and cards into the air. Seeing her man dethrone Heygar was likely to do the youth no harm removing the damsels clothing, he imagined.

After a moment, he climbed to his feet and watched the couple make their hasty escape out into the cool night beyond. Task done and feeling good about the world, he clicked his neck loudly. Then he joined the rest of his comrades in finishing the traditional fight before embarking on their undertaking.

DELICATE WORDS AND UNLIT CANDLES

"My divine goddess, will you do me the honour of pledging myself to you for … No, no, that doesn't sound right. That's no good at all." Heygar looked hopefully into the mirror as though the battered man staring back could suggest something finer to say.

Try harder, Heygar, you idiot.

"Cherrie, I love you. I always have because you're the most … the most … ah, thurk it anyway."

He dropped to the seat of his bedroom, cursing his lack of a silver tongue. He sighed miserably, wiped his brow, and discovered blood and perspiration had left its mark upon his shaking hand. Wonderful. Where was Eralorien to heal his after-fight injuries when he needed him most?

A hundred candles flickered all around him, and he thought them perfect for setting the mood. His fingers still stung from melted wax and ash-eaten matches, but love always hurt and stung. He felt a sudden breeze up his back, and to his dismay, a few little flames blew out in front of his helpless eyes. He listened to the whistling wind outside as it thrashed the single window behind him and thought it lonely, ominous, and perfect for distraction.

Proposing a pledge was to be an exciting time for lovers, but Heygar feared the unknown. The wind gusted again, and more candles flickered to darkness. It had taken a painful span of time to light each one with fingers as arthritic and clumsy as his, but keeping them all burning until she arrived was proving the harder task. As was the actual pledge, but the saga of the lighting of candles was something he might accomplish with success. All in the name of romance.

What was taking her so long, anyway?

"Listen, woman, I'm pledging myself to you, and you will accept," he hissed and dared a chuckle. She would probably prefer that direct approach anyway. She had never been one to hold back on her words or actions.

He knew he should have spoken with Denan before all of this. Denan was the poet among this group, at least with women. The cur could make a faithful woman beg for adulterous play with a few whispered words of wooing.

Heygar spread the rose petals along the bed. They would cost a pretty fortune for this time of the year, but where he might fail with delicate words, he would succeed with passionate gestures. Three of the fragile red petals stuck to his hand.

"She loves me," he flicked one away.

"She loves me a lot," he flicked another.

"She loves me until we rot." He stared at the last one before flicking it away too.

Heygar picked up a candle and returned to the process of illuminating the room in a way befitting her magnificence while ignoring the real question in his mind: was he making the right decision?

A heavy knock drew him from childish rhymes and melancholic worries. He tapped his breast pocket, caught a glance of himself in the mirror one more time, and reasoned there was little he could do at this late hour. She already knew him at his best and worst.

There was a second knock. Why would Cherrie knock a second time? Why would she even knock at all? Heygar opened the door and met the euphoric gaze of Eralorien. The man had been hitting the cuttings of snakewood harder and harder these days. A man his age should have known better.

"I was walking by and felt the sudden urge to speak with you," the older man whispered.

For a pulse, Heygar wondered if Eralorien was more skilled in perception than he had led him to believe. Probably not. Eralorien had never struck him as a great deceiver. Without warning, the weaver waved his hand slowly across Heygar's head. A faint blue trail of source power followed his fingers, and immediately, Heygar felt the healing in his body. He blinked a few times and allowed the bruising to lessen in his aching bones.

"Thank you."

"Some things I can heal just fine." Eralorien blinked a few times and touched his temple. He bowed and wavered slightly as the enchantment took from his soul. It was not enough to age the man but just enough to take his breath for a moment or two. Heygar always thought it strange that healing, though so important in war, spent so little use of the soul while others, such as a lure cast or enchanting concealment, would take so much more. Perhaps a soul's exact purpose in this world was the divine act of healing. As with their history, any weaver was unlikely to reveal their thoughts on the matter if he asked. Perhaps they didn't even know themselves, he wondered. Man was young, but weaving was even younger.

"Just earning my place within the group, General." He looked into the room, raising an eyebrow.

"Was there anything else?" Heygar asked as politely as any general could with life-altering choices on his mind. He could tell that the weaver was worried, and it was nothing to do with their task. A fine general could press matters until those under his command were satisfied, but not tonight. Tonight was his only chance to win himself a bride before they finished their mission. It would only be a week before they returned, but could he hold a ring that long? Could he hold the excitement? Could he even hold his nerve?

"I wanted to …" Eralorien started but fell silent. He had a strained expression, as though struggling with two separate desires, as if something lured him to a different path. He looked far more haggard and sicklier than normal. Such was the appearance of natural age, Heygar supposed. He looked out the door to the large iron gate at the stairs separating the top floor from the rest of the building's levels. Somewhere below, his love was unaware of the question awaiting her.

"You wanted to?" He had hoped for a little peace and quiet. He had bought the entire top floor of the inn to avoid these interruptions. It was also to have one more sleep in comfort and safety before facing the perils of the march.

Eralorien said nothing for a few moments before sighing sadly as if he sensed Heygar's hesitation. "Nothing that cannot wait until after we return," he said, glancing at Heygar's breast pocket, where the ring nestled. "I find it strange to imagine settling down with a female. I would have expected you and Cherrie would feel similar, but still settling with her might be…nice?" He turned away leaving Heygar even more nervous than before. Surely, the weaver wasn't subtly warning him from commitment.

"My love, keep my heat close … and … and warm my bed." Heygar groaned and banged his head on the wall. Another candle blew out. After a few more attempts at discovering his poetic nature, Heygar heard another knock.

"May I speak with you?" Iaculous hissed through the door, and Heygar bade him entry. "I like the candles," the apprentice said, slipping into the room. He looked to the rose petals on the bed and said nothing more. Heygar thought him a nice enough young man, if not a little dim. "You missed a few." He nodded to the many that had blown out.

"What do you want?" Heygar asked, bringing another little silent flame to life while another three candles fell to darkness.

"I know you spoke to Eralorien. I tried to sway his thoughts on such matters, but he is a stubborn old man. I was hoping you might sway his decision to leave the group."

Ah, the brief mystery was unravelled. Eralorien wanted to tender his resignation. Feelings of rejection stirred, but Heygar showed nothing but calm on his face. The lure had swayed the old man's predilection towards leaving for now, but it would not hold for long. He would march one last time, and after, they would sit down and speak of things.

At least if Eralorien perished during this undertaking, there would be even less guilt than normal. And more gold to share. The man had no family to care for, so there was no further responsibility. And Iaculous? Well, he was welcome to do whatever he wanted to. He was a fine enough killer, and his healing was as good as any other weaver at such a fee.

"You should get rest, Iaculous. Maybe grab yourself a little companionship before the road," he said as though nothing in the world bothered him, not even a growing

number of unlit candles. The young apprentice bowed, and
Heygar understood his worry. Would he choose a life with his
love or follow the path of weaving?

"Yes, sir," Iaculous said, trying to disguise the
despondency in his face.

"Let's see what happens," Heygar offered as he heard
delicate steps from below. Panic surged through him once
more. It wasn't her. Just steps that sounded like her.

"Let me through," cried Arielle from the head of the
stairs. Her fingers gripped the iron bars tightly. Iaculous
stepped out and swiftly unlocked the gate like a good
potential mate.

"As if anyone would attack us in Dellerin!" she snapped,
and the door opened for her. Her face was redder than normal.
Like her sister, she had fire when she needed it. She stormed
through the security cage and slammed the door behind her.
"See, Heygar, we're all nice and safe now," she mocked,
kicking at the gate that secluded The Seven from everyone
else in the inn. Her voice was slurred from the ale, and he
imagined she would regret that after a few hours in the
saddle's sway.

"I keep my Hounds in fine cages," Heygar growled,
trying and failing to stop the diminutive female as she missed
her own bedroom by quite a distance and slipped through his
doorway.

"Ooh, pretty," she gasped, eyeing the burning candles.
"Get out!"

She glided through the room dreamily. "Incense would be
a fine addition for some playing." He wondered what her
reaction would be to his stealing her sister from her. And
dissolving the Hounds. No man went to war with his wife at
his side. Retirement was inevitable—as was death. At least
one would be a worthy story to tell.

"I reserved a room apiece for a reason," Heygar said, but she still wasn't listening. She was absently tearing a few of the rose petals apart while staring at the little flames with a stupid grin on her face. Despite himself, he thought she looked a little endearing in her annoying ways. She brought out the best in everyone. It was a gift.

"I could help," Iaculous whispered.

"You could leave."

Silvious appeared from behind the gate. He had appeared without a sound. "Lemme in." When no one made any move to unlock the gate, he slipped a tiny pin into the mechanism. After a few pulses, the gate swung open effortlessly.

"Bolt it after you," hissed Heygar and cursed the security on this floor. So much for a restful few hours, knowing they were protected.

Silvious pulled a large wedge of cheese from under his cloak "No need to sleep yet. Look what I … found," He produced a thin dagger and spun it in his clawed fingers. His nose twitched in excitement—for the treasure and for the act in its procurement. Heygar had known many thieves in his time, but none shared the joy of the rodenerack every time he "found" something.

"You aren't exactly breaking the stereotype of your kind," Iaculous said from the doorway.

"I'd love some cheese," Arielle cried in excitement.

"Plenty to share with family," Silvious suggested, gesturing to his master.

"Could everyone please leave me to my thoughts?" shouted Heygar. Then he heard the sharp tone of his beloved as she climbed the last level. "Not with everyone around." His heart hammered, and he grabbed desperately for the nearest candle to finish the lighting.

"I can help," Iaculous said and held his hands out. They

48

glowed brighter than Eralorien's. A flame leapt around the room, and a hundred candles blinked into darkness before swiftly relighting themselves. Iaculous went pale and fell against the door as though struck by a brute twice his size. Arielle gasped in panic and fright and took hold of the apprentice as he steadied himself.

"What did you do?" she cried.

"It's a simple enchantment," he whispered as though lost in a dream. His voice was rough and heavy as if he had spent a night and a day singing without rest. Perhaps he had.

"You look broken."

"We should leave the general to it," he wheezed and leaned on Arielle for a moment, allowing strength to return to his body.

"I will tend to you, idiot," she cried, stroking his chin tenderly.

"I'm fine!" he suddenly snapped. His voice was clear and stronger. "Let's enjoy the spoils of the rat," he added, softer this time, and he offered his potential lover a smile. Making a fuss in front of the boss was unlikely to curry favour it would appear.

They retired to Silvious's room to dine on cheese until sleep likely robbed them of missed opportunities. The sooner they leapt upon each other, the better, thought Heygar. Then he thought of Bereziel's words, that they might create something incredible eventually. But those were just the broken words of a decrepit old man.

"So, are you going to let me in?" Cherrie snapped.

"I don't know, my love. Will I earn a kiss?" Heygar asked, wary that his comrades might hear his sweeter side. He met her at the gate and stroked her hair through the bars with his rough, calloused hands.

"You may have a kiss, I suppose," she said as though it was an expense of great effort.

"Perhaps I would like a little more," he whispered and tried to meet her lips.

She dodged his assault. "Open the gate, Heygar."

"I'm not sure I really want to now."

"Fine, you may see me in a state of undress," Cherrie countered and smiled weakly. He knew that smile. She was troubled. Perhaps when he asked her a quick question, she might snap out of it. Click. She glided into their room, and he left the gate unlocked for whenever Denan and whichever young beauty he had ensnarled retired for the evening.

"Oh, the candles are nice," she said softly and undid the knots at her dress. She groaned under her breath as she did. She was beautiful, and any reservations he felt diminished immediately.

"Oh, Cherrie, you are my …" he said as her dress fell away. He crept up behind her with the ring in hand.

"Oh, that's much better. I can breathe now," she said.

"You are my …" *Soulmate?*

She dropped onto the bed. A few petals took flight and found death upon the ground.

"I hate this thurken cycle," she moaned and prodded at her scarred back absently. "It always starts with the back and then everything really goes to spit. You would think weavers could have figured a way to deal with things like this."

Heygar realised his folly.

"So, I'm no father yet?" He didn't know females all too well, but he knew now was the wrong time to ask for her hand. He slipped the ring back into his pocket.

"I'm not with your child just yet, my love," she said, snuggling her head into the feathered pillow.

"I lit one candle and lost the run of myself," he joked and climbed upon the bed.

"The candles are pretty," she said, sighing as he ran his fingers along her ruined skin. "You don't have to if you are too tired," she added and stretched out on the bed.

"If nothing else, I will always take what pain I can from you," he said and massaged away what pain he could.

"My man."

DAY ONE

Morning struck, and with it came dreary marching weather. Heygar sat in his saddle miserably as his mount carried him farther from civilisation. It was still well before dawn. Sleep was an overrated interest to any decent mercenary, and the sooner they were clear of Dellerin's grasp, the safer they would be.

They had made good time already. It was only a day and a half's ride to the coast and a day's swift sailing over treacherous waters to the unwelcoming shore of Venistra. Still, without a locked gate at their back, there were dangers. Lemier had painted fine targets on all their rears. Leaving under the cover of night was a fine way to stay ahead of potential ambushes.

Silvious was another. The rodenerack's horse was tethered to Denan's. It was smaller than the rest of the warhorses and built with speed in mind. Now though, it ambled in its reins as it awaited the return of its rodenerack master.

Silvious could scamper quicker than any horse for a short time if needed, and scamper ahead he did. With his head arched unnaturally low and claws dragging ever so slightly in the muddy ground, they had charged him with the unenviable task of scouting their route. Not for a swifter path to the coast, however. There was only one suitable road, and therein lay the problem.

Silvious's quarries were assassins and ambushes. Sadly enough, both were a common occurrence between rival companies. The Seven should have been above all this, having become the most reliable group in their field and sitting atop the ladder of rule, but there was always a foolish little brat with ideas above his or her station. They had faced at least a dozen attempts in as many years, which was admittedly well below the average. Still, Heygar was tiring of needless bloodshed and the constant watching of the bend in the road ahead.

He had committed similar deeds as a whippet himself, attempting to become the fiercest Venandi in the courtyard. Thoughts of the last troupe he and his little group had taken out in Fayenar sprung to mind, and guilty thoughts were suppressed swiftly. A mercenary's life was full of sins. Some things he wouldn't miss when retirement came.

"You look tired, friend," Denan said from beside him.

Though the morning was dull, the younger man's eyes were bright and alert. They were hunter's eyes awaiting the first dribble of blood before draining a man dry. Heygar had long since presumed that his old friend cared little for wealth and notoriety. He was a mercenary for the sport and kill. It was something in his lineage, he imagined. Venistrians were always a little too twisted for his taste. Though Denan's absence from such a miserable country had disciplined his friend and tapered his loyalties, he had displayed no real desire to return to his land. Denan treated his homeland as a cold outcast would, from a city of light.

Perhaps it was all the recent tales of collapsing economies, mass famine, and unique monsters rising which stirred his thoughts of desire. Whispered words of dark activities occurring in Venistra were slow to emerge at first, but as months passed and little trinkets of information became known, Denan appeared to reconsider. Eventually, he heard a dark weaver had taken a step towards leadership, which stirred him to act. And act he had, by proposing a task of assassination on this mysterious Mallum to Heygar and Heygar alone.

"We can do the deed, my friend, but why not make sure we earn gold along the way?" Heygar had suggested with a wry grin. It wasn't difficult to imagine King Lemier wanting Mallum taken care of. Anchoring the Hounds in Dellerin for a few days longer than needed had placed them in the king's sights and provided the shrewdest solution.

"I was up half the night with Cherrie," lied Heygar, and Denan laughed.

"She should allow our fearless leader to sleep on the eve of battle." Denan gripped both ropes tightly. His eyes were on the path ahead as they neared the ingress of Ailedroc Forest. The dozen miles ahead would be taken carefully. With clusters of trees on either side, it made a fine staging point for ambushes. He didn't need to mention fears like this to his comrades. They already knew what to expect and exactly how to react.

"I almost pledged myself to her," Heygar mumbled, in case she heard.

"What happened? Did she do something new and lurid?"

"I have a ring," Heygar said. Denan's smile faded upon realising the truth in his words and the ramifications.

Welcome to my misery, brother.

Denan appeared dreadfully unhappy at discussing emotional things with Heygar. "So, she said no?"

"Be still, my friend. The conversation never reared its unpleasant head."

"If you two wed, what becomes of our little troop?" Denan said and spat in the dirt. Leader or not, Heygar saw the hurt in his friend's face. As second in command, Heygar should have informed him. Denan wiped spittle from his goatee and looked down in shame. Heygar patted him on the back.

"If we wed, I will invite you to the affair," Heygar said, grinning.

The first sparks of dawn drew life, but the shadow of the wood enclosed itself over them before they could feel the sun's first warm rays. Instead, the morning chill increased, and Heygar shuddered despite himself.

Denan tapped the magnificent heavy armour. "Will you dress in that monstrosity for the auspicious occasion?"

"I'll have Silvious polish it up nice and proper," Heygar said and caught himself glancing at the path below for any signs of his diminutive comrade's scuff marks in the mud. He had only suggested he run a few miles ahead, and the little thief should have returned by now. Still, he wasn't too concerned. Silvious was crafty enough to spot any danger a few miles off.

"Will you leave us, then?"

"She might say no."

"Let's hope so," Denan said and tried to smile. Heygar cursed to himself. As if the Venistrian did not have enough on his mind. Now his general had pulled the rug from under his feet.

"At some point, you will be the one to take the mantle

from me, Denan. It's long past due you fronted your own group of lunatics."

"I've never craved ruling."

"This isn't running a little group of hunters, trying to avoid your birth right. This is something far less honourable and far more important." Heygar offered a smile.

"I've tried honour and look where it's taken me." Denan released his grip on one rein and scratched absently at the one tattoo he wore on his chest. It was a small, unimpressive symbol in black and red, but whenever Denan was troubled, his hand inevitably reached for it. Heygar knew it was his family crest. If a snake, skinned alive, was an attractive crest in Venistra, they were sorely lacking an artist's eye. Maybe if they spent less time rebelling and more time engaging in artistic practices, Heygar thought, the island might be better off. "You can lead, you can inspire," Heygar insisted, and Denan offered a humourless laugh.

"My friendship has blinded your senses, old man. If I was ever capable of inspiring the lowliest peasant, I would consider my life well-lived. As it is, well, the most I can inspire is a desperate woman away from her boredom for a few nights." Denan shuffled in his saddle searching for a way to change the subject. Talking of his return home was likely bringing down his mood even more than normal. "I wonder where the rat is. He should have returned by now," he said suddenly.

"See, you are already thinking like a leader," agreed Heygar with a little too much enthusiasm.

A few hours later, when the sun was higher in the sky, the casual banter between the warriors of bad bets, salacious jests, and pompous boasts filled the air. Heygar imagined for the umpteenth time whether he could give it all up.

Despite the early hour, they made camp at the side of the

road where there was a big enough break in the tree line. Only a blinded fool would continue without the reappearance of their scout. If a few more hours passed, trouble and nasty, predictable things were afoot.

"We rest here until Silvious returns," Heygar said and dropped to the ground. His armour clanked loudly under its weight as he steadied himself. He still wasn't used to the heaviness of his new armour.

He hobbled his horse near a patch of grass and stretched out, resting his head on a moss-covered log. Around him, he heard his comrades sit, eat, and mutter their irritation at Silvious's absence. It was like trying to manage a troupe of children.

After a time, Heygar fell into a well-needed sleep with wonderful dreams of jewels and rings and beautiful women. But they were lost in uneasy visions of dark Venistrian shadows, unnatural fierce beasts, and feelings of tragic loss. He woke with a start, not from the nightmares but from Denan's call.

"Here comes the little rat now," the younger warrior said, and Heygar blinked the sleep from his eyes.

"He's moving quicker than he needs to," hissed Iaculous.

The young weaver cursed, and Heygar spotted the rodenerack a couple hundred feet down the thin path, scurrying with all his might towards them. He screamed incomprehensible words, again and again. Sometimes, when his mind was elsewhere, Silvious's original language returned. It usually happened when he was frightened, which was rare enough.

Iaculous was the first to notice the arrow imbedded in the rat's shoulder. He dropped to his knees and closed his eyes, and the blue surge of source power emanated from his fists. He wove his healing. The rodenerack continued screaming the word again. It sounded like a drowning man coughing water from his lungs, with a few hisses thrown in between. When he eventually reached his comrades, he discovered his foreign tongue once more.

"Ambush!" he cried out in their language. Then he collapsed in the mud at Heygar's feet as a thin blue veneer of healing covered his panting body.

A COMPANY OF FOOLS

"Spread out, Hounds!" Heygar shouted, and each of his warriors leapt to action.

At the top of the path, Silvious's attackers came into view. Heygar strained his eyes as twenty brutes charged towards them in a cluster of menace and frenzy. They carried swords, shields, maces, daggers and flails. All were perfectly suited to the instilling of fear and dread upon victims. The ambushers roared loudly as they sprinted.

Heygar took a few breaths to calm his beating heart and lowered the guard on his helm. Less vision, but he had to keep himself pretty, did he not? The steel in his longsword was always reassuring, and as he pulled it free of his scabbard, a cold thought ran through his mind. Someday, he would pull this blade and never sheath it again. It wasn't the first time he had such a thought. It was likelier he would one day sheath his blade and never draw it again. He did not know which notion he preferred, for in battle, he felt alive. They all did. That was why they chose this life.

At his feet, Eralorien and Iaculous tended to Silvious. The

apprentice placed his glowing hands over the thin break in the rodenerack's armour.

"Pull it out," squealed Silvious, trying to reach back at the offending arrow.

"The barbed tip hasn't come through the rat's shoulder," Eralorien said, instructing the apprentice.

"Don't call him that," cried Arielle. Her face was flush with rage that someone had hurt her pet. Her friend.

Iaculous bent over the wound and pushed the arrow through Silvious's shoulder. There was a scream and a quick snap as the thin wooden body split in two and the offending arrow pieces pulled free. Iaculous allowed more of the source energy to flow into the wound, which sealed swiftly.

"Just heal him enough to get him back into the fight," Eralorien hissed and pulled the apprentice from his patient. The wound had become a delicate, pale membrane forming over the hole, and Silvious's moans fell silent. The panic was already leaving his face, and Heygar saw the spark of war returning to the rodenerack's eyes.

The assassins spread out along the path. Each of them wore similar chain mail armour with red sashes along their arms. As he assumed, they were just another mercenary group. Money was money, and death was good business.

He gestured to Arielle and Iaculous. They took out their bows and dashed for cover on the far side of the path, taking cover in the tree line. Eralorien moved to the other side and hid himself behind an old oak tree, taking out a bow of his own. He was a weaver of healing and illusion, but in the Hounds, he dug into the mud just like everyone else. With enough gold, one could afford the grandest soaps to wash it all away.

"You did well, Silvious," said Heygar. The rodenerack

grinned and pulled his bow from his horse's saddlebag. "How far have they tracked you?"

"I picked up their scent a few miles in. When I got a closer look, they pinned me with an arrow. I would have been back sooner, but I couldn't shake them."

Heygar patted him roughly on the head. "Let's make these thurken brats pay for drawing Hound blood." Silvious bared his teeth and scampered off to join Eralorien in the tree line.

"Are these fools going to attack us like this?" Denan hissed, donning his own helmet casually. He held his Venistrian sword out before him. Most blades were silver or bronze, but some blades forged from that region were a deep, unsettling green. Heygar had always had an eye on that weapon, but Denan insisted he would never sell a family heirloom. Maybe when they earned their own blood money, he might find a Venistrian blacksmith willing to cook him up a similar sword.

"I think it's the Crimson Company," said Cherrie, stepping up beside Heygar. She had tied her wild red hair up into an unflattering bun and secured an iron facemask. He'd begged her many times to wear a helmet, but this was the most she'd ever do to protect herself, and she'd never given the reason. Perhaps she liked them knowing just who vanquished them. As if any fool couldn't recognise the way she moved in battle.

"High numbers, low in tactics." Denan spat his disgust into the dirt. He had a point. It was easy to send twenty soldiers after seven and assume that numbers would overcome.

"Now!" Four projectiles took flight from either side through the trees, directly into the first line of attackers.

"Like children led to an idiot's slaughter," Cherrie said and secured her leather chest plate. She stretched her arms out casually as though watching four young mercenaries die thirty feet from her was no great thing.

Denan tapped his sword against his forehead absently. "I'm trying to remember their leader's name." Four bodies stumbled and crashed to the ground, limp appendages tripping a few more as they did. Horrific screams erupted from the cluster, but still, they charged down the Hounds, never once assuming this battle was about to turn swiftly before it had even begun.

"I may be wrong, but I think Lorgan is their leader's name," Heygar said. Denan shrugged.

Another volley of projectiles took flight from each side, and three more attackers fell to the ground. Heygar thought back to the brash young cur by the name of Lorgan he had met over a few ales in a tavern a few months previous. It was somewhere up north, but he couldn't be certain. There were so many. The event had been nothing spectacular, just a few civil words among comrades of the money under the guise of a peaceful banner. He remembered the lad was half his age and twice as arrogant. He had only begun to accept death contracts, and that sudden rise in power usually brought out the worst in any man or woman. A few months later and a few more contracts filled, and the fool believed he had garnered enough experience to form a mercenary crew wild enough to attack the Hounds.

"This is unsettling," Cherrie said.

Both mercenaries nodded in agreement at the pitiful attempt on their life. What type of ambush involved charging straight into oncoming fire? Heygar looked beyond the dozen attackers still running to a lone warrior sitting atop a war steed at the top of the path, away from danger.

What type of man concocted a thoughtless plan as this? The same man who left his soldiers to die while he sat back, taking stock, he thought bitterly. Another volley, but only one more fell. It was Arielle's kill. She rarely missed. The brutes finally cleared the line of archers, and Heygar stepped forward to meet their attack. Cherrie stepped with him. She crouched low and poised like a bird of prey. She was built for war, blood, and delicious death. She was perfect for him.

"Kill them all!" cried Heygar fiercely and charged into the crowd. He swung and nothing could hold his strike. With a swiftness that belied his great size, he tore into the attackers and felled all who stood before him. Through chain mail, through skin, through organ. Blood sprayed over his armour, ruined its polished finish, and marred the exquisite image of the hound across his chest plate. However, things like this couldn't be helped when fighting for one's wealth.

Heygar felt the blows from his assailants as they collectively struck back, but his armour was far stronger than any sword could ever be. It would take a sturdy battle-axe and a sturdier wielder to cause worry. He ignored the young screams ringing in his ears as he took their misled lives into the source beyond. He tried not to think of these young men signing up to a fool's gambit, hoping to make a life for themselves. A catchy title like the Crimson Company must have seemed like quite the idea. Little did they know, the Crimson Company would likely be disbanded by day's end.

"Fall to my vengeance!" Heygar roared—for that was the thing living legends infused their legacy with. It instilled confidence in those he fought with. He also liked to scream out in triumph when winning the day. He had a very impressive roar.

Cherrie was equally mesmerising to watch in battle. She never forced the attack, instead relying on her reflexes to earn her victory. Every time a strike came near her, she slipped from the terrifying blow easily as though she dared the aggressor to end her life. She leapt between two attackers, ducked, and dodged under each failing strike before countering swiftly and drawing blood. He imagined the smile on her luscious lips as she leapt away from danger. She took his breath away.

Within a few moments, all who charged Heygar were brutally felled. What remained at his feet was a handful of broken mercenaries fit only for carrion birds. He caught sight of Cherrie spinning under one last strike and sweeping up behind her attacker. With blood-soaked hands, she took hold of the young man and held her blade to his throat.

"Lay down your blade," she hissed to the second attacker, who hesitated at the potential for mercy. That was all she needed. Quick as an eye, she slid the blade across her prisoner's throat. Through the spray of blood, she leapt forward and sent her sword through the second man's heart. The easiest kills of the day.

On the other side, Denan cursed loudly and struck down the last attacker. "Why didn't you use your heads?" he screamed to the dying man at his feet. He plunged the sword through the man's face and fell to his knee, leaving the blade standing upright. Heygar heard the low mutter of Venistrian prayer and left him to receive the one remaining Crimson soldier up the road.

"You failed them all. Come redeem yourself," Heygar called out, but the figure remained motionless atop the steed. Frozen in panic at the thought of his diminished guild of idiots, Heygar almost felt bad for the thurken cur. Almost. "Coward."

The rest of his Hounds emerged from the trees to loot the dead, leaving both leaders to settle up. Arielle joined Denan in prayer, but after a few verses, he knew she would scavenge too.

"Just you and me," Heygar said, raising his blade in challenge.

"I have hardly any chance against you, Heygar," Lorgan countered from atop his horse.

"Better that than a dishonourable death."

"I fancy a dishonourable life."

"Strike me down and live," Heygar said, playing and enjoying the part of the honourable warrior, gifting a broken man one last chance at redemption. Such things added to his mystique. The bards would soon be singing tales of the Crimson Company's last march. A fitting end would be a fight to the death. He would hold the man's head as he died and whisper reassurances as he passed into the source's night.

"And if I do, none of your Hounds will bite?"

"You have my word," Heygar said and waved his blade.

Lorgan drew his loaded crossbow swiftly and shot the legend in the head.

WATER LILY

Thunk! It was a fine sound. Heavy, metallic, and reassuring.

Heygar fell to a knee as the bolt rebounded and embedded itself in a nearby patch of flowers. He shook the dizziness from his senses, and something else replaced the arrogant triumph he had felt. Something cruel, fierce, and volatile.

Lorgan turned his steed and charged away. In his panic, he dropped the crossbow and Heygar grinned. That mistake would cost him.

"No, you don't," he hissed, climbing to his unsteady feet.

The short battle had taken a toll with such heavy armour. Still, it had earned its value. Who knew how well a lighter helm might have fared?

"My horse," he called as his quarry reached the top of the path and disappeared around the corner in a haze of cowardly dust. It felt as though an ethereal force had taken hold and infused him with a terrible fury. How dare this thurk impede his task?

With a heave that spent the last of his energy, Silvious assisted him into the saddle.

"Leave it be," said Cherrie from somewhere behind, but Heygar paid the woman little heed. A legend could not allow an animal like Lorgan to live after such a treacherous act. A legend would chase down the fool and bleed him until he was dry.

His horse, free of the rodenerack's hold and the smell of death, charged onwards willingly. Heygar gripped tightly with aching hands and roared aloud, for there was one more death to come that day. He loved a fine skirmish, but the hunt was where he truly came alive.

They broke from the clearing, and soon enough, he caught sight of the cur. Lorgan's ineptitude as a general was not his only failing. He struggled with his horse, and Heygar grinned under his helm. This hunt would be short. He gave frantic chase through dark woods until they broke into a burst of sunshine as the forest path opened to a clearing. Heygar came up behind his prey, close enough to strike, but like the snake he was, Lorgan pulled his horse sharply wide. He broke across the waist-high grass back into a wilder, pathless charge. Heygar's turn was slower, and his quarry earned a few more breaths of freedom before both men raced back through the wooded tree line.

Ducking and dodging between trunks and thick shrubbery slowed the pace, and Heygar cursed loudly between each breath. The chase continued up a hill, and he felt sweat pour down his forehead. Perhaps he really was getting too old for this. A few years before, he would have recovered from the fight and chased down the last man standing without enduring exhaustion like this. Maybe this was a young man's game.

Lorgan roared, pleaded, and cursed his beast forward. Heygar took pleasure in his frantic, desperate yelling. The assassin willed the beast beyond its limit and paid dearly for it. As they reached the top of the incline, the exhausted animal dropped its sprint altogether. Heygar wondered if it would rear and kick Lorgan from his saddle for good measure. Heygar eased the charge and came alongside the beaten man at the top of the hill.

"It's over. Let us end this as warriors!" he shouted, offering Lorgan one last chance at honour. The festering anger simmered within him again.

Lorgan reached for his blade, and Heygar met the strike with his own longsword.

"You dare attack my pack?"

It was foolish thugs like Lorgan who gave the mercenary profession a bad name and caused the senseless deaths of impressionable young warriors. Their only sins had been desires of fame, prestige, and exquisite things. Or maybe just full bellies.

Lorgan slashed again, and Heygar allowed the strike to clash his helm and rebound away harmlessly against the thick steel. Unlike the arrow before, he was prepared for the strike, and Lorgan could only drop his assault and look around pitifully. There was nowhere left to run but for a slope, a drop, and a river far below.

Without the rush of wind or the clash of metal piercing the day, Heygar enjoyed the silence falling around them. The world recognised silence when death was walking its land. He found it oddly settling. His heart raced, his head hurt, and he was more fatigued than he had ever remembered, but Heygar felt at peace.

"Please," Lorgan begged and dropped his sword to the ground.

"I'm sorry."

Heygar raised his sword, but the snake surprised him once more. Without warning, he leapt from the saddle and struck Heygar. His momentum sent both men careening down the slope. Heygar felt his leg shatter on the second tumble. He screamed. The world spun, and Heygar spun with it. Heygar felt a second something snap in his wrist, and more pain shot through him. He fought unconsciousness until, mercifully, they reached the bottom.

There was a moment of painful weightlessness before he fell headfirst into the river. Blinded by darkness and freezing water pulling him deep, Heygar struggled to right himself as his legs touched the riverbed. Pain shook him to alertness. This river was too deep, he thought. He pushed back to the surface with his one good leg. With a flailing hand, he touched the surface and seized hold of some water lily roots. They tore away in his grasp.

For a second time, Heygar sank downwards again. His lungs burned. His suit of armour was too heavy. Was this how he would die? He tore his helmet free and let it disappear among the murk. He blinked in the darkness and strained to see the surface above. He touched the bottom again and groaned aloud as water filled his mouth. He held, swallowed, coughed, panicked, and pushed his injured body up towards the surface, agonizingly slowly.

Not like this.

His lungs felt molten. The world darkened, and his hand reached out of the surface and touched the edge of the riverbank again. He felt river reeds in his grasp and pulled himself a foot short of delicious air before the terrible weight tore them from their roots.

Above him, Heygar saw a shadow and he reached for it. It was Lorgan. The shadow made no move to take his hand, and Heygar fell back to the bottom, where it was darkest. He kicked back up, but his legs failed him completely, and he fell on his side. He tried to tear his armour free, but it was no simple task done alone. It was nearly impossible without the help of a rodenerack or bride-to-be.

This is it. This is how I die.

He thrashed, screamed, and suddenly, an explosion of bubbles erupted around him as a rodent-like human leapt into the water beside him. His eyes opened, and he felt the claws ripping desperately at his armour. Heygar couldn't make out whatever Silvious screamed beneath the water, but he fought with all his might to stay alive. He had a ring to give to Cherrie. He wanted to live. He wanted to kill Mallum.

Heygar struggled one last time to push himself to the surface. With the help of Silvious, he rose towards life, but his gloved fingers broke the surface and could not take hold. He slipped below again, and his bladder released. He tried to scream, but there was too much water in his lungs. He felt the rat's claws rip and fight for him, but all strength left him as he sank to the bottom.

Heygar closed his eyes. After a few empty breaths, he stopped feeling anything at all.

THE RAT

Silvious ripped into the armour with his long, jagged nails, but the leather straps would not break. It was sturdy, thick leather, expensive and expertly wrapped and worthy of grand armour. His lungs, built for dreadful, hostile conditions, finally betrayed him, and he swam back to the surface for the umpteenth time.

"Help us!" he screamed and gasped precious air into his lungs before dipping back down into the cold water.

Might it be cold enough to slow Heygar's heart? he wondered miserably, thinking of heated debates he had heard between master and apprentice healer. He tried to remember the arguments, but the weavers may as well have been speaking in a foreign tongue.

Silvious moaned in the water and ripped at the leather straps again. The man he owed everything in the whole of Dellerin to was just too heavy for a small rodenerack like himself. One of his jagged nails cracked and split painfully, but he continued with his horrific task. He was a Hound, and Hounds never gave up or admitted defeat. They always found a way.

Heygar bobbed and swayed in the current, and Silvious swayed with him. He avoided looking at his strained face. Eventually, he tore a gauntlet free and rose to the surface, leaving the piece of armour at the bottom of the river. One piece down, plenty to do. Where were the rest of his companions?

"Help us!" Silvious swallowed the gnawing desolation in his stomach before diving back down once again. He had never felt as alone as this, with his best friend only a foot away.

Even in the water, Silvious could smell the familiar scent. It seemed different now though. He had smelled the dying aroma of family before, and it felt tragically familiar, but still, he worked at the leather. It became a task of miserable repetition, tasting the delicious air, then diving back down and attempting to cut through stubborn clasps.

Silvious never knew how long it went on for. He'd never grasped the finer things in the world, such as the steady keeping of time, for that was not his people's way at all. Theirs was a simple, tormented life after the great and unsuccessful Roden War. Even though he lived among humans, there were plenty of things he still followed instinctively. Telling time was one of these things. His day began at dawn, when he broke slumber's grasp. His day ended with the darkening of the world, when slumber embraced him once more. The humans desired to count the moments in between—as was their privilege. Time just passed differently to rodeneracks.

How many hours had passed since Heygar had ceased his struggling? Maybe it had been only a handful of breaths. A human would know for certain. And what Silvious knew for certain was that enough time had passed that his friend was dead.

He surfaced once more, and his eye caught something in the distance. Something returning to view the devastation left behind. He gripped the side of the riverbank and pulled at the sunken warrior.

"Help us! He isn't moving!" Silvious cried to Lorgan as he emerged from the undergrowth with his horse's reins in hand. It didn't matter that the man approaching was the enemy. What mattered was saving Heygar. Somehow.

"Nor will he move again," Lorgan hissed and stood over the rodenerack. He was pale, and his body shook from battle, grief, and cowardice. "There is no honour in a death like this." The assassin made no move to help.

Silvious dropped underneath the water and tugged at the body once more. With the absence of the gauntlet, he could slip his arm further in. Before he had lost his breath, he pulled the chest piece free and dropped it in the murk. Silvious surged above the lily pads once more and met the tip of a sword's blade.

"Leave the dead as they lie."

Silvious saw the agony in the young man's eyes, but it paled compared to the agony he felt.

Silvious swiped the blade away in disgust. It should have terrified him, but facing a sword was hardly a thing to him. "I will never leave this man."

Without warning, Lorgan dropped into the water and pulled Heygar from the river. Silvious helped him as best he could, and they left the body to dry in the sun. He didn't look any less dead from his bed in the dry grass. His mouth hung to one side, his teeth bore a manic grin, and his dull eyes stretched wide open. No warrior deserved to die like that.

"Here lies a fallen legend," Lorgan muttered and sheathed his blade. "He can't be saved. He's too far gone, rat," the assassin said before reaching for Heygar's pockets.

"You will not take a thing from him," Silvious said, leaping across the body of his friend and pushing his vanquisher away.

"You are a brave one, little rat."

"We'll hunt ye for this," warned Silvious and met the doomed eyes of the assassin, who shrugged at the threat.

"You tore all that I had built this day, but I will live well for quite a time as the man who killed Heygar before any of you Hounds track me down." He climbed atop his horse. "My fate's sealed, rat, but I will wait with a sword in hand." Kicking his horse sharply, he disappeared deep into the undergrowth.

"You will die a thousand deaths." Silvious placed his pointy ear to his friend's chest.

If Lorgan heard his weak, defiant retort, he said nothing. Instead, the assassin thundered off, leaving him to the hum of the forest and the silence of his friend's chest.

"The others'll know what to do," Silvious whispered to the dead man and patted along the cold body.

In the distance, he heard the first voices of his comrades. They had tired of waiting for their return.

His hand touched upon a small pouch in Heygar's chest pocket, and Silvious froze. *Better this way.* He removed the pouch and carefully took the ring. Glancing at its beauty in the clearing sun, he tried it on once before slipping it back into a pocket of its own. Such a piece would catch a fine price in any land. Even Venistra. Such things couldn't be taken as chance, and she would never need a ring like this anyway.

From above the slope, he heard their voices louder than before. With the ring safely away from prying eyes, Silvious called out for them, wondering if it was all too late.

WEAVING FROM THE SOURCE

It was the young apprentice Iaculous who first appeared atop the slope, covered in blood from scavenging and weary from battle. The young human dropped from his horse and stumbled down the slope, scattering half the rocks on the decline as he did. Somehow avoiding breaking a bone, he scrambled over to the body, pushing Silvious away.

"How?"

"He fell." Silvious pointed to the river.

Iaculous closed his eyes. Immediately, there was a turning warmth in the air. The surrounding ground hummed slightly, and Silvious felt dizzy as the weaving spun his thoughts awry. Though he couldn't be sure, he felt something dark and menacing near him. It licked its lips, and Silvious shook the dizziness from his head.

Screaming filled the air. The lamenting wail was from Arielle. She fell to her knees beside him and cried like a heartbroken larker beast after mating season. A shaken Cherrie stood behind her and looked about to break. He had never seen her cry. He doubted he would. She was tougher than them all combined.

"How long was he under?" hissed Iaculous. He placed his hand across the other and came to stop over Heygar's chest. After a moment, he heaved both hands down, and a thin stream of water erupted from Heygar's grinning face like a geyser.

"Long time that his breath was taken." Silvious didn't think the sun had moved that far across the sky. Would that help?

The young healer groaned and pushed again, and even more fluid surged from Heygar's mouth. Silvious allowed himself some hope as a thick veneer of blue weaving source energy covered the legend. However, this was no enchantment for a sprained knee or sliced flesh. Even Silvious knew that.

"Wake up, Heygar!" screamed Denan, and tears streamed from his eyes. Silvious wondered what it was like to cry. Though he knew sorrow and melancholy, his kind could not let precious fluids slip from their eyes on demand.

The warrior took hold of Cherrie and held her as the young healer went to work. Cherrie merely stared unblinkingly at the body.

"He is lost," Eralorien, the master healer, muttered quietly. Weakness brought Silvious to his knees. Beside him, Cherrie moaned, and Denan spun her from the sight. She fought him and struck his chest but did not look back.

But one Hound was not willing to let things be.

"Nothing is ever lost," cried Iaculous in a strange voice. He dove his hands down a third time, and the last of the resting water was expunged from the dead body. "I can save him." He choked back the dreadful desolation of finding a loved one in such a state. "I can save him." He groaned as though some unseen force moved through him. "No one dies today."

Iaculous grimaced as though fighting an invisible beast with eyes upon their souls. The heat around the weaver grew fierce. Eralorien had always berated and belittled the young healer, yet Silvious couldn't but notice the master kept a distance as the apprentice attempted to save their leader. Perhaps even with such costs, it was best to let the student perfect his art. To push the darkness back at whatever cost. Or else, the master healer was too scared to take part. If Bereziel were here, that would be different.

"I can step into the source and pull his soul right back into his body," Iaculous said, looking every day his youthful age in front of his master.

"You shall not take back what is lost," Eralorien warned, but his words felt hollow. He stood behind Iaculous, watching intently.

If Silvious could have stepped into the source beyond and found Heygar's soul, he would have done it in a moment's breath, whatever that meant.

The young healer held his fingers out over the body, and the air thinned to nothing. The ground shuddered, and a piercing heat encircled the two. A soul. Silvious thought an ethereal wraith of conscious energy locked inside the meat of a human body as something strange. He wondered if he had one. Was he more than just meat? They did not believe in anything like that among his people, but then again, he had known no rodenerack capable of weaving from the source.

"You've got to wake up, Heygar," Arielle begged the dead body before pulling away from the rising heat. The rest of the Hounds followed, apart from the weavers.

"I can save him," Iaculous said in that strange voice. It was older, wiser, and not meant for mortal men. Silvious had heard the same tone many times before, and terrible things usually followed. All of this was before Eralorien had joined their pack.

"Be wary, young one. Weaving like this is treacherous!" Eralorien cried. If the surging heat troubled him, he showed little on his old, wrinkled face. Instead, he stood like a statue and kept his hands firmly under his cloak. Perhaps he was worried they would get burned.

"I can save him," Iaculous groaned again in the tone that sounded older than the mountains. His hands separated and focused over the heart of the great man.

Silvious watched the source reveal itself upon the healer's hands. It was both mesmerising and terrifying. He'd seen illusions many times before, but this was something new. A tendril of blue flame surrounded the apprentice's hands, and the ground shook as though a great earthquake was upon them. A sudden wind enveloped them. Trees swayed wildly all around them. Silvious could hear nothing but its roar until Cherrie broke away from Denan's grasp. She wavered and looked ready to collapse, but she did not fall.

"Save him!" she screamed, but Iaculous was already lost to the source. His eyes were misty and grey—as if burned out by a poker's tip—and his face contorted in a painful grimace. The source covered his body in the same blue veneer. He faded like an artist's masterpiece left to display in a decade of uncovered sunlight, still there, yet less so.

"Do not step far into the source," Eralorien cried as he fought the erupting storm. Still, he kept his hands under his cloak as it flapped in the unnatural wind.

Another surging pulse of heat erupted from the young healer. It struck as an invisible wave, and the remaining Hounds cowered from the blast. The tendril of flame had grown to a furnace. Silvious saw the young man's hands bubble and burn.

"I can see a darkness," Iaculous moaned and stood up. Somehow, he seemed taller. Perhaps he was levitating.

"Can you see beyond the black?" Eralorien pulled his hands free and gripped the young man's shoulders. His hands, too, were glowing, but not with flame. His were a controlled ember of light, white, and calming. He healed himself as his own skin burned.

Silvious heard his comrades screaming and cursing and wailing, but it made little sense. He felt the fire burn his rough face, but he couldn't help himself. Something great and ferocious lured him to the energy. He had not felt this way since Heygar had pulled him from that den almost a decade ago. That same sense of power as Heygar ripped into his jailors one by one, tearing and cutting, unstoppable and divine. He had loved his master then. Seeing him now, he loved him even more. He prayed to whatever was among them with words he had heard spoken by man and not a rat. He prayed for his master to blink his eyes once more and drink merrily with them that night.

"What do you see?" roared Eralorien. The flames engulfed his robes, yet still, he stayed with his protégé. He was a good man, Silvious thought.

"I see Heygar, trapped, waiting," Iaculous whispered. His voice carried like a deity's roar. He reached out as though Heygar was in front of him. The flames grew ten feet high, and he became immolated in the blue fire he was creating.

"Come back, Iaculous," cried Eralorien. The flames overcame him, and he released his hold on his apprentice. The flames struck out like fireflies and struck the terrified Hounds.

"My love," screamed Arielle. She leapt into the flame and knocked both healers from their feet into the cold water. Immediately, the storm passed, and the flames dissipated away. The only sounds were that of three burned warriors as they pulled themselves painfully from the river and the dull hiss from Heygar as parts of his body glowed an ember red.

Eralorien administered healing to himself first. Iaculous, though scorched and scarred, refused his help until he had removed the blisters from Arielle. By the time the healing took the last of the burns, Iaculous was already kneeling over Heygar's body. His hands were a faded blue as he weaved healing back into himself.

"I'm not strong enough, Heygar," Iaculous wept. Arielle knelt with him, her own tears matching his own.

"He is gone," Denan said.

"He is at peace," Silvious said sadly. Iaculous shot him a look.

"No, rat, he has found no peace. He is just beyond the dark. Something has hold of his soul, and he is waiting for us to save him," the young healer said. "I'm not strong enough to step into the source, but I will try. His body is just a vessel. If someone returns the soul, it can undo everything." He spun on Arielle. "If you hadn't knocked me in the water, I might have reached him."

"You would have burned up," Arielle replied in a cutting tone only a spurned lover could use. Iaculous looked contrite at his misstep.

"Can Heygar be saved?" Denan asked, his voice a whispered wheezing breath. As he spoke, he fumbled for a little pouch of spices from his belt. He undid the clasp and inhaled deeply a few times. His breath returned a moment later. "Can Heygar be saved?" he asked a second time more confidently.

Eralorien spoke quietly as though wary of revealing a terrible truth. "A weaver strong enough might, but neither one of us are strong enough for returning a soul back into this world." He stood over the young man and took hold of a few strands of his hair. "Grey," he muttered.

Cherrie finally knelt by her man and stroked his features tenderly. "If neither of you can do it, then we will bring him to a weaver who is strong enough." She kissed his forehead. "Wrap him up, Silvious."

WHAT TO DO?

Silvious wrapped the body up in some sheets and tied it securely at both ends while the rest of the Hounds sat in silence around their temporary campsite. Death was no stranger to all mercenaries. It followed them every step of the way. It was a constant ally and the most deceitful of friends.

None of the Hounds should have struggled to accept Heygar's passing, but they did it easily enough. Perhaps it was Iaculous's suggestion that Heygar was not at rest that influenced them so. Heygar had led this troupe for two decades, in both war and peacetime, as flag-waving patriots, as expensive knives for hire, and occasionally somewhere in between. They were unwilling to let him go.

Silvious looked at the wrapped body and wondered how they would treat him now that his champion was silent. He sewed the last stitch and bit the thin thread, leaving the body as snug as possible. Denan and Iaculous hoisted the burden onto the back of his horse. They spoke of resurrection, and Silvious knew the unlikeliness of such a thing, but his opinion carried less water than the others. They did, however, speak of a man capable of unlikely things.

"We bury Heygar here, or we bring him to Venistra and seek Bereziel to cast the enchantment of all enchantments," Denan said carefully. Those were words from a man unsure of himself as a leader. Perhaps he would grow into the role, Silvious thought.

"Is it a choice? If so, we must give the great man every chance," Iaculous said.

"I agree," Arielle said.

Though Silvious's mind spun, the only reassuring thought was that Venistra called. His initial desire to complete their treacherous task had grown since Heygar's passing. Whatever was discussed or decided, Silvious thought it imperative that Mallum fall to their blade. Everything after that was up for discussion.

Eralorien placed his hands upon Cherrie's shoulder as a father might with a lamenting daughter. She did not fight his touch nor accept his warmth. She merely stared blankly ahead, and he held her. "We cannot trust Bereziel to return Heygar to you … to us." His fingers squeezed her shoulders ever so delicately. "This is madness."

"No one is ever truly gone," Iaculous said, eyeing the ground to avoid the contemptuous gaze from his master. There would be another screaming argument shared before the day was out, Silvious thought. They seemed to fight more frequently these days. The apprentice had attempted stronger enchantments these last few months, and Eralorien was having none of it.

"Even if his soul was retrievable, his body has already cooled and is decaying," Eralorien said.

And cooked, thought Silvious, thinking of the fires burning at the flesh.

"Is it possible to heal a dead body if someone returns the soul?" asked Denan to the master weaver.

"I've heard of things returned to life within a few days, but that was an enchantment which drew the souls of a hundred weavers and aged them as many years. If you step into the darkness searching like that, something unnatural to our world will seek you out. If returning a life was easy to accomplish, death would be nothing but a hindrance to mortal man. I know what you ask. You seek my predecessor, Bereziel? Nothing good will come of this. Bereziel is a deluded fool obsessed with finding eternal youth."

"Perhaps he found other things," Iaculous muttered.

"We don't even know where in Venistra he is. Leave the dead as they are. Let us finish his last mission and be done with it," Eralorien said, but his words were empty. If it had been a vote, it would have been all to one.

As it was, Cherrie's voice was loudest. "I know I could find him. Wherever Bereziel is in Venistra, I will find him." She was assured, and it settled the matter.

"Heygar would do exactly the same for us," Arielle said and climbed up on her horse.

Eralorien spat into the scorched ground. "If that is your belief, then you never knew the man."

Denan, ever the quiet and reserved one, led them out and nobody argued. Cherrie rode behind him, as far from the body of her lover as she could. Arielle rode between master and apprentice, lest their growing irritation rises to the surface in the form of nasty words. They followed in a single, cheerless file, with Silvious the last to ride out. Trotting behind him and led by a rope was Heygar's horse with her heavy load.

Silvious didn't mind his place in this line. He said nothing. The humans just wouldn't understand. No man or beast had a sense of smell like a rodenerack, and the aroma emanating from the body was tantalising. It was only a little cooking by the young weaver, but the skin had charred perfectly. Silvious licked his lips and twitched his nose as the flavour of cooked legend permeated around him. No, Silvious didn't mind being in this line at all.

Once they emerged from the Ailedroc Forest, the road opened, and they brought their horses into a swifter charge. The pace wore them down, but they continued until nightfall, wherein they came upon the first taste of salt in the air. They did not set down at the first town they came upon, for the fear of another attack was fresh in their minds. Like wisps in the night, they passed by without notice until they reached a little fishing village called Delfina.

Denan and Cherrie left the exhausted Hounds to rest while they sought passage to Venistra. Blessed with better vision than humans, Silvious watched the two figures make their way down through the darkness towards the harbour. Cherrie took Denan's hand in hers as they walked, and Denan kissed her hand in reply.

"Humans," he whispered to the wind and returned to camp.

SAILING TO VENISTRA

Arielle speared a few slabs of meat with a charred cooking rod and held it out over the heat of the little campfire. Iaculous stared into the little flames with a vacant look upon his tired face. Silvious heard him whisper a few words to himself but not their meaning. The young healer's injuries were long-healed, but there were bright grey strands shooting through his dark hair.

Arielle ran her fingers through Iaculous's hair, and he smiled. "I like this new look," she said, moving to his chin, where a few bristles caught her finger. He said nothing and rested his head on her shoulder.

Their courting was a strange thing, thought Silvious. They said rodeneracks weren't as intelligent as humans were, but in some ways, he thought his own kind far ahead when bedding a lover. You see, you desire, and you enjoy. He understood love, and he had always believed the young showed the most reckless daring, yet both young humans were afraid to even kiss. Was Iaculous not an excitable youth with bounds of juice? Was Arielle not a fine piece of fruit, ripe for plucking?

Perhaps someday. Perhaps tomorrow? Perhaps never at

all, and that would be a shame. He imagined Iaculous would make Arielle incredibly happy. Happier than Heygar and Cherrie at least.

Silvious touched the ring as though it held source energy. It didn't. It was a feeble declaration between unsuitable mates, and he thought of the grand price it would fetch in the next town. Better this way, he reminded himself.

"You look like the source has torn you limb from limb, child," Eralorien said.

"Yes, Master."

"You should never have allowed yourself to lose control like that," the master said.

"I could feel his desperate soul... I still can," Iaculous said and fell silent. Arielle spun the cooking meats, and fat dripped down into the flame and sizzled loudly. "I wish you hadn't knocked me from the flames," he said to her, though he said it without anger.

"She saved you," Silvious said, and Iaculous's eyes narrowed. He knew the look all too well. He was about to be called a rat. Silvious waited, and Iaculous merely shrugged.

"There is something dark in the source, and the farther you stray, the stronger its lure," Eralorien said.

"Yes, I felt something else. I can't explain what it was, but it knew of my presence."

Eralorien sat down beside the young man and patted his shoulder. "We know little of that world, but we know something ferocious awaits those who weave carelessly. Do not present yourself in such a way. Leave it to fools like Bereziel."

"Is that why you never stray within?" Iaculous asked.

His master shrugged and ran his finger through his hair absently. "I have my reasons, but more than that, I have my senses. You will be an accomplished healer. Be satisfied with that." Eralorien took Iaculous's shoulder in a vice-like grip before squeezing sharply. Such strength from one so old was unexpected, and the young man recoiled but did not argue the assault.

"Yes, Master."

Silvious wondered if the younger man would have progressed further had he received even a delicate touch of support these last few years. Still, Silvious had little knowledge in these things. Perhaps that was a master's way with instruction. Bully the young until they are strong enough to bully right back.

"Now away with you, and go fetch water," Eralorien said. Iaculous fled into the darkness.

"Why settle with the young man when you could have any man you want?" Eralorien asked of Arielle when the sounds of Iaculous had faded.

"I'll settle with whoever I choose, be it Iaculous, the king, or Mallum himself," she said and tasted the meat before throwing a piece to Eralorien.

"You are just like your sister." Eralorien laughed and gratefully accepted the meat. Though Iaculous was bent to his will, Arielle would never be.

"I'm exactly like my sister only prettier," Arielle sniggered. Then she caught sight of Heygar, and her smile faded. Eralorien must have noticed it too.

"The man was great, but the man has fallen. He's already rotting. No legend deserves this."

"Iaculous thinks differently."

"We will spend the next few weeks dragging a decaying corpse around Venistra, searching for a madman who might not even be there. Eventually, the smell will steal our appetites, fighting off the buzzards will ruin us, and we will bury what's left of him in unfamiliar lands."

"We are the Hounds. We will find a way. All we need to do is find Mallum, and the trip will be worth it," she countered.

Silvious found himself excluded from the conversation yet still nodding in agreement.

"Venistra is already a dangerous enough place without this added load weighing us down. Part of me believes we should just dismiss this entire endeavour as a bad bit of business, turn our tails to home, and … and …"

The weaver's face changed as though awoken from a trance by a click of a mischief-maker's fingers. Silvious had seen the entertaining trick many a time as proud men fell under the spell of a heavy whisper and acted as moronic beasts or delicate damsels, all for a crowd's entertainment.

"No … we will finish this mission. That is what we will do," Eralorien said, and a strange comfort struck Silvious. Once more, the thought of travelling to Venistra and completing their mission seemed like the ideal plan.

Cherrie and Denan finally returned a few hours later with word of travel. Cherrie's eyes had a taste of red, and Denan appeared miserable, if not a little relaxed. They led the group down into the sleeping village of Delfina. Their horses' hooves echoed loudly in the night as they made their way through the small village, and all around them, a thin mist formed. With around a dozen neatly bricked buildings with thatched roofs clustered together, it was almost surprising to see a long quay leading out into the deep sea.

Silvious sniffed the air, and he found nothing but the aroma of bitter salt and freshly gutted fish. He licked his lips, and his nerves settled. If there was an ambush waiting, their killers emitted little scent. Such a thing was improbable. Denan had thought on the matter and chosen a fine place to cast off. Using the head was how a leader became a solid leader, according to Heygar. Perhaps Denan was capable.

They walked along the stone quay and passed many vessels docked for the night. Each worn vessel bobbed gently in the calm water. These were no colossal galleons, but any decent barge would be swift and sturdy enough to face the journey.

They said the waters between here and there held challenging tides. They also suggested horrid sea creatures roamed their depths, but Silvious had never believed the tales of barges falling to the charge of a grand cantus, or entwined and sunk in the scaled body of a colubra. They existed, but most nasty little fish monsters fled under the appearance of a sea vessel—even in mating season.

At the far end, where the sea broke against the dock, a sturdy sea barge was waiting. Sitting by the edge of the water was its old barge captain. He was as old as Eralorien and twice as intimidating. He extinguished his pipe with a worn thumb and waved them aboard.

The vessel creaked gently in the waves. The smell of mould was weak, the wooden body was polished, and the worn deck had little warping. It looked seaworthy, which was enough for any passenger.

"I had hoped you would keep that room for the night," the old man said upon seeing Denan and Cherrie. He placed old, gnarled hands on sturdy hips and shook his head.

"Better to leave in darkness," Denan said and led his black horse aboard.

"I've been thinking. It's a long sail to Venistra in this season at night," the captain said and looked at the sky. "There's rain in the air, and the last thing I want to do is sail in any type of rain at night."

The old man made no effort to stop Arielle or Iaculous

from loading their horses aboard the large barge. Silvious knew this play all too well. Would it be storm season? A colubra's mating time? Something equally precarious to push up the price?

"The weather looks like it'll hold just fine." Cherrie knew this play too.

"You don't know the sea like an old serpent like me." This time, the captain stopped Eralorien as he led his horse aboard. He eyed the man warily until his eyes caught sight of Heygar's wrapped-up body. Silvious stepped in front of the body, but the captain stepped forward. "What is this?" he cried.

"Cargo," Denan said, but the captain tore at the sheets before Silvious could stop him.

"Are you thurken mad?" he cried out upon discovering the body. "How long is it dead?"

"He's not lost yet," Iaculous muttered.

"You want to bring a body out into the sea at night? I hope it's for feeding a grand cantus because if they catch a smell of a carcass, the *Celeste* won't survive a frenzy."

Silvious thought the argument convincing. Most bartered, but this old man was convincing enough that for the briefest of moments, the thought of embarking at dawn seemed a safer bet.

"We agreed a fair price."

"It's no longer about money."

Denan produced a few coins and put them in the barge captain's shaking hand. Apparently, it was about money when the fare would cover a month's expenses. With a curse, the old man pocketed the coins and looked to the sky above.

"Better to leave at dawn," he muttered and allowed them passage.

They climbed aboard the barge and, after securing the

horses for the unstable dozen hours, set down for the journey. The captain took his place at the wheel as they cast off. A few deckhands manned the tall sails, and Silvious watched curiously as a little wind caught in the massive sheets and the vessel surged forward through the waves. In a few breaths, they were clear of the quay, and they quickly lost the lights from the village in the waves, sea mist, and spray.

Silvious felt oddly comfortable in the tide's hold and spent quite an unknown amount of time with his hood over his head, walking the length of the barge, watching the waves crash and break. Eventually, he found himself at the rear. Beneath the dancing flame of a long wooden torch, he sat down and allowed his feet to hang over the edge.

His body moved with the wonderful sway, and the rushing water below him felt familiar. He had always loved the water. His people were natural seafarers if nothing else, and most of the larger galleons patrolling the Four Seas carried a handful of roderneracks. Their agility and balance were essential when facing the more precarious of tasks. His people said they often gave respect out among the waves when none was found on land, and Silvious had wondered on this many a time.

He removed the pledging ring from his pocket and eyed it in the light. It was a fine enough ring, and for only a moment did Silvious think about gifting it to its rightful owner. It was better Cherrie never know the entirety of her betrayal.

"This is a bad night to sail," the barge captain's voice muttered from behind him and roused him from his thoughts.

Suddenly, a hand flicked the hood from Silvious's head, revealing his heritage. If the barge captain was disgusted with what he discovered, he concealed it well. Silvious hissed at the invasion of privacy. He had been happy alone with his thoughts, the waves, and regretful shiny things.

"And here I was thinking you were just a little boy playing with the adults," the barge captain mocked. Silvious bit back a reply as the old man left the barge wheel and propped himself against the waist-high safety rope, which ran the length and breadth of the boat. He must have trusted that rope something fierce as he hung out over the raging water like a child swinging against the trunk of a mighty weeping oak. His feet were all that kept him anchored at the edge.

"You are a long way from home, rodenerack, and where you are going is farther still."

"I go wherever I need to, waterman." He had long discovered that on first meeting with any human, it was best to show teeth.

"Please, call me Dirion," Dirion said, feigning pleasantness.

"If you like." Silvious pocketed the ring carefully.

"That is a fine piece of jewellery. Does it have a price?" Dirion asked and swayed against the edge. He produced a pipe and stuffed tobacco into it. As he did, Silvious realised his eyes never left the ship's wheel for more than a breath. There was a thin strap of leather holding it in place. Whichever way the wind blew, the captain intended to go straight.

"Everything has a price in this world. It can convince even a captain to sell his own ship's safety with the right amount of silver in his pocket."

Dirion snorted at his wit. He even chuckled for a few moments before lighting the pipe with a match. His eyes fell on the bundle in the deck centre. "Let me guess, you travel to Venistra to seek a creepy shaman to steal illicit life back into that broken form?" he asked.

Silvious shrugged. It wasn't the worst cover. It was even partly true.

"That ring won't even cover the costs of a soul bandoleer," Dirion said and puffed smoke into the night.

Silvious didn't know what a soul bandoleer was. It didn't matter either.

"That may be so, but it's no business o' yours, old man," Silvious said. The captain shrugged and watched the wheel.

The barge creaked loudly, and both fell silent, listening to the rise and fall of the vessel in the ocean. Silvious didn't know how long the sea captain rocked back and forth over the water or how long he stood in mute silence, countering the balance of the waves, but when the barge captain spoke again, it felt as though they had sailed a thousand miles. It may have been only a hundred feet.

"Tell me, little rodenerack, do you truly know how precarious Venistra is for a mercenary like you? They would slaughter, eat you, and think of it as nothing more than feasting upon a swine. You would make quite the delicacy for the Venistrian tastes."

Silvious suspected the old sea captain was playing a fine teasing game with him. Despite his better senses, he warmed to the man. The wind took the smoke and dragged it as soon as it exhaled, and the captain purred in contentment. He offered the pipe, and Silvious took the piece and inhaled shallowly. He held for a moment, exhaled, and watched the smoke dissipate in the sea breeze. A storm was likely brewing. Far away, in the distant dark, a shrill cry floated in the night and was lost in the wind's reply.

"I'm more bone 'n' ligament. Chewy like. I'd cause choking," Silvious mocked and offered the pipe back.

Dirion did not accept the piece. Instead, he stepped back to sturdier ground and eyed the darkness where the cry had come from.

"Cantus."

Dirion removed the leather holding from the wheel. With barely any effort, he spun the wheel and the vessel immediately swayed to the right.

"We'll be fine. It's just not a good time to be sailing these ocean waves. It'll be better if the rain holds off, for those vile creatures frenzy when there's rain in the air." He watched the dark sky above.

Silvious pulled himself up from the edge of the barge and took hold of the safety rope. The sudden uneasiness of the barge captain set him on edge. After a few breaths, another cry erupted. This one, however, was much farther away and on the far side of the *Celeste*. Its tone was deeper and melancholic, and the sea barge captain cursed quietly.

"What is that cry?"

"A second fierce terror, little one," Dirion said warily. He whistled, and a deckhand looked up from his task at one ship sail. "Pull her wide and light her up," Dirion called, and the deckhand nodded swiftly.

Silvious watched the young sailor release a heavy rope. The middle sail opened fully and caught in the wind. The speed of the *Celeste* doubled, and Silvious took hold of the rope tighter.

He seemed to relax. "Don't worry, little rodenerack. This is just precautionary. It won't be as smooth a ride now though."

With a flaming torch in hand, the deckhand ran from bow to stern, lighting torches. Within a few moments, the *Celeste* lit up the night sea.

"They don't like flames either." Another cry from behind made both figures jump. "You were right to pull your feet up out of the spray," the sea captain joked, but Silvious could see the fear creeping into his wrinkled face. He offered the pipe again, and Dirion snatched it and popped it in his mouth.

Suddenly, the three eerie voices cried in unison, a cacophony of monstrous beauty and terror. He had known the scream of the cantus was a terrifying thing, but this unnatural wail sent shivers down Silvious's spine.

"It's that dead body."

The barge suddenly met a strong wave head-on. Dirion moved with the sudden jolt, and a few silver coins chinked loudly in his pocket. The wave crashed and sprayed harmlessly across the front of the bow.

"We'll be fine. It is just the interest of a few sea beasts eager to know what sails atop their realm. As long as the sea don't tempest, our speed will be enough." Dirion pulled the wheel fiercely as though attempting to avoid unseen creatures standing in their way.

Above them, where few men or women ever cared to stare, a few clouds clustered and broke.

It started to rain.

SEA MONSTERS

"Ignite the catalights!" Dirion cried.

Thunder erupted far above their heads. With the roar came a heavy downpour, and Dirion cursed as only a salty barge captain could. Primal shrieking filled the air. Silvious gripped the rail as the barge caught a violent gust of wind and swayed against it.

Below him, Silvious saw his comrades emerge from under the deck, looking confused and dishevelled as sea spray and a torrential downpour roused them to their wits. Perhaps they should have waited until dawn, thought Silvious.

Deckhands screwed little glass bowls to the end of six metal poles, ten feet long. They filled the glass bowls with a white powder and ignited each. The *Celeste* became illuminated in a glaring, bright white light, which burned Silvious's eyes when he looked directly at them. Each deckhand held these catalights out over the edge of the water and secured them tightly, leaving a bright glow on either side of the barge.

It was only in that moment that Silvious saw the true,

terrifying height of the surrounding waves. They towered the height of the barge at their pinnacle, yet somehow, they did not thrash the vessel to a thousand pieces as they struck her hull without respite. Instead, they broke and soaked the top level. Silvious marvelled that they washed away no deckhand along the edge.

Dirion spun the wheel and turned the *Celeste* into the largest waves, allowing the pull of the wind to drag them over many of the aggressive swells. He did so with the skill of a man no stranger to a deathly squall. Water gathered and flowed to the under-levels, and deckhands went to task with little more than a bucket to halt their sinking. The world surged wildly, and Silvious held his stomach as the barge rose and fell repetitively, all to the symphony of unknown screaming beasts.

"It's not the waves which worry me." Dirion grasped Silvious roughly and dragged him to the wheel. He pointed to the sky. "Climb to the pouch and tell me where they are."

Silvious, seeing no other deckhand able to help, obeyed like a good little rodenerack. Though the deck was slippery, he matched the turning of the planks underfoot and reached the thin wooden mast swiftly. He eyed the wooden pouch far above. Strangely enough, he didn't hesitate and took each metal rung by two. The waves rolled the barge, and the wind caught in his cloak, pulling tightly at his neck, but he kept his footing.

Below him, he lost the shouts of his comrades in the violent gusts and splattering of rain. Silvious wondered how difficult Dirion might find it swimming with such heavy pockets. He peered out through the storm into the night and saw nothing but terrifying waves on all sides. Then he saw something else. He thought it similar in appearance to the black river eels he and his kin had fished a lifetime ago. Slippery, gelatinous, and delectably bitter, they had been quite the treat. These fearsome creatures were a thousand times bigger though. He shivered as one as long as the barge slithered past.

"To the right," he cried, pointing.

Dirion spun the wheel furiously. The barge left the grand cantus behind, and the creature rose out of the water and screamed in frustration. The piercing cry was deafening without the water to muffle. It moved like an eel within the waves, but above the surface, it behaved more like a snake swaying to a piper's whistle. It differed from both in that it had a large fin thrice the width of its body running from its head all the way to its tail. It shrieked once more before dropping below the surface and giving chase once more.

"Another on the other side."

A cantus dipped near the *Celeste* before disappearing under the water. After a moment, it surfaced on the far side and barely missed a collision with its brother. Or sister. Or whatever.

"Get it right!" roared Dirion as though Silvious should have predicted the movements of the big fish. Typical humans. He heard the barge captain curse Heygar's body, but he lost everything else in the wind.

The beasts swarmed in unison, and the *Celeste* answered by swaying with the waves and pulling away. The creatures fell a few feet behind and a few more after that. Dirion spun the sea barge across the stormy surface as though he were a god of the open waters.

Then a large beast twice the length of the barge appeared from the depths below and struck them headfirst. The *Celeste* rose high into the air before rearing and crashing back into the swell. The sudden jolt knocked Silvious from the pouch. Somehow, he caught the edge with his claw and hung on. The catalights rocked wildly in their places, and the sea glowed and pulsed in reply.

All three massive monsters met the barge as one terrifying battering ram along its hull. Silvious was whipped back into the sky as the barge almost capsized to the sound of splintering wood and concussive animalistic shrieking. He found himself briefly weightless as the attack tossed his body. For a terrible moment, he saw nothing but water below him, and he plummeted down only to see the returning sway of the barge fill his vision.

Darkness. Wetness. Screaming. The entire world shaking.

Silvious opened his eyes as a wave broke over and covered him entirely. How long had he been unconscious? It felt like hours. Days? Moments? He fought the urge to throw up and lost. He spat the bile over the side and used the safety rope to help him to his unsteady, clawed feet. The world spun, but that might have been his mind.

Somewhere among the clamour of screaming Hounds, wailing beasts and driving storms, he heard Dirion bark out commands.

"Pull the sails in," Dirion ordered and left the wheel to spin freely in the wind.

He pulled a chain, and an anchor fell from above into the water below. Within the counting of three breaths, the *Celeste* turned about and veered sideways. She came to an unsteady stop, and all on-board shuddered from the force.

He leaned out along the edge of the vessel. A long iron pole with a serrated end was in his grip. "Anyone that can, grab a whaling pole and stab those thurken curs."

Behind him, the deckhands and willing Hounds took hold

of their own poles from a long chest and went to war. They stabbed any beast that neared, but the creatures were elusive and dove away from the defenders' attacks with little more than grazing cuts on thick, leathered skin.

"We must do this until the demons lose the taste for battle!" Dirion roared. Silvious heard the deception in the old man's voice. The beasts would not give in. They would not tire. They were a doomed vessel.

Silvious believed, however. The *Celeste* carried The Seven, did it not? And when Denan struck success and plunged the pole deep into one of the cantus's necks as it charged by, it felt as though this would be just another thrilling tale in their legend.

However, this tale would not be without its tragedy.

The beast spun, thrashed, and struck itself fiercely against the boat, knocking Denan from his feet. As he fell, he reached for Arielle's outstretched hand in desperation. She was swift, nimble, courageous, and far lighter than most others were, and he took her overboard with him.

They plunged into the unforgiving waves. While Denan stayed and matched the current with powerful strokes, Arielle was helpless. Silvious remembered her telling him she could not swim one afternoon, and he had never put a dark thought upon such a fact until this moment.

The deliriously grateful beasts circled her. Far away, Silvious heard Cherrie scream. To die and get eaten was no fitting end for anyone.

Silvious snapped the safety rope with a clawed strike, tore it free, and leapt from the edge to the struggling girl below without haste. She would have done the same, he thought as the water rushed up to meet him.

Suddenly, he was among the storm of waves. He was not

alone, however, for Denan reached her first, and she almost took him down as she reached for him with panicked, flailing arms. To compensate, he struck her fiercely in the stomach and pulled her roughly by her long hair. The girl screeched, but as he took hold from behind and held her afloat, her arms relaxed, and she listened to his screaming, calming reassurances. Perhaps he could be a fine, fearless leader after all.

Silvious, with rope in hand, was two waves from his drowning comrades when a cantus suddenly surfaced between them. It rose out of the water and eyed both floating delicacies as a lord would over a choice of feast. It desired rodenerack this night, spun, and crashed down on Silvious, pushing him far beneath the surface with its snout.

He screamed his lungs to filling point and still clasped the rope in hand as he tried to kick out from the creature as he plunged deeper, but the beast held him fast.

Then, without warning, the halting rope still clutched in his claw wrenched him free of the beast. He was left floating alone in darkness as the grand cantus continued its surging charge to the depths below, not yet realising its quarry had escaped.

Far above, he made out the dim lights of life. He swam upwards swiftly, leaving the life-saving rope to float alongside. He felt the sway of the massive beast as it realised its loss and tore the current apart in search of him. He dared not look below, lest he somehow drew its attention.

The few moments swimming towards life were the worst he had ever known. Knowing the beast could discover his graceful gliding and pull him back, he wondered if this was the same panic that Heygar had felt.

He focused on the light growing brighter above him. His

lungs ached, and he had never known fear like this, but he never wavered. He kicked fiercely until the rush of water left his ears and he broke the surface of the sea, spitting water from within and tasting wonderful, salty air once more.

And then the night exploded in fire.

HUMAN SACRIFICE

The flames thundered down upon them like a terrifying deity bent on vengeance and destruction. Each ball was larger than the last and lit up the night and the sea beneath its gaze. Silvious could only stare in awe while Denan grabbed the swinging rope and wrapped it around all three of them before calling desperately for salvation.

Around them, the sea was alight with fire, close enough to warm the bones in the freezing water but not enough to burn. That was reserved for the wielder Iaculous, who brought the fight to the beasts singlehandedly. He stood alone at the aft of the barge. His hands were ever-moving spheres of flame, and they waved erratically with every gust of wind and shake of the fist. They burned his clothes and skin, but he offered only a war cry as he burned himself away.

Once again, Silvious felt something from beyond this world. He imagined a brutal beast clawing at the darkness between god and man, trying to unleash itself on an unprepared world or fleeing a prison of its own. Sometimes his kind could feel things that were not there, and sometimes his people were dreadfully mistaken.

Repeatedly, like a machine of other worlds, the immolated form of Iaculous fired spheres of flame down into the water. They continued to burn for a few deadly pulses around the trio like an unnatural net holding off inevitable death. They filled the air with the shrill scream of both beast and burning weaver, but Denan's commanding cry was louder than all others were.

Suddenly, the rope pulled them from the water. Silvious felt the leathery brush of fin upon his feet as they came aboard, but he also felt the burn of fire as Iaculous made the attacking creature pay. Within a few breaths, he was free of the water and in the grasp of warm hands. They pulled Silvious and his comrades aboard, where the heat was tenfold.

With the trio on board, the volley came to an abrupt halt, and Iaculous fell back from the edge to the deck. He cried out in agony, and Silvious licked his lips because the delicious smell of charred meat was in the air once more.

The apprentice crumbled in a heap of ruin and burning embers beneath the mast of the barge. He patted down the small fires along each arm weakly as though it was the hardest task ever attempted. No deckhands dared near him as the blazing heat still emanated from his broken form. It was only Arielle who ran to him, screaming. Her soaking body put out the last of the fires around his body, and she cradled him in her arms.

In the light of the catalights, Silvious saw the full devastation. It was far worse than at the river. With no healer reviving him as he brought alive the source weaving, Iaculous had burned himself to charcoal. His hair dripped from his head in a caramelised liquid, and his skin peeled away, leaving dreadful blotches of raw muscle and tendon. He tried to speak, but his tongue had burned and charred to a stump.

He tried to look into her eyes, but his own were melted away. All he could offer were a few low moans of anguish with the last few breaths from scorched lungs as he faded away.

"My Iaculous," Arielle wailed and tears fell among the drips of seawater. She cradled him so that he wouldn't know he was alone as he died. "I'm with you, my love," she whispered. He reached up to touch her face and left a smear of gore upon her cheek. She took his ruined hand in hers. "You saved us from the monsters."

Behind her, Denan fell to his knees grasping his pouch breathing deeply into the contents within. Another man down, the first on his watch.

"You saved us all," Silvious said.

The barge lurched, heaved, and almost overturned as the sea monsters rallied and attacked once more and struck the side of the barge.

"Pull the anchor and crank the line," cried Dirion, grabbing the wheel and spinning the barge towards the call of the wind. Whatever misery was happening among his fares, he was disinterested until the appearance of the old healer and his burden. He appeared to read the old man's intentions, for he nodded and eyed the sea and said no more.

"We have to send Heygar over the side," Eralorien said, dragging the dead body up the steps from the deep below of storage. The exertion was too much for the old man, and halfway up, he stumbled and collapsed.

"Where were you? Help him," screamed Arielle, holding her dying burden in her grasp as though love alone could save the boy from a terrible fate.

"Oh, Iaculous," he gasped and took his head in his hands as though someone had driven a shard of venomous pain through it. The beasts struck again, and the *Celeste* shuddered and spun. However, the Hounds noticed none of this, for one of their pack had been stricken, and Eralorien was slow to save him.

"I could feel the darkness from below."

"He still breathes," Denan hissed.

"I could feel the darkness, and I knew he'd gone too far. I could feel the fire," Eralorien said and looked upon the ruin of the young man. Silvious saw the sorrow in his face, the regret of a man who knows full well the distance walked was a step too far. They were five now.

"Why aren't you healing him?" Cherrie demanded.

The barge took another strike, and the world faltered, creaked, and splintered in parts.

"His wounds are from the source's touch. There is nothing I can do."

"Try."

"We have problems greater than this," Eralorien hissed, wiping tears from his eyes. An apprentice was the closest thing the old weaver had to family.

"Save him, you thurken coward!" screamed Arielle, leaving the still body of Iaculous to its death. She leapt upon the old man, striking him fiercely across the face, chest, anywhere she could.

"I will not!" he roared and pushed her to the ground. He returned to his burden. "The creatures can smell his body."

Silvious shook his head. That didn't matter. They were his Hounds.

"It must be done." Cherrie took her lover's legs and dragged him across the deck, with Eralorien as her accomplice.

"We can't do this to Heygar," cried Denan, but he did not stop her. Heygar was hers to put to rest.

"No, no, this is wrong!" screamed Arielle. She drew her sword and leapt between sister, weaver, and ocean edge. A lone fighter heroically defending the condemned. It wasn't just Heygar she fought for either. They would not stop with one sacrifice. They would feed two Hounds stinking of roasted ambrosia to the beasts this night.

"You can't do this," Silvious said, stepping beside her. His head was spinning as though he had just made a mockery of a barrel of sine, but still, he knew he wasn't ready to feed his master to a fish. He almost fainted but somehow stayed upright. A great exhaustion came upon him. Behind them, Dirion collapsed heavily against the wheel as though struck by a phantom pugilist, and the *Celeste* pivoted in the waves.

"He deserves better than this," said Denan weakly as all fight left him. He stumbled with the barge's sway.

"He left this world a long time ago. We carry a husk towards our death," Eralorien cried. He struggled under the load, and Cherrie collapsed beside him, her face paler than ever before.

Arielle dropped her sword loudly before falling backwards onto the glowing form of Iaculous. "This is wrong."

"THROW HIM OVER!" cried Iaculous in that strange, terrifying voice. The world went quiet. The wind fell still, and the sea calmed around them. The continuous squeals of the grand cantuses were silent. Iaculous attempted to rise to his feet.

"It can't be," Eralorien said, as though a god had taken form in front of his eyes. Whatever ruin Iaculous had been a few agonising moments before was now disappearing in front of their eyes. His broken, ripped skin was crusting over as though a thousand days' recovery was happening in mere breaths. That same crust was falling away swiftly, revealing fresh, pink skin beneath.

Though it ached to stand, Silvious helped the young warrior to his feet. The closer he came, the weaker he felt.

"I feel better." It was a whisper, though it felt as if a giant from the lost forests of Velmar had roared each word through his chest.

"You are taking what is ours. Stop," gasped Eralorien.

Cherrie stumbled against the old weaver, and he shielded her from the tearing of her soul. He shielded and embraced her completely as though he was a man in love. She groaned, and only then did Iaculous realise what damage he was doing to his comrades. For a few pulses more, he took deep breaths as though his lungs were reborn. Then he allowed the glow around his body to fade and disappear, leaving everyone on the *Celeste* struggling to rise from where they fell.

"What have I done?" he cried out in a voice far more recognisable.

"What you needed to do," Arielle said and wheezed and coughed as she caught her breath. She had been closest and was most affected.

"You took from our life force. You took from all our souls, and you did it carelessly!" Eralorien screamed. Cherrie pulled herself away from his protective embrace, into the hands of the equally stricken Denan. He stumbled over and struck the younger man across the face before falling to his knees once more. "You could have killed any of us. You could have killed all of us."

Arielle took Iaculous's shaking hand and kissed it. "But he didn't kill us."

Dirion was unmoved. "I don't know what dark enchantments you have done to calm the water, but the beasts will be upon us. The old weaver is right. Sacrifice the body."

Both weavers eyed each other as only a master and apprentice could, sharing a silent argument amid miraculous events. Eralorien glared his disapproval, but he softened after a breath. His apprentice nodded and assisted the older man in their unenviable task.

"We still shouldn't do this," Arielle whimpered. "It won't even change a thing." She sighed as though the effort of speech was exhausting.

Somewhere out in the night, there was a fresh cry of frenzied beast, and Silvious's heart dropped. Whatever Iaculous had done, it had not involved slaying the sea monsters.

"The smell is just too much, and we have too many miles," Dirion muttered.

The weavers carried the body to the edge of the barge. Far away, the screams grew and the waves, wind, and terrible times grew with them. Silvious patted the ring in his chest and dropped his head. This was how it would be.

"Goodbye, old friend," Denan said. He took the weeping Cherrie in his arms as both healers dropped the body into the water, and the saga of the legendary Heygar ended forever.

DAY TWO

The body floated across the surface, bobbing in the waves for a time. From the stern, Silvious looked on. He was the only one that would. The rest of the Hounds turned away, disgusted and relieved with what they had done. It was only Arielle's melancholic mutterings that suggested remorse.

A large wave took the body and turned it on its side. It looked as though Heygar were sleeping. Then a creature from beneath took it completely. Silvious glimpsed a fin and then he saw nothing at all.

The *Celeste* sailed through the storm, and soon enough, they were alone with the waves and their journey.

Silvious sat beside Dirion as he had little desire to face his comrades after the event. The old barge captain said nothing, and Silvious appreciated the silence. The deckhands returned to their duties as though little had happened at all. Hammers from below deck sang their song of patching up leaks, foot-long metal spikes and careful prayers. They secured the cracked mast to a near-sailing condition. In that time, Silvious did nothing more but stare into the ocean, waiting for the sun to rise.

Eventually, Dirion took his hands, placed them on the wheel, and pointed south. "Hold her steady there," he said and left Silvious to steer them onwards.

With the wind in his face and salt on his lips, Silvious felt the movement of the barge and felt more at ease than he had since he had begun this endeavour. Time passed, though he never watched the moon's movement. He didn't want to. The barge in his grip was a fine experience.

"You did well out there, young one," Denan blurted and startled Silvious from his sailing. He had not heard the warrior steal up beside him.

Silvious smiled to himself at Denan's poor choice of words. Young? He was nearing middle age among his kind. Still, what good was there to point out such a thing?

Denan shuffled his feet as though offering a compliment was a difficult task. "We may have drowned without you thinking so swiftly."

"Nearly drowned m'self. Had I thought on it a moment longer, I might have lost me nerve."

"Hounds don't wait and think," Denan said and laughed tragically. Was that not one of Heygar's favourite sayings when action called?

Silvious smiled and felt the loss anew. He placed his clawed fingers to his chest and touched the ring in his pocket. Would Denan be a better man knowing Heygar's true intentions? The ring felt heavy, and he said nothing more.

"And you will have a fine place at my side among the Hounds, little one," Denan said and patted Silvious on the head as if he were a child. He should have known better. "Denan's Hounds. It doesn't sound right, does it?"

"It has no ring to it," Silvious said, shrugging. He knew

Denan was watching his every move and gesture, but he kept his eye on the way ahead. Easier that than starting an argument with Denan over their lost master. The wounds were still fresh, and Silvious knew well Denan's pain was probably worse than his own was.

"Who wants to walk in the footsteps of a giant?" Denan said.

"At least the road'll be clear."

"If you serve me as you did him, then all will be well, little one," Denan said.

"All will be well."

Silvious gripped the wheel as though it was the only thing in the world which offered comfort. His world was awry. He knew Denan well enough these last few years, yet he did not know the man. He did not know his own fate within this group, nor whether it was a group worth marching with. What he knew was that the sea was beautiful at this time of the morning, with the storm far behind and the breeze driving them forward. He also knew he needed to complete Heygar's last mission. After that, perhaps Denan would be a suitable leader. Perhaps he would not.

"When we make dock, I'll have a task for you, little one. I need your scouting skills, perhaps differently to what you are accustomed to. Walk the town ahead of us and learn what you can of the land. Learn what you can of our quarry and anything of value beyond. I'm wary of Mallum learning our intentions and warier of him learning that a group of mercenaries have made landfall," Denan said and placed his hand upon Silvious's shoulder.

"As you wish."

"Be wary, my friend. Take few risks, and keep your wits about you. All parts of Venistra are treacherous to your kind, and the last thing I want is to lose another brother. There are some who would happily slit a rodenerack's throat and serve it as an exotic meat and think nothing more of it," he said.

Silvious nodded. He was wily enough to avoid a butcher's block. Still, "friend" and "brother" had a nice ring to it.

"I will be wary."

"We will meet you in the tall inn at the far end of the town before dawn," Denan said and appeared happier now that his orders were received well enough.

A heavy mist hung over the port where they made landing. Silvious's heart felt heavy for the cost of the voyage and leaving the barge behind.

With the *Celeste* moored along the old stone quay, Dirion came to him as he prepared to disembark alone. "The *Celeste* could do with a man of your talents," he said.

Silvious wondered if the old barge captain could read the desire openly upon his face. If Heygar was still with them it would have been like any voyage before, but he wasn't with them anymore, was he?

"I can't offer the wealth of a mercenary life, but it pays enough so you can eat. You have the nerve of a giant, and such things would be welcome. We'll be here for another few hours, my friend." The barge captain shrugged as though offering an entire change of life and livelihood was no small matter. "My boys would welcome someone with a little sea to their legs, whatever breed of leg they might be." Dirion shook Silvious's hand as though he were an equal.

"Kind of you, Captain. I'll think on it a while."

Silvious dropped from the barge onto solid ground. The offer moved him. Though his mind bade him accept the role, part of him could not allow such liberating thoughts. He was here to kill Mallum. Nothing else mattered, did it? Did it? His mind spun.

He bowed to Dirion. "I'll think on it a while," he repeated

and wondered if he held enough nerve to return to the barge come dawn. Whatever decision he made would wait until he learned what he could for his comrades.

Silvious walked up along the quiet quay and thought the town similar to the one they had departed from. He had expected creepy lacquered buildings with threatening spikes built into the walls, or ungodly cathedrals decorated in nasty stone gargoyles at every corner. Instead, he saw a sleepy fishing town with a few dozen buildings, just like any other fishing town in Dellerin.

He couldn't help think on the offer the barge captain had made. He had known no great kindness from most humans, apart from Heygar and Arielle. Occasionally, Iaculous had feigned kindness, though that may have been to win favour with his future betrothed. He thought on this and tapped the ring in his pocket. He had two missions to accomplish.

Silvious slipped through the town like the expert thief he was. He was slinking, smooth, and a shadow to any careless observer. Unlike Dellerin under this late hour, where all shops closed with the falling sun, the town of Anbrianne was brimming with energy throughout. Humans went about their tasks as if sleep was a thing to be feared.

He glided through each passageway and every alley in between, keeping an eye and nose out for any menace. Perhaps he might spot a wandering troupe of assassins just waiting in the wings for the Hounds, or a handful of devious weavers just waiting to do Mallum's horrible bidding. Or perhaps the mysterious man himself, out for a midnight stroll.

After a time that may have been an hour, he came upon the most suitable of places to complete both tasks. Though many similar buildings were boarded up, this shop shone brightly with the flicker of candles, displaying shiny valuables in its front window. The outer panelling was black, and the main windows were polished and clean. It stood out from all the poverty in the surrounding buildings. A place like that would have a fine price for a ring like his. And with the money? Well, it would be his parting gift to his comrades. Better the ring bring a little joy to their group and not condemn Cherrie to a life of eternal guilt. Better she never knew the true depth of Heygar's love for her.

He stepped through the doorway of Wildrew's Worldly Wares and slipped the ring onto his largest claw as he did. Trinkets, jewellery, artwork, and a thousand unwanted gifts from lovers, friends or paupers' heirlooms adorned the walls of the shop. It was both breath-taking and heart-breaking. Silvious rolled the ring on his finger as he eyed shelf after shelf of goblets, tankards, glassware, and trophies. He knew the ring would find a fine place somewhere among the riches and forgotten thereafter.

"And what brings a rat into my domain?" the owner said from behind his counter at the far end of the room.

He wasn't alone. There were two raven-haired men standing on the other side of the counter. It was as though he had stumbled upon some great game of bartering. Between them was a thick sack, and Silvious sniffed the raw meat within. He knew hunger had become a commodity in these lands the last year. Meat was likely a fine currency.

"I'm looking for a barter," Silvious said easily enough, though he suspected these men were up to devilment. He would keep his wits about him.

"The rat wants to barter something nice. Well, boys, I think our business can wait until I see to my customer." The middle-aged man had short grey hair and stroked his smooth chin as though in great thought.

Silvious couldn't help wonder if he could purchase the

same shaving kit the man used as part of the deal. His own kit was running a terrible, cutting rust.

"Wildrew is the name. I have every treasure a little merchant like yourself could ever need," the owner said.

His two comrades laughed and made way for the hooded rodenerack at the counter. They busied themselves with perusing through Wildrew's wares, likely searching for an additional treasure to add to their list of demands. Their feet dragged on the sawdust on the ground. Silvious thought it strange for a wealthy domain like this to carpet the floor so shabbily.

"I have this shiny thing," Silvious said and rolled the ring across the counter like a loose chip in a fated battle of cards. This pleased Wildrew greatly, who snapped it up and eyed the pure gold piece carefully.

"The gems are exquisitely cut. I should lie, but I suspect you know this treasure's value." Wildrew held the glimmering ring near the light of one of the dozen candles in his shop. It twinkled perfectly. Silvious smiled.

"Where is your troupe, and might they have need of precious meats?" one man asked, and Silvious was cautious. Who knew whom he spoke with?

"I'm walking with no troupe, my friend. In fact, I'm wanting a little work around town," he said, feigning the wanderer just right. Lull them into a false sense of security.

He was desperate for a quick sale. Wildrew would offer a paltry sum, he would act indignant and storm out, and the shop owner would gloriously over-offer to keep him from losing the sale.

Silvious's eyes suddenly caught sight of a strange thing behind the counter. It was a small leather bandoleer with six glass jars attached to it.

"A little wandering rat, all alone in the world, looking for a little cheese to chew upon," he heard a voice mock, but it didn't matter. He could take the mocking. Besides, he had something far more interesting to stare upon.

He thought the bandoleer beautiful, though he could not say why. It wouldn't even fit his waist, yet he felt lured to it. Something instinctive drew him to it as though it was more than a piece of clothing. As though something destined him to be near it. He wondered whether the ring would cover its cost.

"Now," Wildrew hissed, and something dragged Silvious from his stupor. It was the clutch of one man. And then the other.

"Thurken rat!" one of them screamed, and he felt a rope loop over his neck.

Silvious fought, screamed out, and felt a heavy strike at the back of his head. His senses spun. The rope tightened, and Wildrew appeared in front of him. He tried to claw at his assailant, and another punch knocked him to the side. He stumbled back and fell against a wall, then he caught sight of the ring as it took flight, lost in the melee somehow. He almost thought about grabbing for it, but it was already far from reach.

"Please."

A boot knocked him to the ground, and he thought about the ocean.

"Not here. Get him in the back. Do you not remember the last time? He'll bleed everywhere," Wildrew hissed.

"Please," Silvious cried again as they dragged him into a dark room devoid of trinkets and treasures.

A blade plunged into his stomach and then a second time. Silvious screamed and remembered the waves below his clawed grip on the wheel of the barge. He wanted to sail. He wanted to touch the bandoleer. He wanted Heygar to come save him.

Not like this.

They knocked him to the floor, and the smell of raw meat stung his nose. They wrapped a scarf around his mouth to silence his shrill screams. Punishing hands tied a rope around his arms as he gasped for a respite. They tied a hanging rope around his feet and swiftly pulled upwards until he hung upside-down.

"You'll have twenty pounds and no more from this one," Wildrew whispered.

He placed a bucket underneath Silvious, who had fallen silent as his stomach bled out all over him. With his last breaths, he halted the screams. Instead, he stared at his killers and vowed silent vengeance on them.

"Twenty pounds of flesh is no fair price," one hissed, watching the angle of Silvious's sway. If Silvious's staring intimidated him, he showed nothing in his cruel features.

"He walked right into the den. You hardly had anything to do," Wildrew said and steadied the sway with a careless grip.

Silvious thought again of the sway of the barge from atop the pouch and his nerve against such terror. He wanted that seafaring life more than ever. He wondered if Dirion would still be waiting for him at the quay.

His killer slid the knife across his neck and held him steady as he died.

PILLOW TALK

Arielle awoke and grabbed her chest in alarm.
Something was wrong. Was it her? Was she dying?
Where was she? She wrapped the surrounding bedclothes
around her naked body and attempted to gather her thoughts.

Her heart was hammering, though that may have just been
the absence of her soul. No, that wasn't right. Her soul wasn't
absent. It was just a little eaten away by her man. No, that
wasn't accurate either. He was more like a boy. Her boy. He
might be more someday. So might she.

She wiped her brow, counted the beats in each pulse, and
held her chest as she tried to calm herself. Everything about
this place felt strange. She almost imagined the sky to be a
different colour, but at dawn, it was exactly the same grey as
a cloudy Dellerin.

Arielle lay back in the lavish bedding and stretched out
magnificently. There was nothing like a magnificent stretch to
return a tripping heart to its rightful beat. Sometimes her
heart's irregular beats kept her up all night. Sometimes it
wiped her out completely. She never complained and asked

no one to heal her. Why waste the soul on such a trivial matter?

"Calm down, skipping thing," she whispered and enjoyed her recovery in the comfortable bedding.

Heygar had always insisted they sleep well before heading out into the scary world to earn their bread, and Denan insisted they continue the tradition. "Earn our bread," she muttered. It was a finer way of saying they were in the business of barbaric murder. Sometimes with a cleaver. Heygar would have rolled in his watery grave at how Denan was behaving in the wake of his death. Not to mention her sister too, but any fool who knew her knew that her heart only belonged to one man, and it wasn't Heygar.

"Oh, Heygar." Her stomach lurched. Big Heygar had always been good to her. Truthfully, he had condemned her to this life, but apart from that, he was a decent enough man and a damn fine leader. "At least we'll complete your last mission," she said to the far walls of the rented room, and her stomach and heart settled.

"*Are you awake, Arielle?*" a distant voice whispered in her mind, and she dared a smile. He was still learning the art. It was a rare skill for any weaver to speak across thoughts. Eralorien couldn't do it.

The door opened, and Arielle stifled a smile as Iaculous stumbled across the small room, clumsily navigating her bags, leathers, and womanly things. When troubled, he usually came to her. After the previous night's horrors, it surprised her that dawn had come before he made an appearance. Perhaps he had needed sleep after eating so much of their souls. He should be dead, she thought, and her hidden smile faded entirely.

"Wake up, my temptress," Iaculous whispered, and she

turned in her silken coverings as though in sleep's wondrous grip.

She was a temptress and a little more. She allowed her coverings to slide free of her upper half. Nothing like a glance at forbidden enticements to stir his desires. She had charmed him masterfully but to no avail. At least, not yet. He was an apprentice weaver, and her appreciated distraction was very much a distraction.

Arielle wondered how long she would wait for the fool to act upon her wishes. She wondered how long her stuttering heart would take his delicate rejection. She believed in love. She also believed in love at first sight, and though it had been a slow march from friendship to something more with Iaculous, she believed they were in love with each other. She wondered if he were even aware of this himself.

"Sleeping," she muttered dreamily.

"You are putting on weight." He stroked her cheek. Though he jested, she could feel the conflicting emotion in his voice. His hand hovered and almost touched her chest, but instead, he drew it away and pulled the covers over her, as only a gentleman would do.

She didn't mind him seeing her like this. In fact, after the bet he had lost to her in the Addakkas inlets and the subsequent price of him stripping as her payment, she was always keen to repay the embarrassment. He had a fine manhood. She had fine naked parts.

"I have put on weight in all the right places, my friend," Arielle purred, dazzling him with her smile. How many years had they played this game? One of these days, it would come to a head. They would kiss and beyond, or they would shake hands and stay as close as they had always been. She was comfortable enough to tempt him this way, and he was stubborn enough to reject her so openly. Cherrie did not approve of their relationship—or lack thereof—but she was no person to learn from, was she?

"You don't have to eat every pie they offer you, my beauty," Iaculous said and returned the smile as she opened the duvet. Comrades did this all the time out in the wilderness, didn't they?

"What troubles you?" she asked, nestling into his chest. She had asked of his horrors already, but even death wasn't enough for him to confide in her. She knew he didn't come to her to empty his worries upon her platter either. He came for distraction.

"This place is strange," he whispered and embraced her. His hold was stronger than usual, and she melted under his power. He was less the meek, delicate healing poet and more the first breeze of a growing hurricane. Perhaps she was mistaken and merely enjoying his embrace more after losing him.

"Yes, this room is strange. I think it is the colour. It is a strange-coloured wall, and I don't like it," she said. Iaculous sniggered. The wall in question was a dark olive. She would have chosen red and black. They were strong colours.

"I'm not talking about the thurken colour of the wall," he said, and she knew her wit was having the desired effect. She always knew what her man needed. He needed her, but he was not ready to need it enough. When he found her in the arms of another man, that might change his tune quick enough, she imagined. It would not be hard to find a man, should she need such salacious things.

"I'm sorry I took from you. I feel stronger than I've ever felt before in my life."

"Strong enough to make a man out of yourself?" Arielle said, stroking his arm playfully. She met his eyes and bit her lower lip. Cherrie always said this drove men wild.

Iaculous sighed loudly. She could see the desire to devour her. Wonderful.

"Without you in my life, I'd probably be a full weaver by now. You distract me, woman."

Her hand slipped to his thigh, and he sighed again.

"You love me doing it, my love," she countered and pinched him gently. Usually, by now, he would have smacked her hand away.

"Perhaps that's the problem."

She allowed her hand to glide up and down along his thigh before sliding across to his other thigh, touching his manhood delicately along the way. He gasped loudly and said nothing. That was a little more than usually allowed. At this rate, in two years, they might even touch tongues.

"Enter me," she whispered, blowing gently on his ear. Iaculous smacked her hand away. "Ah, I almost had you." She kissed his cheek. It wasn't just love on her part. It was an itch that needed scratching. She was but a girl with needs, like anyone else.

"Yes, you did."

"Tell me, young healer boy, if you have so little interest in my body, why not allow me to lie with others? Why string me along if there is no chance in life for us?"

He met her gaze. "Do you want me to say it?"

She ran her fingernail gently down his cheek and then scraped him suddenly. She wanted him to say it.

"I've loved you since the morning we met. My body yearns for you and you alone. You are my beating heart, and without you, I would find myself anguished and lost."

Iaculous placed his finger across her lips. She saw the torment and desire on his face, and it pleased her. Yes, sometimes he crushed her, but when he was gentle and open, she knew why he was the man for her. He will be worth it, she told herself.

"Well, that's better, I suppose, but that line will only work on me for so long." She slid free of the bedcoverings to open the curtains and look out at the new day.

"Once I finish my apprenticeship, it will be different," he pledged, as he usually did. Diligent little Iaculous. If he were as dedicated to his craft as he was to her, once they became lovers, those would be fine times.

"Just another couple years?" Arielle asked, shrugging, looking out over the eerily quiet town.

Though haggard people moved through its streets, any fool could recognise a town dying. Boarded-up buildings stretched up and down the cracked road, and the flavour of silence in the town was unnervingly bitter. Whatever wealth this place had known was long since gone. She felt bad for their hardship. It wasn't their fault King Lemier had imposed such steep taxes, nor that the crops were battling a blight.

"After this mission, perhaps things will change," he offered. It was hardly a resounding pledge of betrothal, was it?

"Everything will change after this mission," she said, feeling a great sadness fall upon her. "Come on. I reckon Silvious will have stolen a fine breakfast from some unsuspecting Venistrian chef. I'm starving and bored from absolutely no dirty endeavours whatsoever." Arielle slipped into her clothing and beckoned her future lover to come join her.

"As you wish."

AND AWAY WE GO

L ike a pair of smooth thieves who had apprenticed under a wily old rodenerack, they made their way downstairs, appearing as innocent as the dawn. They were last to emerge from their chambers and met their comrades sitting around a table in the dining hall of the empty inn.

Eralorien offered a disapproving glance to Iaculous, who sat down beside him. The apprentice answered this disapproval by stealing his honey bread. He did so grinning, and Eralorien smiled despite himself. When needed, Iaculous was as charming as any silver-tongued pleasure-earner.

Arielle, however, didn't have to steal her breakfast. As she sat, Cherrie slid a large, steaming platter of thickly cut meat across to her, as a mother would a starving child.

"There may be a famine in these parts, but the Hounds will always eat the juiciest meats. The innkeeper assured me they slaughtered it today," Denan said, taking pride in his generosity.

Arielle didn't recognise these cuts at all. She dared a bite and was pleasantly surprised. It was richer than most cuts, and barely a salty streak of fat ran through it. She devoured the slice and a second after that.

"Ugh, I'll pass. Whatever beast that was, it didn't want to die," Iaculous hissed, and a few of his comrades rolled their eyes.

Arielle grabbed a third slice and ate it at him as pleasurably as she could. She saw the others would have done the same had they not all sated themselves already.

"Perhaps if you partook in a proper diet, you might be less of a skut." Cherrie sniffed, and Iaculous's face turned flush at the reprimand.

"What animal is it, anyway?" Arielle asked.

Denan shrugged. "Meat is meat. Add a little salt and cook it in butter, and it's all the same." His face darkened. "We are yet another Hound down." He took a beverage of steaming brew, grimacing as he did.

"A Hound down" was a term they saved for absentees and the worst conversation to have. The Seven were family, and sometimes family went their own way. Bereziel was the first Hound that Arielle remembered leaving them without warning. She hadn't even been old enough to be a member herself, but she remembered her sister's friends taking it terribly. However, that was the way with mercenaries. Sometimes they fell in a river. Sometimes they slipped away in the night without telling a soul.

Arielle looked around the table, frowned and remembered waking to terrible dreams.

"Where is Silvious?" she asked, eyeing the invisible weight on Denan's shoulders. Sometimes she found it impossible not to read people's emotions. It was something she had always done. Iaculous suggested it was a touch of the source upon her mind, but she supposed it was a skill she had not learned to tap into just yet. She was young though, and it would come eventually. She always believed things happened exactly as if they were written.

"The little rat has scampered away from us," Eralorien said.

"Don't call him that. He can't have left us. What did he say?" Arielle argued.

"I gave him a task, and he never returned," Denan said.

"You think he left us because he's a little late?" she asked.

"He's late, even for a rat," Cherrie said.

"Don't call him that, Cherrie. Something could have happened to him. He wouldn't just leave us without saying goodbye."

It was Eralorien who countered her argument with damningly emphatic words, as though he spoke of a man who fled his haggard, loving wife for a divine, loving queen. "The little rat took employment upon the *Celeste,* and all the best to him. I saw the look in that barge captain's eyes the moment he saw a rodenerack come aboard. He even had him sailing her by the end of the voyage, and I heard him sway the rat at the edge of the quay. A whole new life without blood on his hands? A man or beast can only deal such brutality until they cower away. Rats are simple creatures and born for water," he said.

It crushed her, but Arielle showed no such misery on her face. Eralorien shouldn't have called him a rat, but she lost the insistence in correcting him.

"He would have taken Heygar's passing badly," Iaculous said, and Cherrie nodded.

"He should have said goodbye."

Denan did his best to conceal his disappointment that the rodenerack chose a terrifying new life over his leadership for a few days. "It's half a night now. He should have returned.

Though it's disappointing, to know he's happier among the waves is a fine thing."

Arielle was heartbroken. "I owe him three gold."

"He left his winnings in Heygar's safe. You can add to it when we return. Fear not, Arielle. You will see the little rat again someday," Cherrie said and patted Arielle gently on the back.

Arielle smiled, and Cherrie's face hardened as though it would break and a torrent of agonising pain would erupt from her features. Arielle took her sister's hand in hers and squeezed. A silent moment of sadness passed between them. Two Hounds down.

"He's gone. We are worse off for it. Though it seems bleak, we must complete our mission," Denan said. He seemed to grow in nerve as he spoke the words. Arielle felt better hearing them.

Iaculous poked the meat curiously. "Five is a strong enough number. We can still do this with five."

Eralorien did not appear to agree. "You speak out of line, apprentice. With seven, we were formidable. With six, we were capable. But five? In an island of gutless swine as this, I am wary of our path and the light which guides us."

Denan winced. "Show respect, weaver. These are my lands, and this is still my outfit. Is the sea calling to you as well, or do you wish to continue with our task?" he hissed.

"We are no longer Heygar's Hounds. We are less than we were. You are brave and careless, Denan. A strong servant, but are you fit to lead us ... my friend?" the old weaver asked.

"You think a delicate weaver like you is fit to lead?" Denan growled as though he was a hound standing over a rotting bone. Sometimes it wasn't about the prize. Sometimes it was the battle.

"I do not wish to lead this disparate outfit."

"Five can just as easily become four. Do not dare speak of me or my country in such a way ever again. Ask to leave this table and be done with the Hounds, or else bow a pledge, weaver," Denan said.

Arielle saw his hand drop beneath the table and take hold of his sword, lest Eralorien weave fire like his apprentice. She froze in fear. Only moments before, they were a tranquil group aiming to complete the same cause. Now there was pride, rage, and ill intent in the air.

"Easy, my boys," Cherrie said, placing both her hands on the arms of both men.

Eralorien trailed off as though something deep within took control, and his face flashed a milliard of emotions that Arielle struggled to read. He was furious with Denan but desperate to stay in the fight. Fury, jealousy, sadness and love. All dangerous emotions at the best of times. He also reacted to Cherrie's insistence as most people did.

"Apologies, Denan. I was out of order. Call it an old man's irritability first thing in the morning," Eralorien said and smiled before offering a handshake. After a few pulses, Denan nodded an acceptance. He did not take the healer's hand though.

"See, boys, we are much better when we aren't spitting on each other's plate?" Cherrie said, and the table relaxed.

Arielle had always thought her sister had a way of calming matters with a few easy words when war was in the air, and Arielle was almost as skilled. Often, she had wondered if this ability was a trait they shared with their mother. She had never met her mother, and she knew little of the woman. She had only had her older sister to teach her the ways of the world. To engage in embarrassing conversations about why she bled as she did, or why boys were different to girls, and why this was sometimes a good thing. In all but the title, Cherrie had been a good parent.

It was only Bereziel who had ever spoken of her mother —back when he still had a glint in his eye and a kind smile. He had told her that her mother was an important person that was unable to look after her. He had claimed he'd never known her father, but who knew if the weaver knew anything at all? She had asked many a time, but he had sworn on blood, and it forbade him to reveal anything further. As for asking Cherrie? Well, this was a subject her sister never once spoke of, let alone offered a grain of information on. By her fifteenth year, Arielle had stopped asking altogether.

"You are right, Cherrie. All that matters is finishing Heygar's last mission. It's what the great man would have wanted. May he rest in peace," Eralorien said and touched his temple. After a moment, the table joined him in his silent prayer.

"I will not have us journey as a group while we are in Venistra," Denan said after a time. He rolled a map of the lands across the table. He pointed to a notched inkblot and ran his finger down the page a few times as if reassuring himself of the route. "South to the Green." He tipped a point on the creased brown parchment.

Arielle nodded along with the rest, even though it meant nothing to her. She had never mastered the art of a map or the reading of great books. Whenever she stared intently at the printed works, some numbers and letters appeared to leap into different places, and it made her head spin. Her gifts were the reading of faces—and sometimes using a cleaver.

"We will split up into three and meet up in the town of Vahr in the Blood Red Assassin inn. I will ride on alone first. I know the road. Better we don't appear as a group of mercenaries seeking Mallum." Denan eyed his listeners anxiously. "Iaculous will travel with Arielle at noon. Eralorien shall escort the lovely Cherrie a few hours after noon. As a grandfather and doting granddaughter," he said before rolling the map back up.

Eralorien eyed him for a few moments but said nothing. Arielle thought this interesting enough. She had expected another outburst, but instead, the old healer merely nodded. Perhaps he found the company of Cherrie more enjoyable than that of his own apprentice.

"I'll walk you out, Denan," Cherrie said.

Arielle didn't understand why the two of them attempted secrecy now that Heygar was dead. Perhaps they said nothing because the guilt was eating them up like a dead legend in a large fish's mouth. They may as well wear the lust in bright colours instead of hiding it away as they had done for the last few months.

Oh, Heygar, how did you ever miss what was occurring in front of your Cherrie-flavoured eyes?

How many times were they found in snug little corners, whispering wonderful nothings in each other's ear? How many times had Arielle heard a slight click of the lock as Cherrie slipped from Heygar's room into another? Men could never see what was happening right in front of their eyes.

Poor Denan. He probably thought Cherrie was in love with him too.

A FOX'S SCENT

A rielle watched the gloomy sky and muttered a curse. She doubted Iaculous was even listening. When he was concentrating on a difficult piece of weaving, his face changed, and he lost all ability to communicate.

It was something she should have been used to. However, recently, she grew frustrated as he displayed his desire for weaving over her company more frequently. He would sometimes fall silent for hours until he coerced a dead flower into blooming for a few breaths before withering away or tricking a leaf into slowing its descent from a tree. It was impressive but a little disheartening, although she had never complained.

All of these successes were away from the watchful eye of his disapproving master. Arielle imagined the absence of the old man's burning stare helped the young weaver greatly. Today, he wasn't weaving though. He was concentrating on something else entirely.

"If I'm to be soaked to a bone, I'd like to be moving, so it's a worthy sacrifice," she said, watching the sky for the inevitable rain.

Since he had stepped out of the tavern, Iaculous had behaved strangely. It was afternoon, and they hadn't walked their horses more than a hundred yards from their inn. Now and then, he would bring his horse forward while looking to the sky and back at the ground, as if searching for a scent out on the hunt. Eventually, he came to a definite stop outside a brightly lit shop just down the road from their inn.

"I need to go in here," he said, and she shrugged. Of course, he meant to go in. At this hour, Eralorien and her sister were likely heading on their way. It would do no good to meet them outside.

It was a fine enough shop, she supposed, with all the trinkets in the world on display. Arielle imagined Silvious drawn to its treasures, and her stomach clenched at her friend's absence. He would make a fine deckhand. He had scaled the barge's mast easily enough. She wondered if they would ever meet again.

"Would you at least wait for me?" she snapped as he entered.

A flash of warmth struck Arielle's face, and with it came a slight pain in her head. Weaving was afoot, though of what, she could not say. She thought Iaculous capable of becoming a great weaver, and she desired to know more of their world, but he never offered explanations. Like her sister, he could be irritatingly stubborn.

She followed him into the shop and thought it more impressive within. Her eyes glimmered in the gold, silver, and diamond. She wanted to own it all, but more than that, she wanted Iaculous to do his business and let them be on their way. It seemed foolish to delay, and thoughts of completing the mission offered a greater relief this morning than the day before.

Iaculous walked around the small shop dreamily as if night-blind in a storm. His eyes fell upon every treasure but moved on without a second glance. Arielle could almost imagine him smelling the air. She nearly laughed until he spun and she caught sight of his eyes. They were his usual brown, but there was a film of grey covering each pupil. Then she felt the unnatural warmth pulse off him in waves as though it were his heartbeat. The unsettling eyes looked beyond her and came to stop upon the far wall, where the owner of the establishment busied himself polishing a large brass candelabrum behind an old counter.

The warmth dissipated immediately, and Iaculous gasped, as his mind appeared to return. He offered her his warmest smile, which only appeared when he was inebriated or when Eralorien was nowhere near. She returned the smile and immediately felt at ease.

"I saw it from the window," Iaculous said loudly. The polishing stopped, the candelabrum was put aside, and the most enthusiastic smile appeared across crooked teeth.

"Did you now?" the owner said and looked behind him, searching for whatever treasure the patron so desired. He was forming his sales pitch depending on whatever was in demand, no doubt.

"The bandoleer, I mean," Iaculous said. He reached for the long leather belt with six jingling glass jars.

Arielle felt dizzy when she saw it. It was the effect of the weaving and lack of soul, no doubt. Or else a reaction to too much meat for breakfast.

"The price?" Iaculous ran his fingers along each glass canister strapped in a divot of the thickly cut leather.

It wasn't the prettiest accessory Arielle had ever seen, worn with age and scarred from warring times. Bereziel wore one embedded with amethyst stones, and she thought it far more appealing to the eye. She patted her pockets absently. Not a penny to her name.

The shop owner's eyes were bright with enthusiasm. She'd seen that look on plenty of men when attempting fun and games. "Merely ten gold, my friend. A treasure, it is. Some say Mallum himself cut the leather into shape." Arielle saw through the lie easily enough, but Iaculous wasn't listening. He was rummaging in his pocket, and she knew he would come short and then she saw something else.

"This is all I have," Iaculous said, dropping a couple pieces of gold across the counter. No bartering, no play, just a weak opening bet. It was also his closing bet too.

"That will be enough for a down payment, my friend." The seller reached for the leather piece. Iaculous did not return it. Instead, he eyed the door and the horses outside. Where was there a rodenerack with swift fingers when needed?

Arielle looked down and spotted a little thing at his foot. Lost beneath the strangely covered carpet of the floor, it was almost indiscernible. She bent down and recovered the ring. With a quick application of spittle and the right amount of rubbing on her blouse, she held the beautiful ring up in the candlelight and thought it stunning.

"That's not yours, little girl."

However, quicker than the eye could see, she had it on her finger. She read the sudden rage and his quick recovery of control. She waved her finger as though Iaculous had made her the happiest little girl in the realm, for it was a stunning piece. What owner was foolish or heartbroken enough to barter such a wonderful piece? It was worth at least thirty gold on a weak barter alone, but she was not willing to attempt a fair barter at all.

"My gold ring," she said, beaming her finest smile. "I

can't believe I almost lost it in the sawdust. I'm such a damsel," she squeaked, but her eyes marked her intent. *Make me an offer, and you can still avoid a terrible loss.*

If Iaculous observed or heard any of this exchange, he showed no interest. Instead, he stared at the bandoleer.

"I was sure I dropped it on the ground not two hours ago," the owner said. Arielle read his lie and also his intention. "Would you consider an exchange of wares?" It was lose-lose, so better the lesser loss of the two.

"How much would you offer for my wedded ring?" she asked. Iaculous looked up from his desired object for a moment before returning his gaze.

"I'll give you eight gold, a fair deal."

"But, fine sir, he used a family heirloom when he asked me. Surely, you wouldn't expect me to just hand it back at such a steal?" she countered but removed the ring. Nearly there. On the one hand, it was his ring to start. On the other, a local constabulary might favour the pretty little thing's word over his, especially if they believed they could profit from her favour. She had learned more than enough tricks from her sister to make them believe as much.

"A fair deal would be swapping both, I suppose," Mister Wildrew said and cursed his mixed fortune under his breath.

Arielle recovered the few pieces offered by Iaculous and dragged her potential lover away from the counter, lest he change his mind with the ring in his possession. However, he didn't.

"Thank you. Come again," the owner said dejectedly.

"You are a good man, sir."

Strangely, Iaculous did not don the belt. Instead, he packed it safely away on the back of his horse with the rest of his belongings.

Without warning, a blast of warmth struck her, and

Arielle felt a dreadful surge of sorrow. Thoughts of never seeing Silvious again flooded through her mind, and she felt the same panic she had awoken to that morning. She felt like crying but instead climbed aboard her horse and led Iaculous from the town.

The land they rode upon was dead. The path they took was more miserable than any she had taken before. She had seen weeping oaks in all corners of Dellerin at all points of season, and they never differed. Yet, in Venistra, there was no sign of rich green in their leaves nor wild amber in their branches. They appeared eaten through by a virus of fire, leaving a living husk of ashen grey behind. They moved in the wind like a sickly ocean of cobblestone, and they unsettled her so. If these were the trees, it was no surprise to hear a great blight had taken much of the land.

"It feels like we are riding through a graveyard," Arielle said as they brought their horses through the path in the forest. The path itself was dark despite the day, with tall lines of dreary trees on either side. She wondered if it was the entire forest or if there were shards of green farther in. She had little intention of discovering for herself.

Iaculous offered no comment.

"Are you okay?" she asked.

"I'm fine."

They rode for a time in unusual silence. It unsettled her. Many times, she thought of breaking this silence, but the opportunity never arose. All that mattered was the path and the journey.

It wasn't until sunset, when her rear ached and her stomach grumbled, that he finally spoke. She wanted to believe it was the Iaculous she knew well, but he seemed different.

"Something concerns you?"

The fading rays shone upon the grey and offered what beauty it could to such deathly-looking trees. Arielle had never hated being alone with him in her life.

"I'm concerned about many things, some of which are you," she said, stretching in the saddle.

"There are strange energies in this place. I felt it from the moment we made landfall. It is as though the source is closer to our world in Venistra."

Arielle didn't understand, and she knew better than to ask.

Iaculous let go of the reins and held up his hand. He closed his eyes, and his fingers glowed. She had seen it a thousand times before but never with as little ease. He met her eyes, and his hands became a little sphere of fire. She shuddered and remembered the night before.

"It's okay, Arielle," he said and raised his other hand. As before, his fingers glowed and his burning hand bubbled, but he smiled again. "It doesn't hurt now," he said, and she felt very little heat from his body. "I can do both."

Arielle smiled warily. He healed as he destroyed. It was not a done thing. What was Eralorien really teaching him?

Iaculous's hand ceased its bubbling and, after a few moments, it returned to normal, though it still held the flame. He laughed, and the flame grew until he released it by sending it careening into a nearby tree. It took light immediately. Arielle pulled her horse from the fire, cursing loudly as she did.

"I'm sorry," he cried. Iaculous dropped from his horse and ran towards the tree aflame. With both hands, he killed the flame with a gust of energy, but this time, he fell to his knees from the effort. "I'm getting better," he gasped and laughed aloud again.

He waited for her to join him in merriment, but Arielle kicked her horse forward and rode away from him.

BRIEF CLARIFICATIONS OF PRECARIOUS THINGS

They rode for a few hours more without saying another word. The rain fell down on them, the muddy path and the dreary forest of grey, but Arielle made no complaint and neither did Iaculous. Instead, they fell into an uncomfortable silence usually shared by couples wedded for a decade or more.

Even when they rested for a time, ate the last of the strange Venistrian meat, and washed it down with a bitter limewater concoction, they still said nothing. Again, she thought of an old wedded couple's miserable behaviour. She wondered if this was a glimpse of her future.

Now and then, while in the saddle, Iaculous would raise a hand. A thin, blue glow would appear in the growing dark and fade quickly as he shook the light from his fingers. Arielle knew he was creating and controlling delicate fireballs and extinguishing them out just as swiftly. It unnerved her that he ignored the trauma of what had occurred before, when he had lost control. He viewed it as a challenge to master, and perhaps it was. Perhaps the more he weaved, the stronger he became.

Arielle could have asked him, but he would have never told her. For all the effort it usually took, he showed nothing more but a few deep breaths. However, these were only little balls of flame, unlike the torrent of wrath he had unleashed upon the grand cantuses. She wondered if he were lulling himself to arrogance and would he regret his missteps once again.

The wind blew soundlessly around them, and she rarely saw a bird above their heads. They had seen no towns along their route, and Arielle grew uneasy with so few signs of civilisation in this strange land. In parts where the dense forests of grey gave way to open land, they passed humble farms, which looked lost, desolate, and plagued by blight. A dead land. She knew Venistra was a place of few artists and poets, and now she understood why. There was nothing to inspire them but dreariness.

Arielle always thought Denan intense and broody, but growing up in a place like this, it was no surprise why he was, nor why he had little interest in ever returning home.

"I'm sorry."

She knew his tone. It was the tone Iaculous offered to Eralorien to appease the old man when he felt very little contrition.

"Do you know what for?"

"Setting fire to the tree and scaring you?" he offered in a different tone, one used by broken husbands when facing the vengeance of their dutiful wives.

Arielle wondered if this was a precursor to their life: he a troubled weaver and she a dutiful wife satisfied with his depthless emotional silence. No, she would never settle with that at all. She would be something great herself. Bereziel had always reassured her she was special.

"You scared me on the barge. You scared me when you burned!" she snapped.

Iaculous muttered a curse under a breath in frustration. This wasn't like him at all. He brought his horse to a stop, and she stopped with him.

"I didn't realise what I was doing. I merely did it. Sometimes things happen out of a weaver's control. Sometimes there are terrible repercussions. You can't know what it's like to go through what I did and come out the other side."

"Tell me, then," Arielle countered. Iaculous looked through her as though she was a stranger: a stranger he could open up to, apparently.

"There is so little we know about weaving the source, except that it is manipulating energy from another place."

Arielle knew all this but said nothing.

"They say when we die, our source energy or our souls, walk into the darkness beyond. This darkness is the other world, and a weaver is the doorway in-between. We are not godly wielders of this power. We can touch it momentarily and steal what power we can," he said, and she only knew some of this.

"Tell me more."

Iaculous smiled ruefully as though there was a greater understanding to his words she could not comprehend. "Most of what weavers achieve is through practice. There are few books on weaving, and those written say so little. A man could go mad reading for years and still learn nothing. Eralorien is my only guide in this world, so that is why things are as they are. I have little choice but to listen and steal what I can from him." He reached across and took her hand, a reminder of his love for her.

"You are worrying me," Arielle said and squeezed his hand in reply. It became unnaturally warm, and she released his grasp, lest he inadvertently burn her again. It would crush him if he hurt her again. It would crush her more.

"I know I have behaved strangely. I cannot explain why, nor can I help myself. Sometimes I want to cry out in frustration because I want to know it all," Iaculous muttered. His voice was deep and peculiar, and she realised it was the voice he used when he was invoking the source beyond his capabilities. She remembered his husk of a broken body.

"You weave, yet there is nothing out here in the night to enchant," she said, hoping to pull him back to himself. Perhaps it was just the loss of Heygar affecting him.

"There is something near, calling," he said, and a cold shard slid down her spine.

"We are close to Vahr. Let us finish this ride and sit among our comrades."

"No, Arielle. You go on without me. I must wander a while," Iaculous said strangely and dropped from his horse.

"Iaculous," she called.

She hobbled her horse next to his before chasing after him through the forest of grey. He did not wait for her, yet he did not run from her either. When she caught up with him, she felt the heat emanating from him. His eyes had become grey. With an audience, Iaculous continued talking, oblivious to the low-hanging branches and their grey leaves as they smacked him in the face as they walked.

"It started here only a few hundred years ago. The first weavers of the source were all Venistrian," he said, and she did not know any of this. "They spread out and sowed their oats throughout the seven lands of Dellerin. They wed and made children, and each generation was weaker than the next.

Their source weaving ability diluted and whittled out until few practised the old ways."

"Iaculous, come back, my darling," Arielle cried, but he was not listening. He was giving her a lesson. Hadn't she wanted to know this? The distant glow of Vahr disappeared beneath the clustered forest, and though she was with her future betrothed, she felt alone.

Then she didn't feel alone at all. She felt a dark presence around them and somewhere ahead, something even darker. She patted the sword at her waist and fell in step with him. "What is ahead?"

"You can feel it now, can't you?"

"Yes, and I'm scared." She felt lured towards the darkness. Perhaps beyond the next tree, it waited. Or over a little hill.

"I feel a hundred-fold what you feel right now. It consumes and embraces me." That strange, unearthly tone entered his voice, like a beast hidden beneath his skin was clawing to get at whatever called to them.

"This is wrong, Iaculous," she whispered and took his hand to bring them back to the path.

Iaculous suddenly kissed her, and Arielle felt the energy surging through her body. She had never felt such desire in her life. It was like walking a desert for a lifetime and being gifted a tankard of cooled water from an oasis. She fell to her knees, and he with her. They kissed, and she felt his passion. It matched her own. Arielle drank him in, and he drank her, and whatever fears she had felt disappeared entirely.

Then Iaculous broke the kiss. Arielle felt desperate, cold, and unfulfilled. As far as first kisses went, it was rather impressive, but it didn't feel like a kiss between soulmates. It felt like something equally powerful. Such was the price of imagining something beautiful for far too long, she thought.

"Your soul is more powerful than mine," Iaculous said in that strange tone and walked from her.

"Stay here with me," Arielle called back, but he had already left her.

THE ROCK OF IACULOUS

Arielle followed yet again. She did it because she needed to know what lay farther in. What pulled at him so severely? It also pulled at her.

"I can't seem to shake you, can I?"

"We are Hounds. We stick together."

"We were Hounds," he countered and shrugged.

"The kiss," she said and found no other words.

It had felt like a kiss goodbye and not the beginning of something wonderful. It crushed her—not at it being their last but more that it occurred in such a way. She had imagined their first kiss to leave her breathless without cessation as desire overcame her. She thought a kiss from a soulmate would stop her heart with pangs of ecstasy, but perhaps the anticipation could only ever allow a feeling of anti-climax.

"I've always wanted to. I'm glad I did," Iaculous said and marched onwards through the forest's dark.

The treacherous undergrowth and deathly grey leaves filled Arielle's mind with dread. She could not shake the thought that this would be her last march ever. Her limbs did not feel their own, as though possessed by an invisible being of menace. Yet, she took no rest until they came to a break in the forest overlooking an open glade free of any other growth. No tree was standing within a hundred feet of a tall rock in the centre, and it drew her to stare upon it.

It was black onyx. Smooth, pure, as tall as any man, and as wide as his stomach. It looked like a devil's clawed finger had broken through from the burning depths of its fiery domain below. Every few breaths, a light from within pulsed and shone through the stone until it became translucent. It burned her eyes as though she stared at the sun. What light was bright enough to shine through stone, she wondered. Despite her trepidation, she thought the rock beautiful.

"We should not be here," Arielle hissed to Iaculous, who had fallen to a knee as though in prayer.

"This rock is not of this world. This rock tears the goodness from the ground," he whispered.

Without warning, pain pierced Arielle's head like an angry blade, spinning and cutting. She remembered the worst hangover she had ever felt after drinking three nights with Heygar and Cherrie at the winter solstice, and this pain was tenfold. Blinding and disarming. As though someone had sent a cleaver through her head, into her mind. She screamed and collapsed beside him, and Iaculous did not react.

"You are too weak to be here, Arielle."

The rock pulsed once more, and his hands glowed a bright blue. She knew that of the two loves of his life, he was choosing the other, right in front of her eyes. Just like Bereziel did.

"Let us go from this ungodly place, Iaculous," she moaned and held her head as though she could somehow stop it from splitting in two. His disregard for her pain stung her, and though she wanted to curse him, she scrambled over to him instead. She had seen this happen before. His own weavings blinded him, as Bereziel had been at the end. Desire had driven him from Heygar's friendship, and not even Cherrie could sway him from such actions.

"Wait for me by the road," Iaculous muttered, and his hands became fists. He stared down at the rock like a cat eyeing its prey. "We are not alone," he whispered. He waved his hands in the air nonchalantly, and some pain dissipated. It felt merely like a needle through her skull.

"I can see nothing."

"Look to the edge of the far tree-line and listen."

Sure enough, without the debilitating pain blinding her, Arielle could make out six figures standing among the trees. They were dressed in long, hooded cloaks and stared at the pulsing rock.

"Can you hear it?" Iaculous whispered and crawled a little closer to look down.

Despite her apprehension, Arielle crawled with him. She listened and, after a time, heard it. They were singing.

"This rock is source energy in corporeal form. I could take a thousand wounds a thousand times and die as many times over and take only a fraction of what it possesses."

"How do you know this?"

"My master's teachings," he muttered as though accepting Eralorien's wisdom on such a strange thing was beneath him.

"And who are the figures?" Arielle asked warily. She had seen the lust of desire in men, and she saw it now in his desire for the power in that rock.

"They are acolytes of the darkness who worship this stone. They imbue it with their own souls and kill this land. None of them has any real power. Though I am an apprentice, I can feel their weakness from here," Iaculous whispered.

A wave of clear energy surged from the onyx monolith,

through each figure, and off into the glade and trees beyond. After a moment, there was another and then another. It reached out and touched Iaculous and Arielle as it did. Arielle felt as though an ice dragon had leapt upon her and numbed her senses, while he appeared invigorated with each pulse. His eyes faded over into the grey once again.

"Those fools sing to a rock and believe it to be a deity. They cannot feel what I feel," he growled as though in war.

It terrified her. He was drunk on the energies pulsing in the air. He would wake up the following morning with regret and weakness and realise he was still only an apprentice touching great things for the first time. Arielle knew this because Eralorien warned him loudly of this whenever he caught him pushing too far. Damn the old man, but he had been right.

Each of the hooded figures knelt in front of the rock, and their song intensified. It was primal and beautiful, and each note penetrated her soul like no other song ever had before. Arielle felt a wave of sudden warmth, and beneath her, the ground quaked.

"Do not follow," Iaculous said in that source-drenched voice.

"I will do what I must," she cried.

Despite the pain, she took hold of his shirt. Instantly, an invisible hand dragged her to the ground as though accosted by a rambunctious drunk eager for sport at the witching hour. It pinned her fast, and her body lost all strength. All she could do was breathe and ache.

How dare he.

"*DO NOT FOLLOW,*" she heard in her mind, and fresh pulses of pain surged through her head. It was a warning of Iaculous's power over her, a reminder to know her place.

Arielle felt his mind, his warmth, and his love. She felt

the frustrating struggle that came with desiring her body and soul over the energy of the source. She struggled from these unwanted emotions, but the harder she fought, the more she experienced. Could she ever forgive a man who hurt her like this?

Iaculous released her from his thoughts and left her lying in the damp grass on the verge. He released all holding of the pain in her mind in one last act of cruelty, so she would know never to interfere with his actions again. He left her to writhe in pain as he walked down through the glade towards the figures. It was as if he were out for a stroll in the paved streets of Dellerin city during the season of harvest.

The figures leapt to their feet as Iaculous neared, and a blinding flash of pain took her mind completely. Arielle moaned and called out for him, but he never answered.

Pain.

She finally understood pain like this. She had always questioned the pain ever since the first man. Throughout her life, her thoughts had never been far from the first man. Heygar had chosen the first man, and he had chosen well. Arielle had only been fourteen at the time, and though she had been no deity of innocence, after that night, she had become a woman.

Cherrie had dressed her down to look even younger than she was and added to the deception with the slightest dabs of paint to bring out her youthful features in just the right places. For the price of a bag of silver coins, a worker had unlocked the back entrance to the house of ill repute, smuggled her in among the rest of the frayed whores, and left her with a bag of sweetened almonds to suck upon, adding to the repulsive illusion.

Before the endeavour, Cherrie had tested her how best to entice. As they paraded her out in front of the bald man with the flat chin, she had played the part well. The first man had certain needs, and she was the only one capable of the task. Leaving his entourage of a dozen formidable protectors behind, he led her to a small room with silken sheets, rose petals, and the stench of shameful deeds. He had locked the door and set about destroying her. It wasn't enough he wanted to rape the innocence from her either. His tastes were nastier.

The first strike with a closed fist took her off guard, and she fell loudly to the ground, smashing the bedside table as she did. She had cried out in alarm, and her childish wails elicited a moan of pleasure from him. He picked her from the floor as though she were nothing but a child's doll. He managed two more strikes before she recovered her senses and retrieved the concealed weapon beneath the mattress.

Heygar had given her the option of a tool at hand, and she had chosen a suitable, if not brutal, piece. She recovered the cleaver, turned on him and swung fiercely without hesitation. It was six inches wide and four deep, and its sturdy wooden handle held expertly carved finger grips. It embedded itself in his head, and he dropped to his knees, gripping at the handle, but it would not budge from its place among matter and bone.

Arielle had waited for the screams and the splitting stream of blood to erupt and hasten her escape, but there was neither. Instead, there was a wet gasp and the sound of desperate scraping where his fingers tried and failed repeatedly to pull the blade free. He had slumped back, his face drooped, and his eyes stared separate ways, but the hands continued regardless. Somewhere among the ruin of his split-apart brain, a desperate attempt to survive kept him fighting. A stream of blood finally appeared on either side of the blade and with it, the realisation that the fight was done.

He had dropped one hand limply at his side just as he gripped the weapon. He pulled weakly before ceasing the fight altogether. He tried to scream, and his tongue fell from his mouth and hung to the side. He reached for her but not to kill, not even to hurt. When it came down to it, nobody wanted to die alone. Arielle had knelt down beside the dying man and took his hand. She bade apology to the beast for her doing and whispered how big a bounty he had earned. He hadn't screamed, for his mind no longer remembered how to cry out, but it remembered pain.

For years, Arielle had wondered what it must have felt like in those last few moments. As she lay sprawling in the grass in the middle of a forest of grey, weeping trees, she finally knew.

She held her head as though some nasty young girl had cloven it in two, and she cried for Iaculous again as he fell upon the figures. Their grey cloaks whipped out behind them as they formed up around him. Arielle wondered if they could sense his strength or if they were alarmed at his presence.

They fired black spheres of fire at Iaculous. Each projectile was closer to a cancerous ball of sputum than the fire forming around Iaculous's hands. It was always the dark against the light. She knew this well. The six fierce balls of fire engulfed and knocked him to his knees, and the figures surrounded him. The rock pulsed ferociously, and all the pain left Arielle completely. As all the source energy focused around the seven figures below and not on her delicate mind. It was as though it was a living, breathing beast.

The light in Iaculous's hands became a stunning blue fire around him. Like the pulsing wave from the rock, it shot out through the valley and up past Arielle, who ducked beneath its surging power. She felt a terrible burn across her face and screamed.

The flame disappeared as soon as it appeared. Around the edge of the tree line, branches smouldered, burned ochre, and then fell to ash. Down below, in the centre, Iaculous was the only man left standing. His assailants lay in a circle around him, patting down their own clothes as he had the night before. Arielle felt no phantom hold upon her anymore.

"Who do you serve?" Iaculous roared, and the glade shook. His hands pulsed blue and beautiful, but more than that, they pulsed in time with the rock he stood beside. He touched it absently, and both rock and weaver pulsed in perfect harmony at a frantic pace, like a flickering candle behind a stained glass lantern shade.

Without thinking, Arielle ran down the slope towards him. She feared for his life, his soul, and whatever came after.

"We serve the true leader, Mallum," hissed one acolyte. His hood had fallen away. His hair was silver, and his skin was wrinkled and broken.

"Where is he?" Iaculous demanded as though nothing in the world mattered but their master's fate. None of the acolytes gave answer. "*WHERE IS HE?*"

Arielle felt the air heat terribly as his words burned into her mind. She stumbled and tripped but somehow stayed upright. She reached him as he raised his arms into the air, and all six figures rose into the sky.

"Beyond the Hundred Houses, but you cannot beat him, Hound," another acolyte wailed. An invisible, godly hand spun and rolled him as though he were swimming playfully in a river.

Behind them, the hum of the rock grew, and Arielle saw large cracks appear along its side. The screams of each man rose as they floated higher. She had heard of strange things in tavern talk of great deeds when the source infused itself around a weaver with potential, but never had she imagined such terror. Their screams of fear were mixed with pitiful pleading for their lives as they rose deep into the sky and showed no sign of stopping. She couldn't make out their faces anymore.

"What has taken hold of you, Iaculous?" Arielle cried.

All around her, the world exploded in one final pulse of energy. She saw all six men fly off in six different directions across the night sky as if released by an airborne catapult. She watched in horror, knowing their fate, until a large piece of rock struck her across the face and knocked her from this world.

DAY THREE

The grey world was burning golden fire, and she stumbled around on shaky legs. Arielle could only remember darkness and the echo of their screams. She felt torn skin on her cheek and the warm, bubbling blood seeping out, making a ruin of her clothes completely. She wavered but caught herself before she collapsed. Her bloody hands shook as though she walked the frozen north.

Around her, trees immolated in flame and lit up the glade just enough for her to see the true devastation at Iaculous's cruel hand. Cruel. Just like Bereziel had become. She never thought Iaculous could turn like that, but men were men, weren't they? Perhaps more accurately, weavers were weavers.

Two of the acolytes lay strewn apart on the ground, their arms and legs torn from their bodies. Their last agonised expressions were etched forever on their faces and, in her mind, all nestled up safely with the bald man. The other four acolytes were thrown deep into the forest, and she doubted anyone would ever recover their remains. Being unable to do a thing but scream against rushing air filling your lungs as the ground appeared before you was no way to meet an end. Better you never see it coming.

Arielle shuddered and tried to clear her spinning thoughts.

The large, pulsing rock had disappeared from its place, leaving little more than shattered shards and rubble in its place. Iaculous was sitting among the ruins of the rock with crossed legs. In his hands was the bandoleer. He was placing the choicest cuts of ruined onyx into each glass. The rage he had shown had left him completely. He was a man at peace between ruin and devastation.

"Why did you do all this?"

"It needed to be done, my dear Arielle." He found a shard of stone, placed it into a jar, and resealed it. For a moment, the rock pulsed impressively and then dimmed to nothing. He ran his finger along the glass and returned to his search.

"What you did was brutal."

"We are Hounds," he said and held another shard of stone in the light of one of the burning trees. He grimaced, cast it aside, and reached for another. He was right. They were Hounds and capable of terrible deeds. Still, mercy could have been given. They had begged for it.

She felt her fury rise. As though all her frustrations were emerging once. "You held me down!" she screamed.

He held his search for a breath. "Oh … that. I'm sorry. I did it to protect you." His hands glowed, and she felt the healing of the cuts across her face. The pain gave away to stinging and then to barely anything after that. It didn't change a thing.

They had kissed. It had been lovely. It was ruined. "You will never earn my trust again," she hissed, worried her voice would break.

"You don't understand what it is like to be me," he

muttered and did not get up and go to her, to try and win back her favour.

She thought of the kiss again, and saliva formed in her mouth. She spat at the ground and turned away from him. "You are not the man I thought you were."

"I am a weaver first and a man second." After a moment, he called after her, "If you wait a time, I'll be along."

She cursed his stupidity. How could a man be so blind to what was happening in front of his eyes? He returned to examining his ruined stone, and she struggled to the top of the glade and glanced back over the edge one more time. She looked upon him and willed him to give chase as they did in those vulgar books of lovers Cherrie had read to her as a child. In almost every tome, the heroine always stormed off, and at the last moment, when tears were like rivers, it was then he pursued and rescued her. Foolish stories from foolish books. Iaculous did not follow her, and she found it strange that it did not crush her.

"I have lost you to another desire, it would appear," she whispered and left.

Arielle marched through the forest, spitting curses, allowing the temper she and her sister shared to reassure her it was his loss. She found the hobbled horses and, without looking back, rode the last leg of her journey alone.

By the time she reached the town of Vahr, she had shed tears and dried them. Iaculous's kiss had been examined, criticised, and condemned. She had decided that Mallum's evil head would earn a place on her mantle when the mission was over. She also decided she would keep cats, and this made her happy. Finally, she decided she would drink too much alcohol this evening, order the sweetest honey cakes, and devour them all by herself. This made her happiest of all.

Boys were boys. Arielle would be fine understanding

Iaculous would not be in her future. More than that, she felt a profound sense of relief, though she couldn't understand why.

The town of Vahr was closer to being a village than anything else. A few houses surrounded a tall tower of an inn in the middle of nowhere. She liked it very much.

Leaving her horse in the tavern stables near the rest of her comrades', she wondered if Cherrie and Eralorien might have spotted a flying weaver above their heads as they overtook them on the road. Cherrie would give her an earful for being so late, but she would allow Iaculous to explain what happened. They were his actions and his to explain in unpleasant detail.

Denan and Cherrie met her before she had taken five paces in. Arielle thought she might break down on seeing friendly faces, but she felt strangely liberated, like a pledged bride who had broken free of an arranged wedlock. She insisted that Iaculous would be along. Denan and Cherrie did not push the issue any further. Instead, they bade her a good night and disappeared upstairs.

After months of creeping around, they were finally openly freeing themselves of the guilt of Heygar. Let them have their fun behind four walls and wooden doors tonight, Arielle thought. There wasn't a town between here and their final destination, and though comrades on the march never said it outright, it was of the utmost rudeness to lie with your lover in earshot of those in your party while out in the wilderness.

Arielle watched them ascend the stairs, then she turned to look around the tavern and met the most unexpected of moment of her life. She saw her soulmate.

At first, she mistook him for Iaculous and realised how unfair it was to draw comparisons. Yes, they looked alike, but this man was a little older, better dressed, with a sharper jaw, and a kinder smile. Perhaps it was the way he carried himself, which reminded her so much of the boy. Or else the eyes, which looked as though they had seen an abyss of another world. Or perhaps it was that he sat next to Eralorien in a secluded corner of the tavern as they shared deep words over a couple ales.

Arielle believed in love at first sight, but more than that, she believed in lust at first sight. She very much wanted to meet this man and see what became of it. She mocked her youthful yearnings. She knew she was only reacting to what had occurred earlier, and she knew well the ways people behaved when spurned in love, hurt in lust, or spun by desire.

For tonight, she decided, the man would be the one to occupy her mind. And something strange happened. For the first time in three days, her thoughts were no longer tickled by visions of killing Mallum. Instead, they became settled as though the deed was done.

"To the fires with Mallum. I've had a tough day. It's time to smile," Arielle whispered to herself and felt wonderful. She knew how to play this game, for she had studied under an oblivious master.

She ordered two drinks and made her way through the crowd. Her eyes never left the man with black hair, chiselled jaw, and dark, exotic eyes. She liked his carefully kept beard with a moustache and his brightly coloured shirt, which was a silken red. She thought his fashion intriguing in such a place. This was a man used to standing out in every room he sat in.

"May I join you both?" Arielle said, joining them before either could offer argument. She sat opposite the man and thought him gorgeous up close. He raised an eyebrow at her sudden intrusion and caught a half-smile before it spread across his wonderful lips. She thought this charming and decided he was the perfect tonic to what ailed her.

"This is Arielle," Eralorien slurred and wavered in his

seat. His eyes were bloodshot, and they darted around the room. He was an awful drunk, and for a moment, she fretted for Iaculous having to assist the healer to his room. Then she remembered everything and considered offering the old man an entire bottle of wine for the journey.

"I'm Germanus of the Hundred Houses." Germanus took her hand and kissed it delicately. His grip was firm, and his kiss was dry. His beard was smooth, and he smelled like waterlilies. He charmed her, and she hid it all behind a veneer of disinterest. Not that it seemed to matter. He appeared uninterested in enticing her, and this drew her to him that little more.

"Arielle is the kindest little thing to walk this world," Eralorien said and winked as he did. The task almost knocked him from his chair. He suddenly grabbed at his head as though a terrible headache had taken him.

"Kind things are a difficult thing to find in this land," Germanus said warmly, though his eyes were upon the faltering weaver.

After a few breaths, Eralorien slipped from his chair. Like a flash, Germanus caught him. He held the weaver in muscular arms before patting his shirt as though tending to a loved one. He smiled at her, and Arielle decided he was making quite the first impression. Others might have let the old man fall. Iaculous would have, though he would at least have had good reason to.

"You have had at least three too many," Germanus said, laughing. The uncertain weaver batted him away with withered hands, and Arielle couldn't help laughing with him. She stopped herself swiftly.

Silly girl. Let him work for my favour.

"I've barely had three as it is." Eralorien's eyes were lost in a haze of merriment, but he was sincere. "Iaculous is a foolish one. He still thinks we can save him. Still thinks there is hope. No man can be that powerful." A stream of spittle escaped his mouth and died somewhere among his chest robes. Arielle had never seen him this deliriously drunk before.

"Let him do whatever he needs to do," she said and shrugged. If Iaculous still believed he could save Heygar, he was deluded. If he did somehow become powerful enough to return Heygar's soul, what could he do with it? Whose body could he return it to? Could he return it to another body?

"You bring out the most in him—good and bad," Eralorien slurred and drained his mug before attempting to take his turn with the gambling dice sitting patiently in front of him. He counted a few coins and tried to decide how much to wager before a kind hand held his roll.

"It is late. Perhaps we call it even, my friend," Germanus said.

The old weaver thought on this and, after a moment, decided that even was much better than losing everything.

"My head hurts from the tainted ale in this place," Eralorien declared and stumbled to his feet. "You, sir, are a true gentleman," he offered before bowing theatrically and wandering from the table, leaving Arielle, her two drinks, and Germanus alone.

"Was that supposed to be for me?" Germanus asked, looking at the second drink before reaching for his black cloak hanging behind his chair. In one fluid motion, he wrapped it around his neck. The black and red combination was striking. Was there anything he didn't do well?

"No, they're both for me," Arielle said and sipped the ale delicately. "You can buy the third round though," she added and held his gaze. His eyes were green, like the Everfields of the Fayenar. She wanted to drown in those eyes.

"Oh, but I am tempted. However, I have business, so I must regretfully decline your charming company this evening," Germanus said and bowed before standing to leave.

Arielle was crestfallen, and she didn't know why. She desired fun, laughter, and blissful distraction. Not another rejection, slight as it was. He must have read her face as she read everyone else's, for he hesitated and, after a moment's thought, he sat back down beside her and touched her arm. It wasn't a touch of desire or lustful threat. It was familiar and compassionate, and she wasn't at all prepared for it. Or for the kind look upon his face.

"Forgive my intrusion, but are you all right?" he asked, and her sorrow overcame her. It surged through her at his sudden display of compassion. Had anyone ever asked how she was?

"No, I'm not at all," Arielle sniffed. Before she realised, he was holding her in the warmest embrace she had ever known, and wonderful, relieving tears were flooding from her eyes.

AFTER THE BREAKUP

G ermanus's laugh was kind, but more than that, it was frequent. Arielle attempted wit, jests, and mockery of the world, herself, and everything in between. He laughed every time, even sometimes adding to her wit with a sharp retort of his own. They gleefully disturbed any patrons within earshot with raucous merriment, and it was time well spent.

He made her feel special, and she confided more than she normally would have. She had heard of amazing first meetings and dreamt of such things, but theirs belonged in a saga of its own. Germanus was what she needed when she needed it most. A good man.

The hours passed like fleeting breaths, and Arielle became enamoured with him. Even if he had shown hesitation at the beginning, she could feel his interest grow, among other things, she wondered wickedly. As though caught up in an enchantment, every time she thought of Iaculous or feared for the wasted time taken in Heygar's final mission, she felt more reassured that spending time with this man was for the greater good. She wanted to know him, and he allowed her to.

As interested in her tales as he was, she listened with equal enthusiasm to his own. He told her his life, though only because she charmed it out of him. His parents died in a fire when he was young, and only his younger brother and sister had survived the blaze. He lived in an orphanage until he was eleven, wherein he was sent out to forage for his own meal and shelter. His younger siblings were long since adopted, and he never saw them again. He had shrugged at his own misfortune when she had shown concern, for that was the measure of the man he was.

Growing up on the streets of the Venistra city of Aramas, without a penny to his name, he had flourished despite his wicked luck. Somewhere among the dens of thieves, houses of whores, and dark weaver's shrines, he had somehow earned a penny and another after that. By his late teens, he was rich enough to pull himself from the dredges of Aramas altogether and earn a place among the Hundred Houses in the richest region of Venistra.

Germanus was a merchant by trade and skilled at grinding out a tight barter. Such a skill was gold, and it brought him much, especially in places of turmoil like Venistra these recent years. They thought alike and enjoyed similar pleasures, but they did not agree on all things. He spoke critically of Dellerin and its vast reach throughout the realm. He spoke of Venistra's eternal struggle under the tight grip of the prejudicial King Lemier, and when she argued patriotism, he countered without giving ground. The battle was intoxicating. He spoke of his love for his people and scorn for the royals who stunted their progress, and Arielle listened and offered thought without insult, and he listened and agreed where he could. Though he was as passionate as she was, they never came to blows, for that is how people fell in love. It was through talk of Mallum that their final battle raged.

"He is the one royal with any sense of goodness. You critique a man who only wants to help starving people through treacherous times?" Germanus asked.

"I do."

"Do you even know what sins he has committed?"

"I do."

"Did you know Mallum attempted to meet with the king of Dellerin two times to offer peace between the regions? On both occasions, he narrowly escaped assassination attempts at the hand of royalty, yet still, he would happily return to Dellerin for the sake of his people. Not many royals can claim such selflessness," Germanus said.

Arielle didn't know this at all, but that wasn't the point. It didn't even matter they disagreed. She loved his passion. She loved his pride. Perhaps under different circumstances, his charisma might have swayed her thinking.

"Anyone in power has climbed atop blood and murder. Do you really believe Mallum a deity of innocence?" she asked.

"I do."

"Do you think Mallum would show mercy to the king were the roles reversed?"

"I do."

"I don't think it was honourable that he accepted an invitation twice and nearly paid for his trust. I think he was an idiot. Don't you think he was an idiot?" she asked.

Germanus laughed in defeat. "Your king may be wilier than mine. I find it interesting that a mercenary has outwitted me so easily."

Suddenly, she worried just how much she had revealed to him. How did he know she was a mercenary? Was he a spy?

He must have seen the concern upon her face as he smiled again. "Be still, dear Arielle. You gave little away. The old weaver is a terrible drinker. He told me his entire life over a half-game of dice. He also told me you ride with Denan of the Green. Perhaps I would have liked to have spoken with the great man, but instead, I find myself here with a delightfully charming mercenary. Hardly a disappointing evening."

"I'm no mercenary," she lied weakly.

Germanus took her hands, and they were cool and reassuring. He took them to his lips and kissed them gently. He had enchanted her magnificently.

"It wouldn't take a scholar to recognise a good man like Denan among your little group regardless of what was said. It is obvious why Heygar's Hounds are in this little town. You are here to complete a task, and though I think your quarry is the wrong leader, who am I to judge your service? Truthfully, whatever your intentions to Mallum are, they are your own. I do not know what made me sit back and meet with you Arielle, but know this: I never want this first meeting to end," he said.

Arielle's heart fluttered in excitement. The last few days of misery were fading away in this man's company. She wondered if Silvious hadn't had the right idea. She imagined running from the tavern that night with Germanus at her arm and decided that settling down as a young merchant's wife was a life worth living. Perhaps, after a time, she would bear him a child while she was at it. Maybe a pair of little ones and name them after his long-lost brother and sister. She imagined a life free of murder, death, and cleavers, and she pined for something new.

She shook her head half-heartedly. She would never have that life. She would charm this man, perhaps take him to her bed, and after a final kiss, leave him come the morning. She could have nothing beyond that. Could she? Probably not.

Iaculous entered the tavern late in the night, when most

patrons had disappeared into the bedrooms above or out into the night to walk the drunken shuffle home. It didn't take him long to present himself at their table. His clothes were singed, torn, and muddied; his hair a tangled, sweaty mess; his face drawn and exhausted. Compared to the man at her side, he was pathetic.

"You could have waited for me at the path," he muttered.

Arielle wanted to argue, but her tongue lost the will. She felt the heat emanating from his body, and she was wary.

"You could have followed."

"Are the others here?" he asked, and she eyed the stairs above. "Who is this thurken cur?"

The bandoleer jingled slightly as Iaculous passed it from one arm to the next. Arielle wondered if she could stop him if he flew into a rage and attacked her companion. She could. He had only strayed from the path; he had not lost himself yet.

"You look tired, my friend. Come sit with us and be merry," Germanus said amiably and stood up to offer Eralorien's forgotten seat. He stood above Iaculous and carried himself as though Iaculous was nothing more than a scruffy child, but he showed the boy respect despite the younger man's rudeness. Arielle liked this.

"Are you okay, my dear?" Iaculous asked in her mind. She recoiled for the invasion, and he winced.

"I am fine with the company, Iaculous," she said aloud and felt the heat dissipate.

"I was wrong," he said again in her mind, and she saw the blood drain from his face. All fight was lost. He knew his misstep, and he suffered his first hangover from drunkenly wielding the source's power. He would not be knocking on her door come the dawn to speak of things. He might never again.

Arielle nodded gently and tugged at Germanus's sleeve to return to his seat.

"I am sorry," Iaculous said aloud and offered a deep bow to both. Though the act looked as though it might tear him apart, he removed a silver coin from his pouch. "Please enjoy a drink on me."

For a moment, Arielle wanted to tell him that these things happened. That life was more than just these moments. Though her body might belong to another man tonight, who knew what lay ahead?

Iaculous left them to their quiet awkwardness at the table. Until he had disappeared completely, she could only stare at her ale and wonder if Iaculous's appearance was just one step too far to a beautiful merchant eager for a night's pleasure.

Germanus watched the weaver disappear upstairs. "So, that is the lover whom you fight with?"

"He is just suffering the loss of …" Arielle caught herself before she gave anything away. Stunning lover as he might become, she held her tongue as they had taught her.

"You are no longer seven."

She shrugged innocently enough and stole from his glass. Germanus moved closer to her, a subtle manoeuvre by a man intending to bed. He put his hands on her shoulders and pulled her to him in one more sympathetic embrace. He did not linger, however, and he charmed her again.

The hours passed, and the tavern eventually emptied entirely. Germanus, ever the gentleman, settled the debt, and before she knew it, they were sitting alone in a secluded corner of the inn with only a solitary candle and the dying embers of the tavern fire as their light. She had never felt more snug in her life. She lost all thoughts of Iaculous beneath his eyes and smile. After hours of learning much of each other's thoughts, hopes, and loves, there only remained the delicate dance of desire.

"I know I'm just a piece of meat to make your boyfriend jealous," Germanus said and rubbed her fingers with his own. She couldn't remember how long they had been holding hands. Perhaps since the barkeep had bid them a good sleep.

"Who said I would dine upon such things tonight? Perhaps I've lost the taste for that," Arielle countered and dared a biting of the lip.

There was no one else around. They could do anything they wanted on the floor, in front of the fire, or perhaps even on their table. Imagine turning to her grandchildren and shocking them with illicit tales of their grandparents' first night of meeting, many years from now.

"Perhaps you haven't had the right cook," Germanus whispered and laughed at his own unoriginality.

"Oh, wow. Let me remove my clothes for you immediately," she mocked, and he blushed. This was quite the accomplishment in this light.

Then he turned serious. "Could I convince you to stay in this town a little longer? Can I convince you of something beyond the morning? I'm not one to trip under a girl's beauty, but whatever happens, I will not spend the rest of my life wondering if I should have asked," he said clumsily.

For a smooth merchant, it was rather endearing to see him so uncomfortable. He felt the connection too. What had started as a simple meeting in a tavern might very well have interesting complications. His meaning was clear: he desired more than a night of passion. Cherrie would argue that all every man ever desired was a night of passion and a little more. Her sister would insist that every man might say everything under the sun to get that night. Was Germanus such a man? Did it really matter? Arielle thought of

Silvious's choice once more. He had taken a leap of faith. Why couldn't she? Why shouldn't she?

"Let us see after tonight, my dear," she whispered.

Arielle leaned across, and their lips met passionately. Like Iaculous before, she felt his energy as their tongues touched, and Germanus devoured her with passion. He lifted her from her chair with his strong arms and held her aloft as though she were little more than a doll. He spread her across the table, and she giggled. So did he. Their goblets crashed to the floor and the candle with it. The red glow of the fire behind them remained their only light, and it was perfect.

"The source sent you to tempt me, didn't it?" he whispered passionately.

Arielle wrapped her legs around his waist. "You love the temptation, my dearest Germanus," she replied and ripped his shirt free of its buttons.

He could have left, she thought suddenly. He was out the door, and now he was with her.

He ripped her vest down through the centre and exposed her chest. Arielle froze for just a moment, and then she kissed his clenched fists as they tore the garment away completely.

"That's not my true name," he whispered, and she didn't care. His real name could be the Venistrian king or the high priest of Dellerin. She only cared for this moment.

"Tell me, and I will howl it loudly," she cried and then moaned as he removed his trousers. After a few moments, she felt him pull her own garments free of her body.

Soulmates were to love and lust in silk and divinity. When they offered each other the divinest of gifts, it was to be in a far better place than atop a stained table of oak in a corner of a tavern a few hours after meeting.

Germanus stood over her but made no move to seal their passion. She took him in and touched his chest. He was naked but for a silver chain with an encased crystal pendant around his neck. It glowed in the light of the dying fire. She slid her fingers down to his vigorous manhood, and he sighed at her touch.

"Could love best the presumed evils of this world?" he whispered and held her hand, lest she stop or, better, pull him nearer.

"Could you love an evil like me?" Arielle giggled and pulled gently.

"I feel connected to you, though I'm not sure how," he whispered. He resisted her urging like a desperate drowning man, who, on the precipice of the deep, still attempted to stop himself from pulling his rescuer down into savage, unforgiving rapids.

"Soon enough, we will be connected," she teased.

Arielle desired him more than any man she had ever craved. She loved him. She loved him from the moment they had met. He'd loved her too. She could see it in his eternal eyes, even as he spoke a terrible, terrible thing.

"I am Mallum."

Not like this.

Her mind spun as though torn and shaken, and all she could taste was love. Bitter, cruel love as sweet as a Ciritis lemon. She formed a fist and almost struck—her mind awash with hatred and duty and a luring need to kill this beautiful man. But she felt a similar lure to love him. Did he enchant her? Was he enchanting this lust to spin her wavering mind? He had almost left. He might have understood her fragility and took what pleasure he could. A monstrous thought. Mallum was a monster, wasn't he?

She didn't strike him. Her rage became heaving lust, and she whipped her legs back behind his rear and trapped him there firmly. Somewhere in her thoughts, where duty spun her measure as a human, she fought hard to hate him. Her instincts begged her kill him, to rip his thurken heart out and mount him as he died in front of her. But she did not kill him. Instead, she looked into his eyes and realised he waited for her to decide.

"Enter me," she cried out and kissed him.

He did as she asked. She screamed louder than she had ever done in her life. Far away, she heard her voice and she couldn't help herself. The building itself shook in her pleasured cry, and she knew Iaculous could hear. She didn't care. She only cared about his thrusting and her own with him. It was poetic and rhythmic, and she never wanted him to stop.

Time never mattered. In the dim light of his glowing chain, she saw his beautiful body against hers, and she only wanted this life with him. Arielle lost all thoughts of Heygar's final mission beneath his love, and she climaxed. Deep within, she felt him near his end. He lifted her from the table as passion overcame him like a beast, and she loved every moment.

The glow of his chain and the little crystal at its centre pulsed like the rock, and she felt the splitting of her head and the vision of the bald man. She felt Mallum empty himself, and her breath caught in her chest. His hands glowed like the crystal and blinded her. She felt him kiss her naked body, but she was powerless to move. She felt herself float towards him and above him all in the same moment.

She heard him laugh, and she tried to laugh with him, but tiredness called and with it, an eternal feeling of peace and contentment. All around her, the world shook, and she lost her breath completely. She saw her last breath in a fading white veil of energy as her soul disappeared from her body to nothing. She was not afraid, though she knew she should be.

Arielle watched him pull away from her corpse, and she saw her eyes were open. Her face was etched with lust and completion. He left her naked upon the wooden table. This time, she cried out, but her voice would not come.

She floated above her lover, and something far away called at her. It was familiar and warm, like family. She sensed Silvious's lament, and she floated away from the world she knew until something pulled at her, something unnatural and unwanted.

Mallum the Evil stood below her with one glowing hand outstretched towards her. She floated back to him, and all fight was hopeless. Closer and closer to his chest she came until, in her last desperate moments, she saw his beautiful eyes one last time as she felt him trap her inside the glowing crystal at his chest and then all went to terrible darkness.

INTERVAL

"Ah, now I see what's happening with this story," Rhendell said, leaning back against the bed of old books he had manoeuvred into something resembling a support. Somehow, despite his injury, he appeared perfectly comfortable. Every child liked a bedtime story, she supposed.

Erin wiped her eyes and stretched her neck. She couldn't remember a time she had been drawn into a book so fiercely. It felt as though an enchantment were cast around her. It was a fine way to while away the worry of waiting for soldiers to storm through the doorway, drag them out into the streets, and face a little bit of execution for sedition.

"That the character di—"

"We don't know if Arielle is dead!" Erin snapped before he could finish the words. She didn't want Arielle to be dead. It didn't seem fair. She didn't like this book, yet she thought it amazing. It was a fine distraction altogether.

"Okay, well it sounds like he thurked the life out of her."

"That's just lovely," Erin mocked. She turned the page, hoping to see what became of the innocent and remarkable Arielle.

"Well, does it start with a new character's point of view?" Rhendell asked, though his attention was with the window above them.

"Perhaps."

"She's dead."

Erin heard it now too. The unmistakable sound of a dozen acolytes in armour marching through the streets below. She left the book, hid behind the curtain and peered to the ground far below. They were out searching for stragglers with blades and staffs in hands and nasty hoods upon their heads.

She hated The Dark One's acolytes dearly, for they were weak-willed weavers who obeyed without question. Their crimes were just as cruel as their master's and perhaps worse, for their power and reward was paltry.

She watched them below as they spread out to check the houses of this quarter. She knew it was only a few pulses before they turned their attentions to their sanctuary. She held her breath as they congregated at the front gate.

The sky had opened a little, and she could see a thin slit of blue. Erin smiled bitterly. At least she had seen the sky one last time. She would fight from this room, she decided. There was only one doorway, and perhaps they had little command of the terrible fire.

Her head spun, and she realised her exhaustion. She almost stumbled again, but as before, it passed. By the time it did, something fortuitous had occurred. The acolytes dispersed and continued their hunt, leaving theirs as the only house unsearched. They welcomed such luck after such horrors, she thought, seeing them disappear down through countless alleyways and streets.

"They missed us," she whispered and undid her ponytail, absently releasing the long brown curls down her back.

"It's a big city. They can't check every house," Rhendell

said. His eyes were glassy, but colour had returned to his face.

They sat in silence for a time, grateful and somewhat shaken by how near they had come to disaster. Eventually, it was Rhendell who spoke.

"So, tell me. Who is next after Arielle's death?" he asked, making himself comfortable once more.

"They are The Seven. They are capable of many great things. I bet you three whole rations she makes it through," Erin said.

"I'll take that bet. Skip to the end. Find out who lives."

"No, I don't think we should read this book in such a way," she snapped.

"Well, can I look? I won't say a thing," Rhendell pledged.

Shrugging, Erin passed the book across with limbs she felt were not her own. She realised that exhaustion was draining her completely, yet she couldn't imagine sleeping away what might be the last day of her life. As he took hold of the book, he sighed and nodded thoughtfully.

"No, this is stupid. This is a good way to spend hours. It would be a waste to ruin it. Forget the bet. This book deserves better than childish wagers." He passed it back as though it contained some dreadful disease atop its faded surface.

"I really don't think she's dead. I feel it in my bones. I think something bigger is going on with this tale," Erin whispered and found her page.

"So do I," Rhendell agreed.

THE OLD MAN

E ralorien never slept anymore. Well, that was not entirely accurate. He slept but only when the seeping pain in his body allowed. When the headaches dragged him to oblivion. If he had the skill to cast an enchantment of slumber upon himself, he would. And as for healing his own pain? Well, that was well beyond his skills as a healer.

There was no cheating the natural order of things. This he knew all too well. At some point around the witching hour, his mind finally wandered and tricked his grasp on this world. He remembered strange visions of lurid yearnings and a thousand wounds, and to his disappointment, he awoke just as fatigued. Moreover, he woke to find himself in a compromising position.

Tears of exhaustion streamed down his face, and a desire to complete Heygar's last mission suddenly overcame him. Eralorien gasped and felt a great darkness drawing upon him. Beams creaked around him, followed by the terrible cracking of wood. He roused himself, so he could shake this waking dream from his mind.

He sat up, the room shook, and he felt old. So very old.

He was seventy years old. Some would say he was terrifically old, and he would not disagree. He would not live to eighty.

"Some things age can't slow, can it?" he whispered to his manhood as it stood to attention. He felt embarrassed and a little ashamed. He had enjoyed the time alone with Cherrie. He always had—even if it was torment. He very much doubted she would feel the same way. He wondered could he sway her eventually.

"The room shouldn't be shaking this much," a little voice in his head whispered. Eralorien silenced it with a grunt as he climbed from his bed.

Each time he rose, he gave thanks to the source and the demons who guarded the gateway from there to here. He knew little of the seven beasts or the seven gods in the source —save that some reckless weavers claimed to have seen their movements. It seemed the less he slept, the more he thought of them. He wondered, on his deathbed, might he leap into the darkness and seek them out himself? Would he show daring for once in his life? Probably not. He liked his soul, ravaged and aged as it was. He didn't want a fabled demon chomping down upon it.

The room continued to shake, and Eralorien glanced to his young apprentice asleep among a few cushions and their bags in the room's corner. He had heard Iaculous come in, and he had also heard the hour of weeping once he nestled in for the night. Eralorien should have felt miserable for the pain inflicted upon his young apprentice, but he didn't. It wasn't in him. He hadn't offered warmth to the child in many years, so what point was there in starting when he was finally beaten to a pulp by love? Arielle slipping into the arms of another might be the best thing for the young man.

In one of his less lucid moments, he had considered waking

Iaculous, so his young apprentice could hear the loud moaning rising through the levels of the tavern. He had listened to each passionate outburst as she severed her bond with Iaculous, and Eralorien had enjoyed every moment despite himself.

Then his mind had wandered to thoughts of her older sister. Oh, how he would have loved to give Cherrie that pleasure. Without warning, desire had come upon him as though he were a youth discovering his manhood for the first time. Shameful and exciting. His hand had slid to his lap, and he had thought of bringing alive sordid fantasies.

It had been years since he had needed such reliefs, and tragically enough, he had ignored an old friend and fallen asleep mid-movement. How awkward would that conversation have been come the harsh light of day, had he slept through the night and Iaculous woke him in such a state of undress? He was well endowed; it was hard to miss.

Sorry, Iaculous. I was listening to your future wife get poked impressively by some chance patron, and it was so salacious that I imagined poking her sister in such a way. Now today's lesson will be about enchanting someone to forget unsavoury things ... he imagined himself saying and sniggered despite the juvenile embarrassment. Perhaps that was why he sniggered.

Then the support beam above him collapsed, taking half the ceiling with it. A strange thought occurred to Eralorien. Perhaps the room was, in fact, shaking.

"Wake up, Iaculous!" he shouted. He pulled himself from his bed completely and wrapped his cloak around him.

All around him, a cloud of dust engulfed the room, covering his eyes, and he coughed heavily through blackened, scarred lungs. The world around him shook as though he were balancing atop a charging mount. He stumbled and fell fiercely against the bedding, knocking whatever senses he still had from himself.

"Iaculous!" he cried again, but the young weaver made no stir despite a large clump of plaster falling loose and rapping his shoulder. His sleep was unnaturally deep. As though he was enchanting in a trance or more likely enchanted.

But by who?

Eralorien felt unnatural energies pulsing all around him. There were dark moves afoot, and he was blind without a candle to light his way to the doorway. He climbed to unsteady feet and cried one last time for his apprentice. The floor at his feet cracked. Against his better judgement, Eralorien stepped into the dark world of the source to discover what evils were weaving so fiercely that the tavern itself shook.

Ominous shivers ran up his tainted spine, and for a moment, Eralorien no longer felt like the ancient weaver he was. Instead, he felt renewed by the other world being so close. The teasing call of power whispered to him louder than any voice in his mind, and he resisted it as he always did. He would die whenever he was to die. Weaving would have little to do with it.

He tasted the sensation of a healthy body for a few breaths, and then he rejected it completely and stepped into the shroud of the source. Though his body was still in the real world, his soul travelled through another.

Eralorien felt out into the darkness for what caused such ructions. He rarely took more than a few steps into this misty darkness. He dared not step another as a terrible presence revealed itself to him, though he did not think it meant to do so. He could feel it, sense it, and he somehow knew it moved. He sensed its desires, for they were terrible.

Eralorien felt something draw the beast to this world from

somewhere below in the building. Perhaps this was, in fact, a dream. He peered into the darkness, where the beast would dwell. All he saw were terrible, demonic shadows creeping towards the world of man, called forth by a cataclysmic event, creeping towards the souls of all who he cared for. He thought he sensed Silvious. He knew he sensed Heygar too.

Then he heard the wailing bray of the beast, an ancient cry of such torment and hate and evil, like an entire herd of brahmien bulls crying as one. It cut through his mind and soul.

"Flee, you fool," the voice in his head hissed.

Eralorien suddenly drew himself from the world as though surfacing from a fathomless river. He gasped and felt the divine source energy overcome him as he enchanted a shield of protection to cover himself completely. He did it without thinking, and it weakened his body once more. He fruitlessly attempted to pull himself to his feet and discovered, warily, just how warm his skin was.

"It wouldn't suit to burn this cloak to ash," he said aloud to steady his nerves and instil the steel he needed for his nerve.

Summoning his will, Eralorien climbed to his feet once more. The terrible shaking was subsiding. Whatever evil had occurred was slipping away, but it left devastation in its wake. Outside, he heard some people fleeing the shaking land in panic. Still, Iaculous made no move, and Eralorien left him to his enchantment. With withered, broken fingers gnarled by arthritis and age, he unlocked the door and felt the pure, pulsing wave of energy strike him.

"Someone has taken a delicious soul tonight," the voice in his head screamed. Eralorien grabbed his ear, lest he go deaf. How long had a voice been talking to him anyway? Mere moments, he imagined.

The hallway pulsed with a dozen panicked patrons of the tavern. They stumbled and held the wall for support, but the shaking was fading away to nothing. Most were in a state of undress, and some of them had packs of belongings. Some believed the shaking to be a natural and frequent Venistrian curse of the land and returned to their beds while others dared not stay in this tall building a moment longer.

Their unease concealed the terrible truth of what had occurred, and as they fled the corridor down the stairs, Eralorien sensed the awfulness of her. Or, more accurately, he sensed the awfulness of her absence. He also felt her destroyer, and it terrified him.

And then he heard Cherrie's screams.

AWKWARD INTRODUCTIONS

E ralorien charged out into the hall, his knees popping
angrily with the effort. He couldn't help but follow the
agonising wails of lament, for no man would ever wish to
hear such sorrow and cower away from it.

Despite his age and brittleness, he was reckless in his
desperate attempt to get to her. There was a crowd running
with him as they fled the tavern out of a selfish desire of
survival, and he charged through them all with elbows
swinging, so he might descend quicker. His body resisted,
and his weakening bones cried outrage at the exertion, but he
was relentless. Within a few pulses, he was down the first
flight. A few aggressive steps after that, he was on the last
landing of the stairs, looking down on the killer a few feet
below.

Cherrie stood in the middle of the tavern. Her howling
had ceased, and she gasped in anguish. The guests, bruised
and panicked, flooded past Eralorien and fled out into the
night, lest the building collapse. In their haste, they missed
the scene of tragedy, and why wouldn't they? The horrors

were hidden away in the snuggest corner of the tavern, and none of them knew who the girl was anyway.

Germanus wrapped a robe around his body. His hands glowed an unnatural light in the darkness. Beside him, Eralorien saw the still body of Arielle laying atop the table, legs spread apart as if mid-coitus. Eralorien's head spun as though a bottle of finest sine was downed in one daring wager. He fell against the bannister, and opposing thoughts of Heygar and Cherrie struck his mind. Finish the mission or tend to Cherrie's melancholy?

Something enchanted him. It tore at his mind until a terrible moment of clarity occurred to him like a shattered wall in his exhausted mind. Everything here was wrong. Why were they in Venistra? Now they were three Hounds down, one of whom was their leader. To stay another day in this vile land was lunacy, yet something bound him to finish the mission. Someone lured them like a giant fish to the light.

Eralorien grabbed his head and groaned; he felt a change in the air as though a great beast of the darkness took a deep breath and stole all of his around him. He knew it was the movement of the source, though he could not understand why it focused upon Germanus, the easy mannered trader he had shared a game of chance with, the man who had been overly eager to speak with their leader. Eralorien had sensed little malice in the man, but the great weavers could make things appear as they chose, could they not? Germanus had taken Arielle's life, and it was only a pulse before he turned on Cherrie and delivered the same fate.

"What did you do to her?" cried Cherrie. She struggled to charge upon the vile man, but her body remained statue-still.

Eralorien sensed the weaving and the invisible hold Germanus had upon Cherrie. He was flustered and held out his hand, and Cherrie fought him but to no avail. She was helpless to his yearnings. Ripe for the plucking. He had taken the child. Now it was time for the main meal.

He didn't know why he did it, nor how his body allowed itself to behave so irrationally. Perhaps it was love. Perhaps it was seeing the frozen dagger in Cherrie's hand a couple feet from her prey. She had almost made it to Arielle's killer before he held her in place. Perhaps with the correct amount of lunacy and disregard for his own welfare, he might distract Germanus's hold, so she could reach him.

With thoughts no longer clear, Eralorien leapt onto the bannister and threw himself from the stairs down to the dark weaver below. A fine leap and a decade earlier (perhaps a few stone heavier) he may have collided with his quarry. As it was, something caught him mid-leap. An invisible grasp of energy flung him across the room violently. It was enough to distract his vanquisher though, and Cherrie leapt upon the man, stabbing brutally as she did.

Eralorien collapsed upon the table occupied by a naked dead girl, and both crashed to the ground in a terrible spinning mass of skin, limb, and lifelessness. Her dead body landed on him, and they met eye-to-eye. She still took a breath, and for a moment, he thought she was still alive. Really though, he knew there would be no happy ending for this girl.

She still lived, but her soul was absent and lost to them. Her chest heaved slightly, and her eyes remained vacant and unblinking, stolen by a cur who took his pleasure and then her essence. He had always believed his master was lying when he suggested such things were possible. Arielle had experienced a fate worse than death.

He heard Cherrie screaming as she dug her blade into Germanus, but Eralorien could only stroke Arielle's cheek and slowly drape some of her clothing over her shame. Who would tell Iaculous of his love's terrible fate? Who would tell him that her soul could be used for dreadful things now? He knew why the demon in the source had been lurking near. The energy in such an act tasted delicious.

Eralorien spun away from the girl. Renewed by hate, he summoned a shield upon himself and willed himself to return to the fight. His head pulsed with pain, but he ignored its hold as he did with every battle.

Cherrie had plunged deep into the man a second time when Germanus suddenly struck her fiercely across her brow with a fist. Stunned from his unexpected recovery, she fell back momentarily. She returned with dagger raised again only to meet the weaver's holding enchantment once more. She tried to block, but the weapon was no Venistrian blade. He threw her across the room, leaving the dagger to fall harmlessly where she stood.

Before she landed, Germanus caught her with the invisible grip and hoisted her high into the air, like an angler bringing in a burdened line. The power emanating from his hand was incredible. He swayed his fist out as if in water, and Cherrie imitated the movement. He twisted his fist to the side, and Cherrie spun to her side. Her nightdress spun open, and Eralorien caught sight of more skin than ever acceptable. He was ashamed that he held his attack momentarily as he watched her writhe in the weaver's hold.

The world slowed to a pulse. Cherrie danced for him in the air, and her magnificence hypnotised him. Her hair moved as though each red strand were alive in fire and held by a thousand obliging fingers, all swaying to her movement. She was graceful and beautiful. Eralorien thought about her moaning like her sister, and he wanted to tear the rest of her clothes free. The terrible spinning in his head returned, and he felt an overwhelming compulsion to beg the weaver to grant him her body. Then they would be away into the night with no further trouble.

"Is that what you want? There is no loss in asking," the voice asked nastily.

Eralorien pulled himself from these dreadful thoughts as though woken from a month-long sleep. "Leave her be, you animal."

He threw what little enchantment energy he had upon the dark weaver. It was a clear, faded blue pulse, barely visible in the dim light. It shot out like an arrow and pierced Germanus's heart, who fell to his knee and released Cherrie. It was the first time in a decade that Eralorien had cast a hostile enchantment, and his knees lost all their strength. He felt he aged a year in that moment.

Cherrie fell awkwardly and crumbled beneath a wooden table, discarded chairs, and broken goblets, breaking each one with her beautiful face. Eralorien charged again, picking her fallen blade as he did. It was a fine blade, with a carved tendercat's tusk as its handle, a silver blade of ice-stone so thin that it was near transparent but as sturdy as a bridge's support beams—and sharper than almost all other metals ever forged.

Germanus was slow to turn, and he collapsed to the ground as the old weaver fell upon him and continued the assault begun by Cherrie. Eralorien stabbed violently as Germanus's hands punched, scratched, and blocked his relentless attack. Ten, twenty strikes to his chest, his face, his neck, his groin, and still no final blow stopped the man from fighting back. Eralorien's fingers burned from his touch, and he sensed the healing occur swifter than they dealt damage. How could anyone take this punishment and still live?

The amulet chained around the reaver's neck almost blinded him. Eralorien sensed its dreadful power and what its source was. He stabbed uselessly, knowing this murder would never occur. Blood sprayed into his eyes, and as swiftly as it appeared, the surging spray dissipated to nothing.

"Enough of this," Germanus hissed suddenly. He heaved Eralorien from him as though he were little more than a child's rag doll, sending him across the room to land in a painful heap with a forceful shove.

"Why did you do this?" screamed Cherrie, climbing through the rubble to get to him. Her shredded face should have caused her to hesitate, but nothing would deny her vengeance.

Eralorien could only marvel at her strength and draw his own from it. He reached for anything to support him, and with the mantle of the fireplace as his ally, he climbed to his feet. It was scant consolation, but though he knew he would die this day, at least he would die beside her. More importantly, when she died, it would be at his side and not Denan's. Denan. Where was Denan in all this?

"Why did you come hunting?" Germanus countered, and Eralorien charged again. Germanus raised his hand and fired a sphere of black energy, which struck him and exploded in a deathly plume of pulsing smoke and fire across his chest. Eralorien collapsed against the tavern's counter as the flame consumed his body in maddening pain.

"This is what death is," the voice in his head added.

Eralorien endured searing pain like nothing he had ever experienced before. It burned into his body, and he felt his skin blister, bubble, and split open. Though he tried to counter the strike with healing, his breath left him completely.

"This is what Iaculous felt."

Eralorien tugged at his clothes as they smouldered and melted. The smell of his own decaying flesh was awful. He pulled his robes free and watched his skin burn, char, and continue to cook. He screamed and placed his healing hands upon his chest, but he only spread the terrible burning to each hand.

"Mallum!" Iaculous cried from the stairs, and Eralorien felt a healing wave of energy flow across him and fight the blaze of torment.

BATTLE ROYALE

Mallum eyed the young weaver standing atop the staircase, looking far more impressive than he ever had in his young life. Deep within the writhing mess of his burning chest, Eralorien felt his healing take hold. Suddenly, he could taste air again as the holes around his lungs sealed up and returned to their original state. The healing was strong and reassured and not of his own hand. Eralorien knew it was his apprentice's doing.

Eralorien had always done his best to keep the young man's ability curtailed and focused upon healing, but the child was becoming a man with potent ability. Eralorien doubted he was prepared for that.

As if to prove this, Iaculous struck the first blow. A perfect sphere of burning flame erupted from his palm. He threw it as if skimming a rock across a river's surface, and the room exploded in fire as it struck their quarry upon the head. He followed up with a second and then a third. Each sphere was a perfect circle with just a tail of flame behind it. Though it had only been a day since he had attacked the monsters with wilder fireballs, he threw these as if he had been doing it his entire life. His body did not burn as it did before either. Was Iaculous finally becoming the weaver Eralorien thought he could become?

As if to defy the younger weaver, Mallum countered with fire of his own. He threw three at a time, and they lit up the room like a deathly sunset. Iaculous met each volley with crossed hands, and the flame dissipated as they struck.

It was a fine defence but not without cost. Eralorien felt the sudden decline in his body, and he willed his own healing to finish the task.

Iaculous knocked volley after volley aside, but the exertion was too much. Finally, a stray fireball struck him and knocked him over the edge of the staircase to the unforgiving ground below.

"You dishonourable brutes hunt me down and expect me to give up my life silently. All so you might line your pockets with blooded gold?" The ground shook with Mallum's words.

Eralorien's yearning to kill Mallum brought him to his feet. Though, it was as much the will to save Cherrie, earn her desire, and thurk her until the fifth day.

"You are our quarry. You must die," roared Denan, arriving late at the gathering, as was his annoying tendency. Perhaps had he not exhausted himself with his lover he would have woken sooner to such clamours. Perhaps had he not taken the time to don his finest armour, he could have reached them much sooner. As it was, he charged down the stairs with his gleaming green blade held out in front of him looking impossibly heroic, and Eralorien hated him.

"How could Cherrie not desire such a reckless god?" the little voice in Eralorien's head hissed, and Eralorien believed the voice to be right.

Denan took three steps at a time and leapt the last ten, coming to a smooth landing at the bottom of the stairs. He was a nervous leader but a fierce warrior. Some said he matched Heygar in battle. Some said he even bettered the legend. Neither had ever fought, for it was better they never knew the truth.

"Perhaps if he died, you could take Cherrie as your own," the voice purred, and it was a fine opinion. Each word pulsed like a dagger in his mind. Blinding his will to persistent agony.

"Get out of my thoughts."

"Not yet."

Mallum turned on Denan, and for a moment, he hesitated. "Nothing here can be undone. Is there no point in attempting a peaceful resolution?"

"Peace? No peace," snarled Denan, and only then did Eralorien see the fatigue in Denan's face, as though Cherrie herself had drained all his vigour.

Without warning, Mallum released a volley of fireballs upon Denan, who met each with a confident strike of his blade as though playing a game from another world. Eralorien had never seen such a thing in his life, and neither had Mallum, who cursed and retreated from the charging Venistrian.

"Come die at my blade, cur!" Denan roared magnificently.

"Nice sword. You could slay a demon with that," the monster hissed bitterly and skulked away from the charging Denan.

Be they king, lord, pauper or weaving brute, when the Hounds fell upon someone, it did not matter how many swords they called upon, nor how much weaving they controlled. The Hounds always found a way. Mallum must have known this, for his confidence appeared to shatter. He appeared as though fighting Denan was the last thing in this world he desired. For a moment, he looked less the maniacal dark weaver of deathly demonic enchantments and more a terrified young man facing his death after murdering one of their own.

For a breath of time.

Mallum gestured as he had with Cherrie, but Denan crashed through his invisible assault as though it were little more than a thin veneer of a spider web. Only reflex stopped Mallum's head from being decapitated and ending the matter there. He spun beneath the slash and threw himself backwards over a table before rolling away.

Denan followed, swinging wildly and knocking tables and chairs to splinters. As he did, he appeared to recover his fatigue with each breath while Mallum slithered like a snake and avoided the strikes by his skin and teeth. Though smaller in stature than Heygar, in that moment, Denan was just as imposing. Eralorien cursed, seeing Cherrie rouse herself and look upon her man bringing the fight to their prey. Mallum countered with fire, but all met an end beneath Denan's swinging blade.

Spinning away gracefully, Mallum earned a reprieve to beg for mercy. "I would have offered you all a hundred gold apiece just to sit and speak with me, but I could see the madness in your eyes, Denan of the Green," Mallum called. He slipped out of reach of Denan's blade and manoeuvred himself back towards the main door.

"We would never accept peace with you, monster," Denan growled.

Eralorien agreed despite himself. There was deceit in the man and a silver tongue to him. Precarious things.

"Denan should have killed him by now," the little voice pointed out, and Eralorien also agreed with this.

"You couldn't accept my word. There is a lured madness

upon you all that you cannot see, the lure torments you all, it rips souls away," Mallum roared bitterly. "You fools!"

With Denan close enough to strike, Mallum attacked one last time. He brought a fire fiercer than the fire Iaculous had used. Eralorien felt the burning from across the room, and for a wonderful moment, he thought it might burn Denan to ash. But Denan did not burn to ash. He ducked under a searing trail of fire and slashed the blade down fiercely. Mallum took the strike across the chest and howled like a beast slain. He fell away, leaving a streaming surging river of blood behind.

Whatever enchantment lay in the sword, Mallum could not heal the wound as before. They had him. The mission was at an end. Heygar's last tale was a wondrous victory in a little tavern in Vahr.

Eralorien felt a surge of energy, then something else. A wave of darkness descended upon them, and he wondered if he had stepped into the source unconsciously. He felt a demon near, so close as it picked with claws at the doorway between this world and the next. He felt its hunger, its salacious desire for things still to come, like a cast lure's enchantment diminishing away after its conclusion. Renewed fear stirred in him.

Then a recovering Iaculous spotted Arielle. As awful as Cherrie's laments were, Iaculous's wails were worse—primal and terrible. They were not human, nor beast, yet somewhere in between. Gripping his head in shaking hands, he wept openly. Eralorien's failing heart broke for the young weaver despite his better judgement.

Iaculous fell down beside Arielle and took her lifeless body in his shaking arms. He held her to his chest and cradled her, crying her name out, again and again, as though his words could return her soul to her body. For that moment, he was broken, and Eralorien felt his emotions gush out like a shattered dam.

Perhaps Denan sensed his grief for it distracted him, and that was all it took for the dark weaver. He leapt upon the leader of the Hounds, knocking the sword from his grip. He took hold of Denan's neck in both hands and squeezed. Black smoke erupted from the grasp, and Denan screamed as the weaver burned into him. The pathetic sight of Mallum frantically attempting an escape appeared as nothing but a ruse, for he hoisted Denan upwards with terrific strength, roaring in an unrecognisable tongue as he did.

Only Cherrie reacted. Despite her ruination, she charged at her sister's killer, leaping upon him, striking with fist and knee. But Mallum, infused with a strange, dark energy, did not release his victim. Instead, he slammed him to the ground, and Denan was helpless to stop him. Cherrie attacked and cursed her inability to damage the brute.

Was Mallum a man at all or a spawn of a demon? The same demon of the source Eralorien felt just an arm's reach away? Had it come to watch its prodigy tear them apart?

"You could earn Cherrie's favour," suggested the little voice in his mind.

Eralorien discovered Denan's blade in his hand. He had not even noticed himself pick it up.

"Hobble up behind the weaver, and all of this will be over."

Eralorien gripped the sword handle tightly.

"Perhaps you could wait until he finishes Denan, and Cherrie will be yours."

Eralorien held his attack for a moment. "Let me think," he muttered to himself and wondered how long this voice had been his companion. At least a week. Maybe a month. When he thought about it, his head hurt even more.

"Help me, Eralorien!" Cherrie screamed as she ripped hair from Mallum's head and tried to gouge out his eyes. A lifetime spent in terrible circumstances had gifted her fine skills at defeating a larger opponent without a weapon, but none of these unarmed tactics worked as Mallum strangled the life out of their leader. "Please."

Mallum's head snapped back and struck her fiercely across the nose, shattering many bones. Eralorien shook himself from his stupor and charged as swiftly as his old legs would let him. With one divine strike, he pierced Mallum's belly and plunged until the blade came out the back. Mallum released the struggling Denan, who grasped his neck and tried to breathe amid the acrid, familiar smell of burning skin. Mallum collapsed to his knees beside him. Eralorien pulled the blade free in silent triumph, and Mallum gasped as his breath became a river of crimson.

Can't heal a Venistrian blade's strike as easily, can you? Eralorien thought.

Cherrie stumbled towards him. Her face was destroyed. She spat out one of her teeth, and it hit Mallum in the face, along with a thick globule of blood. The spittle and blood slithered down his face, taking the tooth with it, but Mallum did not notice. He stared into her eyes as though this was merely an unfortunate turn of events. Bubbles appeared around her nostrils where the cartilage was pulped to paper. Blood matching her hair streamed down into her mouth, covering her perfect luscious lips, and Eralorien desired to drink every drop. She wavered ever so slightly on her feet, but no concussion, shattered face, or obstructed airway could impede her vengeance. She shoved Eralorien away and took hold of his adopted sword.

"Pray for mercy," she hissed through a broken mouth. The

skin gave way as the tip of the sword plunged into his flesh, and Mallum moaned in pain.

"Mercy…" Mallum grabbed her hands and embraced them around her own as she gripped the Venistrian sword. He didn't stop her. He attempted to dissuade her anger. An interesting tactic. Eralorien would have imagined the dying weaver would have fought violently to the bitter end.

Cherrie thought little of his pleading and pushed the blade deeper, slower this time. Eralorien couldn't imagine how it had taken up to this night to find her so appealing, but on the cusp of victory, with her body destroyed and face torn apart, he only wanted to take her to bed. He wanted her to fall for him, and he would pleasure her like none of the thousand men before him.

"Have mercy. I am but a man looking to help my people," Mallum offered. Eralorien almost believed the sincerity, if it was not for Iaculous's weeping and their terrible loss.

"Kill him," Eralorien snarled.

Beside him, Denan gasped on the ground, and Eralorien took pleasure in the man's demise.

"Have mercy, and we might undo things that have occurred tonight," Mallum whimpered.

Eralorien knew he deceived. Cherrie thought so too and plunged the blade deep into the cur. A fine, vengeful strike to steal his last breath and end his reign as unlawful leader of Venistra.

But Mallum did not fade and die like any true man, or even a beast. Instead, a powerful wave of fire and energy emerged from him and knocked the Hounds across the room. Cherrie took the brunt of the release and crashed against the far wall in a bloody mess. He threw Denan just as far in the other direction, and he came to rest among the embers in the fireplace.

Iaculous was knocked away from the still body of his love, and as grief took him, he made no effort to save himself, crashing to the ground beneath the stairs.

Eralorien saw all this as he went over the tavern's counter, which saved most of the blast, if not the fall. He crashed among bottles of ale, sine, and whisky. He was torn to shreds, just like the female he desired most. For what felt like the tenth time that day, Eralorien climbed to his feet and set his gaze upon the lone figure left standing.

"So, these are the Hounds I am to fear so much," Mallum said. As he spoke, his wounds sealed and his eyes burned with vigour and power. At his chest, the amulet shone brightly, and he took hold of it and held it until the light dimmed away. Where was Heygar now, when they needed him most? In one great bellow, the man would inspire them to one more charge and a likely victory soon after. As it was, Denan, their fearless leader, was in a crumpled heap in the corner. He was most likely dead.

Good riddance.

"You will fear me!" roared Iaculous. The blast had returned his wits and his fury with it.

Eralorien, touched by its presence, felt the beast move deliriously within the source. It watched, and yet, it did more. It was within them, yet it was not. He sensed it closer to this world. He imagined it banging upon a doorway and earning success. He feared for the world itself and the darkness to follow. He tried to hide behind the counter as though concealing himself would somehow make the beast pass him by. It was a foolish notion by a man who long since should have given up this life and earned a bed to die in.

Instead of hiding, Eralorien stood motionless as an infuriated young weaver attempted to meet his lover's murderer in battle. It was a battle he could not win.

DAY FOUR

"I didn't want this," Mallum growled, watching the young weaver circling him like prey attempting to turn the table on a vicious predator.

It was no contest, and Eralorien thought his apprentice reckless and heroic. Heartbreak made any man do foolish things.

Iaculous let loose a fireball that matched his rage. His body should have burned to nothing in that moment, but there was no sizzle of skin or stench of burned flesh. Eralorien felt the swelling power flow from his apprentice, which he knew had always been there. The fireball flew, and Mallum caught it as though it were little more than sport. He held the ball for a moment in his fingers as though examining its potency before crushing it so that it fizzled away to nothing.

"You are strong," Mallum said and flicked his wrist swiftly. He lifted Iaculous a few feet into the air like a wooden puppet in a seasonal fair. With his other hand, he lifted a long oak bench and brought both floating apparitions together with a sickening thud.

Eralorien heard a shrill cry as they impacted, only to see

his apprentice fall limp amid blood and broken bones. Everything became clear. Each of them would die upon this misadventure. Perhaps all of them this very night.

"As you wish," Mallum said to no one, touching the crystal at his chest.

Eralorien almost cried out for Cherrie's terrible torment, but he remained silent. His opponent was too fearsome. He had tried and failed, so why try again?

"That's the feeble spirit," the voice mocked, and Eralorien hissed it to silence. How long had the voice been in his head? At least a year. Ever since he had learned of his health, he believed. He swallowed his cowardice and bested its mocking.

"Why did you take her soul?" he asked Mallum. He hobbled over towards the dark weaver looking as intimidating as a Blue Lillium Flutterbye. He did it for Cherrie. Everything he had ever done was for Cherrie. He wished he had told her long ago.

Mallum did not answer, and why should he? Giving any reason other than the obvious would have been a lie. All souls trapped were colossal stores of energy, but a soul stolen while the body lived was a fathomless well. Killing Arielle was one diabolical act, but trapping her soul while her body still took a breath was evil. She would never know peace. Her torment would be ceaseless. All weavers of the source knew this.

"Do you really want to continue this fight, old man?" Mallum bent down beside the unconscious Iaculous. Eralorien feared he would slit his throat, but instead, he ran his finger down his face. "He really looks like me," he said, sniffing in disgust.

"Please set the girl's soul free and let her body die," Eralorien pleaded.

Mallum suddenly gripped the pendant and all light from it

dimmed again. "She wanted to say goodbye to him, but he's sleeping, and it's a better thing for us all." He released the grip. The crystal glimmered and shone brightly like a star in his grasp. "Leaving is a game for fools," he added softly and left the young apprentice to his sleep.

Then he turned on Eralorien. "In answer to your question, old man, no, I will not release her to die. She is mine now. Do not continue this hunt a moment further. I have shown mercy where none of you could."

Mallum wrapped his robe tightly and concealed the lost soul of Arielle within. As he did, Eralorien felt a great sadness and realised it was her own.

"Someone has played with your soul, old man. Do not allow yourselves to fall further from the road. If we meet again, all of you will die."

Despite the fear and ache, Eralorien felt a terrible desire to leap upon him and tear him apart. He had an equal desire to heed the brute's warning, flee with Cherrie, and know happiness. He made no move regardless.

"You know, I came here tonight with an offer for Heygar myself. I could have used a few dogs like you among my family."

Eralorien remembered what his old master had once said: *"The beast comes bearing fear and gifts. Accept neither."*

Mallum gestured to the doorway and ripped it from its hinges. It flew across the room, crashing against the far wall. It was loud enough to wake the dead but not a few sleeping Hounds.

Outside in the darkness, Eralorien saw a dozen figures dressed in hooded cloaks. All of them carried torches.

"Are you impressed, weaver? They are my acolytes, followers of the Church of Mallum," he mocked and waved them entry. They did so, and Eralorien tasted their fierce power. "There aren't many places for people to go in time of hunger, and they flock to me, for I am welcoming. I have fields that bear fruit. I am happy to share."

The hooded figures flooded into the tavern in silence as though he commanded their minds. They were fine little foot soldiers. The brute was building an army of weavers all for himself. It was no surprise the king was so wary.

Eralorien cursed Lemier, Denan, and, most of all, Heygar for damning them all by taking a foolish mission. He cursed himself, for he had been ready to leave their services that last night in Dellerin, but instead, Heygar had swayed his better judgement with a few smooth words. He should have insisted his apprentice was up to the task without him.

"You know, this is Bereziel's doing," the voice in his head said. Eralorien knew it was the truth. Bereziel had lured them to this place. He was an old Hound embittered by time and lost love, no doubt.

"Take the body of the girl," Mallum ordered, and two acolytes leapt to task. Lifting her carefully, they swept her from the room through the parting crowd. Arielle was gone, carried off to her new owners. Eralorien wondered if she would know what salacious use Mallum's weavers would have of her. Would she sense each man atop her from her prison, or would the torment of her holding consume all her thoughts?

"Let me take Cherrie, and we will be done with you, Mallum," Eralorien pleaded.

The weaver raised an eyebrow and smiled curiously. "You suddenly have no wish to slay me anymore?"

"I do not," Eralorien lied and eyed the unconscious Cherrie.

Do it for Cherrie, he told himself.

"And tell me this, healer. Will you leave your apprentice and your leader to their doom?"

"I will leave them where they lie sleeping."

"Do you not think such a thing is dishonourable?"

"Love is no dishonour."

"Interesting," Mallum said, sniffing the air as a fox would in search of the scent. "You would forsake your comrades easily enough and ignore the call of a lure. Love is a potent flavour. Perhaps some unbreakable things might shatter?"

A lure?

"*It's nothing*," the voice insisted, and his inner friend sounded so convincing.

"Follow that desire. May you find happiness with the girl. Perhaps I might even offer you a gift."

The amulet blazed brightly from beneath Mallum's cloak, and a surge of weaving energies formed around the dark weaver. Each of the surrounding acolytes hummed, and they, too, wove enchantments. Eralorien's head spun.

"He means to kill her," the voice in Eralorien's head cried.

Eralorien did not hesitate. He was no great weaver of the source, and he was an adequate master, but there was one ability he was better at than anything else. With the last of his might, he threw up an enchanted blue sphere all around himself and his unconscious companions. Immediately, he felt the release of a dark hold upon him, and with it, his head settled. However, the fatigue struck him immediately, and he almost fainted.

"Protect her!" the voice screamed, and he did.

The thin veneer of blue was translucent and unimpressive, but its strength was demonic. Mallum cursed in rage as the glistening blue wall of light lit up the room and separated him and his acolytes from the defenceless mercenaries. It hummed slightly, and Eralorien held it in place as he backed away to Cherrie's body. He whispered his wishes in his mind that it stayed true until his comrades recovered their senses.

Mallum held his fingers over the surface as a child would over a glass-contained candle. Careful and careless. It said much of Eralorien's measure that his most impressive talent was cowering behind a wall of source energy. The dark weaver suddenly struck the surface fiercely, and Eralorien shuddered under the assault. He struck again and then again. Each strike imbued with the force of a dozen acolytes, but a lifetime of mastering such a skill served him well, and the shield held.

Mallum was not all-powerful. Perhaps with Eralorien's skill with shielding, Iaculous's aggression, and Denan's impressive sword, there was hope.

If he were to fight.

"You fool!" Mallum cried and turned from the healer. The acolytes followed, and Eralorien was alone with the beaten Hounds, having somehow survived their first encounter with the monster of Venistra.

He watched them take to their horses. He watched them lead a cart filled with a soulless treasure. He watched them until they disappeared into the night. Only when he no longer sensed Mallum or the dark forces did he turn around and cradle the unconscious Cherrie in his arms.

"There, there, my love. All will be well now. It is time to leave," he whispered and stroked her ruined chin.

MAD ABOUT THE GIRL

"*You know what you have to do,*" the voice said.

Eralorien felt a wave of exhaustion overcome him. *Not enough sleep,* he thought warily.

"*You need not sleep,*" the voice insisted, and the pain was immense.

"Maybe not," he said aloud to the sleeping room.

Carried by weary limbs, he hobbled through the thin protective barrier, shivering from the tingles on his skin as he passed through. He looked out the front door, into the quiet night. The path was clear. No half-dressed guests of the inn; no hooded acolytes; no deranged king. His eyes fell upon the flurry of footsteps and horse clefts left in the muddy ground, and he worried how easy they would be to track. His head spun, and he considered returning to bed and rethinking matters after dawn.

"*Whisht, fool, that'll be too late. You need not sleep,*" the little voice insisted again, and he nodded in agreement.

Eralorien journeyed around the stable and found what he needed. Despite his exhaustion, he was quick to strap up the horse to the wooden cart and left it to wait by the front doorway. Slipping through the shield once more and into the abandoned kitchen, he sifted through the cupboards and found a freshly baked loaf of honey bread, a large wedge of apricot cheese, two jars of dried meats, and a crate of Venistrian Velvet. In the pantry, he found a milliard of different fruits, but he left them all for a sweet cake with glazed icing sitting atop a shelf at the back. Among the fruit, he found one solitary cherry and placed it atop the dark icing. Now it was perfect. He left the treasures in the cart and continued with his task as though a tired man possessed.

"Is all of this necessary, my old friend?" he asked the voice in his head, and it gently insisted it was.

With knees popping and crunching with every step, he finally reached the top floor. Food was only half of the requirements. She would have other needs. He slipped into their bedroom, and the sweaty air struck his nostrils immediately.

"He is not good enough to have that goddess."

Eralorien nodded.

"With Heygar gone, she has reverted to her old ways, and Denan has taken advantage," the voice added.

"Poor Cherrie," Eralorien said.

"Poor Cherrie," the voice he had kept in his head for many years agreed.

He rummaged through her belongings. Certain he could neither discover nor deduce what she needed most, he shoved everything into a bag. His bag was lighter, and he placed all into the cart with the pilfered supplies. His body was haggard and slow from maintaining the shield, but if nothing else, he would keep them protected. The voice disagreed, but it was fine to have arguments with those you loved most. He had always desired Cherrie, but until tonight, he had never taken his chance. Finally, he stood over her and embraced his doubts.

"I should not be doing this," he whispered and moved a few bloody matted strands from her ruined face. Even asleep, he thought her most beautiful, despite the wet rasp she made from blood and mucus blocking her breathing.

"You should do this," the voice said irritably, and why wouldn't it be? It spent much of its time repeating the same affirmations.

Eralorien conceded. He took her hands in his and pulled her along the floor. Her head flopped weakly and struck the floor every few steps. He could have taken more care, but the hour was late. Anyway, a few extra bumps wouldn't matter. With some blankets, he made a kingly bed for her in the cart's back. As the sun rose, he kissed her once upon her torn lips and felt stirrings like before. It was only then he noticed that her sleeping gown had come undone completely, and her breasts spilled out into the morning air. He wondered how such a thing had happened without his knowledge.

"What matters is they are yours to enjoy," the voice said.

By the seven demons of the source, he wanted to cup them in his withered old hands and enjoy them.

"Denan enjoyed them with payments of gold. You do it for love."

Eralorien reached for her and pulled her gown closed. His vision blurred, and fierce pain ripped through his head. It felt as though a hoofed beast stamped upon his every thought, but he pulled away from her and focused himself with the last task. Finding as many unlit lanterns as he could, he drained their oil along the floor of the tavern. Everywhere but around the shield. He stepped through and knelt beside the boy.

He grasped the boy's hand. "I tried my best with you, Iaculous. May we never meet again." Suddenly, an ocean of energy consumed him, and he felt wholly reinvigorated. Eralorien had not known for certain until that moment that somehow, the child had awoken his full potential. A lesser man may have been jealous. As it was, Eralorien felt only compassion for the boy. Perhaps he would be better without an old weaver halting his hand. Perhaps a little freedom might be the makings of a good man. Perhaps it might even save his soul entirely.

"The guild was right to take you in. I'm sorry I wasn't a shrewd enough master to lead you towards a better life."

Eralorien released the boy from his grip, but as he did, an image of Cherrie took his sight. She was in a dress of white, gold, and crystal-blue. There were red and black flowers in her hair. He saw himself younger, in a grey hooded cloak, and a priest blessing them to wed.

"Steal but a mouthful of the child's soul, so you may take her from this place," the voice whispered. Eralorien's hands shook. *"Delicious soul, it's just going to waste in a vessel unsure of what to do with itself."*

For a decade, he had cared deeply for the orphan Iaculous, and at first, he had swayed his young heart. Such a thing was easy enough, for his soul was depthless and consumed by love. But all children grow older, and as they do, the world digs her thurken claws deep into them and embitters them ever so. What could an old weaver do with an acolyte of such prodigious talent anyway? Iaculous had power hidden away so deep and so fierce that he might someday control the world.

The guild had feared the child, as had he, but they had let the orphan baby live, which was a kindness on their part. Eralorien taking his first and only apprentice to keep the child in the way of lighter things was a kindness on his part. Perhaps he should have trusted the child a little more, but hindsight was as cruel as the Dellerin streets after midnight. He had controlled the child as a reckless general would with a thousand surplus warriors facing a battle of hundreds. He gave him enough to chew on without giving him a taste. He had browbeaten and crushed the child into submission. The child had grown to become a capable healer and never known his true talents.

"But this place woke the furnace in him, didn't it, Eralorien?"

"It did."

Like a dry wretch without an ale in a month, he drank from the child. A fist of energy drove through his mind, his soul, his every cancerous part. It was incredible. He stole life as the silent voice showed him, and he could taste rebirth and immortality. Pain diminished to pleasure, and lethargy became vigour. He stole and continued to steal, and the voice in his mind was silent as it gorged deeply upon the energy.

It felt like hours, though it may have been a pulse and then gone. It was as though an invisible hand pulled him from the boy's soul, and he cried out and almost woke both sleeping comrades.

"More," the silent voice hissed, drunk from delirium.

"I want more," Eralorien wailed, but he rolled away from the unconscious weaver to avoid further temptation, his head hurt no more.

He leapt to his feet without effort and glimpsed himself in the mirror behind the tavern counter. He almost expected to see a young man looking back for how great he felt, but instead, he saw the same old withered man with bright silver hair.

"I am no younger."

"No, but you have opened a delicious door into that world," the voice of silence said.

"Bereziel lost himself searching for youth," he muttered. *Curses on that man.*

Eralorien swept away from the shield. He willed it with a renewed energy to keep them safe, even as the surrounding building turned to ruin. He willed them all sleep a little longer. He willed it to deny them escape. It was a fine enough enchantment, sturdy enough that Mallum himself could not crack it. At least for a time.

Then he pictured a flame in his mind, and the voice insisted he do so. He thought on the touch of burning and the energies involved, and he felt his heart beat rapidly. He tasted burning charcoal in his mouth and imagined a spark leaping from his finger. Nothing happened, but he felt something afoot.

The voice of silence whispered he try again, and so he did. Sweat trickled down his back, and he licked his lips. A stunning spark appeared from his finger and died. He invoked it again, and it stayed alight atop his index as though a candle in the darkness. It bubbled his skin, and he took the pain, for destruction born from will was beautiful.

He released the fire, so it would do its task. The spark fell to the ground, caught the oil, and set it alight. It grew and caught swiftly with each stream of spilled oil, and Eralorien turned away.

He locked his eyes upon Cherrie's sleeping form in the cart. Alone at last.

THE TWO LOVERS

With the warmth at his back and the source throbbing through his blood, Eralorien climbed nimbly into the wagon and set his gaze upon his treasure. She was perfect despite the blood spilling from the ruin of her face. He spread her arms wide and wrapped a rope around each wrist carefully.

"Perhaps I shouldn't be doing this," he said and held his hand for a moment.

"It will keep her safe as you ride."

Eralorien thought on it. The road would be uneven, and she was a delicate flower that could crack apart like porcelain. Behind him, something within exploded loudly. He felt the energy shift and drain him a little as the shield stood firm against the flame. How strange the last two Hounds might feel if they awoke with a wall of fire all around them.

"Strange and vengeful."

"They will know why I did it. They will know I no longer wished to be part of their doomed quest." He wrapped her first wrist tightly against the wooden handrail of the cart, then undid the knot and left it a little looser. He took the second wrist and did the same on the other side. "You can sleep in safety as we flee, my love." He ran his finger lovingly down her cheek, down her neck, and at the turn of her chest, he held himself.

"Keep going."

Eralorien shook his head and climbed to the front seat. With gentle persuasion, he eased the beast and cart forward to carry them from their troubles. The air was cool despite the season, and he watched his breath in the rising dawn light. A fine day ahead, no doubt.

The cart moved swiftly enough as the beast was healthy and young, and he thought about giving it a name. Perhaps Arielle? Cherrie would care for that, he imagined.

He met no hidden acolyte out on the road in the early morning. Perhaps they realised Eralorien was no longer a threat to Mallum, and they would be right. As if someone had taken a veneer from his sight, like a bride removed a veil, he saw everything clearer now. Yes, his head spun at deserting his comrades, but the deed was done, and the reward was priceless.

"A small price to pay," the voice named Silencio whispered in agreement, and Eralorien recognised that demonic name. He could have been alarmed, but Silencio was no enemy. It whispered as much.

Eralorien passed the last building of desolate grey and the last thatched cottage after that, and soon enough, the path led them away from the town of Vahr. For a few hours more, she slept, and the sun rose enough that he did not need to squint his eyes against the gloom. He thought of wonderful things, yet he could not think beyond the relief of his mission ending and the realisation of his love for Cherrie.

In his mind, the voice whispered little things, and Eralorien listened and learned like a young apprentice. He wondered if this was how Bereziel had become so fierce in the weaving of energies. It did not matter now, for he was twice the man. Soon enough, he would not need to weave from the source, except perhaps to prolong his life. That was worth dipping into the souls of others.

He set to healing Cherrie as she slept. As he started, a tear streamed down his face, and he wiped it away. The action confused him; it felt as though another controlled his limb, but he quickly shook the thought away and continued to heal his love.

The energy searched like a hound along her body, knitting her skin back together and easing the tenderness in her bruising. He did not believe her teeth would recover, but sure enough, a few little stumps appeared upon her gums immediately, and after an hour, they had grown completely. Her smile would be something he could happily gaze upon every waking morn, he decided.

As it was, it was midday, and they had travelled far enough south that were she to wake, any amount of screaming on her part was unlikely to alert their pursuers, so he released her from her sleeping enchantment. Another tear rolled down his cheek, but his phantom limb did not wipe it free this time.

Something distracted his thoughts for the mildest of moments as he sensed a quiver. It was a delicate sensation in the back of his mind, and it amused him somewhat. Far back, countless miles behind, the shield he had held with a sliver of his will had suddenly shattered.

Had the wall succumbed to the reaching fire, or had the building collapsed upon itself? Were his comrades dying in that same breath—charred alive, with no chance of healing themselves? Would they become one with the ash, little more than a pair of overcooked mounds among the bricks and debris? Had Denan cut through with the sword of green, or had Iaculous recovered from his slumberous mugging and shattered their imprisoning shield into a mist? Were they already searching? Would they even be able to pick up his scent? Did any of it really matter?

Eralorien sighed and thought little more of them as Cherrie shot up awake. Her body jolted from the fright.

"You are fine, my dear," he said and allowed her a few moments to compose herself. To wake up in such a way would unnerve anyone, even a goddess. He turned back and faced the road ahead. He moved the beast to a canter with a gentle rapping of the whip upon its rear. He had never felt as tired as this.

"What is this treachery?" she screamed, and he heard her struggle in the ropes.

"Perhaps you shouldn't have given her that much room," Silencio said, and he hissed it quiet.

Above them, dreary, miserable clouds were already forming, and he thought having her soaked through would do no good at all. Not that she wasn't in need of a bath though. Denan's smell would still be upon her skin, her hands, her mouth, her everything. Eralorien ground his teeth irritably.

Curses on that fool Denan. Curses on his heavy pockets of gold to have his way.

"You have gold too. Just in case."

"Where is Arielle?"

"My love, we are fleeing terrible things. All is well," Eralorien said because the voice named Silencio suggested those words and other things he was not ready to embrace. At least not yet.

"What is happening, Eralorien? Where are the others? Where is my … sister?" she cried, knowing well the truth, he imagined.

"She will come around," Silencio insisted.

"Are you hungry, my love?" Food was always best for what ailed the sickness of misery.

"Release me now." Cherrie wrenched her left arm free.

She screamed as she did, and as though possessed by a demon's touch, he leapt back and pinned her down. She kicked and fought, for she was a champion, and that was one of the many things he had loved about her. He lay across her and held her fighting arm, and she could not struggle anymore. He desired her so.

"What are you doing this for, Eralorien?" she hissed.

He smiled and covered her mouth with his hand. He kissed her forehead and enjoyed the thoughts of entering her. He enjoyed the thoughts of her enjoying him doing so. She struggled more, and the voice named Silencio liked this. After a few more fruitless attempts, she fell still, and this pleased them both greatly.

"After what he did to Arielle, I understand why you behave like this," Eralorien said.

He sat up away from her but not enough to remove his weight upon her free arm. She made no further movement. She didn't even try to speak. She only whimpered a few more times.

"We are safe from Mallum's touch. He cannot hurt us anymore," he reassured her, and she listened.

After a moment, he removed his hand from her mouth. The horse continued to walk on unperturbed. He could stay in the back of the cart with her all morning, and they would still make acceptable time. He didn't exactly know where he was going, but somewhere along the way, they would touch the coast. Then they could be off in a barge back to Dellerin and away from this cursed place. He stroked her hair, and she pulled her head away for a moment before easing her defiance.

"Where is she?" Cherrie asked.

Her voice was strong, and he was proud of her. Another tear streamed down his cheek, and the phantom hand wiped it away roughly. Then it moved to her heaving chest, and he whipped her dress open and took hold of her naked breast. She gasped from fright, but a lifetime of holding her tongue in precarious situations served her well.

"It is excitement she feels," the voice named Silencio insisted, and he desired her greatly.

Eralorien was exhausted. He enjoyed her burning hot skin. She whimpered again, and he ripped the hand away, lest it do more. The horse carrying them along slowed as it came upon a small keystone bridge. The stream underneath was deep enough though it barely flowed with any pace. It was perfect. She held her breath as though he were about to do more, and Eralorien shook his head defiantly.

"No, not in the back of a cart," he hissed.

For the slightest of moments, he saw Cherrie as more than the defenceless woman unwittingly baring her body to him. He saw the danger in her eyes, and he thought on her as a comrade. Why was he doing this?

"She struggles with love. Do not be disheartened, for she will be your bride. And if not, she might die at the hands of that pretty blade she always liked. Yes, stabbing her a few times and healing her would be a fine way to display your power. Strength always lured her, and what greater strength than to hold command over her life?"

Eralorien shook his head. "I love you." He placed his hand across her eyes. Before she could reply, she fell into a deep sleep once more.

PRECIOUS SLEEP

The current of the stream kept her afloat, and Eralorien only needed one hand to keep her steady enough. Beautiful Cherrie was looking more and more enticing with every scrub. He dipped the soap in the water and made fresh bubbles before attacking more marks upon her body. He enjoyed her beauty, but he also enjoyed knowing that he removed Denan's touch from her skin with every stroke. In fact, it was not just Denan; it was Heygar's many-year touch and the thousand paying brutes before him.

Fresh hatred for all who had defiled her coursed through Eralorien. A few flickering sparks slipped from his fingers and singed hair from where few men should ever see. He scrubbed her as clean as the day she was born and pulled her from the edge of the stream onto the bedding he had prepared.

He had chosen a suitable place in which to take her. If rain were to fall, a low-hanging weeping oak would cover them against all but the greatest of thunderstorms. They were far enough in from the path that few passers-by would notice the cart's tracks into the rich forest of grey or hear her screams. Beside her bedding, he had set a small fire to warm the gloom from the day, and upon a spit, he had skewered strips of dried meat. By the time they had finished the act, the food would be nice and crispy, just the way she liked it.

Eralorien wedged the bottle of Venistrian red in beside the fire's stones and tipped its edge to ensure it was warm enough. He carefully recovered her finest gown of blue silk from her pack and slid his fingers across its surface. Yes, this would suffice. He had always liked silken things. He placed her legs into the dress and gently slid it up her body with hands that were not his own. He buttoned each clasp and tightly pulled the supports at her back. It would be romantic when she awoke fully clothed. A girl liked to keep her dignity. It would also be a little more romantic to seduce her out of the grand clothing.

He wondered if he should have bought a ring to ask for her hand before they became intimately entwined. His head spun, tears spilled down his cheeks, and weariness filled his every being.

Cherrie moved slightly in her slumber, and he loved her so. He took hold of his rope, wrapped it back around her wrists, and secured her tightly again.

"Better safe than sorry."

Eralorien nodded before opening her mysterious box of paints. He dabbed his finger in a glass bottle of red oil, like he had seen her do a thousand times before.

"One time for each man."

Eralorien did not rise to the crude jest. Instead, he rubbed his oily finger across Cherrie's lips and was rather pleased with his artistry. Next, he took a jar of dry, black mud and rubbed it around her eyes. This was trickier, and he grimaced as he attacked the task with phantom limbs until, eventually, her beauty satisfied him.

"Her hair is dreadfully tangled," he whispered to the wind and recovered her hairbrush.

She had always taken great care to present herself flawlessly, and he would honour that wish. How many times had he innocently watched her brush her hair in the early morning, out on the march? How many times had the rhythm of her movement almost brought the onset of sleep?

She loved that brush and cared for it as much as she did her mirror. They were a matching set, both with golden bodies, lined with jewels. Likely, they were glass, but they caught beautifully in the sun.

Eralorien dragged the brush through her hair, slowly at first. It caught a few knots, but he persevered and separated them without disturbing her. He watched the strands fall to a perfectly straight line, and he got wonderful, relaxing pleasure as he did.

"Enough of this. Take her to your bed," Silencio said, but it was more distant now. More distant than he had ever known the voice to be his entire life.

He continued to brush her hair and felt the world's weariness take hold of him something fierce. He slid in beside her, pulled the surrounding bedding, and yawned wonderfully. The perfect yawn of a man who knows sleep is inevitable.

"No!" screamed Silencio. Thoughts of entering her body flashed in his mind and stirred his manhood with desire.

"Not now," Eralorien whispered and kissed her upon the forehead.

He stroked her hair again and felt wonderful, innocent pleasure, like silk gloves caressing his mind, pushing him towards unconsciousness. He closed his weeping eyes, and the relief was wonderful. He felt the darkness and there was no sign of the beast. He felt her sleeping breath upon his cheek, but most of all, he felt her hair in his hands, and they were his own. He smiled and fell into a deep sleep.

He awoke to the taste of a late evening, for the fire had long burned out. Thunder was in the air, and he—well, he was Eralorien, and he was under a nasty enchantment. She was still in his arms, and the brush had fallen from his hand. He felt the urge to smell her hair, but he knew such a thing was wrong.

"Wake up, Cherrie!" he cried and released the enchantment, which held as he had slept. Oh, the wonderful power of a clear mind to make thoughts his own again.

"What are you doing?" Silencio cried from far away.

Shards of fear ran up Eralorien's back like spiders upon a web. The voice was no friend for life. No companion to guide his way. Something drew it forth through a terrible lure cast by a skilled weaver, and the dying Eralorien was more open than most. His mind was torn apart by disease. The beast whispered from afar to most others, but it crawled right into his lured and broken mind.

"Would I have been so easily lured if I'd slept more these last months?" he cried out and left Cherrie's side to stand in the cold air of the evening.

He had not slept properly since learning of that terrible prognosis from a far greater healer than he. No amount of weaving could cure such rampant poisons running through his body, desecrating each organ, and polluting every drop of blood. His mind had wandered and fallen to melancholy, and in that time, someone had enchanted him. All of them. There was only man vile enough to do such a thing.

"Damn you, Bereziel!" he screamed to an invisible spectator. His soul was his own to command.

"But you are better than Bereziel," Silencio whispered.

Eralorien slapped his face hard before shaking her, so she

would wake before his derangement brought him near to her again. Near enough to ravage her.

"But she could do with a good ravaging though, couldn't she?"

"Oh, by the seven demons, she really could." He slapped his face again and pulled her from her restraints.

Her bleary eyes awoke to the sudden commotion. Cherrie did not hesitate; she struck him fiercely and rolled from their bedding. She leapt to her feet and bolted for the cart in one smooth motion as he fought the demon that was gripping onto his cancerous mind. Gripping and climbing back in.

"What have you done?" she roared and recovered her dagger from the cart.

"Clever girl," he said and watched her spin the blade in her grip.

An unrestrained Cherrie could take on a pack of wolves and win. Perhaps even more. Her eyes were stunning, and he knew if he took a step towards her, she was likely to tear him from head to toe. He willed himself to take a step towards her but instead settled for climbing to unsteady feet.

"Someone cast a lure upon me," Eralorien cried. Tormented screams of a demon filled his head as it attempted to take control.

"A fine story," she hissed.

He thought she was a fine soldier. A lesser girl would have faltered and fled. He wanted to take her to bed. Oh, how he wanted to pleasure her.

"We all were." Thoughts of her naked body stirred him greatly.

"Where… is… Arielle?" she said coldly.

"Don't tell her, or you will lose her company for certain."

Eralorien tried to speak, to reveal what his demented mind had whispered.

"DON'T TELL HER."

"Arielle's body lives; she might still be saved," he cried and felt the full wrath of the demonic voice. It was like a hammer smashing, crushing, and killing his mind. He heard its anguished cry.

"FOOL!"

"Iaculous can become powerful enough to return her soul, though he does not know it yet," he slurred as though drunk. As though a claw dug itself deep into his mouth to silence him, and he fought it every syllable at a time.

"I'M GOING TO RAPE HER WITH YOUR BODY!"

"Mallum has taken her soul within the crystal and her body with it."

"WHEN SHE IS RUINED, I WILL SLIT HER THROAT WITH YOUR HANDS!"

Eralorien fell to the ground, and Cherrie leapt to his side. She kept the blade ready to strike, should there be a need.

"As long as her body takes breath, her soul is stronger than anything else," he whispered as his tongue revolted. He grabbed his head with hands that weren't his own anymore.

"Much better," Silencio whispered and took control again. Eralorien wept as he longed to tear the clothing from her body. What beast could lure a man to rape?

"Maybe it is because these desires have always been inside you?" the beast suggested.

"Kill me before I come for you," Eralorien gasped. So little time, and so many words and warnings to offer.

Cherrie shook her head because she was a goddess who desired his love more than her welfare, and he knew killing her would be divine. She would scream, and as she died, he would tell her how much he loved her.

"NO!" he screamed and pulled his own dagger from its scabbard.

He thought her hair was beautiful in this light, and he desired to kill her, for all beauty must die at the hands of divinity.

"NO!" He slit the veins on each of his wrists before his demon could stop him. He ripped up along his arm and felt the blood spray into the clear evening air.

Cherrie cried out and reached for him, but he stumbled away, lest he take her with him.

"I'm so sorry," he pleaded.

He hated Bereziel for bringing doom upon them all. He fell back against the tree trunk and felt the blood ruin his cloak, and he thought it was a fine enough place to die. It was better than rotting away in a bed among the sickly and forlorn. His head spun again from lack of blood, and he looked out to see if he would last another sunset, but a bright blue hue had fallen upon their little campsite. To his dismay, he looked down at his hands, and they glowed brightly as they healed the wounds along his wrists.

"Not like this."

"This cannot be," he cried miserably.

Cherrie neared him warily. He willed her to understand and could almost feel her frightened mind as he did. He willed her to know his remorse for all he had done. He willed her to know him for what he truly was, but such a thing was impossible. He wanted forgiveness but could not ask for it, so he drew away from her.

"Run from this place in case I return."

With what determination he had left, Eralorien stumbled away from the girl, into the forest. He ignored the howls of misery as he charged towards the road. Each branch whipped his face violently, but he did not flinch nor slow. However far he could go, he would go. He plunged the blade deep into his stomach and slid its sharp edge as far across as he could. He moaned aloud and felt his innards spill out before immediately healing themselves.

"No," whispered Silencio.

"I will beat you, demon," Eralorien countered and charged forward despite the agony.

Whatever hold this demon had upon him lessened as it struggled to heal, and somehow, he turned stumbling into a fierce run through the forest. The blade was his rope; he was lost at sea, and he used that thurken rope repeatedly and attempted to drag his soul away from the clutches of the beast towards the salvation of death. Each mutilating plunge into his body was an extra stroke. He could taste death in the blood in his mouth, and he never wanted to embrace it as much before.

"This is what I desired," he hissed whenever the voice reasoned for control and attempted to stop his demented death charge.

Far away, he sensed the energies of his apprentice, and he knew there was redemption. He charged forward and fought the urge to return to hunt her down and have his way. At his weakest moment, his cloak caught in a branch and held him. Like a dog mad in heat, he saw in his mind her naked body, glistening in the water.

"You make me see what I desire most? I will look no more." Eralorien drove the knife into his eye. Before he could stop himself, he struck the other and the enchanting vision disappeared along with his sight.

Blindly, he charged towards the energies of his comrades, and a few miles along the beaten path, he met them, charging down upon horses. He leapt out at them, and they reared in surprise and alarm at his sudden appearance.

"What have you done?" Denan roared and fell upon him. He pinned him down, and Eralorien spit in his face and attempted to stab him with half-healing eyes. It was a fine attempt born out of hatred for the younger man.

"HE WILL BE THURKING THE SOUL OUT OF CHERRIE IN A FEW HOURS!"

Eralorien stabbed until he felt the blade penetrate through leather into skin. Denan fell away in shock and coughed up blood where his lungs were speared. He spluttered and died beside him, and Eralorien laughed and faced the young apprentice with glowing hands.

All desire to kill dissipated upon seeing Iaculous. His eyes fell to the countless holes upon his body from where his body had healed the wounds. The skin was pink and new, and it disgusted him. He felt tears stream down his face at his loss of will, and deep within, he summoned one last piece of his own will. He lifted his cloak to show the many attempts at suicide.

"Kill me, before I kill you all." Eralorien charged the boy.

He took hold of him and drained precious energy from his soul. As he did, he stabbed weakly at Iaculous, who, shaken with the assault, had just enough about him to meet the strike, take hold of his wrist, and twist the knife away.

"NO."

He tasted the delicious source, and the voice devoured it too, but it was not like before. The child was conscious and capable of sensing his menace. Eralorien committed his full desires upon Cherrie, upon Denan, and lastly, the selfish approval that Arielle lay with another man. He felt the recoil, and he felt the cruel emotion, so he focused on remembering her throngs of loud ecstasy at the hands of her murderer. He envisioned her beautiful, broken body with legs still spread.

Like a heaving furnace, Eralorien felt his own soul and its enchanted lure burn away to its heat. He felt the hatred, and he felt the knife bury into his heart, again and again. As the demon tried resurrection once more, he felt the child tear his soul from him like a monger would a trout. And then he felt as if he were floating as his body fell beneath him into the dirt beside Denan's, and he lamented for his crimes.

"I'm sorry, my boy," Eralorien whispered, but no words came.

He felt an invisible grip take hold. As the world drew black forever, he felt himself drawn towards the bandoleer of his young apprentice and the shards of rock upon it. He watched Iaculous weep at his own dead body's bloody feet. He felt nothing at all as the final precious sleep called him to the night.

THE GIRL WITH REGRETS

The cheese was precariously close to melting into a delicious slush of flavour on the top spit. The lower-tiered meats bubbled and sizzled just enough fat from each cut. Cherrie spun each piece in the fire and watched the meal take shape.

It was an underrated skill to prepare and cook out on the march. Cherrie rarely tasked herself with the deed, lest her comrades believe it a regular duty. Sometimes it was better not to show one's true talents, so she had always let her daughter do most of the cooking.

Daughter.

She stopped spinning mid-turn and caught the gasp in her breath as soon as it occurred. The fire didn't care for her hesitation and began over-charring the long piece of meat in its heat. Whatever it was, it was salted and easy to cook. The dry sizzle ceased, and a flame appeared where it touched the fire's tip for too long. She blew the catching flame dead and lifted her head from the little pirouette of smoke.

"Oh, my Arielle."

Cherrie ripped the ruined piece of meat from the spit and

flung it into the tree line. Let it become a feast to an army of diligent worker ants, she thought.

"Oh, my beautiful, beautiful Arielle."

She fought true desolation and held her stony expression. She grabbed her chest at the mention of her daughter's demise and felt her heart attempt to tear itself apart and end her misery.

"Why did this come upon us?" she quietly moaned and tore a fresh piece of dried meat. She dipped it in oil and wrapped it around the spit. Her fingers burned as she did, but it was a pain she accepted and appreciated.

Sometimes pain was a friend to the best of people. Pain reminded her she still took a breath, her heart still beat, and her mind still hoped. Pain warned her, but more than that, pain could be controlled and gifted when the rest of the world cut the spirit too deeply. Sometimes though, pain was all a torn apart person could feel as they gave themselves up to a world of darkness.

Cherrie glanced at a revealing scar at the cuff of her gown and pulled herself from lamenting thoughts. So many scars. So many that there was never enough clothing to conceal them all completely. "War was tough," she said to any man curious enough to ask why she had as many as she did. It was half a truth, which was better than the truth. War was tough, but a life in the brothels of Dellerin was truly devastating to both the soul and the skin. Sometimes it was a brutal patron who desired blood and thrust, while other times, when shame took hold, a few little cuts soothed her fragile mind. She was scarred, but it made her stronger.

What scar would Arielle leave upon her soul?

She removed her fingers, placed them to her lips, and enjoyed the deliciously salted anguish. Was there anything more reliable in the world than pain? Cherrie watched a drip of cheese melt completely and fall to a premature death in the burning embers below. Another fell after that, and she did not catch the delicacy or save it for later. There was no point, she thought and poured a glass of steaming wine. The thurken dinner was a ruin, and she didn't give a spit for it. She cooked the meal because she had nothing better to do while she waited.

"We will return you," she whispered to the wind.

She drank a bitter mouthful of wine and felt its burn on her empty stomach. Not too much, she told herself, lest he came back to sit and eat at the feast she had prepared. She tried to hate him. She wanted to hate him. She wanted to lash out and maim. Gift a scar of her own. Perhaps kill. She wanted her daughter to return whole. Therefore, she would wait for him to return and ask him the prudent questions until it sated her. And then, if he still wore the demented gaze, she could take out her frustrations on him.

"My beautiful child," she wailed in her mind, but her eyes barely flickered, for she was proficient in hiding emotions behind her face. And what a pretty face they told her she had.

She poured the wine into the fire and realised she was suffering a state of shock. She accepted this easily enough. What point was there in clutching her knees and rocking back and forth until the pain ebbed away? Instead, she ripped the second piece of meat from the spit, and after a careful bite, she threw that into the trees. Nothing would ever taste agreeable until she had recovered her beautiful daughter from that monster.

"Mallum will die by a Hound's hand," Cherrie whispered, and a thin smile fought its way to her lips.

Her head spun, and she felt the lure overcome her once more. Let it, she thought bitterly, remembering the lost battle with Mallum. She had had her chance and was no measure to the cur. His skills were terrifying, and hers were instinctive, instincts tainted by an ethereal enchantment.

Eralorien had spoken of the lure, and she knew enough to feel its presence. There was a power in knowing its potency and not even fighting it. Better it drive her forward. Kill Mallum, save Arielle. Simple plans were always the best.

She understood Eralorien's attempts at redemption, and she understood his pathetic plea for her to run from him. In his madness, he must really have thought she was a pathetic damsel awaiting ravaging, or worse—in need of saving.

Cherrie poured more wine into the flame and watched it die again. It was also something for her to do while she waited for Eralorien to return and face her questions. What else did he do to her as she slept? Her knuckles turned white, and she ground her teeth painfully. She sloshed the bottle of Venistrian red in the fiery light and poured it over the cheese, down into the flames. Though the embers fought hard, the vintage smothered them, a good year as it was.

She shuddered as darkness swathed the camp in eerie loneliness. She watched the embers burn away in the damp mound of cheese and alcohol. After a few breaths, she kicked the entire spit over and trod it into the ground with her heavy boot. For good measure, she stamped it to nothing, cursing deep within as she did.

Thurk Mallum. Thurk Eralorien. Thurk Heygar. And by the demons of the source, thurk Bereziel above them all. He should have been here.

Without the fire, she felt the cold immediately and relished the alertness it would provide. She pulled her dagger from her belt and the accompanying whetstone from her pack and sat atop her cart. Higher ground was always a habit. She scraped the blade along the grainy surface and enjoyed the gentle screech as she made her perfect blade a little more perfect. Perhaps if she sharpened it enough, she might pierce Mallum's heart right through and kill him before he healed. She cursed her foolish hope, knowing full well the power in that invisible grasp and its ability to thrash her against a wall until she was mush. That was no way to die. Better to go out in a battle with many felled opponents at her feet.

Cherrie regretted many things. Mostly it was the lies to her daughter. There was no sweetening of such a truth. She had lied to her for an entire lifetime, and she could never take it back. It didn't matter that she had lied out of kindness, out of necessity.

Cherrie's own mother had also spent a lifetime on her back in countless different chambers, only for one fertile patron to leave more than smeared makeup and a river of sweat upon her. Cherrie had not died from the tonics prescribed, and so she had been born into a cruel world, inheriting the same occupation as her wretched, cold, and gloriously deceased mother.

Arielle was conceived in love though, wasn't she? Conceived in throngs of passion with the only man Cherrie had ever loved, in the hours before war called brave young men back to blood and death. Business disappeared for a time by her choice, and she was grateful that it was, for a child by any other man might have meant little. She hadn't been ready to allow another to empty himself in her while her love's memory was fresh. What was a month anyway after experiencing the true act of love?

And in that last night, she had seen love in the boy. They had held each other until dawn, whispering their thoughts, fears, hopes and sorrows, and it had been incredible. It hadn't taken long to discover a change in her body. When the time came, as it usually did for all in that profession, Cherrie couldn't bring herself to drink the deathly black tonic of her own. She had held the bottle in her hand after end of business for three nights in a row before flinging it from her grasp and accepting the consequences. The gift.

She refused to curse her daughter with her lineage. Better the little one believe her mother died in a plague. And as for her father, well, his tale could be the first lesson that a trapped man was likely to bolt with the wind. She had never proven Cherrie wrong, and now she never would.

Fleeing from Dellerin with a child had been easy enough. Less so, birth, but Cherrie found a way as she did with all great things. Starting a life with no noticeable skills apart from her staggering beauty soon brought her back into that world, albeit closer to the front line, where soldiers were willing, gold was plentiful, and business was very profitable. A few years renting a room in a clean tavern, earning her place on her back to doomed men as Arielle grew was the life Cherrie settled for.

Then came the fateful rekindling with one of her highest paying customers and the entanglements surrounding him. Meeting Heygar that night in the tavern had reaffirmed the deception to her daughter and, inadvertently, condemned them both to a life of dishonesty.

Tears fell from Cherrie's eyes to the damp ground at her feet, and she halted the assault on the blade. She wished the only man she had ever loved were with her now, but he had left her without saying goodbye. A lifetime of silent lies still sat between them. Would things have been different if she'd have spoken the truth? Yes, she never would have become a Hound, and after Arielle, that was the greatest achievement of her life. She took a breath and continued sharpening her dagger.

The discharged Heygar, weighed down with countless

medals, had discovered her from across the room and charged through the crowd, roaring magnificently. He had whisked her into the air with sturdy arms, and despite herself, she had giggled—not in excitement but in the comfort of familiarity. He had professed his love for her as most drunkards did, and he had returned to her so many loving memories of Arielle's father before war had separated them.

It had been wonderful until he had opened his little bag of impressive coin and insisted he pay her thrice the rate for a week of her company. Cherrie had ignored the shame and accepted the offer, terrified to ask the prudent questions. Instead, she hoped the truth would reveal itself and, with it, a conclusion to the tale of the man she loved. So, she had taken the gold gladly, met the kindly fool every evening, and enjoyed herself as best she could until the last night.

"I should have told him," Cherrie said from atop her cart to the silent darkness. "I should have told them both."

Heygar's best and oldest friend had appeared at the tavern with him, and her heart had both surged and plummeted in that same dreadful moment. So beautiful. So kind. So loyal. He had only ever had to pay the once and never after that. Nothing had changed about him apart from slightly premature grey in his hair and eyes, which burned with more passion. He had known Arielle was no little sister immediately, for that is what great weavers do, but the tale she spun that first night remained to this day.

Oh, if she could turn back time and add a few little details, she might well have, but that was not how true tales of regret usually went. For they sat at a table and reminisced of times in Dellerin when both young soldiers, one of the blade and the other of the source, had raced each other to earn a night with the stunning young redheaded girl. Heygar had mocked their weekly argument over price, and she had laughed as though her insides did not curdle within.

That wonderful night could not last forever, and an eager Heygar had earned enough vigour to take her to bed one last time, so she had nodded and concealed her remorse. Cherrie had played the dutiful whore for one night more and promised herself that come the morning, she would whisper the truths to her love. How well would he take the knowledge that he was the father of a whore's child? Still to this day, she had no answer.

She had bid her oblivious love a perfectly polite bow and walked with her patron through the town to dine upon some fine delicacies before a nice thrust. She remembered that Heygar had always liked to hold from behind, with her red hair grasped roughly in his fist as he got his fill. Bereziel, however, had pleasured her for hours with every limb and appendage he could offer before meeting her eye-to-eye for their inevitable conclusion.

Were it not for the ambush on Heygar by four brutes along the quays that night, her life may have been different.

They had crept up on them at the docks, where he had shown her the barge that would take his merry crew away on their first ever mercenary mission come the morning. The assassins tore him to shreds, searching for his gold, and she had watched on in terror as he had bravely fought them off. However, he was not the man back then he would become. He soon fell to their strikes and covered up as they plunged blades into him.

It was the crimson blood streaming from his body, which shook Cherrie to life, and so, to death she went. She seized one of the fallen and some rather fetching daggers and set herself upon them ferociously. They never had a chance. She moved as if assisted by a beast in the source. Though they rallied after the costly surprise that a feeble whore could inflict such terrors upon them, they still died at her brutal hand.

She had imagined they were her patrons, and her seething rage had driven each strike home. Even to this day, when war was upon them, she leapt into battle and tore apart memories of those thousand men who thrusted, lurched, and burst inside her, and she killed easily enough.

That night was the first time she had swung a weapon in anger. When the red mist cleared, there were four dead men at her hands, and she had earned Heygar's trust for life. She had never even considered revealing the truth thereafter. Instead, she had accepted a proposition from Heygar.

"A pretty girl with knife skills could make a proper living in my fledgling mercenary outfit," he had whispered as they had healed him back to life.

Only a fool would have rejected securities like this. Who ever heard of a dead mercenary's young kin turned out into the streets? It would never happen. A whore's sister would soon slip back into that whoring world, but a mercenary's younger sister would always be taken in and homed by the mercenaries' guild. It was law, and one of the few she approved of.

So, Cherrie had fallen in line with the man she had loved a lifetime, behind the man who controlled her destiny, and she had said nothing more. She did it partly out of loyalty to Heygar for offering her a life above what she had endured but also knowing how swiftly Heygar could take it away, were he to discover the truth of her heart. She chose deceit and never regretted it.

THE GIRL WITH MANY THOUGHTS

"Oh, my Bereziel, where are you when we need you most?" Cherrie cried, lamenting the double-sided blade of a life thrust upon her.

Eralorien was a weaver with adequate skills, but he was the lesser replacement to the greatest man she had ever known. If Eralorien was a light of source power, Bereziel was a furnace of darker energies. If Bereziel were here now, things would be very different. Bereziel would have taken the fight to Mallum. Bereziel was far too wily for a lure. In fact, he was more likely to cast the lure than anything else.

She had always suspected Eralorien might look upon her in that way but never enough that an enchantment could turn him to a monster. In all those years, did he really know little of her will or her temperament? He didn't know her at all, for that could never be her fate. She would never give up her life and spirit for anything or anyone.

Instead, she would fight for every breath, and she would know success. She was no waif in these matters, and with a blade at her side and her wits about her, there was nothing she could fear of Eralorien. When he returned with glowing, luring fingers and suggestions of love, blood, and rape on his mind, she would do what she had intended to do from the first moment she had woken up in the cart: find every detail she could of Arielle's fate. She could easily slit his throat and bleed him until he stepped into death any time she liked. It only mattered what she learned before that.

Her tears for Arielle had long since dried up. Lamenting with tears served little in this world unless a patron was paying for such behaviour. Better to embrace the anger and engage in strategy. It was the Hound in her.

Cherrie heard the sudden breaking of twigs and leapt from the cart with her dagger in hand. The crack became a cacophony of branches moving, muffled talk, and heavy boots. She held her breath and hid behind the wide trunk, where the leaves hung low enough they touched the ground. The voices grew loud, and she recognised them as her comrades'. She took a moment to make certain the unwanted tears were gone from her eyes. She would never be the victim ever again.

Iaculous broke through the tree line first. As he did, he immediately spun around to where she concealed herself. He peered into the darkness to see if he could make her out within the shadows. A few breaths later, Denan followed. Both had their horses with them. The beasts ambled, laden with great weights. One carried baggage and supplies, while the other carried something she couldn't make out in this faded light.

Denan limped as though he had spent a night playing the ridiculous game of "belly punch" with Heygar and come off the loser. Few had ever beaten him at that game, she thought sadly.

She missed Heygar something fierce. What had been a service to his kindness became comfortable as the years passed. She loved him in a way, and like Bereziel, she wished he were here. In all missions and matters, he had always somehow completed the impossible or recovered the irretrievable, until the impossible task became such an innocuous thing as floating. A whore and her two favoured patrons soon became a clan of skilled mercenaries. They had other brothers and sisters who joined the ranks over the Hounds' life, yet the trio were the only ones to remain until Bereziel abruptly disappeared.

"Have we found her?" Denan asked, crashing into the young apprentice's mount and grabbing his stomach as he did.

Cherrie slipped from the tree trunk and glided through the hanging leaves like a forest sprite of the night. She stepped into the moonlight, so they could see her. She kept her blade behind her back. It was reassuring and steady.

She was no fool to come rushing to them. Who knew what evils had occurred out on the road, since the tavern? If it came to it, she knew she could tear Denan apart in a fair fight, even with his fantastical sword, but the apprentice had a threat about him. She had seen it in the flashes of Eralorien's thoughts. She believed her own thoughts terrible upon seeing her casual lover and youthful comrade, but after Eralorien's behaviour under the lure, who knew how they would behave?

"Cherrie!" Denan cried. His injuries didn't stop him from taking hold and squeezing the breath from her. "I'm sorry, my love. Eralorien enchanted and trapped us beneath a wall of fire and doom." He kissed her openly. She was not ever used to public displays of affection outside of the bedroom, and she felt herself blush as he cupped her face in his grubby, bloody hands.

"Are you okay, Cherrie?" Iaculous asked.

She wondered why his face glowed in the dark as it did. It

was like the crystal upon her daughter's killer's chest. No, she remembered Eralorien's words and reminded herself of the hope for the girl.

She saw the bandoleer and one of the glass canisters glowing brightly upon it, and she thought it more beautiful than any jewel or golden coin she had ever come upon. It drew her to it immediately, and once Denan's affectionate manhandling lessened, she walked to it. He must have sensed her curiosity, for as though he were a child with a new toy, Iaculous whipped his cloak around his chest and concealed the glow from her eyes.

"I am well now that I am among my comrades," Cherrie said, curious how they had discovered her in the deep forest. She suspected they had run afoul of Eralorien and, most likely, forced the truth from him. That appeared rather serendipitous, however.

"We thought he might have done something terrible," Iaculous said and took her hands pitifully. She wondered if an apprentice were responsible for a master's actions, as a master was for an apprentice's. "He was a madman when he came upon us," he added.

Despite herself, Cherrie embraced him as a mother would a wounded child who had played too brutally with the bigger children. *Be still, little one. Plenty of time to grow up. Let's go find your little girlfriend, shall we?* She held him for a moment and felt the cold emotion taking over once more. They were still a pack, and there was still a task at hand.

She spun her dagger absently before returning it to its scabbard at her waist. "Where is Eralorien? He and I have unfinished business."

Denan dropped his head and opened his shirt so that she could see the damage done to his clothing and the recovering skin beyond. "He struck me down," Denan said as though she would fall at his feet and weep, eternally grateful that the gods had kept him safe. She reached out and caressed his cheek mechanically.

"Are you okay, my poor boy?"

It was easy playing this part for Denan. He carried the weight of the world on his shoulders and was desperate for a reprieve. He was brave, beautiful, and blessed with the soul of a poet, but he was no leader. She enjoyed his company, but far too swiftly he had lost confidence in himself. Such a thing was a turnoff to a mother in need of a man who could help rescue her daughter. It took a whore to notice these things and, where possible, ease the doubt to better their situation. A confident leader was what the Hounds needed right now. They were falling like flies, and there was a girl that needed saving. She looked at each of them and realised they needed her strength as much as she needed their skill at murder.

Cherrie felt the lure and wondered what the benefit would be if they knew. She knew a lure could lead an unaware man to death, and he would know no better. She agonised over the decision for almost a pulse of blood before deciding against telling them the truth. Did that make her evil? Not at all. Just a little heartless. They were her comrades, but she couldn't take any chance they would turn and flee. Therefore, she kept her peace and felt wonderful at the thought of killing Mallum.

"Does Eralorien still breathe?" she asked, knowing the truth already. The shape upon the horse's back was like that of a weaver's broken body.

As if struck in the same game with Heygar and Denan, Iaculous collapsed on his rear by the dead fire. He tried to speak, but no words came. Instead, with a simple wave of his fingers, a spiral of flame flew and found life. It rose, warmed them all, and lit up their camp.

"Find a place to bury him," she said to Denan, who

looked like a man accepting a rope from a lifelong nemesis as he hung from a cliff face.

Take the rope and fall in line, she thought to herself.

"I have no shovel," he argued, though he reached for the body upon the horse. A fine man in need of a leader. She should have taken control after Heygar's passing, but there was little point in arguing the matter now.

"Bury him in rocks. He was a Hound and deserves his rest," Cherrie hissed, and Denan nodded in acquiescence. When he disappeared into the night with his load, she turned to the young apprentice.

Alone at last, the last ever leader of the Hounds thought and sat down beside the broken healer.

THE GIRL WITH PLANS

They said nothing for a time. Instead, they listened to the struggles of the faraway gravedigger as he battled the darkness and the carrying of rocks.

Cherrie watched Iaculous as he watched the fire. The flames danced upon each other as though they were a beautiful orange ocean during a wild squall. It was only after a few moments she realised he was controlling the fire with his will. His hands barely glowed, and for her lack of knowledge in those mysterious arts, she found this peculiar. She said nothing. She merely sat and waited for him to speak.

A man always had something to say—especially at the more pressing of times in their lives. While sometimes it was wiser to sit and think up devious plans, a man frequently spoke his thoughts until thoughts fell away to plans. Perhaps speaking aloud was exactly what helped them form devious plans, she had always thought.

As she had expected, the sky finally opened and gifted the world a heavy downpour. Immediately, large droplets fell all around them. Far away, she heard Denan curse their bad luck and his own more than most. Iaculous didn't notice the rain as it fell until the fire withered in a soothing hiss. He grimaced, and Cherrie felt the drops soak her head through. She eyed the low-hanging tree and was about to break the silence when he did something he had never done before.

Iaculous whipped his hand swiftly out in front of him as though there were an irritating insect looking for purchase on his skin. A blue sphere was born into existence all around them. She almost leapt in fright, but instead, she gasped in delicate awe, and she knew this pleased him. It was translucent, shimmering, and formed around them in a comforting cocoon. She saw Denan through the hazy veil as he worked diligently with heavy rock, oblivious to her watching. She had seen Eralorien create such a shield before, but she had only remembered the old healer's struggles. His young apprentice barely showed effort.

Cherrie watched the raindrops land atop the sphere and roll down its side. The smoke from their little flame passed right through as though it were a clear afternoon without a breeze. On another day, she might have asked more, but this was no ordinary day, was it? It was as if a cruel god had taken one of their adventures as his own and twisted it for his and other's pleasure. If that were true, she thought the god a thurken cur. She thought the others just as bad.

"My shield is not as strong as Eralorien's." Iaculous's voice was weak and lost, and she wondered if the enchantment were affecting him. "I bring this shield to life so easily yet only a handful of days before, I could barely ensnare a daisy with these hands."

He looked at the guilty hands in question. They were covered in blood, and Cherrie resisted the urge to know more. When he was ready, he would say. So, she said nothing.

"It is this place which draws the source closer," he said, finally looking from the flames to her and then to the world all around them. "Every day that I walk these lands, I become infused with an unnatural power. Perhaps it is in the air or the water. Perhaps it is something in the food. Venistra is a place for an apprentice." Though these words pleased her greatly, she said nothing.

Far away, they heard the heavy clunk of a large boulder upon another and a faint curse again as the rocks Denan had gathered toppled away from the mound he was building. Cherrie would have found her lover's misfortune humorous were it not for the tragedy involved. The rain lashed against the shield, and she shuddered at an imaginary breeze, which would have accompanied the wave. Nice to have a weaver for unpleasant things like rainstorms.

Against her better judgement, Cherrie reached out to touch the wall of energy beside her. Her fingers hovered over the wall of delicate light, and they quivered like a limb suffering a bout of needles and stings, having sat at the wrong angle for too long. She dared a touch, and her entire arm vibrated. It wasn't an unpleasant sensation, yet as she pushed, it felt as though she pushed against an eternal cliff face.

"When you wish to leave this shield, you need only ask," Iaculous whispered, and she said nothing.

Instead, she pushed once more and, certain it would not budge, she rested her quivering arm in her lap. After a moment, the sensation left her hand. The source was a strange thing. Again, she said nothing. She looked into his eyes and saw the torment at play. She almost wilted and took hold of the boy and reassured him, lamented with him, and vowed vengeance with him.

Cherrie wondered if Bereziel might have made a fine master to the boy. Perhaps not. The boy desired to know of the weaving world, and Bereziel had driven himself to near madness searching to make sense of unnatural things. He had earned a fortune as a weaver and spent a lifetime's fortune on every scrap of parchment scribed with words on the source. She wondered if the boy were likely to take the same route.

Was Arielle likely to have her heart tripped by him as she had? She had almost forgotten Arielle's soul was raped from her body. Fury struck her, but she blinked it away and said nothing, for the boy had more to say.

"There is a nasty little deceiving voice deep within my mind, and it whispers everything I need to know. Things Eralorien could never fathom," Iaculous said. His voice broke, and her resolve almost did. "It tells me of terrible things."

He gripped the bridge of his nose as though a beast attempted to rip itself free of his skull. The flames flickered and grew, and the heat in their cosy little tent of light grew a little uncomfortable. The shard of stone within the jar upon his bandoleer glowed. He placed his hand over the glass, and all returned to normal.

"I could burn every single one of those grand cantuses now if I wanted." From the steel in his voice, she had little reason to disbelieve. "It is as if a great barge gate has opened in my soul, and it has released everything," he whispered. "I search to fight the current."

Cherrie knew well the doubt in all men when they said too much. Though she wanted to, she still said nothing.

"I do not know what Eralorien did to you, but when he came upon us, he stabbed Denan to near death, turned upon me, and then attempted to devour my soul. I didn't know he could do that. He never told me could do that. I wasn't ready. If I'd have known, maybe I could have saved him."

Still, she said nothing, despite the air suffocating her breath.

"His mind touched mine. He showed me things, terrible

things, and then tried to kill me. So, I killed him, but that wasn't all. I think I took some of his soul—like Mallum took Arielle's."

She thought this was incredible. He opened his cloak and tapped the jar.

"I feel powerful with him next to me," he said, and she wanted him to know power like that was nothing to be ashamed of. She embraced him and offered words of her own.

"Should Denan really be burying his body?"

"I could not return his soul and return him to life. I felt the cancer which had taken his mind. There was nothing to save. I stabbed him from this world, and it was all I could do. Tonight, I mourn my master. I would have no man or woman return him to the world of living now. He should be buried." Cherrie felt his tears upon her hands where they fell.

"Would you return the soul of Arielle?" she asked.

"If there was one thing in the world I could ever attempt and have success with, it would be returning Arielle's soul to the living," Iaculous said. "I miss her more than anyone can ever know."

Cherrie made no further attempt to ease his suffering. Regret and sorrow were powerful tools to wield and control, and she would wield him as any other devastating weapon.

She stroked his head. "Rest in my arms for now and feel as the world of Venistra makes you stronger. Tonight, we go hunting, and we will know success. Listen to that nasty little voice inside your mind as we save her."

"As you wish, Cherrie."

THE LEADER OF TWO

The young apprentice said nothing as they stood over the grave. He was no apprentice anymore. He was their weaver now. He had graduated by surviving their first encounter with Mallum while his old master did not. It was the tale of legends. It was also the only tale shared from this day forward to all who would listen. His master slain, he was an apprentice rising to the challenge.

Better that than the truth, Cherrie supposed.

A low sphere of light hung above their head, where the old weaver lay beneath a burial cairn of stone. She felt like a giant overlooking a mountain range, and she thought it a fitting place to forget an attempted rapist. That was probably unfair, but she had always felt men were a few breaths away from committing devious acts. Eralorien had been old, but he was no different.

Denan chanted a few words in Venistrian, and though she couldn't understand a word, she implied the sentiment. When he finished, Iaculous touched his chest, where he kept Eralorien's soul, and they left the grave. The time for words had passed.

They climbed atop their horses at the edge of the forest. The shock of losing yet another comrade by the wayside had already worn off. A side effect to the enchantment cast upon them? Did it matter?

With a shield above their heads, they turned to a night march. They had spent long enough sleeping as it was. There was a girl's soul to recover, a dark weaver to slay, and the hour was late.

Despite the lure, Cherrie had her wits about her. There was one more port of call to replenish what they could. Perhaps they would pick up a battalion or two to aid their mission, if they were on hand. The time of silent assassination was long past.

There was a dignity to wielding numbers, and as fierce as Iaculous was becoming, they were no longer seven Hounds. While Denan was anxious about returning home to the Hundred Houses, Cherrie would have been a fool to ignore taking advantage of his family ties. Few in Dellerin knew his true ancestry, but he had told her long ago in a secluded corner under the glow of a solitary candle. He had some royalty to him.

Each of the great islands had their own king, and they were free to rule any way they saw fit—as long as they answered to King Lemier, for he who ruled Dellerin itself ruled the entire world. Venistra had suffered under Lemier's rule far more than the other great islands. Perhaps a stronger king might have done more for his people, and Denan agreed. Perhaps Denan could still play his part in their future. Perhaps their luck would change when Denan finally returned home after exile.

"If we stick to the path, we should be all right. The beasts only travel in small packs," Denan said from atop his mount beside her. He had said it a few times now, yet still, she was wary. Apparently, so was he. She knew his worries, for those beasts were something she feared. He frequently reached for his pouch to ease his breathing, as though it gave him strength. She had never seen him reach for the salts so much before.

Iaculous, however, was brave. Cherrie saw the effort and passion in his drawn features as he charged his beast forward. He looked like a child holding all the worry in the world, letting nobody know of his melancholy. How hard must it have been for the young weaver to find his way in this world with a master who hated him? Perhaps Eralorien didn't hate him, but it would take a master of the mind to discover any other possible sentiment.

Perhaps, if they did ever find Bereziel in these forsaken lands, she might request Bereziel offer one year of his life to care for the boy. She sensed the goodness in him now, more so than ever, and she knew Bereziel capable of kindness. It might serve the boy in the last few steps before he became a man. Perhaps it would make Bereziel see there was more to the world than becoming all-powerful. She thought these strange thoughts, which comforted her, rather than thinking deeply of childhood traumas involving monsters.

"Only in small packs?" Iaculous asked, and his voice was weak and faded. The shield above their heads was taking its toll.

Cherrie thought for a moment of leaving him to rest but said nothing. After she wielded him as her weapon, the last fire had burned out, and they counted the dead, as long as they rescued Arielle, nothing else mattered. Not even the young weaver himself.

"We have nothing to fear from the Venandi night hunters," Denan said, and a shiver ran down her spine. Even the name brought back memories to her.

"We are the Hounds," Iaculous said.

The accompanying sphere of light shone above his head and lit the way for them all. It hovered and floated as though it had a mind of its own. He kept it lit as though it took little energy, and once again, Cherrie marvelled at the power he was displaying.

They stuck close together and, with the wind at their backs, they began a dash towards their journey's end. Like an itch they couldn't scratch, they followed their instincts in search of relief, and she knew the cause. The dim luring sensation to achieve a difficult task from a few days ago, in a different life, had now become an impossible, ensnaring obsession.

Cherrie suspected something else. With every member to pass from this world, the lure had increased its grip upon the survivors. What a cruel fate to gift upon any man, she thought, but not for a moment did she entertain enlightening them.

"They are monstrous hounds," Denan hissed. It was he who led the three riders, as he knew these parts and its threats.

She thought of him confronting Mallum, and she smiled bitterly. This was where he was at his best, throwing caution to the wind and thinking little of his actions, only his ability to complete his task. He was every general's wish—a fierce fighter willing to listen and to overcome where he saw an issue.

He had been a capable enough leader until Heygar's rat had disappeared. Until that moment, he had believed himself capable of that mantle, but when the most accommodating and loyal servant fled with no explanation, so began Denan's downfall in confidence. She wondered if he had lost his nerve sooner. Was it too much to lose

Heygar, having taken his best friend's lady to bed a few months before?

"They are the hounds bathed and born in the blood of demonic forces," he said, and she nodded in agreement despite herself.

Poor, brave Denan. Cherrie was aware he thought there was more to their illicit dalliance. He believed himself capable of her heart. He was a fine lover with a warm touch and generous ability, and she had kept with him and enjoyed the thrill and excitement of a young buck. Yes, he made her laugh, and he listened to her woe, but part of her did it so that she might hold it over Heygar for his own whoring ways—for there were plenty.

Had she known Heygar would perish as he did, she might have ended their relationship sooner than she had planned. It couldn't be helped now, and when the dust settled and Mallum's head lay upon a silver platter, she would rightly take Denan aside and delicately rip his heart out. He would be fine. She was capable of easing a lover away without disaster. It took a whore to know these things as well.

"They have sharp teeth," she whispered to herself and shuddered.

The hours passed, and though exhaustion was their companion, they never slowed their charge. They pushed the horses to near death, yet neither one of the three thought it prudent they rest. Night engulfed them, and with the many hours passing came tenfold the volume of rain. However, even when the path had turned to a steady stream, and their beasts struggled in the unforgiving terrain, they refused to stop their night march. Nothing else mattered. Even when thunder and lightning struck down fiercely on the deathly grey trees on either side, and the sweet smell of burning oak filled the air, they kept their eyes on the path ahead.

By the tenth strike, Cherrie had stopped noticing the explosions of nature altogether. Beneath the shield, no natural entity like this would stop them on their way. The fires erupted and died in the torrential rain, and still they brought their mounts forward.

Then they heard the threatening, guttural growling of hidden beasts all around them.

MEMORIES FROM THE FAIR

It was Denan who reacted first. He pulled on his horse's reins fiercely and brought it to a sudden halt. After a pulse, Iaculous and Cherrie slowed their own mounts and brought them alongside.

The growls were low, threatening, and barely audible above the driving rain, the hooved thuds of their horses, and her own panting breath, but still they were very much there. Bile churned in her stomach. She looked to either side of the dark path, into the tree line, and she counted several distinctive sounds. She recognised the growling, as she knew she would. For just a moment, she was no longer Cherrie, legend of the Hounds. Instead, she was a little girl facing a monster again.

She remembered the travelling fair even now—when it had settled itself upon land at the outskirts of Dellerin. The entertainers knew well how to draw a crowd. They had paraded through the city's bright boulevards and dark alleys and everywhere in between, advertising their amusements loudly. It hadn't taken long before the streets were littered with promotion slips, colourful posters, and pledges of wonder.

Cherrie couldn't remember the name of the fair thirty years gone, but she remembered it announced itself in bright golden lettering. She remembered images of trapeze artists, flying fireball shows, and drawings of fierce exotic beasts she had never seen nor heard of before. She remembered running her fingers along printed letters she could not decipher, and it had excited her. A break from the dreariness of grey and gloom was rare to one so unfortunate.

An unnaturally tall man in a green suit and a black top hat had walked the streets magnificently and spoken excitedly into a large wooden cone. His voice had magnified unnaturally, much to her cautious amazement. He had promised her and all who listened the world, with the "purist of performers," "the furriest of freaks," and so much more.

Cherrie had been mesmerised and drawn to the collection of tented buildings, like so many other children and adult alike. She had wandered unaccompanied towards the transitory constructs and thought little of the gathered families laughing, enjoying, and paying for wonder, for that is what a child of eleven was prone to do while her mother earned their food. She followed the sounds of jubilee until she had been among the shimmering tents, with stripes of gold, white, red, and blue. Her young mind thought it was the most beautiful, enchanting place she had ever seen.

She had walked among the entertainers as they weaved illusions that made her gasp in awe, and she had giggled with wild jesters who juggled fire and turnips and sometimes even turnips on fire. She had never wanted to leave—until she came upon the last monstrous construction of tarpaulin farther away from the rest.

Someone had called it the tent of "The Forbidden Beasts".

Tragically, it was a copper a visit, which was far too rich for her blood. But Cherrie couldn't resist the lure of the unknown, and as young as she was, she was equally brave. Swift as the wind and far from watching eyes, she had slipped beneath the heavy canvas wall and into a dark, wondrous place of terrifying delight.

Like every other tent, there was enough room to hold a tavern within. This tent was full of massive cages, each with a separate flavour of wild, exotic animals, like those promised to her on the posters. The unusual, acrid stench was unfamiliar to her nose, and she loved it even more, for she was careless, alone, and excited. These incredible animals of all shapes, colours, and sizes hissed, spat, roared, and panted, all for her entertainment.

Cherrie was most entertained with this part of the fair—until she heard the growl. Low, heavy, and menacing, it was not of this world. She recoiled yet could not help following its call. If asked, she would have said it was one of the seven fabled demons of the darkness stolen by a burly warrior hunter who had ventured into the source one full-mooned night with nothing but an iron mesh net and nerves of steel. She had imagined him thieving himself a monster as evil as the night, with a growl as twisted as a knotted loomis tail.

She had foolishly stepped farther into the tent, searching for this creature. She had searched with eager ears, past countless cages. Then, as far from any other pen as possible, the growl grew in volume and intensity. Though Cherrie doubted there was a wild animal running throughout the tent, she had instinctively felt she was its prey. The growl never seemed to break or pause to take breath. She remembered needing to release her bladder from fear of the sound.

Even though the exit called to her, she searched farther in, for that is what foolish children of eleven years of age were prone to do in tales of old. Then she came to a cage bigger than any other, twice the size of her and thrice as long, with bars as thick as molten candlesticks. She couldn't see within, for a large, woollen tarp covered the massive enclosure. She remembered her hands quivering as she split the covering when curiosity overcame fear.

She remembered little else but the releasing of water down her legs. She knew the beast had leapt forward, and glimpses of dry, grey skin remained in her mind for years after. Mostly, she remembered the finger-long incisors snapping at her throat, trying to dig into her flesh and tear her apart.

Years later, she had discovered which beast she had met that day. Though she had seen none of its kind since, she had never forgotten the haunting growl. It had vibrated in her chest, and she had felt an unholy fear that followed her for thirty years. It wasn't a reasonable fear, like that of dying. It was far worse and shared only by the children who had the misfortune of meeting a demonic monster beneath the stairs or in a webbed, dusty cellar.

She had felt it then, and now, in the middle of a forsaken island of ruin and starvation, where monsters roamed freely, Cherrie felt this familiar fear once more.

Denan fought his horse as it reared, for it knew the danger it found itself in and thought it better to flee without a heavy load upon its back. "Keep the light upon us, Iaculous, or we are doomed."

All three horses formed up beneath the blue glow of Iaculous's light as if a little blue light could save them from the things of nightmares moving around them, behind the cover of trees.

"Night hunters. They fear burning light and little else." Denan looked to rear and break like his horse. He knew these beasts better than most, even more than she did. He had a right to show panic, didn't he?

Cherrie felt her bladder scream in protest, and a cold question appeared in her mind. Was this how she would die? She heard the things of childish nightmares spread out and surround them, and she looked into the night, expecting to see teeth leap forward, snapping for her throat. She saw nothing in the wave of the leaves as they caught the wind and rain around them. The only suggestion of their presence was the growling.

Cherrie took hold of her dagger and waited for movement. Any movement, any place she might focus her defence upon. Her horse spun in a circle, fighting her control. She hissed for it to obey her, and finally, after a hastily taken breath, it relented.

Denan's horse nearly threw him, sensing its rider's panic. "This makes no sense."

To his exhausting credit, Iaculous raised his arm and their illuminating orb rose into the air and doubled in size. This time, she caught sight of the effort in his face, and she was grateful for his calm bravery. Perhaps there really was greatness in him.

The world turned to a hazy blue version of day, and though it was only a light, Cherrie felt braver. Then she realised holding the illumination was more than Iaculous could take. With every passing breath, he grew weaker and weaker.

The light gave away the monsters' concealment, and what she saw was terrifying. They were walking sacks of crude muscle, with limbs that were twice that of any man's. Their furless skin was grey like the forest, and they were exactly like she remembered. The shackled beast had towered over her cherry red curls that day at the fair, and as a woman, they only reached her waist, but it still did not diminish their threat. They were as if a god had forced a mountain lion upon a wilding wolf and produced a vile spawn of the source. Their teeth gnashed with hatred, rabid hunger, and spitting saliva.

Venandi night hunters roamed in packs of four or five, but Cherrie counted dozens on each side—too many to fight. The light flickered, and all beasts as one looked upon its struggling glow. Iaculous leaned on his horse, suffering a fierce strike to his will.

"Stay strong, little one," Cherrie called. It was an order and a request. The sweat on his brow streamed down his grimacing face.

"They are in a pack like I've never seen before," Denan cried, shaking his head. Iaculous's light flickered at hearing his panic.

Come now, Denan. Find your nerve.

"Possessed by a dark hand," he cried, and she hissed him to silence. He calmed his horse with a firm grip and looked into the night, towards their ambushing beasts.

"We are fine in the light of Iaculous," Cherrie said, feigning a confidence in him that only Arielle would have suggested possible.

"Iaculous creates imitation sunlight and nothing more," Denan countered warily, and the beasts turned from growling to barking.

If the growl was threatening, the bark was truly terrifying. They roared, and the forest became a deluge of noise. It sapped most of her nerve. Cherrie remembered the tarpaulin and the snapping teeth but also the loud roar and the sound of bending metal bars as the monster thrashed itself against the cage to get to her.

There were no bars to protect her this time. She felt like a pathetic little girl needing to relieve herself all over again, and her fear turned to deep anger. The roars grew, and Iaculous brought his orb higher and brighter. Perhaps he was powerful enough that he could bring an entire day to them and send the beasts on their way.

"I can bring fire too," Iaculous moaned. The light spread out and shone well enough that she could see each beast as they circled them on both sides. She wasn't sure if the child could keep their way lit until dawn.

"Can we outrun them?" she whispered to Denan, lest the beasts be clever enough to speak their language.

"On a clear night, we could, but in this rain … I don't know, Cherrie. I really don't."

Cherrie imagined the beasts listening and understanding. She looked up their path, and one of the night hunters sauntered across the muddy surface from one set of trees to the next. As it did, it snarled menacingly. It was moving to the other side to get a better angle of attack. She had seen that same casual demeanour in a thousand cats back in Dellerin, in the quiet moments before they pounced upon the unassuming rat and tore it to shreds.

She really didn't want to be torn to shreds. Who, then, would kill the dark weaver and rescue Arielle from her prison? Bereziel would, she thought and hated her self-deception. He had never loved her. He had charmed her. Emptied himself in her a few times and desired little else—especially a wedded bride and child.

She cursed the unwelcomed thoughts, and as Iaculous cried out in fatigued pain, she tried desperately to form a plan. Any plan. Anything better than running. Where was there a good rodenerack to cut deeply and leave in the mud as they fled from death?

"I am failing," Iaculous moaned.

He held the sphere's light high, and the beasts leapt back

from its spread. He dropped his reins and held both hands in the air, and his fingers glowed brightly. Cherrie could see him lose his grip on his ability. He was not ready for such power.

Without warning, the sphere fizzled away to a delicate spark and then that, too, fizzled to nothing. The reaction was immediate. All around them, the night trembled with terrible howling as the beasts realised the untimely daylight had returned the dark to its rightful place. Cherrie knew the next part to their concerto. They charged from both sides as their quarry presented themselves.

"Go!" she screamed and kicked her beast blindly forward.

Shrill barks of primal frustration filled the night; she knew death followed with relentless fervour. She knew the Venandi would never stop until the sun rose and burned them back to their caves. A cold thought occurred to her. With herself and her mount leaking aromatic blood all over the path, the hunters would not give up. Instead, they would frenzy and soon enough, they would catch up with a lame horse.

Cherrie ignored her own injury despite its maddening grip. Pain was pain, and she could manage pain in the quiet with a few bandages and no monsters in pursuit. If Iaculous could not regrow a couple of toes for her ... well, there were worse injuries to bear. That was the future, however. For now, she needed to escape and race the horse to its doom while she could.

Both comrades caught up with her, but their reunion was no happy occasion despite the dwindling sounds of their hunting pack. Both riders charged along with her for a time, but neither man said a word, for their eyes were on the ill-lit road ahead and their ears upon the beasts behind. They raced the night against their hunters, and her brave horse kept up its miserable charge as best it could. Perhaps with the other two beasts running alongside, it drew in the last of its will and raced its last ever race, determined to make it its best.

Soon enough, she fell a mount's length behind her brethren and swiftly a length beyond that. Cherrie willed her beast forward, but dreadful exhaustion affected her every move. She realised, like Pageant, she was bleeding herself to death with this charge.

She called to them, but her voice was weak. She felt dizzy and fought a precarious tumble from her saddle to the mud below when the horse bounced her over a dip in the ground. Up ahead, the path turned slightly into a corner. Both riders went ahead, but when Cherrie took the turn, she took it too widely and struck a branch as she did. Miraculously she did not fall, but she wavered and dropped the reins, relinquishing the hold on her horse.

"No!" she screamed, feeling the beast embrace the respite.

Cherrie whipped her hands down and caught the leather straps once again. She charged her horse forward as the blurred world of darkness slowed to resemble a deathly forest of grey at the witching hour.

"Not yet!" she cried, watching her comrades charge off into the darkness ahead. She didn't want to die alone. "Wait!" Her head spun and she felt weak.

They left her far behind.

She kicked Pageant fiercely in the ribs, and the horse answered with an exhausted snort before running forward, though only for a few steps. The damage was done. The beast had forgotten what hunted them, and it came to an agonizingly slow trot, gasping loudly, for whinnying was too difficult a task. And then it stopped altogether.

Not like this.

"Oh, please," Cherrie whispered and patted the horse, but it was barely listening.

She dared not shout out for her comrades again, so she allowed her horse to move at its own pace. She shook the reins gently. Slowly, the horse walked forward, but as before, it slowed, stopped, and snorted loudly between desperate gasps. Then she heard something else in the wind's turn, something beautiful and hopeful. She heard the rushing of a river and hoped once more.

"Be swift, Cherrie," she whispered to herself and dropped painfully to the ground, moaning as she did. She pulled a rag from her pack and wrapped it tightly around her ruined foot. "Take the pain, little girl."

She pulled tightly and almost fainted from the fresh shards of agony shooting up like fiery bolts through her foot. She pulled her pack and her weapons after but little else from Pageant's back. In the distance behind, she heard them again. The pack was on the hunt, howling as they raced down upon her. The blood would drive them wild; she knew what last horror she needed to endure.

She could have taken a moment to tend to the horse's wound as she did her own, but instead, Cherrie held her reins tightly. She pulled at the horse's wound with her dagger, drawing further spillage down its smooth, brown skin. The horse cried out and reared but trusted her hold and did not flee her master. Cherrie felt worse as the fresh river dripped down onto the path.

"I'm sorry, Pageant."

She dragged the horse around and smacked it fiercely on the rear. Without her weight and following its bolting instincts, it charged back down the path they had taken, towards its doom. She knew it a cruel thing to send such a magnificent, trusting animal to its death, but a girl had to do what she needed to do. She had to survive the night, kill a dark murdering weaver, and recover the beautiful soul of a lost daughter.

Cherrie turned from the road and hobbled into the tree line in search of the river. The thundering hooves had already faded. She found herself less graceful than usual, and her feet caught on the marshy ground. She prayed to the gods of the source that her scent dissolve in the rain. She struggled to keep balance but used branches as support as she crept into the forest. She kept going, swallowing the pain of every step in grim determination. Then, somewhere far away, the howling rose into a shrill, excited cry, and she felt shameful as she stumbled down a slope towards the sounds of nearing water.

"I'm so sorry, Pageant."

By the time she had reached the bottom, Cherrie heard something else, which broke her spirit. It was a low, recognisable hum. It grew, thundered and tore the night apart. She recognised it as a magnificent retreat.

"Oh, to the thurken fires with you, Pageant."

Somewhere along the road, the horse she had sent out as sacrifice had realised its erroneous charge and spun away from the threat. As it raced by without a burden upon its back, she realised it could easily outrun the Venandi. There was only one more scent for the monsters to follow, and she was the easiest of prey.

With panic threatening to consume her, like a Venandi would an injured legend, Cherrie charged towards the river, ignoring all pain and weariness. Unforgiving branches snapped and stung her face, and her foot bled and blinded her with pain, yet still, she ventured after a phantom sound like a child searching in a fair.

Suddenly, she broke through the clustered trees and unforgiving shrubbery and came upon the river. She caught sight of its black surface in the concealed glow of the moon and thought its glisten beautiful. It was fierce and deep, and without a thought, she leapt from the riverbank. Mercifully, she was carried from the edge, and for a moment, she believed she might survive. It embraced her in its icy grip towards salvation, and all the river asked in reply was a few feeble kicks to keep herself afloat as she surged away from monsters and easy trails. Drowning was a thing reserved for fools and children.

After a time and a few floating miles, Cherrie swam towards the edge of the bank and lay among the reeds, attempting further attention to her ruined foot. She was no healer, but a lifetime of removing cuts and bruises from overly enthusiastic patrons had gifted her the ability of a steady hand, even while enduring terrible pain.

For hours, she hobbled along the riverbank with the flowing water and the great southern star above as her guide. The rain ceased its fall, and the forest fell to reassuring silence. She feared for her missing comrades but focused most of her thoughts on besting the night. The only respite she offered herself was as dawn approached, when she allowed herself a time to brush her ruined hair, repaint her lips and eyes, and reapply a fresh shower of her perfume. It was the little things to make a girl feel like herself again, and she felt better.

As dawn whispered its reassurances, Cherrie rested beside a large boulder and allowed herself a few precious moments, imagining how grand it would be to slay Mallum. Then a growl from somewhere in the surrounding trees shattered the last grip the terrible lure had upon her mind. Somehow, she knew, this was the end.

DAY FIVE

C herrie backed away from the growling. She was not scared but merely numbed, as though the lure had finally diminished from her mind. With this clarity came an acceptance of death.

She had lived long enough for any whore; she had lived her life well. It would end in the middle of a dreary forest in the middle of an evil land, but it was still a finer place to die than at the hands of a displeased patron who desired one more malicious sensation of ecstasy. Over the years, in a plethora of brothels, she had discovered dozens of friends, cold as stone with spent seed still inside them, lying naked upon silken bedding. They had been strangled, skulls shattered from nearby utensils, or their throats slit by a demented lover. It was common enough and an inexpensive consequence to those with eternal golden pockets or political influence.

"Always be wary of the better dressed gentlemen, for they have no boundaries," her mother had told her as a child. Then she, too, had fallen to the hands of a royal that very same month.

All whores had an inescapable hourglass upon their

beaten and broken crowns. Cherrie thought it likely she would have met the same end, were it not for Heygar's influence, so she was thankful for each day. She had nearly provided a brighter future for her daughter.

Yes, it was a better life lived, and she knew it would end as the growling took shape in the form of four Venandi night hunters. Brave, betrayed Pageant had taken most of the beasts with her as she fled. Most.

"Couldn't shake all of you, could I?"

She drew her mask from her pack and left the rest of her belongings where they lay. She thought about leaping for the water, but the deluge was nowhere as impressive as in the hours before. A weaker current would grant her nothing but a hindrance of movement, and they would easily rip her apart. So, she backed away and awaited her fate. Death was inevitable, for her last chapter was written. There would never be another tale of Cherrie and, like Heygar, this was one legend too big for her luck.

She slipped the metal mask across her face and immediately felt more confident. She was one of The Seven Hounds, and a Hound never slipped into the source quietly. They screamed, cursed, cut and fought to survive, just to take that next breath and kill a little more. She drew her sword as the beasts surrounded her.

The first rays of light appeared in the sky, and the world slowly turned from the darkest of night to the reassuring pink of a new day. But Cherrie knew well that she would be little more than shreds of meat and bone long before the sun's burning light shone through the trees to drive them away. Her foot's searing fire was blinding, but she ignored all but the growling. She crouched low, with the dagger in her left hand and sword in her right, waiting for the attack. She remembered that child in the dark with those teeth snapping, but her nerve held, and she pledged that she would make at least one pay for her downfall.

"Come at me, you thurken curs." They howled, snarled, and circled her, and she watched each beast. "*Come on.*"

She leapt at one of her killers, who hissed in irritation and stepped away from her. Its ears flicked back and forth, and its furless grey tail swished like a cat tired of petting and ready to strike.

"*Come on*!" she screamed again, begging them to dare end her life. Challenging them to face her blades. "Come meet your end!"

As if her fear and hate were too much to hear, they attacked.

The first came from the left. Two massive leaps and it was upon her, snarling ferociously and snapping at her throat. But Cherrie was no horse, blessed with nothing more than sprinting speed and a primal instinct to survive. She was fierce. She sidestepped the charge and plunged her sword through its ribs. It tore open the beast's sternum, like a stuffed carcass of veal in a solstice feast, and it careened away from her.

It was an easy counter in the most basics of combat. Even though the creature had such muscle and power, with skin as thick as leather, her blade went deeper than she had expected. With one shrill screech, it stumbled away from her, leaking blood and viscera until its heart fell still and the beast died in the long grass.

Cherrie stumbled away on unevenly planted feet as the second caught her from behind and knocked her to the ground. All too late, she realised the first charge had been little more than a diversion. She desperately rolled away, but the beast took hold at her shoulder and gnawed through her leather and steel armour coverings as though they were nothing more than toasted honey bread. She felt teeth tear into skin, and she screamed. The remaining beasts howled in unison in their victory.

Her vanquisher snapped its head back and forth, shaking the fight from her before slamming her to the ground as a dog would with a blooded beast. She cried out, feeling her shoulder rip open, and she fell free from the beast's grip. It did not finish her but merely chewed on the bloody lump of muscle, skin and collarbone remaining in its mouth, leaving her writhing and leaking in the grass.

"Oh, please, not like this." She could hear the crunching of savoury bones. "Let me take one more with me before I die!" she screamed to any god or demon who was listening, but the deities were silent.

The beast swallowed the mouthful and craned its head to seek the next succulent piece upon which to sate itself. It tipped her metal facemask in curiosity, then rested a massive paw upon her chest and took what breath she had with its casual weight. She felt the blade in her hand, but her body would not obey her will, for the beast's breath was hot, and the stench of its meal stung her nostrils.

"May the sun burn your kin to ash," Cherrie cursed and felt burning tears stream down her face.

She had only managed one kill, and it had been a tactic on their part. To be outsmarted by a primal monster's strategies was a dreadful thing. She felt the impossibly heavy dagger; it had been with her from the beginning, and it was only right it be in her grip at the end. She was the little girl once more, alone with the monster. Her bladder released, and all she could do was lie in the grass and weep silently.

A third beast snarled from afar and distracted her captor. It replied in a fearsome roar and stepped from her chest, lest its comrade seek an undeserved morsel of flesh. The show of force was enough to dissuade the newcomer, and it sat back down to wait its turn.

Cherrie caught her breath and felt Bereziel beside her. She did not feel his love, nor his hope. She only felt an eternal sadness, and she almost cried out for him. For the regrets, for their child, for the terrible distance between.

"I only ever loved you, Beezee," she whispered as the blood loss caused her mind to wander towards defiance. He was not there. He never had been. She was alone.

But she would never slip away silently. She summoned the last of her will and plunged her blade through her assailant's throat, slitting the leathery skin open. Its blood showered her as it died, and she imagined Heygar would have liked this.

"I still have a fight in me," she challenged and climbed to her feet.

Cherrie pushed the dead beast away from her and, once again, she took both sword and dagger in hand. The sitting night hunter leapt upon her, and she swung with both weapons. Her mind no longer recognised pain as a thing to fear or endure. She was beyond thought like that. She inflicted devastation on the hunter and sent it scampering away, yelping, with three long gashes across its face. She thought it fled from her like a terrified child in a fair after meeting a monster in the dark, and this last thought pleased her.

The last night hunter circled her swiftly. She struggled upon her feet, matching its wide arc. Around and around, it charged. Then she stumbled, and like a crack of lightning, it slipped beneath her defence and knocked her to the ground one last time. She fought weakly, but it pinned her down and ripped her sword-bearing arm from its socket, leaving it to flap uselessly at her side. With a second bite, it ripped her arm free, and Cherrie squealed like the slaughtered swine she was. The beast was wise to spit her arm away, and it bit down heavily upon her mask. It knew a bite to the face was fatal to any man.

But for its knowledge, it was not to know the metal mask Heygar had gifted her was from the heart, and it was the one gift she still treasured. Upon its impenetrable metal surface was a painted face of such misery and beauty, she named her Muillil, after a demon of the source. It bore a white face and a stunning red smile as alluring as a damsel with lust on her mind, and upon this mask, Cherrie added her own signature. She had painted a large tear for all her pain, and when she wore the mask, she felt more alive than ever before. Stories of Cherrie the Red among those mercenaries who knew her less suggested she was ugly underneath its surface, and the mask itself was her true face. Perhaps this was true.

To a Venandi, however, it was a face to be bitten, and it lost three teeth upon its Venistrian metal. The beast howled in frustration and confusion, and a large piece of tooth fell free into her hand. Such brutal incisors, as fierce as any blade she had ever known. She struck from the side, through its leathery ear, and suddenly, there was no biting anymore. Instead, the monster fell away from her as the tooth penetrated skin, muscle, and brain.

Cherrie gasped from the sudden weight falling away. She felt herself slip away, accepting death as she had seen brave souls before upon the field of battle. With little strength left, she attempted to crawl away from the dead beasts and pools of blood, but the simple act was beyond her, so she lay in the grass and slowly bled to death.

Time stood still, however. The sun rose, and there was no release from her agony. Her heart was as stubborn as she was, and it refused to fall still, so she lay in ruination and allowed

her mind to drift. She thought of Heygar's attempts at
bumbling romance, and she remembered, for a time, it had
been nice. She had smiled and loved him in a way. She felt
Heygar near once again, and this thought warmed her
something wonderful.

Dawn lit the land anew, and she gasped her last few
breaths. Cherrie felt a great darkness around her as her life
finally seeped away. She felt a terrible coldness of the soul.
Blood-laden tears fell from her eyes, down her beautiful face,
to join the blood-soaked ground underneath. And then she felt
his hands upon her, and her eyes focused.

"Hush, Cherrie. You are among friends," Iaculous
whispered, and she shivered from the cold.

He held her remaining ruin of a hand and hid the horror of
seeing her in such a state well enough. His hands glowed
blue; they matched the sky behind him. How strange. She
hadn't seen a blue sky in an age.

"You need to kill Mallum," she whispered, and he nodded
sadly. She felt so cold. The sun was shining, the sky was blue,
and death terrified her. She gasped again, and he hushed her.

"I can't heal you, though I try," he said pitifully. His
hands glowed so brightly, yet still, she felt the darkness. So
close, she could touch it—or close enough that it touched her.

"She loved you, Iaculous," Cherrie whispered. He nodded
and placed his healing hands upon her broken chest. "All she
wanted in this life was you."

Cherrie felt herself drift into the darkness. *Not yet!* she
screamed in her mind.

"I will do what is needed," he said.

"You should have stayed with my girl and protected her,
but you failed her, Iaculous. This is all your fault," she
hissed with her last few breaths. He dropped his head in
shame, and she was glad. "If you do nothing else in this

life, save my girl from that monster," she hissed, and he nodded.

With the last of her strength, Cherrie squeezed his glowing hand and looked into his broken eyes. She saw nothing but ferocious power behind those eyes, and this pleased her.

"He stole her soul …"

She felt a beast clawing at her mind, at her soul, at all she was. Not in this world but in the world where Heygar waited with Silvious, unable to move, trapped by a dreadful enchantment, by the lure.

"Take my soul, Iaculous, and wield it," Cherrie pleaded before surrendering to the demon of the source as the cold engulfed her completely.

INTO THE GREY

The Venandi charged through the undergrowth, and Denan followed behind as swiftly as he could. He swung his sword at every branch careless enough to get in his way and cut them from his path in each sweeping motion.

"Come here."

The fleeing beast did little but snarl in frustration as it attempted to escape his wrath.

The sun between the grey leaves shone brightly, and the night's heavy rainfall left the world glistening something fine. Denan ducked under a branch and tripped over the same tree's root. He tumbled, rolled, and came to a nasty stop in the middle of the wet mud.

He allowed himself a moment's reprieve from the night's exertions before continuing the dreadful race. His chest ached, and his breath was fading, but he was determined to catch the beast. He knew it was capable of greater speeds, but with the sun's rays reinforcing his charge, the beast was attainable. Though the smarter plan was to leave the Venandi to its recovery and he to his own, Denan wasn't capable of mercy. Not today. If he did little else after killing Mallum, then eradicating every single one of the Venandi night hunters was a life well lived.

"Get over here!" he roared to the endless forest of grey. He received only the dull thrashing sounds of an injured beast breaking branches in reply. He would kill one, and then he would kill them all. He would return to his father a hunter, and for his dead mother's sake, there would be deference given to the man.

Denan cursed again and attempted to scramble to his feet, but his strength had left him. His body was torn to shreds from skirmishes, but no blow had felled him, so he continued this demented hunt as though possessed. Perhaps he was possessed by grief, misery, and a bitter madness to boot.

Oh, how he missed the colour of green. He remembered when these forests were greener. He also remembered seeing the first tinges of grey appearing. It was a disease of nature, he suspected, despite prophets and shamans claiming it was the great mysterious stones' doing. As if a stone could spread out the cancerous grey, stealing the life essence from the world around it, like a blight did upon a crop. Like a bad king upon a failing nation.

"Oh, gods of the source," he moaned suddenly and grabbed his chest as an attack came upon him.

No, not like this. He squirmed in the mud and struggled to rise. *No, not yet.* He had so much more killing to do. He couldn't allow a simple act of suffocation to get in his way. Besides, he had a little time before the attack brought him to unconsciousness, and the beast couldn't survive another hour being hunted. So, he struggled onwards.

Each step was agony. Denan's chest constricted with every deep breath, but a few miles in, he saw the first leaves with a glimmer of green and felt wonderfully renewed. A few miles after that, a few leaves turned to teeming branches of green. Eventually, he scrambled through a stunning forest, just as he had as a wild, youthful royal, earning his skills as a hunter.

He considered taking a rest until he discovered the fresh stream of blood from where he had struck the beast. His anger flared, and he thought of her.

Cherrie had fallen behind and was lost in the grey as he was. No, he was not lost, just desperate. He wanted to call out for her, but he knew the dangers. He wanted to call out for Iaculous too, but he also knew the futility of it. He had feared returning home for decades, and now, walking these lands, his heart was heavier than the day he had left. He had hoped to return as a saviour. He had hoped to return to something more than this.

Iaculous had discovered Cherrie's absence first, and he turned his mount around without regard for sense or himself. Denan had not followed. He wasn't familiar with fear, not from an army of drunken gelderings, a storm of sea monstrosities, or even the vengeful wrath of Heygar for stealing his bride. Fear, however, had taken his will these last few days, and he was a worse man for it.

He had left his comrades behind to the darkness, only to face an ambush from three Venandi further on up the road. They had fallen upon him from either side of the path. One had taken him from his saddle with a crunching strike, denting his chest plate, and he had rolled from the beast instinctively. His cursed horse had sprinted off from his life forever, leaving him to his doom, just as he had done with Cherrie and Iaculous.

His old master of skills had always suggested, "Carry all you need upon you and all else upon a beast of burden," and it had served him well in that fateful moment. With sword and shield, Denan had fought the first as the second waited its turn and the third after that. He had always despised their brutality but respected their animalistic code of honour. He had taken advantage and reasoned where each attack would come from, for if one knew the beasts and their ways, one could stand toe-to-toe with many of them—at least for a time.

He had taken the first by dazing its initial attack with the edge of his shield and piercing his sword through its clouded grey eye. The second had attacked from behind and managed a claw to the chest before Denan had knocked it away. He plunged the blade deep into its belly, tearing a gash so deep the snarling animal had wailed loudly until it had faded to nothing. The third beast was wary, and though its grander brethren had fallen to the human's blade, it still attacked. Denan had answered the challenge and killed it at the cost of little more than the exhaustion of battle and a spinning head.

He had left the three earless bodies to rot upon the road. He had kept his wits about him and recalled the rules of survival taught to him as a child. He had skulked from the path with the distant sound of howling in his ears. With nothing but his belt and weapons to his name, he had disappeared into the forest and discovered a sturdy tree deep within.

He remembered climbing high enough that no hidden set of vicious teeth would appear from the dark and tear his ankle free. Concealed and comfortable enough among the thick branches and clumps of aroma-quenching leaves, he had thought himself clever, with the wind as his company and little else. He'd felt confident, as high as a three-storey tavern, and with every hour passed in silence, the only worry he'd had was that of fighting slumber, until the monsters tracked him down.

They had come from the path where he had slain their brothers, sniffing the air knowingly. They had gorged upon their dead brethren and sought the next course. The alpha male that had led them was broader than any other monster Denan had seen. Each step taken was an effort and taken with deliberate composure. The beast behind it had been nearly as impressive but was younger, patient, and waiting for its turn to lead. That was how it usually was in a pack of five or six. He had counted thirty at least, and he wondered if his heart had hammered loudly enough to reveal his concealment. They had known their prey was near, but better than that, they had known their prey had ceased running, as though some entity had whispered in their ears of his whereabouts.

He had gripped the branch tightly and peered through the foliage as each of the monsters sniffed the air around his tree. All thirty in unison had stared up at him with unblinking eyes, and he had dug his head into the unforgiving tree bark as though avoiding their eyes might dissuade them from their nasty primordial intentions.

One monster far below had stared at the tree trunk like a champion meeting an ill-matched opponent in the arena. The beast had lifted its paw up against the sturdy bark and dragged its long claws down, ripping through the wood as though it were little more than paper upon a blade. The surrounding pack had howled triumphantly.

Buoyed on by the clamour of success, the beast had bitten slowly into the thick bark and tore it loose, leaving the skin of the tree unprotected and raw. By the third bite of the tree, Denan had known well his fate. Above him, a nest of birds had known also and took flight, squawking loudly before disappearing into the night. A second beast had gone to task on the other side of the trunk, biting and spitting the bark clear before tearing strips of wood away as though it were little more than a stalk of cornwheat. With each successful piece torn away, they had each taken a moment to snarl a challenge for him to drop and meet them in battle.

"Leave me be," he had cried in reply, and the panic in his voice had brought forth a renewed drive to fell the sanctuary quicker. So, he had climbed higher into the tree, knowing a fall from five feet would be as fatal as from fifty. Each step up had been more treacherous and trickier as the thinning branches clustered tightly together.

Far below, he had heard the terrible splintering as the trunk faltered under the assault. He remembered breaking the surface of branches, then looking out into the cloudy night sky at the top and hearing only silence. It had almost felt like there were no dangers below, but it was a fool's con, like placing a covering over his eyes as the hangman drew nearer. But that blindfold tore free as the branch he clung to shook suddenly, and a terrible snapping filled his ears.

With the terrible thrust of the ground calling him back to her unforgiving grasp, Denan had done what any damned man would do. He had leapt blindly to the nearest adjacent tree and willed the power of the source that the branch he caught could take his weight. Within a pulse, he had discovered that it couldn't.

His head had struck a thick branch and knocked him senseless; he had fallen helplessly from the crown, hitting every branch along the way. He remembered the terrible spinning, the stinging slap of leaves upon his face, and the tearing of spindled branches on his skin. Then he had landed painfully on a large, hanging bough a half-dozen feet above the ground. He remembered gasping for air and feeling for broken bones. A terrible darkness filled his vision, and he remembered nothing more until he opened his eyes to the coming dawn.

As he stirred his mind from the unfortunate sleep, he had

discovered, to his amazement, the beasts sitting quietly beneath him as though listening to a master's instruction. Unsure of what else to do, he had watched them as the night turned to day. Every now and then one had broken from their trance to scrape at the tree trunk weakly, but after a few attempts, each had offered nothing more than a low frustrated growl before sitting back down. This went on until the sky had turned to early morning and with the first whiff of burning touching his nostrils, the beasts fled from the tree leaving four of their brethren behind. Fearing he might lose their tracks, Denan had dropped to the ground with sword drawn, craving vengeance.

THE FURY OF SUNLIGHT

To be his father's son was a difficult thing, but to come home after exile and beg for a battalion of the king's finest would be an insurmountable undertaking altogether. But he would do it to save Arielle. It's what Cherrie would want. But when he thought deeper on the matter, enlisting his father's help was the only way he could kill Mallum. He had come so far on this ill-fated trip, he couldn't stop now.

Being in Venistra was intoxicating, with so many poisoned memories stinging his every step. It had all gone wrong confusing duty with honour. As a prince to an unforgiving Venistrian king, it had been his duty to cull the packs of Venandi night hunters, and he had performed that task admirably. He remembered leading a group back then and leading them well. What a glorious life of hunting, slaying, and camaraderie it was with his entitled royal companions, and for a handful of wonderful years, he had delivered such devastation to the vile creatures that few of them remained. It was then that his father ordered he return home and take his place at court. Perhaps things might have been different had he answered the command. Instead, he had earned the people's favour by choosing to continue his war with the monsters and very nearly winning it completely.

He was denied victory, at the latest hour. When the beasts numbered only a few dozen packs and facing complete annihilation, a battalion of his father's most persuasive troops had appeared at his campsite bearing false smiles and somewhat pressing orders. After being "convinced" to return home, he was met with his father's full kingly wrath. Unfortunately, the king approved of a few roving packs—for they were a fine reminder that a king was a necessary protector, and therefore beasts were a necessary evil. If a few families disappeared every now and then, well, that was a shame. This was where the first real arguments between prince and king began. As a youth of fifteen arguing with a king over moralities, honour, and compassion, he should have become a more confident man in the years following, but he did not. Once his father's dominance prevailed, every argument after became more and more heated. In a way, Denan was glad to understand the world for what it was beyond living in the riches of the Hundred Houses. Perhaps was he not so disillusioned, he might never have stepped from beneath the shadow of his father's kingdom and understood the courage of peasants struggling to earn a life for themselves without entitlement to cushion their fall. As he grew older and more naive, so too did his desire to better the people less fortunate. He fought for their livelihood, spoke out against Dellerin's strict taxes, and became a thorn upon his father's crown. The arguments turned to venomous skirmishes, and after a time, they could no longer be contained within the privacy of their own company, but instead, they spilled out into the court. He was not alone, for he was fierce, honourable, and attractive, and he stoked the fires of betterment in many of the other youths in the

Hundred Houses—at least for a time. His eighteenth birthday should have been a time of celebration, but instead of receiving a king's blessing as was traditional, in the presence of all royals of the court, he was stripped of his title, his inheritance, and everything he believed he was. Those who had followed him swiftly fell silent, along with all of their radical thinking. The fear of the king taught him the loyalty of the Venistrian people. Perhaps, standing alone at the harbour awaiting his exiled embarking, he might still have felt a spark of hope in his heart for his country. But no friend or follower had spoken for him nor offered him help; no comrade had taken his sins as their own and walked the lonely miles with him; no peasants had offered him shelter or a warm meal. Perhaps if even one person was inspired by his selflessness he might have felt that his life wasn't a complete failure. As it was, it took the carnage of war for him ever to find himself again.

Denan looked towards the burning brightness of the morning in the unnatural path ahead, and the smouldering desire to hunt down the entire pack of monsters engulfed him. Let the dying beast show him the way. He desired Mallum's head, but something drew him to hunting the pack. With the dawn came a terrible creeping presence to his mind. Something invasive and cruel. He felt as though a hand split his mind between reasoning and desire. It played with his fearfulness, it stole his better judgement, and it gorged itself upon his will. It could not be human, it was something else, and he wondered was it desolation come alive?

"Cleanliness and perfumes are a curse in this part of the world. Why else did they attack her first?" he pointed out to no one in particular. Ahead, he heard the beast's desperate struggles as its skin burned. Not long now. "She might well have survived this," he said aloud, allowing his deepest thoughts to surface. Strangely, he had believed until the morning that she could not survive the night. Yet, hope had sprung anew as though it were an infection of the soul. "And Iaculous's flames might well burn away the curs," he muttered as an afterthought. Denan looked back the way he had come as if, far behind, his comrades still breathed. Perhaps they did. In the light, anything was possible. It was only in the night where nightmares could be real, and in the day when they hunted them.

Denan counted to ten slowly and forced himself to relax. Sometimes this tactic worked, and sometimes it got so much worse. He reached for his bag of spices, opened the little knot, and realised his hands shook fiercely. It really could be a bad attack. Holding the pouch to his nose, he breathed in the bitter, salty aroma and fought a coughing fit. He felt a break in his lungs and nothing more. Holding his hand across his chest, he poured the last of his water over his head, down his tight chest, and over his groin. Sometimes that helped. Taking one more deep inhale and feeling a little stretch in his constricting lungs, he cursed his own weakness and resumed the race. If he died, he died. What mattered was hunting the last beast, the one still bearing his dagger's plunge. He had never seen a Venandi flee mid-fight with its brethren dead and left unavenged, but this one had. Strange behaviour indeed.

The blood streaks stood out a great distance in the vibrant green as did the many broken branches and clefts in the drying mud from his prey's pack. He was getting closer.

Hours slipped to moments as Denan became little more than the careful hunter, watching the ground, the trees, the world, and all that was above him. All deathly grey clouds dissipated, revealing the stunning land of Venistra in all its glory. Deep down, he knew he should stop this frantic lunacy.

His bones felt ready to shatter, and something crushed his chest in the invisible grip of a vice. All the agonising effort was worth it, however, when he broke through a canopy of stubborn branches and faced an unprotected flash of sunlight. On the hard, uneven ground, he almost tripped over the corpse of the beast, long forgotten by its kin. Denan covered his eyes from the glare, stood over the dead beast, and cursed his bad luck. The edge of the forest had faded away to mountainous stone. The beast had tried desperately to make the last charge, but without the cover of the trees, it had succumbed to the day and died. Somewhere above, among the dips and caves of the rocks, his principal quarry had hidden themselves away from the day.

"Couldn't make it home, could you?" he hissed to his prey, then he sliced one of its ears off and placed it in a little pouch attached to his belt. He hadn't done this in years, but he couldn't help himself. Some habits couldn't be eliminated, he supposed. Even if they were habits from youth. "Should have stayed among the trees and died at my blade." Denan patted the pouch absently. "Would have been a better thing for both of us. Would have been a fine fight."

His chest heaved, and he understood what the beast must have felt, suffocating and burning from the deadly rays. They were such incredible monsters from nightmares, yet weak to the world's most natural thing. Perhaps this was what kept their species contained? Freedom to run the land in night and day would swiftly place them atop the food chain.

Around him, the forest went still. Immediately, he reached for his resting blade at his side. He peered into the tree line, searched for prey or threat, and found nothing.

Crack.

Denan's eyes narrowed. Something moved from behind him. Something menacing and vile. Something that caused the birds to fall silent, lest they draw its wrath. He sat on a rock and waited for what hunted him. In the light of day, with aching chest, he would run no more. He watched the trees in reply and waited for whatever hunted him to reveal itself. The sword was steady in his grip, even if his body was a ruin.

Crack. This breaking twig was closer.

"I can see you there, cur, hiding like a coward among the trees," Denan lied, wondering if he sounded convincing enough.

After a few moments, a figure emerged from behind a tree and walked into the light.

DELUSIONS AND GREATNESS

"Oh, thank the gods," Denan cried. The young weaver stood at the edge of the tree line, covered in blood, with eyes stretched wide in a mania. Denan caught him as he collapsed. "Are you okay, Iaculous?"

It was as though the warmth in his heart had disappeared, like an old broken mercenary who had seen and done things no honourable warrior should ever have to. Iaculous was broken. Denan embraced him as a father would for a time. He waited for the youth to speak of the horrors he had faced since their parting. Evening was half a day away. There was time enough for this.

"Why didn't you follow me?" Iaculous said after a few breaths.

"It was a fool's errand." Denan felt shame for his cowardice. The child had raged into death willingly; he had not. He thought of Cherrie, then he shook her image from his mind and focused on the only thing that settled him.

"A fool's errand is exactly what it turned out to be," Iaculous said.

Denan released him, leaving him hunched over as if in

prayer on the dusty, hot ground. He recovered the dagger from the shoulder blade of the beast.

"So, you were able to kill at least one of those monsters." Iaculous eyed the monster with unrivalled disgust. Some men were built to kill, others to heal. Others to rule everything.

"I slowed her down."

"I wasn't able to kill any of them," Iaculous mumbled and climbed to his feet.

"Do not feel bad."

"I don't feel bad. I know I tried."

Denan saw a terrible story on the young man's face. The shock, the misery, the hesitation. He wanted the young man to hold his tongue more than anything else in the world, but Iaculous had words to share.

"I charged towards those beasts in search of Cherrie, but I couldn't find her on the road," the young weaver said, catching a weeping gasp in his throat.

Denan felt his chest tighten. He clutched his bag of spices once more and inhaled deeply. He felt better, but the child was still speaking. He wanted to grab him and scream him to silence. He wanted to concentrate on killing the Venandi. He wanted to reach his father's house, engage in peace talks, and he wanted an army to kill that thurken Mallum. Everything would be all right as long as they killed Mallum.

Do not speak of Cherrie. Speak of our task, he almost cried out.

"I found where they cornered her …" Iaculous trailed off, and a coldness drew itself upon his listener.

Denan turned away and eyed the mountain where the murdering creatures had taken refuge until nightfall. It could be an exhausting climb for them, but they would make it long before the sun set. The slumbering beasts would be easy enough to slaughter where they lay in the cool, musty darkness. Those that might groggily wake to the sound of fire and steel would offer little threat if they both were swift in their massacre. His eyes fell to the stone, where many sets of claws marred the rock from frequent use.

"If we'd been together, we could have killed them all," Iaculous said and spat on the ground. His mouth may have been dry, or he might have been cursing him.

All Denan could wonder was why there was so much blood upon the younger man's hands and shirt. There didn't appear to be an injury to explain so much blood. What had Iaculous discovered after finding where they chased her?

Kill Mallum, his mind whispered reassuringly. *Worry about other things after.*

Denan buried his inquisitiveness. He buried it all, deep down, along with the guilt of thurking his best friend's bride for half a year. If he climbed this mountain and killed the sleeping beasts, everything would be fine. He didn't know why, only that he was compelled to kill them. "That's where they'll be, most likely," he said, pointing to a cave far up the rocky incline, where greenery and life feared to tread. "After we climb to that ledge, we can continue on and come down the other side of this mountain. We might even recover lost time." It was a plan, and any plan was better than listening to the truth.

"They found her by a river," Iaculous whispered. It was the loudest scream he had ever heard in his life.

Denan dropped to his knees, struck in the chest by the truthful pangs of shock. He tried to close the door in his mind, tried to catch his breath, to shake the words away. He thought of her perfume, sweet, unnatural, and wonderful.

"No. Please, no."

"She struck them down, and she was incredible," Iaculous said. He stood behind Denan, whispering in his ear, as though he enjoyed punishing his leader. Perhaps he did. His voice was stronger than it had been. He took hold of Denan's collar with grubby, ruined hands, and Denan could smell the blood on the young man. Cherrie's blood.

"Shut up, you thurken cur. Just shut up," Denan gasped, reaching for his pouch of spices. His hands shook, and the pouch's contents spilled out all over the dusty, unforgiving ground.

He had to get back to the green, where he could breathe. Get home, so his father would embrace him in discreet pride.

"They tore her to shreds, and we weren't there to help her," Iaculous cried, and each word struck through his mind, into his soul.

"*No*." How could she be dead?

"They tore away her limbs and ate her as she still took a breath, yet still, she killed all of them, alone!" Iaculous screamed into his ear.

Denan's body shook as though wandering in a snowstorm of the Southern Isles. He wailed and felt the force of a dark being infect his mind. Something fought for his will as it fought for all men's wills, and he wanted to allow it.

"We could have saved her together!" Iaculous screamed. It was as though an aggrieved Cherrie influenced his mind, taking out her disgust upon him, and Denan could take no more. He fell to unconsciousness, and in darkness, he felt a terrible, annexing monster ebb away fruitlessly.

Mercifully, when Denan awoke, Iaculous left him with his misery for long enough that he could cry for her without embarrassment. Perhaps the younger man felt ashamed of his outburst, even if he had been right. Especially as he had been right. Denan cried more for her than she had for Heygar, and as he did, he thought of the events that had drawn them close after years of nothing more salacious than subtle glances and suggestive banter.

It had all begun with a solitary death contract for a merchant in Danzaran, where Heygar had suggested a clean approach wherein they might complete the deed without alerting the local constabulary. Performing a little reconnaissance in the merchant's mansion as a Venistrian art dealer had been the right move on the legend's part. Getting caught in bed with the soon-to-be-dead widow by a suspecting Cherrie had not been the right move on the legend's part. It had begun a cascade of gory disaster, with Cherrie killing the returning merchant, his adulterous wife, and about twelve bodyguards in a wave of swift and scorned violence.

Perhaps, had they stuck to the original plan involving the honey, the chandelier, and all the abdop beetles, there might have been one more epic tale for the bards to boast about. Moreover, if Heygar had let on that the dead widow was, in fact, the actual client fronting the entire bill, there might have been a payment to ease the tension.

As it was, Cherrie and Denan found themselves separated from the rest of the Hounds amid chaos, bloodshed, and worst laid plans. They were forced to conceal themselves in the hold of one the dead merchant's trading barges. With little to do but sit in the darkness and seethe and rage about Heygar's behaviour, Cherrie had been an easy plucking. And oh, how he had plucked her that night.

She had been the finest lover to lie with him, and he knew she had felt their passion too. So, instead of never speaking of the dalliance again, it had continued for seven wonderful months. It had been divine love, and he would forever be the worst for it.

When he could cry no more, Denan steeled himself and

began the climb. He didn't bother to scout the route ahead; he aimed to reach the beasts and kill each of them brutally. Behind him, the scrambling of Iaculous, who still desired a leader and tried desperately to catch up, infused Denan with confidence. He led like the champion he once was and could become again, higher and higher, above the forest of green until he could see its cancerous grey far along the horizon behind them.

"Is this really what we should do?" called Iaculous after a while.

Denan felt a compulsion to question himself. He felt a pulling at his mind, and he ignored it.

"We climb this mountain and come over the other side, then we keep going," he called back, and the pull slipped away.

Eventually, with his body soaked in sweat, his chest constricting, and his hands torn open and bloody, they came upon the domain of the Venandi night hunters, near the summit. He knew for certain the beasts lay within the dark cave, for at its mouth lay torn clothing, human bones picked clean, clumps of waste, and the unmistakable stench of territorial markings. They had come to the right place.

"This is vengeance, isn't it? You want to kill all of them for killing her?" Iaculous said as he took the last few steps.

Denan aided the young weaver onto sturdier ground with an offered hand and allowed him a moment's rest. The weaver waved away the suggestion of a pause, and Denan realised that after the climb, the younger man appeared fresh as the morning, while he felt like cold death.

"Is it any matter I desire to kill them all? They have caught our scent. They will hunt us come the night, no matter how far we run." Denan unsheathed his sword quietly. Again, he felt the pulling.

Iaculous took hold of Denan's wrist. "You are not thinking straight. Grief has taken your mind. We cannot kill so many."

Denan understood the words and caught himself nodding in agreement. It really was madness, but his eyes watched the cave, and the desire to punish was overwhelming. He had carried this hatred for the beasts so very long now. She would still be alive if he had killed them all decades before.

"Why did you follow me up here, Iaculous?"

"Why did I return for Cherrie, knowing I would not kill a single creature?"

"Why did you return for her?" Denan snapped.

"I had no choice."

Denan remembered the poem all children memorised before being taught how to hunt the monsters. He recited it as he had from the age of seven.

"The Venandi cluster no closer than this."

"The night hunters hunt in only six."

"They scream, they hiss, they rip, and they fight."

"Only slay them in day, never at night," he said. They didn't hunt in small packs any more, did they though? What else had changed since he left?

Denan tried to step towards the cave, but something pulled at his mind. Iaculous, with glowing blue hands and misty eyes, squinted in deep concentration and gently pulled him from the cave.

"Let us leave this place," he said, and Denan wanted terribly to agree. "Let us leave and heal yourself at your father's house."

Denan couldn't pull his eyes from the cave as though its compelling darkness would offer argument. They killed Cherrie. "With your ability to burn the beasts, we could kill them all in a pulse."

"I am like a fine glass of ale. I am drunk merrily until I run dry, and only when enough time has passed can I replenish fully," Iaculous said.

It wasn't the finest explanation, but it was more than Eralorien had ever offered in the years he had known him. Iaculous brought his hand to his chest and tipped a second glowing glass canister at his bandoleer but said nothing more. Instead, he waved his other hand gently in the air, and a thin blue shield faded into life around the entrance of the cave.

"Why did you do that?" Denan cried loudly as though stirred from a daze. He stumbled over to the shield and collapsed clumsily in front it. All strength left his knees. He reached out and touched the hazy blue barrier, and it shocked him to the touch.

He dimly remembered waking after a brutal battle to a similar shield surrounding them and discovering his lover stolen from him by a mad weaver. A different mad weaver to the one they sought now. He remembered Iaculous shattering the shield and the shell of the burning structure with a wave of his hands, and it had amazed him.

"Let's be on our way, Denan," Iaculous said, and his voice had taken a strange tone.

Denan reached for Iaculous, who helped him to his feet.

"We need not kill any of these beasts. I can keep them trapped within this cave for as long as needed," Iaculous said. "All we need to do is get to your father's kingdom."

Denan nodded, as it seemed the smarter plan. "My father's corrupt kingdom," he said with a voice he hardly recognised as his own.

"And attempt to control your father's corrupt army too, so we can kill Mallum and finish the last task of Heygar's Hounds," Iaculous said, and Denan agreed completely.

DAY SIX

They followed the sun as it turned on its side, making their way slowly down the mountainside, back into the deep forest. Denan couldn't will himself to take any rest, despite his blistered feet breaking and bleeding. Parts of his unexposed skin were torn to shreds from briars and branches, but worst of all, the suffocating chest pain worsened with every mile he forced himself to march. Every step was a test of measure upon his own will, and despite it all, he bested himself.

They walked in defeated silence. No longer the brazen mercenaries of the famous Seven, they were instead a pitiful troupe of the vanquished two. From marching passionately on a mission of steel as fierce heroes, they were now on a miserable wander back to ask a rich father for help.

Denan felt the terrible desolation stirring deep down, where he locked away his agony. But as the day moved on, he emptied his mind of many horrific things, like a man fighting a clutch of ketu and their interminable tentacles. If a man didn't learn to slip away from their grasp in the first few manoeuvres, while he had strength, that man would be held there for a lifetime until they absorbed him up, leaving a shell behind.

He had lost comrades before. All mercenaries had. He had even lost lovers, but it had never broken him to a shell, and he vowed not to break now. As with the climb, he would lead his army of two and see what came. Cherrie would have been proud. So would Heygar.

Behind him, Iaculous walked in silence but for the breaking of trees. His mind was elsewhere—probably with Arielle and thoughts of what was being done to her body. Would it help the young man to know returning her soul to a raped and soiled body was a thousand times better than knowing Cherrie lay torn to ruin in the middle of a forest, sating the appetite of carrion birds? He doubted it would help.

"We will recover her, Iaculous," Denan said and thought his voice sounded unfamiliar to him. Deeper, twisted, lost. He coughed and drank from his water skin and felt a little relief.

"It was Cherrie's last request," Iaculous muttered and said nothing more after that.

As the evening set, they came upon the familiar sight of the great hanging cliffs eternally overlooking his father's kingdom.

"Oh, thank the gods of the source," Denan cried out in relief, and he broke Iaculous from his thoughts with a slap on the back. It was a fine strike of camaraderie between companions of the march, and the slap echoed loudly in the forest. It also caused Iaculous to trip forward and catch his foot on a gnarled root, leaving him to fall awkwardly.

He didn't know why, but the pathetic sight of Iaculous struggling in the mud shook Denan. As though a defensive wall against terrible things shattered in his mind, a surge of misery struck him right to the soul. He saw the anguish of their predicament and felt the grip of his failing chest, and it brought him to his knees. He wailed aloud with a voice not his own, and it cut short as his chest wheezed. He gasped for breath, but his lungs seized and closed over, leaving smothering in their wake.

He had never had an attack come upon him as swiftly. He dimly heard Iaculous curse, and the dreadful exhaustion, which had matched his every step, dissipated. There was a sudden respite as Iaculous stood over him with glowing hands. He reached out for the healer, and the younger man took his hands tightly.

"It is precarious to heal any natural affliction. It is against the natural way of things," Iaculous warned.

Denan nodded as a sliver of air entered his straining lungs. He saw the effort of the healer as a bead of sweat dripped down his forehead. His hands burned at the touch, and he released him, but the healing continued, and Denan recovered his ability to breathe.

"Rest now," Iaculous whispered, and a looming tiredness fell upon Denan like a wave, and he closed his eyes.

Denan awoke to the whistling of the wind and a cool breeze upon his face. Night had fallen, and he was stretched out upon a bedding of blankets. He looked up through the trees, to the stars above and counted their positioning to the time of night. A solitary fire was burning behind a circle of stones, and some meat was cooking across a spit. Denan thought it strange to make camp so close to their destination.

Iaculous sat cross-legged beside him. His face was a deep furrow of concentration, with tightly shut eyes as though in a terrible dream. Denan stared at him for a time, though for how long he couldn't say.

Then he caught sight of something eerie at the corner of his eye, and even though he didn't understand, it sent a chill down his spine. There was a thin veil of black energy covering the entire young man's body, subtle and hidden, like a fine concealing enchantment. It was not settled and still, like the surface of a quiet lake. Instead, it was a wandering brook, moving in waves of pulsing, bubbling energy.

Denan watched from the corner of his eye in silence, wary of breaking the younger man's concentration. Eventually, Iaculous whispered a few words aloud, yet no sound came from his broken lips, and Denan dared to speak.

"Iaculous."

The healer immediately woke from his trance and looked around groggily. His face was pale as though terrified, but after a breath, he composed himself.

"It is good to see you have recovered well enough," he said, staring disapprovingly at Denan as only a successful healer could ever do. Denan had received that same stare many a time after Eralorien had tended to his wounds post-skirmish, and Bereziel before him, though he gazed upon wounds with unrestrained mirth, as if denying death another life was a game of chance and he a gloating master.

"Thank you, apprentice," Denan said, bowing, and he discovered his chest felt far healthier than before: healthier, yet not healthy. Still, he felt better than he had in an age. All the fear from before had left him, replaced with a perfect calm. He felt as though everything would be fine, as though a deity had whispered to him in slumber, reassuring him that everything could return to the way it was.

"Everything can be right again," Iaculous said.

Denan recoiled in astonishment. Had the youth been in his thoughts? Was he capable of such a gift?

Iaculous laughed strangely. "I'm not in your thoughts, Denan, but there are moments when I understand the thoughts of others. It is a simple use of weaving and nothing more. Your mind is your own."

Denan noticed the dark veneer had shimmered its last and vanished. He wondered if there were any weaver powerful enough to turn the passing of time on its head when great and terrible things had befallen the world. So much was unknown to him.

"I think I am more than an apprentice as there are only two of us." It may have sounded as a jest, but he offered no smile.

"Does the shield still hold the beasts at bay ... weaver?"

The title pleased the young man.

"They will be no further trouble," he said, displaying his fingers, glowing faintly. "The more I weave, the stronger I become. To hold the shield for a day and a night is hardly a test of my ability anymore."

"How strong are you now?"

"I'm stronger now than when Mallum tore us apart. But he will have become stronger too. A living soul to call upon is tenfold what any weaver in this world could be. Even Bereziel. Even me," he said. The stones glowed at his chest, and he wrapped his cloak around him to block the cold.

"You fool yourself, apprentice. A week ago, you could barely heal a broken bone," Denan countered.

"I am a master now. Call me a master."

"You are a child, blinded by grief as much as me. Arrogance will lead us to further misery!" Denan shouted.

"I can kill him. I can burn him away to a thurken charred ruin if I want to!"

Denan saw the hurt in his face. "If you were so strong, Cherrie would still be alive." The child went pale at her mention. "My heart wouldn't be broken."

Iaculous sniffed, shrugged, and his fingers pulsed. Denan felt compelled to apologise for insulting the child, not because the young man had enchanted him, but for speaking the cruel truth so harshly. If truth be told, he had improved enough in the last few days. Not enough to save them from the horrors, but enough to bring fight to their quarry with the help of an entire battalion at their hands.

"I only need your father's help to make things easier," Iaculous muttered weakly.

"I'm sorry, Iaculous. I despaired for all that has happened," he offered.

Iaculous stared into the growing night with unblinking eyes. When he spoke, after a time, his voice was thoughtful, as though he addressed himself alone and not his companion.

"Every weaver has a limit to the power they can wield, but I see no boundary in what I can achieve," he said, hugging his cloak tightly against himself. Denan listened as though he were listening to an old storyteller in a tavern. "I have surpassed what Eralorien spent an entire lifetime trying to be, and I have done it with ease," he said to the darkness. "I can be greater than Mallum. I need to do what I must."

Denan felt the young man's own despair. And why wouldn't he despair? The Hounds were defeated, and Heygar's final task seemed insurmountable.

"I will do what I must," Iaculous repeated, and his fingers blazed blue for a moment before returning to normal.

"What must you do?" Denan asked. His words startled the young weaver as though caught in the bedroom with industrious thoughts and exploring fingers. As though he had forgotten Denan was even there.

"I must save them from the beast that's watching us in the darkness. I must save all our comrades lost on this ill-fated crusade. Only then, when we are seven again, will I kill Mallum."

HOMECOMING

It was dreary, cold, and a dreadful last day marching back home. After midnight, the first few raindrops sizzled upon their fire until it died. Though Denan thought about making a shelter, an unusual desire to reach his home compelled him to walk through the night. It was a strange to have no fear of the beasts despite the risk of a few roaming packs, but Iaculous didn't seem to worry, so neither did he.

The young weaver had been right about his increased ability. The light above their heads was twice that of the brightness which had held their ambushers at bay, and he held it now effortlessly. Denan suspected the young man was still upset, as he ignored any attempts at broaching conversation. The child walked as if he were soulless, always forward, matching Denan's steps, weaving a delicate enchantment in his fingers as he did.

Eventually, Denan ceased attempting conversation, instead focusing on what he would say to his father. His father had loved him, just never enough to show it and certainly not at the end. Perhaps their distance apart might have warmed the old cur's heart. Perhaps Denan might have the words this time to sway his thinking. Perhaps it would be different this time.

The last hours had been the harshest. Denan had expected to see the familiar signs of civilisation like beaten paths and tilled fields, but all they found was sparseness. He had hoped to make it home by noon, but as evening approached, they struggled through barren farms of mulch and weeds and unforgiving paths of grey briar, grown swift by abandonment. This was the richest, most fertile region of Venistra, and it had tasted blight.

This time, it was Denan who fell unusually silent. His feet became little more than clumps of mud. Each step became more laboured than the last, with the sun fading behind their backs. Then they reached the region of the Hundred Houses, and with it, the confirmation that all was lost.

To the peasants, it was a walled-off stronghold, imposing and menacing, standing against the relative green of the surrounding countryside. Built by their long-forgotten forefathers in sturdy ash stone, it would last a millennium. Even though it only housed one family, it had a dozen pavilions and twice as many domes of silvery grey in its impressive construction. All of these parts stood beneath the shadow of the largest structure of them all—the grand throne room.

This stronghold was not alone, for behind the outer wall were Hundred houses. All of them were three stories in height and roofed in yellow thatch. All of them were meticulously painted in the same whitewash, with walls of sturdy brick, black timber frontage, and matching sills on all sides. All of them housed the royal gentry of Venistra.

The only allowance for individuality were the doorways, which they could paint any chosen colour as was a royal's right. Denan could have taken any house when he had come of age and left his wing in the palace. He would have insisted on a bright, garish green door to irritate most neighbouring relatives and impressive wealthy merchants, who favoured crystal silver or amber gold.

To the lords of the region, it was the "Royal Court of Nobility". To Denan, it had been his home. To something else, it had become a brutal hunting ground.

The first tracks had appeared east of the eternal caves, and shivers had run up Denan's spine as he dug his fingers into the soft mud to examine the tracks. They were old, a foot in depth, double as wide across, and notably shaped in a clawed hoof. He knew them well. Further on, they had discovered clusters of trees crushed underfoot, where the beast had forgone its careful meander through the land in favour of a terrifying charge at the smell of human in the wind.

He recognised the beast as the crustacuus. However, he had never come upon tracks as large as these. It was rare for these monsters to rouse themselves from the tunnels of the deep, but it wasn't unknown for starvation to send them out into the ocean to attack a barge or, worse, set themselves upon an unfortunate little village every decade or two. Were they to come inland towards any under the royal's watch, just like the Venandi, it was a duty to put the beast down or at least send it fleeing and take the credit for it.

He had only seen one great hunt in his lifetime, but his master of skills had not wasted the opportunity to train the then nine-year-old Denan in the finer arts of tracking them. It wasn't difficult; they just had to look for destruction everywhere they went. Looking back, he didn't think his master's old mind was entirely stable. He remembered watching an entire battalion of his father's soldiers hunt down and attack the beast in the wide-open region of the wetlands, under the watchful eye and whispered instruction of his old master. The vision of the beast never left him.

"Watch how its flailing tail can swing and tear a soldier from neck to groin as though it were fruit upon a stalk," his master had said. He licked his lips and pointed at the magnificent, spinning beast as it struggled under the hail of arrows and spears.

Denan had watched from the cover of a few bushes and trees as the hunters attempted to break through its carapace of scaled armour. "It's vicious and terrifying."

"Look there. What did I say?" his master said. The beast flayed an unfortunate hunter across the front of the body with one flanking tail strike in front of Denan's disbelieving eyes.

"I can hear screaming."

"See how he sliced through the armour and skin as though it were a maid preparing a succulent fillet of rodenerack?" his master had said casually. He behaved as though they sat in a beautiful meadow of green on a bright summer day, rather than learning of murderous things in a treacherous downpour of hail.

"I think it was a woman."

"I wouldn't mind a bit of rat."

"I will be sick."

Denan's stomach had turned as the dying person struggled to cry without the use of a tongue or even a face. He remembered she managed an entire step forward towards one of her comrades before crumpling in a mush of blood, bone, blonde hair, and entrails.

"Yes, I think you are right. I'm quite sure that was Vala from down the coast. Such a nice young girl. I instructed her for a time, but I could only accept duck eggs as payment for so long. I hadn't seen her in, oh, at least a year. I think she had two children. Such a shame," the master muttered.

Denan had stared as the beast killed a few more hunters with its four massive claws. He couldn't remember the names of the other hunters who had perished, only that the four claws moved independently of each other. It was an awe-inspiring sight as the beast reared and fought for its life and its next meal.

If the source had mixed an arachnid with a sea scarab and allowed it to grow for a thousand years, the crustacuus would be that beast. The only advantage hunters had was that for all of its impressive bulk, its mind was that of a limbless serpent. But great, lumbering brutes like this needed little intelligence to trample and stab those that threatened it. It had taken a hundred hunters a dozen hours to pierce all three hearts at a cost of nearly twenty brave but slightly careless souls.

"The right handful of warriors with the right weapons could have easily slain that creature without the loss of life," his master had said, tapping the large green sword at Denan's waist. He had been correct. "But if all is lost, take its eyes and hope it stumbles upon a pack of fevered Venandi." This, too, had been sage advice.

They had walked home that night, and Denan had thought for too long on the horrors. He hadn't eaten more than a couple bites of his meal, so his master had eaten his smoked fillet of rat for him.

The two Hounds followed the tracks and those of its hunters until they found themselves atop the hanging cliffs. The cliffs had always been a fine place to bring a young damsel to charm. They were not too steep, just a minor climb, with a stunning view over the stronghold and the surrounding forests at its pinnacle.

From here, they saw where the great hunt had met the beast in battle and failed miserably. The monster had returned the violence tenfold upon the palace and the royals within. It must have been terrifying to see the soldiers fall under its might, the ramparts tumbling down, and the monster tearing itself an entrance and laying waste to all trapped within. Half the wall lay in great mounds of brick and ruin a half-mile across. Many of the mansions within were crushed to mounds of brick and the dead.

Denan had seen prettier battlefields. Through teared eyes and the fading call of nightfall, he saw the outline of the behemoth and its slumber between the last two remaining turrets of his home. Its head rested somewhere in the throne room, where his father had once presided. Its swishing tail flailed delicately in the air as it slumbered and knocked down anything foolish enough to be at its height as it waved back and forth.

As the tracks suggested, the beast was far larger than anything ever seen before. Around the massive creature lay many dead. Three hundred or more. Men, women, children. All royal, and all dead. All of them were entrapped behind the walls without weapons. Some were sucked dry, leaving only skin and bone behind, while others were mushed to a sticky pulp.

Many more still lay where they died, turning to a sickening rot after a week or two out in the sun. Denan wondered if the monster would still feed upon their rancid meat. Probably, the crustacuus would only stay here until it consumed all nourishment.

"Well, so much for controlling your father's army," Iaculous said.

Denan once more wept openly for all he had lost. Pitiful and wretched, his weakness disgusted him. He saw the disgust in Iaculous's eyes, but he couldn't help himself. A week ago, he had the world at his feet and a legacy in front of him. Now he had nothing at all. All lost, all gone. It wasn't fair. None of this was. How could a beast turn upon a place in such a way and cause such destruction?

"I'm sorry, Father."

"Mallum must have willed that beast to attack in such a way. Another brutal move by that thurken cur," Iaculous growled. His eyes focused upon the sleeping beast, though he looked shaken at the power showed in controlling such a creature.

Maybe it was his own use of the weaving upon his body, but in that moment, Denan caught sight of a few strands of grey in the young man's hair return to their original colour. He didn't know why he thought this unusual. Then, without warning, something broke in his mind, like a vase containing a man's will. Like an enchantment tested beyond its own strength and forced to step aside in the way of vengeance. Any fear he had felt before, disappeared in hatred. All he could see in his mind was the young face of Mallum. Cheerful. Cruel, young, and beautiful, like Iaculous, but drenched in immorality.

"He … will … pay," Denan hissed.

Suddenly, he felt as though he had emerged from a lifetime beneath the waves of an unforgiving ocean. His mind spun, and a searing pain tore through it. It felt good, though he couldn't understand why. He drew his sword, and passion overcame his rationale. He felt the crushing absence of calmness from his mindless trek, but more than that, he felt like Denan of the Green. He felt like Denan of the Hounds.

He leapt from the cliff to a steep slope below, with the screams of Iaculous's protests in his ear. He landed smoothly as he had done a thousand times before as a child and ran towards the fallen house of his family. Quicker and quicker he ran, with gravity as his ally and hatred as his engine. He knew he would die, and though Iaculous's cries gave way to compelling thoughts of retreat, his will was stronger than it had been for quite a time.

Destroying the beast was all he allowed himself to desire. Though his master would have shaken his head in disappointment at his plan, with every step he took, Denan felt more and more assured.

MALLUM'S GIFT TO THE ROYALS

Denan slid gracefully down the slope and came to a stop at the bottom. He dared a glance to the shocked weaver far above, and a weight fell from his chest. He didn't stop moving. His chest was loose, and his head was free. He would die this day in the claws of the crustacuus, but he didn't care anymore.

All fear ebbed away like the afterthought of a horned demon after waking from a dream. He gripped his sword. The light was fading, and he would never see dawn again, but there was more than enough light to kill the beast. All that mattered were these last few moments. This was an unexpected freedom from a prison he had been oblivious to.

His feet left damp grass and met the bloodstained foundations of a destroyed stronghold. He climbed a mound of debris as a free man and wilfully leapt through the large break in the wall, into the place of his birth. He was no longer afraid of anything in the world. He was Denan of the Green, proud second in command to Heygar's Hounds. He had his mind back, and he would be reckless one last time.

Mallum might well be hidden in this fallen place

somewhere, slithering like the vile serpent he was. Even with his sword, Denan could not best the dark weaver, but he could take on this behemoth. He would die, but better with a sword in hand than unarmed and helpless.

As dreadful as it was to view the carnage from atop the cliff, nothing prepared him for the devastation once he stepped into the district of the Hundred houses. He'd had the misfortune to come upon several slaughtered villages during wartime—horrors were tragically common in those dreadful periods. Denan fruitlessly imagined this some arbitrary location on a battle map, unfortunate enough to be in the way of an invading army's march, and not the place he had loved at one point in his youth. He tried to separate himself from the anguished, crushing sorrow he felt for his people strewn at every corner, down every alley, lining the streets in crimson collections of ruined remains.

Massacre was never a tasteful sight. Many of his brethren had been crushed as they climbed from their beds. Many others made it to the street in a shameful state of undress, and they had fallen to the indomitable beast as it charged through, stamping and swishing through any bodies, battlement or building in its wake. Some poor fools had attempted to retreat through the far gates or even through the grand oak doors of the palace, but they had died long before reaching either.

An attack by a frenzied crustacuus was as ferocious as an army of night hunters. It had been swift in its dreadful execution of an entire race. The beast had been wily enough to corral its victims from all four outer corners towards the centre, where the bodies were most plentiful. Even in the dark, Denan could see the grey stone at his feet, cracked and fragmented where the monster had taken every step, and its tale of merciless invasion.

To reach the beast, he had to climb greater mounds of

rubble the nearer he ventured. Each mound was vast and reminded him of running through a sand dune in warmer seasons as a child. They were unsteady, precarious, and each told their own miserable story.

His resolve and anger were tested when he tripped over a child's half-buried hand, which he had perceived to be nothing more than a jutting root between brick and beam near the pinnacle of one rise. A few steps on, he discovered the frozen features of a parent as they reached for the child. He couldn't tell if it was the mother or father because of the decomposition, and this thought made him feel even worse. How long would they lie in this state before receiving a suitable send-off into the source?

Eventually, Denan reached the slumbering beast. Without hesitation or cause to question, he scaled one of its long, spindly legs, took a careful foothold at its back, and hoisted himself atop. The monster was too large to notice a waking threat as small as he was and continued its sated sleep.

In some parts of Dellerin, the richest of people frequently dined upon a similar-looking beast, though the delicacy was far smaller. Admittedly, at first, he had prejudicial misgivings when offered some, but when he tried it, he had discovered its pink meat softer than a good rat's and perfect with a little seasoning of lemon and salted butter. Perhaps, in this world, the greater predators should dine upon their prey. Perhaps if he dined upon this dead monster's flesh as the true act of vengeance, he might compare flavours.

His feet echoed loudly on the hard shell, and he slowed his charge and caught his breath. "I'm breathing better than I have in years," he whispered to himself and thought this strange before the silent, precarious world turned to bedlam.

From almost three stories in height, Denan took a moment to enjoy the taste of pure air in his lungs, and he wondered if

Iaculous were powerful enough to heal something as severe as his particular ailment. At least his last few breaths would be with eyes wide open and a fate of his own. It didn't matter that he knew he would lose. It didn't matter that he heard Iaculous screaming for him from far away. It didn't matter that the young weaver would be the only Hound left to finish the task. It didn't even matter that Mallum would not die at his hand. What mattered was giving Iaculous the chance and trying to kill Mallum's brutal monster. It was a fitting last chapter to this life.

Denan saw the many signs of failed warfare upon its shell. It had met countless strikes and survived all skirmishes it faced. Brave warriors had struck with blade and fire, and none had struck it down. None had caused any significant damage, and Denan knew why. For a moment, he wondered if the Hundred Houses would still be standing were he part of its great defence. For all his master's eccentricities, he had taught him more than all the dead warriors had learned. Perhaps they'd only had duck eggs to pay with.

With renewed breath and a will of his own, Denan crept along the monster's back until he reached its head. He wondered if there was a certain nerve he could sever along the neck to paralyse it or a collection of thick, bulging veins beneath the neck joint, which might cause some splendid cardiac arrest to all three of its hearts. Few men had ever been this close to try.

Denan slid across to the beast's sleeping head, which rested upon a large mound where his father's personal afternoon suite had been. He drew his sword.

"Come back, you fool!" roared Iaculous in his mind, and Denan almost slipped from the precarious edge from fright. He looked out into the darkness and saw the young weaver still scrambling down the hillside. *"Don't kill yourself so*

foolishly. " There was a terrible anguish in his tone. It was as though it wasn't Iaculous at all but instead a demon of nightmares he couldn't remember.

"This is what Hounds do!" Denan cried out and plunged down. If he couldn't kill the beast in one blow, he would make it easier for any warrior thereafter.

Pop.

It was a strange sensation to feel the black, gelatinous eyeball explode in such a way. It was as large as a frying pan, and Denan smelled bitter fish as the disgusting globules burst over his sword, hands, and clothing. He wrenched the blade free as the creature woke and screamed deliciously. It vibrated through Denan's body and infused him with hatred and a renewed desire to do deeds worthy of a freethinking hero.

"Thurken fool!"

The beast raised its head and roared loudly again. The world beneath Denan's feet shuddered as it clambered to its dozen feet. It spun around swiftly, and Denan fell back down its jagged back. Only reflexes stopped him from falling to the ground and losing his life beneath the thundering legs as they trampled around, searching for whatever attacked. It shuddered and charged in wild agony, smashing mounds and structures around it. Denan moved with the swaying charge, hoping to catch the beast one more time and deliver a second strike to its head. He moved desperately with its thunderous sway until, eventually, the monster suddenly whipped its neck backwards and sent Denan flying into the night sky.

Flying. It was a strange feeling to know he was to die. A fall from such a height would be fatal to any man, but being thrown with the brute force of a crustacuus's rage was likely to leave him little more than a pulped ruin of royalty. He had tried; he had failed.

Denan felt the wind in his hair and a cold gale of pure air rush down into his lungs, then something else. It was the crashing through of glass, followed by an awkward landing upon a lavish, four-poster bed. He tumbled, rolled, and took half the bedding with him before he came to a painful stop at the foot of an impressive wooden door. He might have knocked himself out for a pulse, but he couldn't be sure.

He allowed himself a moment to gather his wits before taking in how impressive the bedroom he found himself in was. Through the broken window he had been flung shone a bright light, and Denan climbed to his feet, expecting to discover broken bones or severed arteries. Miraculously, he was unhurt but for a few gashes and bruises. He scrambled out into the upper hallway and down the three flights of stairs of the abandoned house. Without taking breath, he charged out into the night to meet the beast in one final battle.

He wasn't alone. Iaculous had joined the fight, and he had joined it spectacularly. He fired sphere after sphere of black fire at the beast from atop a mound of brick and rubble, with glowing blue hands of flame. He was magnificent.

Denan charged forward with sword in hand. He roared threats of battle, but they were lost in the thundering screams, the explosions of fire, and the crack of the ground where the monster shattered and broke through stone from its impossible weight. Fireballs crashed against its shell but made no impact apart from lighting up the battlefield and dazzling the frenzied creature. Iaculous was not killing but was merely holding the beast in position.

Denan ran beneath the beast as it staggered awkwardly towards the bringer of unnatural fire. With an outer shell as thick as stone in some parts, the beast was almost invulnerable to assault, apart from the underside, where long legs crushed indiscriminately. Denan attacked there once the beast got the better of Iaculous.

The crustacuus spun around with flailing tail. Iaculous ran clear of the unexpected attack easily enough, but the small break in bombardment allowed the beast to track him down despite its failing eyesight. It swiped with all four claws. Iaculous dodged the first, leapt clear of the second, rolled under the third and met the fourth claw directly head-on. The dreadful sound of torn flesh and broken bones echoed as the young man's body flew thirty feet before coming to an unsettling stop among some ruin across the street from Denan. The crustacuus immediately screamed triumphantly and, like a giant meeliopede, scuttled over to finish its task.

It would have crushed Iaculous in that moment had Denan not intercepted the beast and sacrificed himself for the broken young man. It's what any Hound would do, for they were kin, they were comrades, but more than that, Iaculous was the only man capable of defeating Mallum. This thought repeated in his mind, again and again, like a mantra.

Denan leapt through the legs and held his nerve as they stamped down all around him. It was only when it lowered its abdomen enough to eat what remained of Iaculous that Denan took his chance. With both hands, he plunged his blade deep into the fleshy underparts of the beast and held tightly as the crustacuus skewered itself in his hold. He pulled the blade across, like gutting a swine for the roast. Viscera and blood fell freely from the creature and drenched Denan through.

The beast roared, reared, and rushed away from the fallen healer, tearing itself further as it did, allowing Denan to tend to his companion, who was lying deathly still among the ruins of his home. His torn chest leaked a seeping river of blood. His arms and legs were shattered like a body thrown through a bedroom window. Denan knew the young hero would not survive.

He took hold of his arms and dragged him across the ground, doing his best to ignore the terrible stream of crimson he left behind.

"I will not leave you like this, little one."

THE COMING OF ALLIES

Somewhere off in the distance, Denan heard the slow movements of the crustacuus retreating to tend to its wounds. His master would have suggested he pursue injured prey instead of tending to a comrade, but Denan refused to leave the dying boy to his unconscious demise. He'd seen him recover from burning alive before. This was more severe, wasn't it? It would be, if the young man didn't wake up to heal himself.

Whatever the severity, Denan pulled him from the ruins of the battlefield towards the house with the nice bedroom and the broken window, leaving a river of blood behind. Instinctively, he bolted the door behind him, and then he dared a smirk at the thought of a closed door stopping such a monster. He kept it locked and turned to his patient.

"I'll do all that I can, my friend."

Denan set to work on the ruined Hound. The problem was that Iaculous's wounds were so great, he didn't know where to start. The claw had obliterated his chest, and Denan was amazed that even now, the young man still took weak, gargling breaths. He pulled the cleanest linen from the beds

330

and stripped, ripped and cut to make suitable tourniquets. He applied them to each limb before strapping the thickest around the crevice of what should have been a torso. When he finished, he wasn't at all certain he'd done an adequate enough job, but the young man still took a breath, and he'd plugged the holes. Whether there was enough blood inside him would soon be answered.

"Open your eyes. That's all you have to do," he whispered, and he willed the young man to save himself.

He didn't know how long he sat with the unconscious boy. The only light in the house was the eerie glow from the bandoleer, which remained undamaged despite the surrounding carnage. From his bed of wooden floor at the foot of the stairs, Denan covered his companion in some blankets to warm his freezing skin, and the delicate rasp of breathing suggested the child fought for life. Denan never left his side—until the crustacuus returned.

It started as a low cracking sound. The ground shook once more, and Denan crept upstairs to look out through the shattered window, into the night. It moved slower than before. From behind the cover of a mouldy curtain, he watched the beast walk past their building as it hunted its attackers down. It lowered its spiny head near the front door, and Denan ducked away, lest it spot him. The monster tracked the blood and followed the route Denan had taken from the battlefield, walking further into the darkness. Who knew how long it would be before it realised its mistake?

"Not too smart."

In the falling silence, he thought of miserable things. He wanted to cry once more for his people and all he had lost these past few days, but he was an empty shell.

The crustacuus's cry pierced the night, and with a heavy heart, Denan prepared himself for war. He had another lunatic plan. It wasn't dissimilar to the plan he'd had before. When the beast passed by next, he would take one more leap of faith and attempt to finish what he started.

In the main hall below, he saw the growing illumination of Iaculous's bandoleer once more, and he worried the glow would alert the beast before he was ready. There came another shriek from the darkness. Denan steeled himself, and then he saw the reason for the crustacuus's cries.

It was not hunting. It was being hunted.

He thought them heroic. He thought them terrifying. He thought them the end of all things.

The Venandi night hunters streamed through the break in the wall. Their frenzied squeals of primal rage soon overcame the crustacuus's war cries, and Denan watched both factions meet in a terrifying melee. There were at least sixty of the snapping, brutal hounds by his guess before their swarming numbers became too many to count as they charged. Denan thought it frightening how well organised they were. They behaved as one entity again, moving in a tightly controlled pack.

He watched in amazement for a few wonderful breaths until Iaculous stepped into the room. His face was pale, and he appeared fragile, but there was a purpose to his movement. His chest shone brightly, and his torn skin appeared no more worrying than bruising after a tavern brawl. Once more, Iaculous's healing abilities unsettled him, even if he welcomed the young man's sudden resurrection.

"Thank the gods of the source you woke."

"I slept too long."

The crustacuus fought ferociously. With every strike from its monstrous claws, two or three attackers went to the source. However, they drove it back with vicious bites to its many legs, through shell, through membrane, until they hobbled it.

Stumbling away from the building, the creature swung its tail along the ground in one last attempt to save itself. It knocked away a dozen Venandi, but just as many took their place.

Enraged from the loss of their own brethren, the night hunters leapt upon the beast's tail before it could swing a second time. A few scrambled atop its back, biting and striking whatever they could, and their jagged fangs and fierce claws soon broke impenetrable shell and more.

"Who needs an army of men with an army of demons?" Denan said wistfully.

The massive beast reared wildly in primal panic, screaming loud enough to cause Denan to wince, before it fell to its vanquishers. The great battle had taken place in mere moments, and after that, they set about tearing their prey apart, mouthful by savage mouthful. So much for Denan himself dining on the creature in vengeance.

"They deserved their feed after that," Iaculous said from behind him.

Below them, the beasts tore the monster apart quicker than a human army. Denan wondered again what a force wielding such animals as weapons could be.

"They will still come for us after they feed, regardless. I would rather have died at the hands of the crustacuus," Denan said, wincing at the beasts gorging themselves upon the fleshy pink meat. The locked door would hold them at bay for a few moments and nothing more.

"They will not feast upon us both," Iaculous said.

"How do you know?"

"They are difficult to control, but give them what they need, and I will sate them. They will listen further. They will bow to their pack leader easily enough," Iaculous said.

Denan felt the warmth emanating off the youth, yet it was nothing like before. It was as though the heat was from deep within. His fingers blazed brightly, and something laced his voice in a terrible darkness.

"She gave it willingly," Iaculous said and touched one of the brightly pulsing rocks upon his bandoleer.

"Who did?"

"She touched my mind and knew," Iaculous said and placed his hand upon Denan's chest for support.

"Cherrie?"

"A gifted soul is a fierce thing."

Denan felt a great weight fall upon his chest. He attempted to push the youth from him so that he might catch his breath, but all strength left him. He fell against the windowsill. Below him, he caught sight of the beasts as they fell unnaturally still, like a hound would during the trials of its early training, desperate to move but not until master allowed.

"I'm not feeling myself," Denan whispered, and the healer nodded in agreement through a veil of blue.

"Let go, Denan," Iaculous whispered.

There was a dreadful pull from deep within. Horrific images flooded into Denan's mind, and he gripped his chest, but Iaculous never let go. Instead, he held him down, and only then did Denan understand the depth of his betrayal.

"I need it to kill him." He struck Denan across the face.

"Don't do this."

Denan struck out with fist and foot and landed flush, but with almost all his energy diminished, the strikes felt feeble and futile. This was no way for a royal prince to die. Denan rolled away, but the healer held him, and Denan felt himself floating as though in a river.

"No!" he screamed and twisted the youth's hand as he remembered Heygar once showing him.

"A fine twist of the wrists was all it took," his friend had said of the benefits of weapon-less combat. Denan had countered that any blade was superior to fists and grips. They had only known each other a dozen hours at that point and been inseparable since.

Denan twisted and snapped ligaments in the healer's hand, and he heard a scream and earned a reprieve from the hold. Both Hounds fell to the ground. Suddenly, every beast howled in unison and went to war from far below. Denan rolled from his cursing comrade and searched the darkness for his sword. It didn't matter what source energy the youth attacked with. His blade cut through anything of this world or the next.

Iaculous hid in the darkness somewhere. "The soul is stronger from a living being."

"You have lost your thurken mind!" Denan cried and took hold of his fallen blade, resting on the bed. Below him, he heard the hammering of the front door to a hundred clawing paws.

Not like this.

"Please, Iaculous. We are brothers. We are comrades. Whatever you have done, it is the effect of Mallum!" he cried and stood to meet his comrade in battle. He held his blade out in front of him and felt strength returning to his body.

An invisible hand took hold of him and swung him violently against the far wall. Then another phantom hand took hold of his sword-bearing arm and ripped it free from his body.

"Please," he gasped as shock took his pain.

Without warning, the invisible hand threw him from the room, down to the street below.

Falling. Landing. Darkness.

He awoke paralysed and broken beyond most healers' repair. He lay among his own blood and that of the beaten monster, and Iaculous stood over him. He looked twisted, like a wraith of the Rime marshes.

"Why did you do this?" he gasped and felt the world slipping away.

"You look exactly as Cherrie did."

"Do not do this," Denan whimpered, knowing well his doom.

"You won't live long like this, and I can't heal a soulless husk," Iaculous said as though faced with a conundrum of choosing which crop of vegetable to purchase for the farming season ahead. "It would have been so much easier if you had let go."

Without warning, all the pain in the world flooded into Denan's body. He screamed aloud.

"I can make it end," Iaculous whispered, and Denan cried out as a shard of flame penetrated his body. "I can numb it all, and you can give me your soul, and we can kill Mallum together," he whispered, and then he reduced the pain to a mere mind-destroying throb. "Give me your soul, and I will ensure you spend eternity by Cherrie's side."

In that moment, Denan felt her presence. He felt her torment, and it was something terrible. He reached for one of the glowing orbs with his one remaining hand, and Iaculous knocked it away dismissively. With his last efforts, he spat into the healer's face. Iaculous nodded and wiped it away, then he returned the offending sputum of blood and spittle across Denan's forehead.

"No matter at all," he said.

Iaculous took hold of Denan's chest, and all the pain disappeared. A great tiredness overcame him. He felt himself floating. His vision darkened until all he could see was a pulsing piece of rock upon his vanquisher's chest. He cursed aloud, and then he felt nothing at all.

ANGUISHED

D enan's hand fell loosely to the ground, and he exhaled one last time. Iaculous cursed under his breath. The surrounding animals snarled, hissed, growled, and salivated, and he willed them to fall silent. This they did swiftly enough, and why wouldn't they? He was their master and had been for quite a time.

"What a thurken waste," the weaver known as Iaculous whispered aloud in his shadowed voice.

Sometimes it spoke in his mind, deep within the source where devils tread freely, and sometimes, when it felt stronger, it crept into his words, and he allowed it. And why wouldn't he? It was no phantom whisper in the back of his mind like it had been to Eralorien. It was something far more potent and mutually beneficial. Or at least that is what both he and it had agreed.

It called itself Silencio, the seventh demon of the source.

One of the larger Venandi challenged its mental leash and neared the weaver. It sniffed the ground around him, but Iaculous was untroubled. He felt the hold upon the creature, and he met its eyes and saw the thin veil of blue shimmering within them. He held all beasts in this region of Venistra. He allowed this beast to nudge the dead body and lick at the limbless hole slowly draining the last few drops of crimson onto the ground.

Without the benefit of a beating heart to drive the blood, Denan appeared more of a leaking water pouch strewn aside than the warrior of countless legends. For that's all bodies were—weak vessels destined to tear and empty. Probably not a fitting end to a comrade, but most mercenaries ended their days in a pool of their flowing blood, urine, and faeces.

Iaculous reached out and slid his grubby fingers along the defiant beast's leathery back. He sensed the incredible will fighting his hold, and it amused him so. These beauties didn't mind how famous their prey was. There still lay within the unquenchable instinct to feed upon an easy meal. He closed his eyes and willed himself to feel what the creature felt. Though he thought it distasteful, he embraced it and the disgusting craving to feed upon flesh.

Playing within their mind was becoming easier, just as Silencio had whispered it would. And the easier it became, the stronger he grew. In his mind, he tasted Denan's blood, and his mouth watered for its savoury taste. He placed his hand upon the chest of his murdered companion one last time, as he had with Cherrie, and whispered the mercenary's prayer of the dead.

"Steal into the night, comrade," he whispered, and the beasts listened. "Keep your wits and sword sharp. Find your way in this final night. May you find the gold where you seek," he whispered and left him where he lay.

That Denan had died was a terrible waste altogether. A living soul trapped was tenfold the power of the souls he already possessed, and a battalion of ready warriors would have been a fine thing for killing Mallum. But Iaculous was philosophical if nothing else. He matched Mallum as it was, and an army would not be difficult to assemble. He only needed a little more power surging through him, and that would come soon enough.

He waved his hand, and a thin shield covered each of his wondrous beasts. Such a use of energy immediately struck him, and he wavered as his vision blurred. A week before, a thin shield held for a few breaths upon one man would have left him gasping for air and life itself—not to mention the swift ageing of his body. But he had come so far since then and still only taken a few steps. He held his fingers over the shield and felt its potency.

"Can't have you hiding in a cave all day while I walk into a pit."

If his beauties understood, he imagined them nodding in agreement.

"Can't have you burning up in the daylight though, can we?"

After a little time, the drain upon his reserves maintaining the shield faded and disappeared altogether. He was getting stronger with every enchantment weaved, just as Silencio promised.

"Feed."

All those closest leapt upon the royal's body, tearing and ripping. The rest fell upon the fallen crustacuus. Iaculous, meanwhile, found a barrel to bathe the blood and ruin from his body. With the scent of Denan washed from his hands, he felt better. Killing was getting easier. He had never expected it to.

He found the ruined settlement of the Hundred Houses to

be strangely beautiful. Its architecture matched the age of anything Dellerin offered, and perhaps it was this pride in their history, which suggested Venistra's historic distaste for the king. It was an old land with old values. Perhaps, had there been richness in its soil or wealth in the mines of below, it may have been a force. Still, though he didn't know why, he loved this place and the Hundred Houses most of all. All men desired to be king of whatever rock they stood upon, and Venistra was no different.

As dawn emerged from behind the night, Iaculous sat upon an abandoned throne of silver and gold. He wondered what it would be like to sit upon this throne and know full dominion over all man and beast, and he wondered if this thinking brought Mallum to the point of madness.

He watched the dawn through the gaping hole in the throne room where a beast, infused and changed by the spilling of dark energies from a failing monolith, had ruined and slain an army promised to him by a foolish prince of nothing. He watched the stirring burning of amber and red in the sky and almost fell asleep as it turned to blue, but he held off the exhaustion. He enjoyed the chorus of birds incited to frenzy with the discovery of fresh, delicious carrion waiting for them.

He thought he would be a fine king without a queen at his side. This thought soured his mood, for it led to Arielle and her unfaithfulness. She had behaved as a whore would. Rape would have been an honourable end to her, but Mallum had not even needed to sway her thoughts or lure her to his manhood. She had willingly given that cur everything without a thought for her true love, and Iaculous would spend the rest of his days lamenting such an act.

He took his time and did not feel bad for rummaging through the kingdom of the dead until—with clothing of silk and decorated in garish jewels—he garbed himself as a king should. Eyeing himself in a slightly cracked mirror as tall as any man, he thought himself impressive. The demon agreed and whispered as much. Iaculous enjoyed the compliments for a few moments before severing the connection of their mind, much to the irritation of Silencio.

Perhaps the demon was unimpressed or even wary of his aptitude in swiftly learning the darker weavings of the source. Throughout his life, it had never taken long for any of his instructors to become wary of his ability to learn. Silencio was now his only instructor, and he had come so far since he'd been that charred husk of a boy lying dead atop the barge's deck.

"It is not too far now, my beauties." He left the throne behind. It was a comfortable seat, and perhaps he would rest upon it on his return.

Iaculous walked fast and held tightly his cloak in his crossed arms as it whipped out behind him, caught in the early morning wind. He marched forward, and one by one, the beasts marched with him. Some led, others on each side kept watch for threats against master, and finally, the older more reluctant alphas begrudgingly accepted his will and trudged along behind. He respected these most of all. They still had fight. They still had pride.

He did not eat, rest, or even take in the world around him or the decisions he had made to take him to this place. Instead, he calmed his mind and weaved invisible enchantments all around him, all the while making himself stronger and stronger. He immolated trees in an unforgiving flame every now and then before pulling all heat from them, leaving a charred crust in their wake. He elevated boulders from one side of the path to the other as he came upon them. Just enough to practice and improve. Just enough to make impossible weavings second nature to him. Eralorien would have been proud, but when he tipped the bandoleer, all he felt was the old man's senseless grief.

He walked for many hours, from day until night, and he did so with no sleep. He allowed the lure to tease his desire, for he thought it a pleasurable thing. He could shatter the enchantment into nothing, like a twig in a giant's grasp if needed, yet he never did. It made each mile more enjoyable, each hour passed more exciting. He kept that nastiness swirling in his thoughts and in his soul, for it was a welcomed reassurance.

To anyone else, it might have driven them mad, as it had with Eralorien, or sapped all bravery, as it had done to Denan. He knew this because he had felt both men's minds. He should have felt more for them now, but each had forsaken their comrades, all in the name of a whore. Again, he thought of Arielle thurking a man out of spite, and then he thought of the repercussions with the lure.

Iaculous spat into the dirt at his feet and spat Bereziel's name a second time. That foolish old man had doomed the great Hounds, for there was no other weaver skilled enough, reckless enough, or even stupid enough to cast a lure using soul stones as their binding enchantment. It didn't matter that Bereziel was unaware of the potency of such things, but Silencio was aware and had taken its demonic opportunity where it could. When this mission finished, Iaculous would meet Bereziel one last time and repay upon him his sins.

"That thurken lure."

He felt no need to shatter it, for he had need of it too. The lure had bound all their souls together, and when Heygar had died, his desire to complete the mission had been shared out among them all. He knew the rodenerack had passed into the darkness. He would unknowingly have felt it when it happened, yet only now recognised why. So too, had that little beast's yearning joined their collective desires, and Arielle's after Mallum had taken her soul. On and on, they had fallen like flies in a thresher, and with each of their passing, the cruellest of all lures had grown stronger upon those still enchanted by it and oh, Silencio had loved this ever so.

He felt a different presence beside him, yet distant, from across a void, in another world, in another time. *Another time.*

"I will repay what you have done, Bereziel, seven times over," he said aloud, and the unnatural presence of Bereziel dissipated completely.

Iaculous knew the truth. It was another trick by the demon to unsettle him. He ran his fingers along the blade, but the sound of music shattered his thoughts, distant and melodic. He listened and wondered how far he had walked without respite. The sun had set upon this open land, and his beasts were itching for meat.

"What day is it anyway?" he said to the wind.

He smelled the air as they did and sensed many flavours of man, woman, and child. With a delicate wave of the hand, he released the enchantment and freed the Venandi night hunters of their shield.

He expected to feel a surge of relief at the release of such power, but there was nothing. Maintaining so many shields for an entire day against relentless assault should have drained so much of him, yet it felt as little as stretching after a night's rest. He remembered sensing the ferocious power in Mallum, but it was nothing compared to what he felt now. Mallum had reached his pinnacle and would fall well short of Iaculous's will.

He felt the hour change and a new day begin. The music was no farther away than a hill beyond, and somewhere beyond that, he could sense his quarry. "It is time to end this all," he whispered to the demon Silencio and allowed it to touch his mind once more. It was like opening a fist in a stream and allowing the current to pass between each finger. Who knew opening the mind could be so easy?

SILENCIO

He could remember the burns well enough, and not just for the pain. He remembered the potency of the fire as he released each volley into the ocean. He had tasted power as it consumed him, and in that moment, the demon named Silencio had come to him. It had felt every strike and instilled in him the unbridled energies of the source. It must have taken pleasure in his aggression, for he had tasted its hopeful delight as he had lost the run of himself.

He knew well it had influenced his recklessness, causing his doom, and what a fine doom it should have been. He had felt his breath disappear, yet still, the unrivalled hate drove him forward. Each strike was fiercer than the last, and it was intoxicating. It was only after he threw the last strike and fell to the unsteady deck of the *Celeste* that he realised his folly. That was the moment Silencio had begun instruction.

With all his will drained and excruciating pain consuming him all the way to his broken soul, he had attempted to heal himself, knowing he was lost. He remembered her sweet aroma above his own charred skin, and he had tried to tell her he was sorry for killing himself in such a way, but his tongue had burned like a steak left too long upon a cooking spit. He had tried to look to her one last time, but his eyes had melted away like snow after a wave of warmth. But he still had ears to listen, and they heard much beyond her delicate lamenting. He heard Silencio from a great distance, and the demon had laughed riotously at his actions.

"And why shouldn't you have laughed?" Iaculous whispered in the wind, in his mind. The demon had tricked another young weaver into self-inflicted torment for its own pleasure. Or else in its hope that the right young weaver might rise to meet its presence.

He had listened to that guttural, nasty laugh for an eternity, and he had tried to meet it. He never knew how long his body lay there upon the deck, smouldering away to ash, for his mind travelled far. The cruel dark of his blindness became a haze of mist, and he knew well of his passing. This was not the first time he had walked where men were not supposed to walk. Unbeknownst to his master, he had stepped into this world ever since he had come of age. Something had called him for many years, and only at the moment of death, had he finally met his suitor.

"You knew I dared to step into the source and venture like Bereziel. You knew I was there, but you could not find me, could you?" Iaculous whispered in his mind.

Stepping into the source was akin to inviting death openly as a friend, but he had always felt a connection to the darkness and the unknown evils within. In the beginning, he would take only a solitary step as a coward might when entering an unlit cellar hatch. A step was all he dared with the warmth of the living world at his back and cold eternity laid out before him. As he grew older, the will to step farther was too alluring, and eventually, he did. Every time he returned, he carried with him further ability, as though his body became infused with ethereal vitality.

Though Iaculous had always been brave, he was also careful. He was no fool, for after taking a third step, the darkness became a hazy, fog-filled world of death and treacherous things. With heightened senses, he felt the movement of great monsters around him. Though he could not see them, he knew they were there. He viewed the shadows of large, spiked beasts with countless limbs and terrible trunks, as tall as mountains and likely just as old. They drifted in the haze, miles above his head, as only gigantic monsters could, but these creatures were little more than otherworldly beasts of burden to the true rulers who lay farther in.

Though he had never known how he knew this, he had known, as though someone whispered it to him as he slept. Neither Eralorien nor any of his guild had ever walked beyond three steps into the night, yet somehow, he knew Bereziel had taken six. This world existed on another level of his thoughts and his notion of time, and even though it was terrible, he wanted it more and more.

He desired to take seven steps in, for all fools and wise men knew seven was the strongest of all numbers. Perhaps he might have walked that far in but, though she never knew it, Arielle kept him steady, for that is the power of love. So, he had settled with what he had discovered. As his powers had grown, he had kept them secret from Eralorien, who struggled with demons of his own: demons of the rotting body, to be more precise.

It wasn't until the death of Heygar that Iaculous's movements within the source finally birthed repercussions.

Struggling to deny the inevitable with his futile calling of Heygar's soul had finally drawn the demon to them all. Silencio had taken Heygar's lured soul as it struggled to free itself of the enchantment. It was no small thing to feel the passing of a man, but it was worse still to see his soul denied its rest.

Heygar should have enjoyed his eternal sleep in the place beyond even what Silencio and his six kin held dominion over, but the lure had been cast in soul stones, so it denied his soul free passage. A lost soul within the realm of Silencio was just too tasty a delicacy to allow to wander freely. So, it had taken what it was entitled to. Iaculous had seen all this and fled in terror back to the world of the living, for that is what any man or woman would have done. He had kept the truth of what he had seen and hoped to any other gods they could save their leader from a fate as terrible as this.

"I hadn't escaped your notice though, and you knew I would come when I burned," Iaculous said in his mind.

He had felt Arielle's anguish in the barge's sway, and he had turned away from her. Though his body lay broken with fading breath, his soul had marched into the darkness. Unlike Heygar's wild spirit, unable to comprehend its fate, he still had his mind and his ability. One step, two, three, and many more he had taken, and after twenty steps, he had stopped counting. His eyes had fallen upon a beacon of such silver beauty, and he had recognised Heygar's soul for what it was. An energy of fierce power, linked eternally to all of their souls until Mallum was no more. Only then would the enchantment shatter.

Iaculous had come upon the demon, and he had come upon it brazenly.

"You expected me to beg like a dog, like a human," Iaculous said in his mind.

Even then, the demon had sensed the growing power in the young weaver, for as he drew near, the laughing had fallen silent, and things he had only felt finally came to his eyes. Though the demon never spoke aloud, it spoke in his mind as a crude voice in a maniac's head. Iaculous allowed the beast to know his mind and had felt the veils of consciousness stirring with his own. Knowing his sealed fate, he had pushed right back through a river of resistant consciousness and found an ancient creature as old as the world, imprisoned and desperate to return to the world of the living.

"You were just as they said you were, and you were beautiful to my eyes," Iaculous said in his mind. The Venandi around him shuffled uncomfortably in their march. They sensed the coming of a beast fiercer than their master.

Silencio had appeared as an upright figure at least seven feet tall, with horns atop its head and hooves upon each limb. Along its arms were long blades of serrated bone, likely for battle among dreadful gods. Even in appearance, this beast was bred for death and war but not for battles imagined by any great storyteller. Of its dark kin, Iaculous knew its number among its brethren, and even though he strained to see through the mist, he knew its menace was terrible.

But it was a beast, and he was a Hound. So, he had formed fire in his thoughts and upon his hands, and he had thrown the sphere into the darkness and struck the beast across the chest as it stepped towards him. It was a strike capable of burning a grand cantus to nothing, but the demon took the strike and took it well. It did not cry out nor beg for a reprieve or peace between them. Instead, it merely held its march upon him for a moment before drawing near once more and laughing loudly.

He had thought his power was being mocked, but as it

349

grew louder, he realised it was not the laughter of a victorious deity but more of a child who had accepted a playful nip from a puppy. Untroubled, yet a little upset at the defiant act. He had not attacked again and waited for his silencing, only to meet the beast's mind once more, when it spoke of its desires.

And what pathetic pleas they turned out to be.

WALKING WITH GIANTS

I aculous took a deep breath and walked into the darkness. His ethereal soul walked deeper, while his material body continued walking the path, though he took each step at a fraction of the speed. Time moved differently in the source's world and, from what he understood, not entirely in proper sequence. Mostly, time passed far slower in the veil of darkness. So, while a pulse of blood may have passed in the world of the living, an age may have lived and died in the darker world.

Iaculous felt at ease in this place now, without the fear of death walking with him. He had a companion who had taught him so much, for that is what good companions were used for until they had no further use. His power surpassed that of the charred waif from the barge, and he could easily heal the ravages his body suffered, having the source bent to his will. Even as he had slept after the crustacuus's attack and been attended to by Denan, his will had kept him alive until his mind recovered and returned himself to the world of the living. What weaver could claim such an ability?

Iaculous imagined the blade in his hand, as it was in the

world of the living. With all his might and those of his
ensnared comrades, he willed it to pass into the source with
him. Such an improbable thing took most of his energy, for
inorganic objects could not pass into another realm. He knew
this because the demon knew this.

Though they were never actually aware of what an
incredible feat they achieved, most weavers could manipulate
a blade to exist between both worlds using a simple illusion
enchantment. Eralorien himself had frequently enchanted a
blade to appear—invisible yet still deadly—for Heygar
whenever he went to do business. The old fool never
questioned what became of the weapon's appearance to make
it no longer visible. He did not understand he tapped upon the
darker world's door with the blade, and that simple
enchantment could lead the way for very interesting
weavings. Like his masters before, Eralorien never embraced
the potential of the source or saw it as more than a tool for
healing and hiding from battles. None of Eralorien's masters
did.

Iaculous considered those who should have been peers
were little more than inept children. Like little munkets
learning fire for the first time, the weavers before never
questioned. They accepted what was, and the fire warmed
them and little else. They never challenged but accepted the
mundane. Iaculous challenged everything. Perhaps the only
one to weave as precariously was Bereziel.

Iaculous looked to his wraithlike hand and watched the
green sword attempt to appear in his grip, all the while
knowing in the world of the living, the blade was shimmering
and disappearing in his husk's grip. Who knew a healer could
become the most powerful wielder of the source Dellerin
would ever know by following the teachings all acolytes
learned in the first year of study? Everything was attainable

through the eyes of a millennium-old demon as long as the apprentice would practice. Iaculous was willing.

The demon wondered why he had returned so soon and so close to his quarry. Iaculous knew this because he sensed it as though it were a thought of his own. Their bond was strong, but age had weakened Silencio's caution, and its sanity. Iaculous concealed his nervousness and marched into the darkness recklessly, doing all he could to ignore how fast his heart was beating in the world of living. It was so fast and so loud that he wondered if it could beat all the way across both worlds. Deep down in the husk of his body, it knew the peril it was in.

"I had to see you before the end," Iaculous said, and Silencio appeared in front of him.

Spread out behind the creature was the world of darkness. Blurred and murky, yet Iaculous could make out mile-high buildings long since ruined, with broken roads leading out to the dark horizon, and great machines littering the landscape all the way. This was the world his eyes could see, yet the demon saw an entirely different world. Iaculous pledged to see it someday—perhaps when the demon allowed him.

"Is it fear which brings you here, dirty little Iaculous?" it hissed, as though a snake itself had learned the common tongue of man. Iaculous winced at its tone.

"You know the journey I face. You know the power. You know the treacherous path I have to choose," Iaculous hissed in reply, and the demon revealed itself completely. Everything in this world appeared as a blur, but the demon was as clear as a goblet in his grasp, and he aimed to drink from it.

"So, be done with the deed, shatter the lure, and continue our agreement," Silencio said and stood over Iaculous menacingly.

Its tail whipped back and forth, and its beastly nose snorted in disdain. A fine performance of dominance. Despite himself, Iaculous took a step back.

"Or return to your pledge to march upon the six remaining monoliths," Silencio said and poked Iaculous's chest as a master would a disobedient pupil. Perhaps this was what the demon intended him to feel, but a lifetime under the watch of Eralorien had steeled him somewhat. Iaculous knew far more about the source than the demon did of the qualities of man.

"I desire something else." Iaculous felt his fingers take hold of a corporal handle in an ethereal world. The demon snorted and eyed the blade as it appeared, for it knew its strength.

"You dare challenge one of the seven kin of the dark," it hissed.

"I will do what I must."

"I should tear you to shreds for this impudence."

The ground appeared to shake. Perhaps it was the world of darkness itself. Regardless, it was a fine display of intimidation, but Iaculous sensed the lie and the demon's frustration. Silencio had much to lose in killing him, while Iaculous only had his feeble soul. Iaculous was the instrument of Silencio, was he not?—as he had been when the monolith had shattered at his touch. It was no simple rock that shattered. It was a godly lock sealing away the demon, its kin, and the others from returning to the world of the living. But there were more, weren't there? Seven locks in total. Six now.

Iaculous held Denan's sword out in front of him, and Silencio could see its green shimmer. Venistrian steel. So pure and unique. Such a steel unaffected by enchantments, source weavings, or demonic misdeeds. To find enough of this precious metal to smelt a signet ring was rare. To find enough to temper a blade as fine as this would take the lifetimes of a dozen skilled miners. It was a sword for a king's chosen son. It was one in a million. It was the one thing his father had allowed him to carry in exile.

The demon swiped its tip away as an instructor would when facing a delusional apprentice. Iaculous summoned the energy from the three soul stones strapped to his bandoleer in the world of life. He wrenched what he needed from them and felt his former comrades' dreadful torment as their cries echoed in his mind and soul. Their minds were crazed at the loss of their bodies, and for the briefest of moments, he felt ashamed.

So, he closed his mind to their torment and gorged himself upon the re-surging energies as they flowed through him, and the shameful moment passed. He could feed upon them for a thousand years without reprieve, and they would lose little of their lustre or vibrancy. They would feel every breath passed, but it was a small price to pay for eternal life, he supposed. Was this not how the demons of this world leeched life from the departed?

"I've come for their souls."

Silencio roared in anger, and Iaculous attacked.

A DIFFERENCE OF OPINION

He swung the Venistrian blade, and the demon locked its muscular arms in a defensive cross. Silencio deflected the blow away with the two protruding blades of bone running along its forearms. They were as large as a great sword on either side, as strong as any metal, and the demon wielded them masterfully.

Iaculous hadn't expected the lumbering opponent to be as swift as he was. He struck again and met the same stubborn defence successfully used by a creature for a millennium. The demon glided around him as if countering a human's display of swordplay was the most natural thing in this world. Iaculous moved with him and pressed home his attack, eager to overpower the beast in the first few volleys and end the duel swiftly. But it never took long for a fight to turn on its side.

Soon enough, after an over-extension, Iaculous suffered for his error. Silencio caught his wild lunge with a fierce block, and a surge of energy pulsed through Iaculous, fiercely enough to wind him. He stumbled away and narrowly avoided the counterstrike. Silencio swung like a pugilist in a contest with frantic combinations, where each potential hit was a mortal blow, even to an apparition. Iaculous ducked and weaved from the demon's strikes, desperately knocking back any strikes that neared. The demon's style was awkward, and Iaculous was no master, yet still, he somehow kept the serrated edges from cleaving a limb from his body. This was no impressive thing; his form would have enraged his first teacher of the blade.

Heygar hadn't spent so many evenings out on the march, instructing the younger man in the art of swordplay, only for his student to fall at the first hurdle when facing a superior swordsman. Or an eternal demon of the source. It really had not mattered to the legend whom he crossed swords with. "Every battle is winnable regardless of the opponent," he had always insisted, and Iaculous thought them to be fine words from a dead man undone by a few feet of water. Heygar would be just as disappointed as Iaculous felt in surrendering the element of surprise without the benefit of any success at all.

Silencio moved like a cantus beneath the waves and slipped nearer with every strike. Iaculous retreated and felt his strength ebb away to the unrelenting barrage of brutality. "Read your opponent's attacks. Rarely does any man, woman, or beast change their tactics which have kept them alive to this moment," the voice of his old leader said, though less a memory and more an active thought.

Iaculous held his ground as the beast moved around him. Its tail twitched irritably like a hunting cat in the moments before it launched a fresh assault. He wasn't sure noticing such a thing would help him, but he felt a little better. He watched Silencio take deep, heavy breaths, and he wondered how long it had been since any fool had taken such a monster to war.

Iaculous willed the souls at his chest to infuse him with strength and met their lamenting cries. He had gifted them a terrible fate. What type of man was he? Did it matter? Not at all, for they answered his will, and he felt a fierce stirring of power. Perhaps the three imprisoned souls knew a fate at his chest was greater than a fate to a demon. They released their energy to him, and all weariness left his phantom limbs. He felt renewed as before. He remembered his power and his confidence.

He had come to this place knowing the demon would terrorise and bully but never kill him. He held that thought, and he opened his guard to allow the demon to strike his head clear from his neck. It was a dead man's gambit, but it might be another thousand years before another human with his aptitude, his will, and his needs came upon the demon again. Not everyone was like the fool Mallum, who showed promise but fled in terror. He knew this because the demon had almost found fortune with the dark weaver.

The tail twitched, and the beast came at him again, but it staggered the attack as it aimed far from his head, lest it be a killing blow. It snorted in frustration as he fell back, blocking each strike easily enough. Iaculous countered recklessly and sliced an inch deep all the way across Silencio's chest. It was a fine strike capable of devastating any man, but there was no wild spray of blood upon the demon's wound.

"*Vermin.*"

Silencio shook its head in frustration and ran its long claw down the edge of the wound. It tapped at the dry flap of skin as though it were a piece of leather upon a tanning rack. Deep within, Iaculous could see the ruined innards of the monster. For the briefest of terrifying moments, he despaired that the eternal beast might be invulnerable. Then it fell to one of its knees and roared out in pain.

He felt a flood of thoughts surging through his mind that could easily sway a man towards mercy, and Iaculous sensed the fear behind the desperate suggestions. Being so close to freedom from an eternal cage was a pain far greater than never nearing freedom at all.

"I gave you my mind, dirty human." The demon willed Iaculous to experience shame and sorrow. Far away, he felt the pain of Heygar and the rat. Their lured souls were waiting for salvation.

"Yield their souls," he said coldly.

"You think yourself capable of slaying one of my kind?" the demon snarled. It attacked once more, but Iaculous matched each strike recklessly. The demon's attacks laboured as it fought its own nature and bloodlust, all in a glorious cause, until Iaculous struck it down a second time.

"Yield their souls or die."

"I have walked this prison for many thousands of years, dirty human. How can you possibly think yourself capable of matching my stride?" it gasped before circling once more and striking as before.

Again, Iaculous countered and sent his sword through its shoulder, then withdrew from the beaten thing of nightmares. "I am man and capable of many things a demon like you can never understand."

Silencio spat in disgust. "Do not use such an unimaginative term, human," it said in that terrible voice as it broke their melee.

With a tired, torn claw, it evoked the source. Iaculous felt a barrier form around them. Within a pulse, they were both encased in a sphere of dark energy as black and bubbling as a drum of burning oil. He struck at the edge of the cage and felt the effect of draining.

He felt the invasion of a foreign mind as Silencio

attempted to take control of his will. Like cold water streaming through his mind, he felt it enter his thoughts but he held it at bay, he denied it control, he denied it understanding of his motives. The beast launched an attack once more, and with less space to manoeuvre, Iaculous struggled under the beast's dual assault. They fought within the small cage until time became nothing more than a flickered notion shared by men of lesser stations. It may have been a pulse or a day. He couldn't say, for there was no cessation to the attacks, and exhaustion in the source was different to that of the world of the living. It was a weakness of the soul and a fight against despair itself.

Eventually, they separated. Both stood at the edge of the cage, only a handful of feet apart. The hazy world beyond the black wall had disappeared completely. Iaculous wondered if he did kill Silencio, would he receive true vision to this realm and its secrets, or would the demon's brothers and sisters slay him a breath after he walked clear?

"For a dirty human, you have a will." Silencio glanced down upon the multitude of strikes upon its body. Any man would have bled themselves dry from so many cuts, but he was unburdened with such human things as a beating heart or the fluid to drive its mighty machine. The injuries suffered by Iaculous were insignificant.

"You have given me your mind without taking from me. Let me do the same," Iaculous said and opened his mind to allow the demon see his true desires. Let it know man and what he was capable of. If the demon was unturned, then so be it. They would fight for eternity until one of them yielded.

Silencio was still and ceased its attempts at overcoming the weaver's mind. It fell back to its knees once more, allowing the full exhaustion to show upon its ruptured body. Iaculous fell to his own knees and gasped for air, which he did not need. Though the demon had given its mind to Iaculous willingly, it had never felt the compulsion to understand what workings stirred in a lesser being. Perhaps they could have had this shared conversation sooner. It had taken a Venistrian blade to earn the demon a moment of deference.

"We think alike," the demon growled after a time and released the hold on Iaculous's mind completely.

"Give your word, and we will meet again in war, in the world of the living," Iaculous said and threw his blade down at Silencio's feet. Their march was not done, but he was no pawn. Silencio knew this now.

Around them, the cage pulsed brightly and faded to nothing. Iaculous felt the pull of the world of the living once more but also the pull of the two lured souls. The demon held out its clawed hand and produced two floating spheres. Iaculous felt the tormented souls screaming their madness as the demon released them to him.

For a flicker of a moment, Iaculous saw the world as it was, and shudders ran down his spine. But as swiftly as the vision appeared, the world returned to its haziness, and he immediately forgot what dazzling beauty there lay within. The last image to fade was a great city of impossible light, and he knew there was no soul from this world capable of walking the great distance to it. He thought this was no tragedy. And then there was nothing.

"I will wait for you," Silencio whispered and faded into the mist, leaving Iaculous alone with those he had begun this dreadful mission with.

"It is time we march into battle, my friends," Iaculous said as each beautiful soul faded into the stones upon his bandoleer.

DAY SEVEN: THE LAST DAY

I aculous emerged from the source feeling elated for his success but also from the infusion of energy from the two shimmering rocks upon the bandoleer. Around him, the beasts marched obliviously. Iaculous realised he had only taken a dozen steps in all the time he had battled the demon. It did not appreciate being referred to by such a title, he reminded himself, and he deigned never to refer to it as anything but.

The path was barely worn, and the hills were wild on either side of him. This place was not a place used by many Venistrians, yet Iaculous sensed Mallum near. The music still played in the darkened distance, and he thought it beautiful, tragic, memorable, and fitting for his triumphant arrival.

At his feet were the dried tracks of a wandering troupe, and he wondered if they were from Mallum and his acolytes as they'd carted their prised treasure to his domain. He passed over a few fallen trees and recognised their innocent appearance as a way to slow any trespassers. Mallum expected an army to come find him, and instead, he would meet just one man.

Above his head hung the healthiest weeping oaks of this land. His fingers reached out and took hold of a few hanging leaves as he walked. He tore them free and brought them to his nose. Fresh, vibrant and far from the ashy grey he knew well since their arrival. He left the leaves to fall away in the wind and embraced the feeling of five fallen souls surrounding him. He would need their strength for what was to happen.

He reached the top of the hill, and his eyes widened at what lay before him. Secluded from the rest of the world, it was a fine place for a monster to hide away from greater monsters. The valley spread out for a mile across, with a great lake in its middle. The moon and a hundred stars lit it up, and he thought it peculiar that there was such beauty found in this wretched place.

At the centre of the lake was an island that housed a small grey castle, only four floors in height and as much across. There was one large entrance and one large tower from which nervous eyes likely looked out, eager to see little disturbances. Somewhere within this unimpressive stronghold lay a devious cur.

The distance between the island and lake edge was far enough that a man would need to paddle across on one of the small rowboats hitched to the docks. It was the edge of the lake, which interested him most, however, for along its edge, he counted at least a hundred tents and half as many flimsy shacks clustered tightly together. Mallum, it would appear, had gained a little army all to himself.

"They won't save you though, will they?"

Among the transient hovels, Iaculous heard the music much clearer now. People of all sorts and ages sat in front of little cooking fires or stood among comrades, talking happily of pleasant things. The more enthused were singing, dancing, or laughing along with the cheerful mood, rising above the awfulness of their miserable encampment. Children played, ate, and chased each other through the many alleys of old sheets, pegs, and rope. Others were down by the edge of the lake, engaging in a heated competition of skimming stones into the dark water.

Iaculous hated them all, for they were under his quarry's rule. A little itinerant group of refugees all huddled together, making what they could out of what they were given.

He eyed the settlement for any soldiers and saw few standing watch. There were only half a dozen; their complacency would be their downfall. He felt the ground beneath him change, and he looked to find his feet had touched upon freshly tilled land. The entire valley was tilled all the way across, unlike the many other regions tainted by blight and the deathly grey.

They are a beaten people, he heard in his mind, where the stirrings of souls protested their loudest, and he wondered, as he grew stronger, did the souls grow stronger too? He hushed them to silence with a touch of his resolve. His five fallen comrades tasted the death in the air. So could he. They rebelled, yet their fight was done. His tasks were only beginning.

"I must do it. There is no other way."

Iaculous looked upon the group of Venandi surrounding him. They sensed the taste of man in the air. They drooled at hearing the squeals of children at play and women conversing with husbands and comrades. The beasts were poised and needed his release.

"Leave none alive. Then you may feed," he said aloud and into their minds. The peoples' sins were Mallum's, and their penance was eternal. He waved his hand, and the beasts charged as one.

At first, he'd struggled to even bring the Venandi all together. Each of them were fighting spirits of primal anger. That night, when they had fallen upon Cherrie, had been the turning point of their subservience. He delivered flesh of man, ripe and with a fight to it, and he would deliver it again. He felt her unrivalled hatred, and he patted her to silence.

Hush, Cherrie. It made me stronger, did it not?

"Is that not what you wanted?" he whispered aloud, and she ceased her wailing.

There was no howling to announce their way, no primal snarling or growling, for he willed them to silence until they did the deed. He felt the land rumble slightly as they fled from him down the slope, towards a noiseless massacre.

He felt screaming in his mind from the soul called Denan. It raged and begged for mercy, and he ignored the pleading. Some things were part of this life. Some things were as natural as birth and death. Perhaps it was that Denan recognised his kin among the wretches, through Iaculous's eyes.

"They made their choice," Iaculous whispered and patted the stone to silence.

The song still played through. In the dimness, he saw his beauties spread out along the outskirts of the camp, surrounding it in a soundless line of death. He recognised that song, and he was no great fan.

"I have come for you." His voice carried through the valley, across the water, into Mallum's mind. He touched his consciousness and felt a strange kinship to the brute for a moment before severing his thoughts from the man.

The music stopped, replaced with the panic of two hundred voices in unison as they fell under the assault. The beasts were fierce, and with Iaculous's instructions, they were unstoppable. In a few desperate moments, he had eliminated Mallum's followers. Without the desire to feed upon those they had slain, the night hunters bit once and moved to the next target, leaving death or the dying in their wake.

Iaculous watched without prejudice the slaughter of all around him. His ears were deaf to the high-pitched cries of dying children. His mind was cold to the vision of their distraught mothers attempting to hold the flood of death. Demented fathers who attempted vengeance upon the hunters tested his nerve. Only a brave man could undertake such a task.

The beasts ripped through the camp, leaving utter devastation in their wake. Iaculous felt a collective desire to feed upon the dead or dying, but instead, he willed them to circle back and finish all who still stood with blade in hand. Deep within, he felt the pleading from the entrapped souls to allow mercy. He ignored this too as he followed his beauties down the valley, towards the ruined army's base.

By the time he reached the camp, the cries of the doomed had fallen still, and Iaculous thought these hunters worthy of his praise. He sensed only a few of his pack had fallen to hastily and inevitably doomed resistance, and this pleased him greatly. Each of his magnificent hounds sat among the dead but did not move. Instead, they watched and waited for their master, and as any good master would, he rewarded them.

"You have done all that I asked, and we have only just begun. Take what you want, my little ones. I will be along soon," he said, and they fell upon the dead ravenously. The delighted growls of sating filled the air, along with the crunching of bones and the tearing of flesh.

Iaculous shut his mind off to their delirium, for he had no

further taste for it. He walked through the ruined camp and came to a stop at the water's edge. Beyond, he felt the lamenting mind of Mallum and her delicate soul. Fury surged through him.

He walked on, and the rocks at the bottom of the lake answered his will. Each one large enough to fill the size of his boot rose to meet him a foot above the still surface. Every step took a little of his will to maintain. The shrewder move would have been weaving a solitary stone large enough to fit him and carry him all the way across, but after such a long journey, he would not be carried. He would march right up to the thurken gates.

The souls at his chest had fallen quiet, for they knew the importance of these next few moments. They were silent in melancholy, and he thought it amusing they lamented the evils, yet fell silent when it suited them. Killing Mallum suited them down to the water-covered ground. Even in their form, they were still mercenaries. Whatever they felt with his actions, they still infused him with incredible power.

It was colder out on the island. The wind ruffled his cloak, and a deathly silence hung around him. The castle had sturdier walls than he presumed and an imposing portcullis to keep wandering weavers from getting in. He opened his mind and felt over a dozen minds within. Something terrified them, and he licked his lips like a night hunter would before the kill. They knew death was at the gate.

He pushed further from their minds and focused upon that of his prey. He discovered it open and deeply intertwined with Arielle's mind. A terrible fury overcame him in his anguish, and flame erupted from his hands, darker than ever, darker than the black fire from Mallum's own hand. He had seen its colour once before, in the cage he had shared with the demon.

He was getting stronger.

"Open the gate and only Mallum falls," he said aloud, and his voice echoed through the courtyard. A few breaths before he shattered the gate with fire, he heard the cranking of chain and, suddenly, the rising of their last defence against him.

LIFE

I aculous half expected the gates to drop suddenly as he passed underneath, but they did not. He stepped across the threshold, into the enemy's domain. He found himself in a small, barren courtyard beneath a set of steps leading to the keep and thought it a fine place to set up an ambush.

The sound of footsteps reaffirmed his suspicions as a dozen of Mallum's acolytes emerged from the keep's main door and from a passageway behind him. Each of them were warrior weavers, and they carried both sword and shield in hand. They marched in unison and within moments had spread out in a circle, surrounding him. They had come for war despite inviting him in so readily.

Even closer, he sensed their terrible fear. It permeated off them like the stench of death in the Entombed Graves of Elvea in warmer seasons. He saw it in their faces, for fear was the hardest emotion to conceal. They were alone. Without their leader to lead them, they appeared as lost children. Unlike Iaculous, who had grown in the face of terrible things, they had faltered. Mallum had sent them to their doom, and they knew it.

"I have come for your master," he growled and felt his fingers twitch with anticipation. He was not the waif from the tavern anymore. He had come so far in the world of the living in that short time since then. Wonderfully outnumbered, he never felt more in control.

Eventually, one acolyte stepped forward. Though dressed in similar attire to the others, his dark grey cloak held a black sash running down along his chest. Perhaps his grovelling was better than the rest, Iaculous mused. He removed his grey hood, and Iaculous saw he was a young man no older that he. A child among giants. He was pale, and his lips quivered, yet he attempted to address him with deference.

"Our master will treat with you, if you lay down all weapons and intent."

Iaculous despised the wretchedness in his voice. How dare Mallum send him cowards to broker peace while he locked himself in a stone keep? Was this what Arielle had truly desired? A man who hid away when facing unwelcomed odds? Unlike his quarry, Iaculous was unafraid to present himself exactly as he was.

"Where is your master, so I may slay him?"

"Please, Dark One, you must listen to reason," the acolyte pleaded and fell to his knees in subservience.

Dark One? He walked among the darkness. He desired to know the other realm in all its beauty, power, and darkness. So be it.

Iaculous fired a volley of flame at the kneeling man. There was a deafening scream, but it fell silent in a pulse. In the time it took Iaculous to take a breath, the acolyte's skin had burned away to bone and, within another breath, from bone to ashes. Far away, Iaculous felt the torment from Mallum, who felt his passing.

"Where is your master, so I may slay him?" he asked

again. The souls at his chest had fallen silent as they understood his brutality, or else they realised his actions were unaffected by their will alone. Someone could do great things with them answering to his desire. The Hounds would be eternal.

"The lure bends your will to madness. You must fight it, Iaculous," Mallum suddenly whispered from within his mind.

Iaculous recoiled at the invasion. This was not the familiarity of the demon. This was something else entirely, and he hated it as it gave its mind to him.

"Meet me now, and I will spare your flock," Iaculous said aloud so that all could hear. He might be The Dark One, but he was no monster, like Mallum.

As one, the acolytes gripped their swords and held their shields out in front of them. He thought this both admirable and foolish. What hold did the dark weaver have upon their young minds?

"We can return Arielle to the world as she was, if you lay down your wrath," the voice inside his mind whispered.

Iaculous gripped his head as fierce shards of ice shot through him and blinded him with pain. He stumbled to his knees as the dark weaver attempted to tear his will from him. He searched for Mallum's hatred, and he cried out in pain when all he could feel was a pathetic desire for Arielle. He had no right to her.

"Come back from the brink, Iaculous."

"I will kill you all!" Iaculous cried.

He attempted defensive enchantments to hold back the assault, but Mallum was wilier than he had expected. The world darkened around him, and his entire body went numb. He saw the acolytes forming up around him, but he couldn't react. He caught sight of Arielle in his mind, and for a moment, he thought her beautiful as he always had. But then he realised this beauty was something different. This beauty was beyond what he knew or even remembered. It was as though he were meeting her for the first time. He felt his deep wells of confusion stirring within him, for he also saw her as the enemy. And he saw himself as her quarry.

"Get out of my head, monster." His voice echoed through the courtyard, through the castle, and through the entire thurken valley.

The dark weaver's trick was the cruellest of all. Iaculous was living the thoughts and reasoning of Mallum, and it disgusted him. He felt Mallum's stomach quiver as his own as he kissed Arielle for the first time in the tavern. He tried to fight the control Mallum had over his mind, but it was impossible, for he enjoyed the pleasure of this act. He could taste her, feel her warm breath, and he felt many desires to take her. And then he did.

"You will pay for this!" he screamed but lessened his struggle, for knowing this pleasure was incredible. He felt himself tearing at her body, wonderfully and distantly. He felt himself ripping apart what they had once had as future lovers, and he couldn't stop himself. This was the desire shared by those who shared a soul.

"Please, not like this," he moaned pathetically as tears of sorrow and realisation struck him.

Then he felt the first blade enter his chest as one acolyte pierced him with a sharpened blade. No finer way to die.

He felt his fingers rip the clothing from Arielle's body and the taste of her lips upon his as she gave herself over to him completely. Though he knew this was a borrowed memory, he loved it so. As much as he reviled it, because he heard her giggle, he laughed along in a voice that was not his.

A second blade pierced him through the stomach. He felt

himself attempt healing as a dagger of bronze ripped across his throat and tore it apart.

He felt himself inside Arielle. He felt satisfaction like he had never felt before as she moved in delirious joy with him. He felt the completing love of intertwined souls, and it brought coldness, for he realised that it was Mallum who shared this eternal bond with her.

He felt himself falling to the ground as the acolytes killed him, and he could only think of Arielle. His lost Arielle. And then he felt something else as he spent himself gloriously inside her. Something incredible and historical. Something powerful enough to tear a lure from its guided path. Something to tear a soul from a welcoming body in that terrible moment. Something demonic ripped apart from love. *A new life from love.*

"Oh, please no!" Iaculous screamed madly. He tore himself from Mallum's mind and lay upon the cold stone of the courtyard.

He lost all desire for the whore, for she was tainted and weighed down by responsibility now. It would have hurt less had Mallum taken her by force, but he had not. He felt the wounds closing up on his body as he willed his blood to replenish. He felt the souls stirring in anticipation of the next few steps.

Around him, the remaining acolytes lay in eleven piles of charred ash. Even his own subconscious was more devastating than anything Mallum's apprentices could use.

"It's time to end this." He climbed to his feet, and, with a delicate flick of his wrist, he tore the keep's heavy oak door from its frame.

THE LURED QUARRY

So tired. So exhausted. Not just the body but also the soul in its entirety. Iaculous stepped through the doorway and knew it was all at an end. It was time to complete the task and see how strong he truly was.

He thought of Silvious and thought it strange how strong the rat's soul was. He had imagined him possessing a frailer spirit than the others, yet there was a great nobility within. Perhaps he should have given the rat a little more respect as he had lived.

Cherrie stirred in her cage, and he willed her to silence, though it took more effort than it did for the rest because she was stronger than all of them put together. She was the only warrior willing to sacrifice herself for the greater good and for her sister. He patted the little container at his chest.

"Soon my betrayal and your sacrifice will bear fruit," he whispered and walked into the keep.

What good could Denan really have brought to the fight anyway? The lure had twisted his tremendous courage into deathly fear, and only Iaculous's testing manipulations had granted the fierce warrior a reprieve from his unnatural

cowardice at the end. Had there been no army waiting for
them at his father's fallen kingdom, as he had promised,
Iaculous might well have practiced on the warrior sooner with
more success. Still, it was no matter now that he had faced
the demon and gathered what he needed. Denan was a royal,
and the world needed no more royals in power.

He thought of the rotting mind of Eralorien's soul and
cursed the wretched old man for what he was. How easy the
lure had twisted his fragility into insanity. How brazen he had
been to see Iaculous's talent and temper his skills their entire
life together. The first soul entrapped was frenzied and lost,
and despite him knowing this man the longest, he felt least
bonded to the burning source of near eternal energy. Perhaps
his master's madness would serve him from his prison.
Maybe he had it better than the rest of them combined.

Last, he thought of his leader, Heygar. His soul was the
weakest of them all, yet still fierce enough to instil energy
within him for a lifetime. He should have hated the man for
enchanting them all, but without his foolish task, Iaculous
would not be so powerful this glorious night, would he?

With Mallum's whispered memories still floating in his
thoughts, Iaculous knew the truth and reason behind it all.
Heygar's interfering had brought about the true devastating
effects of a lure, and Iaculous thought such a thing was
incredible with far-reaching consequences. He understood
why the lure had behaved as it did. With the creation of life
and a beautiful new soul, the lure became more than a cruel
piece of weaving, for inconceivable circumstances had played
an incredible part.

What if the creators of a child with a beautiful soul were
soulmates themselves? What if a careless weaver bound those
soulmates to hate and kill each other? In that moment, such
weavings had caused the world to shudder. Such weavings

might have repercussions spanning the rest of times. Such weavings might cause a power between both worlds so fierce that all seven keys that separated them might shudder, crack, and await the right weaver in the right moment to shatter them completely.

"All the soul stones, lured in a row; seven souls with nowhere to go," he whispered to himself and to the souls upon his chest. They stirred with excitement for the end of their torment.

The keep was nothing more than a chapel to pray to the seven gods of this land. The chapel was long and cold as most chapels were, with stained glass windows that were thin, tall, and darkly coloured. Iaculous couldn't make out the tales they told, nor was he interested. Preachers spoke of seven gods and seven demons. He had met one of the demons and thought a little less of the beasts because of it. He spat his disgust for this place and eyed the man standing at the altar like a pious leader of faith awaiting his flock. The man watched in silence, and he was not alone.

A shield of energy suddenly formed up around Iaculous and blocked his way. It was the same energy used by the demon and the fire of his own will. Mallum had learned from the demon as Silencio had claimed. Did he cower when he learned the demon's true intentions as Silencio also claimed? Did it really matter?

The shield covered the entire room, separating him completely from his victim, though Iaculous was untroubled. Beside Mallum lay Arielle. They sprawled her out along a stone bench, and she looked to be sleeping peacefully. Her bedding was straw and silk. They brushed her hair, and her face was flawless and as beautiful as he had ever seen her. Upon his chest, the souls stirred. One of them screamed and raged so much so that Iaculous took hold of the canister upon the bandoleer and willed its fury to peter away.

Mallum approached the shield silently. As before, he was impressive. He carried himself with dignity and fearlessness despite knowing the inevitable. "Perhaps we would not have found ourselves in such a place if I had the power to tear that lure from your mind, Iaculous," he said and looked through the younger man as though he were as translucent as the shield itself. "I attempted to tear it from the mind of…"

Mallum trailed off and looked back to the comatose Arielle. Upon her chest was an amulet. It glowed brightly, and he nodded as if listening to her suggestion. Iaculous could not imagine what trickery it was on his part not to have the soul at his grasp. How deluded was he to think he could stand with Iaculous without her power to call upon?

"Eralorien," he said and turned back to Iaculous. "Yes, Eralorien was the one I attempted to free first, but any enchantment as fierce as this must run its course unless undone with the darkest of weavings," Mallum said. His eyes fell upon the glowing orbs on Iaculous's bandoleer. "Denan of the Green no longer walks?" he asked, and his head dropped as though learning of an idol's demise.

"Why were you there that night?" Iaculous's fingers twitched with murderous intent.

"It was no surprise King Lemier enlisted the wrath of the Hounds to take my life. I came to offer Heygar's Hounds a new deal. Venistra needs all the help it can get. I came to seek your help that night, unarmed and humble, as I do now."

Mallum offered his hands openly. Iaculous saw tears streaming down his eyes, but the man did not wipe them away. What weakness was this? For a moment, he felt the terrible sadness that afflicted the dark weaver.

"I need your power to free her from this dreadful event," he pleaded and looked to the shell of Arielle.

"You think I would help you, Mallum?"

"You have taken everything from me this day, so why not take my life, so they may know theirs?" Mallum said. Iaculous believed him, and it angered him further.

"You are a murderer and a fool." Iaculous struck the shield fiercely. Not to tear through it but merely to show he still had fight. Mallum hissed and struck the shield right back. He still had a fight in him too.

"The lure deludes you," Mallum cried with the broken frustration of a man with the finest hand in a game of death-chance, when no one else was playing the round.

"You think a lure commands my mind, as it did the rest?"

"I have seen your mind as you have seen mine. You have seen all my sins, yet still, you see none of your own," Mallum hissed.

Iaculous struck the shield with a weaving fist and shattered it. The eruption of energy was violent, and it blew Mallum across the room. He fell among some praying benches. Before he could rise, Iaculous placed a holding enchantment upon him and stood over him.

He felt his mind spinning as the lure tasted the victory. Somewhere in the world, seven soul stones rattled and shook, and all that mattered was finishing the task. Iaculous felt the souls surging. They desired blood, death, and payment. Even in death, they could be no different. They were the Hounds.

"Arielle begged me not to kill you. It was the first thing she willed from the stone that night," Mallum gasped and forced the enchantment away.

He formed a field of energy around Iaculous once again, but with a flick of Iaculous's wrist, that, too, shattered to nothing. Mallum retreated to the altar. His movements were panicked. He was the same master who had torn the remaining Hounds apart a few days previously, but Iaculous was no longer an apprentice conjuring a spit of fire. He had met with the demon and bested its brutality. He was now closer to a god than a man. He felt the power of the bandoleer, and it was endless. It was righteous. It was worthy of him.

Iaculous took hold of the man's mind and tore it asunder, and then he reached in towards his darkness. Mallum did not fight the invasion. He allowed him to know this mind, and Iaculous was worse for it. Terrible, enlightening visions of a man's desperate will to save all that he could washed through Iaculous. As he had experienced the act of Arielle and her throngs of passion before, he again felt and saw through the eyes of Mallum.

He saw Silencio's first meeting many years ago and experienced Mallum's revulsion as the demon granted him knowledge and failed to coerce the youth into darkness. He saw the demon come to him, time and time again, and he fought the demon's advancements best he could. He saw the land turn grey around him, and he lamented Venistra's lost beauty, for he saw the terrible greyness grow and consume the earth of its riches.

He saw the collapse of the economy after the king of Dellerin ceased all exports in reply to a lower yield of fortunes. He felt the desperation as a new year's taxes were tripled, which brought ruin to nearly all men and women— rich, royal, or peasant—and he hated Dellerin for all that it owned. He saw his country split into penniless towns of criminals and murderers, and open farmlands turned to desolate abandonment as a third crop failure in as many seasons brought Venistra to its knees. He felt a terrible pity for his people as the winter took hold, and he saw the ravages of the famine as it threatened to end what chances of life they had.

He was, however, not silent nor idle to any of these things. For he learned from a disgraced prince who valued honour over duty. Perhaps had Mallum been more than a child when Prince Denan had fallen he might very well have stood with him. Instead, Denan had inspired Mallum to grow up with eyes wide open. Though nearly two decades late, he spoke up for this oppression, this misery. Stirred on by what had happened before he banded together the Hundred Houses, and with their support, and what failing coin they had, they fed and farmed the land, all under one banner. Somewhere along this miserable way, the people listened to his views of hope. They watched him give up all the fortunes he had earned to feed those he could. They prayed for war and rebellion, but still, he wished no death upon any man, woman, or child, and the people with hungry bellies loved him more for this.

He saw himself kneeling at King Lemier's feet, begging for negotiation and receiving assassination attempts in reply. He saw himself rally the people as any decent leader would as thousands more fell to starvation, and no one from Dellerin came to help in their hours of need. He felt the love of the people as they fought the injustice in silence, and he watched helplessly as they tried to save themselves after the point of ruin was crossed. He watched the vile king of Venistra fall to their silent revolution. He watched the wretched settle in the regions of the Hundred Houses, where the grey had not yet poisoned.

He felt the ground rumble as a source-infused beast emerged, ravenous, from the dark caves in the dead of night to lay waste to his home. He saw so many people he loved fall at the claw of a beast as it tore through his city, driven mad by one of the cursed monoliths of this world. He saw his country's fiercest hunters give up their lives to the enormous crustacuus as the people retreated from the once wealthy region they had hoped to be a sanctuary. He had seen the pathetic numbers gathered and led them to the last stronghold with fertile land.

Iaculous pulled his mind from the weaver but not before he saw the last visions of the great and kind man he was to slay. He saw the few hundred survivors build for them a life and regrow. He felt their love for him, but he felt his own love for them greatly.

Then he saw Arielle for the first time. He felt the awfulness of her lured soul becoming bonded to his own soul in tragic punishment for denying the lure its quarry, for creating life instead of bringing death. He remembered the demon laughing as he begged for a way to return her to the world of the living. He remembered the demon mocking him for the father he had become and the vacant wife who was but a silent voice in his mind. And still, she never blamed him, for she only saw his beauty, even from her cage.

"No!" Iaculous screamed. He fell from the dark weaver as the pain of the recent slaughters brought his guilt into physical pain. He fell away from the fallen man, his mind shattering as the realisation of his actions struck him. He searched for any emotion beyond hatred and found nothing else. Mallum was a good man that needed to die.

"Please, Iaculous. Turn from this lure and help me save her, so they may live," Mallum begged and fell beside the still body of Arielle.

Iaculous hated them both for their crimes. For their immediate bond, which he took a lifetime trying to attain. He heard her screaming from far away, and a hunger to punish overcame him.

"You think she is worth saving?" Iaculous cried out.

The imprisoned souls, stirred by his confusion, fought his intentions fiercely and lost. They knew his actions before he knew them himself. With a whispered enchantment under his breath, he silenced them completely as he had done before. He still felt their raging power but none of their protests.

"My life for hers." It was a strange thing to see a man so dominant, beg so pathetically.

"I am anguished," Iaculous hissed in a voice less his own and more that of deity whose primal desire for power rose. For what was greater than five souls to command for an eternity?

Seven.

Iaculous lifted her body into the air with an invisible hand and walked upon Mallum, who clawed desperately for her floating body. Without using Arielle's soul, it limited Mallum. Invading Iaculous's mind had taken its toll. He was beaten, pathetic, and no manner of nobility or goodness would ever change the outcome.

Iaculous opened his palm flat and entwined her in a weaved grip. He willed her body to mimic his hand's movements, and she lay flat in the air. He snapped his hand shut as though catching an irritating, invading insect and her body mirrored the action with dreadful consequences. In one horrific moment, she was no longer the beautiful creature he had spent his adult life desiring. No longer the whimsical girl with a warm heart. No longer anything.

He heard Mallum wailing as her mashed body fell to the floor in a pool of liquefied ruination. No healer could recover her heartbeat. No undertaker could ever place her in a coffin of weeping oak. She was gone. Gone. *Murdered.*

Iaculous brought the fallen amulet with her screaming soul across from where it lay. He held it to his forehead and heard her agony but felt little. Mallum's suffering pierced his ears, and he barely noticed the weaver climb to his feet and leap upon him.

"No," The Dark One said as his body surged from the spinning of a lure and the torment of the souls. He caught the third fiercest weaver ever to live in the air and held him for a moment.

"You thurken monst—"

The anguished Iaculous placed his hand upon his chest and wrenched his soul from him before he could say any meaningful last words. As an afterthought, he flicked a spark upon the broken body and threw it across the room to burn away to ash.

"Soulmates," he cursed and placed the little bright sphere of a soul upon the amulet, which held the tormented Arielle.

He felt the souls converge in the little stone crystal within. He felt them entwine. Bonded in misery. *And love?* He flipped the lid in the last jar in his bandoleer, removed the stone and replaced it with the little rock. As he did, he felt all seven souls, lured and twisted, surge through him. He felt the lure eviscerate as the body of Mallum burned away to nothing, yet still, he felt little relief. He fell into a blissful unconsciousness.

After a time, Iaculous felt his body return to him and with it, a tremendous wellness. It was dawn, and a new day was upon him. The deed was done, and he had attained the seven souls, as he had desired. What demon, weaver, or god could claim to hold such a thing, he wondered and stirred himself to rise.

The world would know his power. The world would know his name. The world would know a strong leader.

He was The Dark One, and Dellerin was his.

BEREZIEL'S NOTE

My name is Bereziel. I greet you possibly from the grave, for I do not yet know my fate. Regardless, to those in the world of the living, this is my last will and testament, my revelations upon the sins I have committed and gifted to the world.

As I write these last few words, it is late and I am almost spent. My soul is ripped, and my will has left me. For too long now, I have cowered in my sanctuary as The Dark One has searched for me. Every year that passes, I sense his strength increase. Soon enough, he will find me, no matter how many enchantments I cover myself and my sanctuaries in. I hope this same enchantment has sought and called one worthy of its need, for he does not know you, and as long as you hold this book, he cannot find you.

I have tried—the demons know how hard—to undo my mistakes. A wretched act has doomed all of us, for I did not know well enough the darkness of the source. That thurken lure has been the shadowing of the world, and I have lost everything because of it. Yet, I have cast one more lure to this book itself, and I pray as you read now, you know The

Anguished Dark One as Iaculous of The Seven, and you understand the source that little better.

Within these pages is the key to his creation and to his downfall. This is no tale from the mind of a broken man, aged many years more than he should be. This is my account with my own eyes. For a soul stone is an eternal glimpse into the living, and I had them all. I have weaved the source to my will, and it has gifted me their last day. I have felt everything; I have died with every one of them a hundred times over. I have been each of The Seven, and I am greater and poorer for the experience. They were magnificent. They were heroic, and I loved them. And though they are dead, their fight is not yet done. I know this, for if this is their end, there is no hope at all.

I have shattered the soul stones to almost nothing, and I have ground and mixed them down to the ink I have written these words upon. What you hold in your hand is the last of them. What you hold is the last link to the goodness and perhaps even the sanity of Iaculous the Innocent. It is the last link to the lure that binds them together, even now. When this book is destroyed, so must begin the final attack upon him.

These years have been cruel, but they have taught me far more of the dark world than I have ever imagined. I have achieved things within that unforgiving realm that Iaculous can only dream to desire, yet I am no match for him and his many ethereal allies. I tell you now, the stories of Iaculous's wrath and Silencio's brutality are true. He walks with many demons, and yes, he has granted them steps upon this world. I have tasted the future, the past, the now, and though I sense I am still to play a part, I am tired. I am old. I am without allies. I am without hope, and I am so very, very scared.

As I write these words, it is near midnight. I prepare to step into the darkness one last time with both soul and body, leaving nothing of me behind. I seek others who cower in the deepest darkness from The Dark One and his fury—I seek those who outlived the dead gods. I seek their help.

Know this: as long as I still live, the enchantments remain. If I return, I will not be the weakened man I was, and I will not be alone.

The Last Weaver of Dellerin,

Bereziel of The Seven.

EPILOGUE

E rin closed the last page and left the book sitting on her lap. She felt deflated and sad, but she also felt something she hadn't felt in many a year. She felt hope.

The room was falling dark as the day neared its end and the night closed in with promises of shadows and concealment. She knew the time was nearing to slip away and regroup with any of her comrades who still lived, or any who still had a fight in them.

"So, that's that, then?" Rhendell asked and stared at the book upon her lap. His colour had returned to its fullness. He resembled more the fierce fighter she knew him to be and less the beaten leader who'd watched his platoon scattered and slaughtered beneath demonic horrors. He looked like she felt. Better.

"A good tale," she whispered. She ran her fingers across the cover and thought of Bereziel's final words.

"But it's just a tale."

She nodded in agreement. Just a tale.

"It's a heavy book, and we have little space within our packs," she said and lifted the book back onto its place among the others. She felt a terrible sadness as she did, like saying goodbye to a friend.

She'd had enough practice with emotions like this. Still, she ran her fingers one last time along its spine and climbed to her feet. With the darkness and luck at their backs, they could get out of the ruined city of Dellerin without notice, and who knew what would come thereafter? He had destroyed the rebellion, and the people would suffer further misery for their unsuccessful insurgence. It would be a time before their forces could recover, let alone consider marching once again. Her heart was heavy, but still, looking upon this book gave her strength.

"It was just a tale. Bereziel is a myth, lost for thirty years or more. If he lived, he is dead now," Rhendell said. He touched the book once more before strapping his pack upon his back and testing the weight on his leg. An injury like his should have taken more movement than it did, but he grinned as his knee bent fully with very little tearing. "It'll last until we get back to camp," he whispered and smiled to himself. It was the little things any warrior accepted as good fortune, as was thieving something forbidden.

"If The Dark One wants none of The Seven's tales told, perhaps this is a reason to make allowances," she said, fearing that she sounded like a child in front of a superior officer. Or worse, in front of a friend.

Rhendell exhaled. "It is just a tale, but … perhaps we would be fools to leave such a tale to die alone in a hovel like this." He sounded like a man bitten by the savageness of hope, for any hope could rebuild anew. Any hope could light a spark to the fires of a new rebellion.

Smiling, Erin pulled the book from its place and emptied her supplies before slipping the book into her satchel Seeing this, Rhendell nodded in agreement. Both warriors gathered their wits and slipped from Bereziel's study, in search of escape from the ruins of Dellerin and its immortal leader, Iaculous the Anguished of The Seven.

THE END

Erin's story is not done…

THANK YOU FOR READING THE SEVEN

Word-of-mouth is crucial for any author to succeed and honest reviews of my books help to bring them to the attention of other readers.
If you enjoyed the book, and have 2 minutes to spare, please leave an honest review on Amazon or Goodreads. Even if it's just a sentence or two it would make all the difference and would be very much appreciated.

Thank you.

EXCLUSIVE OFFER FOR NEW READERS

When you join the Robert J Power Readers' Club you'll get the latest news on the Spark City and Dellerin series, free books, exclusive content and new release updates.

You'll also get a short tale exclusive to members- you can't get this anywhere else!

Conor and The Banshee
Fear the Banshee's Cry

Join at www.RobertJPower.com

ALSO BY ROBERT J POWER

The Spark City Cycle:

Spark City, Book 1

The March of Magnus, Book 2

The Outcasts, Book 3

∼

The Dellerin Tales:

The Crimson Collection:

The Crimson Hunters, vol I

The Lost Tales of Dellerin:

The Seven

ACKNOWLEDGMENTS

Special thank you to Jen, Jill and Poll for all the amazing support. You ladies are just brilliant.

For Cathbar telling me it was a good idea. True praise indeed.

To Jean and Paul for their incredible support.

To everyone who helped with feedback throughout this endeavour, it was greatly appreciated.

I can't believe I get to do this but, a special thank you to all the incredible fans who have shown such wonderful support. I really hope you guys enjoy this new world.

ABOUT THE AUTHOR

Robert J Power is the fantasy author of the Amazon bestselling series, The Spark City Cycle and The Dellerin Tales. When not locked in a dark room with only the daunting laptop screen as a source of light, he fronts Irish rock band, Army of Ed, despite their many attempts to fire him.

Robert lives in Wicklow, Ireland with his wife Jan, two rescue dogs and a cat that detests his very existence. Before he found a career in writing, he enjoyed various occupations such as a terrible pizza chef, a video store manager (ask your grandparents), and an irresponsible camp counsellor. Thankfully, none of them stuck.

If you wish to learn of Robert's latest releases, his feelings on The Elder Scrolls, or just how many coffees he consumes a day before the palpitations kick in, visit his website at www. RobertJPower.com where you can join his reader's club. You might even receive some free goodies, hopefully some writing updates, and probably a few nonsensical ramblings.

www.RobertJPower.com

facebook.com/authorrobertjpower

twitter.com/RobertJPower

instagram.com/RobertJPower

#SaveTheSeven

Manufactured by Amazon.ca
Bolton, ON

25343762R00229